Mary Brock Jones lives in New Zealand but loves nothing more than to escape into the other worlds in her head, to write science fiction and historical romances. For many years, she was a sedate office worker by day and a frantic scribbler by night.

Her parents introduced her to libraries and gave her a farm to play on, where trees became rocket ships and rocky outcrops were ancient fortresses. She grew up writing, filling pages of notebooks and filling her head with stories but took a number of detours on the pathway to her dream job. After raising four sons, a career as a government veterinarian and more than one house renovated, her wish came true.

To keep up to date with her latest news and releases, sign up to her newsletter here:

www.marybrockjones.com/

Or find Mary here:

http://www.marybrockjones.com/

https://www.facebook.com/MaryBrockJonesAuthor

https://www.instagram.com/marybrockjones/

By Mary Brock Jones:

NZ Historical Romances

A Heart Divided
Swift Runs the Heart

Hathe Series

Toil and Strife: Hathe Book One and Two
Aftermath: Hathe Book Three

Arcadia Series

Torn
Taken
Exiled
Broken

BROKEN

Arcadia Book Four

Mary Brock Jones

Mary Brock Jones

Auckland, New Zealand

Author: Mary Brock Jones
Published by Mary Brock Jones
RD 1,
Warkworth, New Zealand 0981
www.marybrockjones.com

Publisher's Note: This is a work of fiction. Names, characters, places, and incidents are a product of the author's imagination. Any resemblance to actual people, living or dead, or to businesses, companies, events, institutions, or locales is completely coincidental.

Book Layout © 2017 BookDesignTemplates.com

Cover design by Amygdala Design. www.amygdaladesign.net

Broken/ Mary Brock Jones
ISBN: 978-1-0670139-1-2

DEDICATION

To my writing community. For being there when I needed you and making me believe I can do this.

CONTENTS

CHARACTER LIST AND GUIDE TO PRONUNCIATION

Mountainer region names describe a person's closest family connections. The emphasis is usually on the first syllable, but this can vary.

Mountainer Language Sounds:
- 'kh at the end of a word - like the Scottish ch (as in *loch*)
- 'h in the pronunciation guide indicates a degree of aspiration in the sound.
- ' a further, slight aspiration is shown by an apostrophe just before the letter in the pronunciation version (italicised stress syllable shown in bold).
- Bh – a soft jz sound as in persua**si**on.
- Mchd – aspirated 'v
- Mhn – v
- Uine – 'win

- Hch – 'h, i.e. like a muffled Scottish ch, an h sound with a slight throat sound at the start

CHARACTER LIST

MAIN CHARACTERS

Cumchdach mar Bram duine Anna den Coille: Second den Coille child and eldest den Coille brother. Presumed heir to the leadership of the Den Coille company. Married to Anna ingh Eolas bean Cumchdach den Coille.

Coo-'va'kh mar Bram d'win Anna den Coyle

Cumchdach son of Bram, husband to Anna, of the family Coille.

Anna ingh Eolas bean Cumchdach den Coille: daughter of Eolas, married to Cumchdach duine Anna den Coille.

*Ann-ah ine **Ee**-o-lass bee-an **Coo**-'va'kh den Coyle.*

Anna, daughter of Eolas, wife to Cumchdach, of the family Coille

Birth name: **Anna ingh Eolas an Sumhneas den Falasch**. (Anna, daughter of Eolas and Sumhneas, of the house of Falasch).

*Ann-ah ine **Ee**-oh-las an **Soov**-nee-as den **Fah**-lash.*

Also can be termed: **Anna ingh Eolas an Sumhneas o Falasch bean Cumchdach den Coille** (fullest legal name, used rarely and only in official forms to prevent confusion).

Ruiseart mar Cumchdach an Anna den Coille (Roo): Baby son of Anna and Cumchdach.

*Ruwsh-airt (as in air) mar **Coo**'va'kh an **Ann**-ah den Coyle*

Den Coille family

Bram mar Gliocas duine Scathach den Coille: Father and head of the Den Coille company.

*Bram mar **Glee**-o-cas d'win **'Skar**-thar'kh den Coyle*

Bram, son of Gliocas, husband to Scathach, of the family Coille.

Scathach ingh Coibhneas bean Bram den Coille: Mother and doctor. Head of Manascraoch Hospital.

*'**Ska**-thar'k ine **Coy'**-nee-ars bee-**arn** Bram den Coyle.*

Scathach, daughter of Coibhneas, wife to Bram, of the family Coille

Samhchair ingh Bram an Scathach den Coille: Eldest sister and doctor.

*Sarm-'**hair** ine Bram an '**Ska**-thar'ch den Coyle*

Samhchair, daughter of Bram (father) and Scathach (mother), of the family Coille.

Cumchdach mar Bram duine Anna den Coille: Second child and eldest den Coille brother. Heir to the head of Den Coille. Married to Anna ingh Eolas bean Cumchdarch den Coille.

Coo-'var'kh mar Bram d'win Anna den Coyle

Cumchdach son of Bram, husband to Anna, of the family Coille.

Anna ingh Eolas bean Cumchdarch den Coille: wife of Cumchdach duine Anna den Coille.

*Ann-ar ine **Ee**-o-larss bee-**arn Coo**-'var'kh den Coyle.*

Birth name: **Anna ingh Eolas an Sumhneas den Falasch. (**Anna, daughter of Eolas and Sumhneas, of the house of Falasch).
***Ann**-ah ine **Ee**-oh-lars an **Soov**-nee-ars den **Far**-lash.*

Seolta mar Bram an Scathach den Coille: Second brother, currently exiled from Arcadia. Married to Anyara a Prithand2, formerly of the planet Surned.
*See-**ole**-tar mar Bram an '**Ska**-thar'ch den Coyle.*

Anyara a Prithand2: A biome scientist formerly from Kevand Station attached to the planet Surned, and an Esteemed Scholar of the Alliance Academy. Married to Seolta mar Bram duine Anyara den Coille.
Name in mountainer style: Anyara ingh Gevard bean Seolta den Coille
*An-**Yar**-ah ine **Gev**-ard bee-**ahn** Bram den Coyle*
Anyara, daughter of Gevard (father) and wife to Seolta den Coille

Ceart mar Bram an Scathach den Coille: Third, largest and quietest brother.
***Kee**-'airt mar Bram arn '**Ska**-thar'ch den Coyle.*

Fioruisghe ingh Bram bean Caleb den Winter: The younger den Coille daughter. An ecoengineer with the Survey and head of the Mountain zone Survey team. Married to Caleb Winter. AKA Fee den Coille Winter.
***Fee**-or-'**hrish**-gay ine Bram bee-**arn Kay**-leb den Winter.*
Fioruisghe, daughter of Bram, wife of Caleb, of the family Winter.

Aigherach mar Bram an Scathach den Coille: The youngest den Coille.

Aye-*ger*-*ar'kh mar Bram an* **'Ska**-*thar'kh den Coyle.*

Den Coille: name of the festia pollen company owned by the den Coille family. A wealthy food company in the central continental zone, Protos.

DEN FALASCH FAMILY

Eolas mar Driach duine Gria den Falasch: Anna's father and head of the Falasch company.
   Ee-*oh*-*lahs mar* **Dree**-*ah'k d'win* **Gree**-*ah den Fah*-**lash**

Sumhneas ingh Eagrai bean Eolas den Falasch: Anna's mother and first wife of Eolas den Falasch. Died when Anna was a child. Daughter of Ceana ingh Diomhain bean Eagrai den Guire.
   Soov-*nee*-*ahs ine* **Eah**-*gry* **bee**-*ahn* **Ee**-*oh*-*lahs den Fah*-*lash*

Gria ingh Ovirisch bean Eolas den Falasch. Second wife of Eolas den Falasch and Anna's stepmother. Originally came from Urbis. Mother to Anton, Verianna and Charmante den Falasch.
   Gree-*ah ine* **O**-*ver*-*ish bee*-*ahn* **Ee**-*oh*-*lahs den Fah*-**lash**

Anton mar Eolas an Gria den Falasch: Anna's half-brother. Eldest child of Eolas and Gria den Falasch. Also referred to as **Anton ghar Driach:** Anton, grandson of Driach

Verianna ingh Eolas an Gria den Falasch: Half-sister to Anna and twin of Charmante.
   Veer -*ee*-*ann*-*ah*

Charmante ingh Eolas an Gria den Falasch: Half-sister to Anna and twin to Verianna.

Shar-man-tay

Driach mar Ramach duine Deana den Falasch: Deceased. Eolas father and Anna's grandfather. Previous head of Falasch Shipping (usually shortened to Falasch) and a renowned businessman.

Dree-ah'k mar Ram-ma'k d'win Dee-an-na den Fah-lash

Aonar mar Ramach an Cinna den Falasch: Anna's great uncle and the reclusive brother of Driach den Falasch

Ouw-nar mar Ram-ma'k an Sin-nah den Fah-lash

WINTER FAMILY

Sol Winter: father and head of Winter Solaris.

Helena Bascombe Winter: mother.

Caleb Winter: Eco-engineer with the Survey. Married to Fioruisghe (Fee) den Coille Winter.

Ethan Winter: Middle brother and head of Solaris.

Sarwenna Beren Winter (Sar): Eldest daughter of the Beren family and married to Ethan Winter. Previously the union representative for the Sulwith solar field workers.

Silas Winter (Si): youngest brother. Systems programming genius.

Winter Solaris: the solar energy company owned by the Winter family, usually shortened to Solaris. The dominant supplier of solar sourced energy on Protos and owner of the Sulwith solar field.

OTHERS

Marshal Marco an Fallon: Supreme Field Commander of the Federal Marshals of Arcadia, the elite planetary police force.

Ceana ingh Diomhain bean Eagrai den Guire (Grandam): Anna's grandmother and head of the den Guire family, an old Rubhaicreach administrative family.

    *Kee-anna ine **Di**-van **bee**-ahn **Eah**-gry den Gwire*

Biarsuin: Ruiseart's nursemaid.

    ***Bee**-ar-shin*

Joseph mar Freshet an Sonrai den Braich: Survey supervisor of a change crew near Manascraoch

    *Jo-sef mar **Fresh**-ett an **Son** -ry den Bra'kh*

Dabha mar Tuath duine Biadhe den Garadh: A Den Coille forester, working with Fee's survey team to change the Manascraoch forest lands.

    ***Dah**-yah mar **Too**-ath d'win **Bee**-'ahth den **Gar**-ah*

Professor Yakacshka: Anna's old professor at the Urbis Higher School of Biota Studies

Shelda: Anna's junior lab assistant in Deuteron and Urbis.

Gerrig: Prominent business vidcaster (journalist)

Meriac mar Toilich: A guard in the den Falasch household.

    ***Meer**- ee-ack mar **Toy**-li'kh*

Ceirden: A Den Coille agent working as Grandam's factotum.

    ***Kyer**-din*

Dhionna ingh Creag: Head of Rubhaicreach scientific institute.

    ***Thee**-on-ah ine Kreg (Th as in There)*

Paolu: Head of the Rubhaicreach dockers.

    Pow-loo

Deputy Malgrave: A past deputy to the Alliance representative on Arcadia.

Hilmar a Kevand3: representative of the off-world company Kevand3 from the planet Surned.

Meth Varkan: A major Alliance banking consortium.

Fongma Consortium: A major Alliance chemical company.

Representative Joe Gibbs: Planetary Upper House representative for the plains region.

Councillor Seilach ingh Craobh bean Stobach den Bunachan: Lower House government representative for the Mountain region.

Si-lah'kh ine **Krow'ch bee**-*ahn* **Stow**-*bah'kh den* **Boo**-*nah'-'han*

Representative Coinneas mar Coille duine Falamh den Cleireach: Upper House Representative, Mountainer region.

Coy-nee-as mar Coyle dwin **Fell**-*ass den* **Clai'r**-*ee-ark*

Caltan Smierg: Senior executive in an Urbis corporate trading company.

Kal-*tann Smeerg*

Gebre of Shiron: Deuteron farmer

Ge-*bray of Shee-ron (Ge as in get)*

Firama of Shiron: Deuteron farmer's wife

Fee-*rah-mah of Shee-ron*

Luchaia ingh Neart an Slanach: The technician in charge of Anna's Manascraoch lab.

*Loo-**ki**-ah ine Neert an* **Slan**-*ah'kh*

Marshal Dunan: Head of Anna's marshal security detail in Rubhaicreach, a Senior Commander in the Federal Marshal police force.

Ianno and Mari: elderly coaster villagers. The last remaining residents of their coastal village.

Sarmadur mar Obar: Union representative for the Falasch dockers.

Yarma: Secretary-General of the Alliance Council.

Other Terms

PLACES

Upper House: The upper house of the Arcadian government. Members are titled Representatives (e.g. Representative Joe Gibb).

Lower House: The Federal Assembly of Arcadia. Members are Councillors.

Regional House: Local government body, governing a particular region, e.g. Protos Central, which includes the Plains, Mountainer country and Deadlands zone.

Alliance Council: central body of the Alliance of Human Worlds. It is the overall government of all Alliance worlds, enforcing laws laid down as required to maintain the Alliance, interplanetary concerns such as trade, and maintenance of human life.

Galactic Ministry: Arcadia's extraplanetary affairs department.

Urbis Higher School of Biota Studies (UBS): A university in Urbis specialising in flora and fauna studies. It also houses the training and research branches of the Ecological Survey and the Institute of Agritechology.

EA – Earth analogue planet: Fully engineered or very similar in type to Earth and fully adapted to human settlement.

Habitable world: A planet that can be wholly or partly bioengineered to make settlement possible. Often includes a mix of habitats and open-air settlements. Alliance Central is a partly bioengineered world.

Habitat world: A planet with gravity, daylength and temp within acceptable limits to allow for artificial habitats.

Moons of Arcadia: Jacopus is the dominant and most functional moon. The other, small asteroid-like moons are only visible to the naked eye in certain geographic locations, depending on the coordinates and a clear sky, e.g. the Deadlands beyond Sulwith.

Protos: main (eastern) continent.

Deuteron: second (western) continent.

Feldwesten: third (southern) continent.

Mountainer Country: The west coast and western slopes of the Western Ranges of the central zone of Protos. Home region to the den Coille family.

Deadlands: the desert region of the eastern part of Protos central.

Manascraoch: home city of the den Coilles. A fabled Mountainer city, built entirely in the branches of enormous baullnia trees.
Man-ass-crow'kh

Rubhaicreach: Anna's home city and the name of the peninsula on which it is built.
Roo-jza-cray'kh'

Urba River: The main river of the three flowing into the estuary that Urbis is built on.

Dridust: The largest town on the Plains. Site of the Solaris head office and the main hospital for the Plains region.

Urbis Basin: The rolling area north of the ranges separating the central and northern parts of Protos, before the land becomes a wide spreading estuary. Identified as the most fertile area on Arcadia by the first settlers.

Mangolon: Southernmost town on Deuteron

PLANTS

Festia: A mountain bog loving tree and source of the edible pollen sold by the Den Coille company.

Festin: A food ingredient derived from the festia tree's pollen. Good source of protein and a taste enhancer.

Chaullnia bush: The flowers are the source of a famous perfume. The crushed leaves also have an aromatic scent.

Rete (the *me-too* flower): A small, low-growing and thorny flowering plant native to Rubhaicreach peninsula.

Sorphlex: Grain crop grown in Deuteron. Wheat-like, it is used for bread and has a high plant protein content.

Costa: Giant grass with a notoriously long ripening period. An excellent source of readily digestible carbohydrates.

Mainna: Marsh seaweed found in the coaster region. Prized edible plant.

Chastne grass: Coastal grass covering the river flats.

Drach: Tough coastal scrub bush with vicious thorns.

Fraustin: coastal tree. A distant cousin of festia but quite different in form and habitat.

ANIMALS

Rakter: A vicious, ground predator of the Plains desert. Cunning and devious. A smile like a rakter bite means one that is untrustworthy and dangerous.

Glitchit: A small, ant-like bug which stores water in an underground communal nest.

Falk: The flying predator of the plains.

Foxllar: A Plains ground predator which hunts nieten.

Chapper: A ground-dwelling animal used for food.

Nieten: native grazing animal farmed for meat and hides.

Wernet: small bloodsucking animal (like hornet equivalent).

Spealach: A scavenger of mountain ranges.

Raiten: distant relative of nietens, native of coaster region and farmed for their fibre.

Ganda: a small, ground-dwelling animal of the plains which hides in burrows from avian predators.

THINGS

A chiad: First of all others. What Cumchdach has called Anna since they were young, though she has no similar one for him, except *mo stochri* in her heart.

Mo leanadh: Term of endearment for a child.

 *Mow **Lee**-ah-nah'*

Mam-duine: husband's mother.

Mam-bean: wife's mother

Da-duine: husband's father

Da-bean: wife's father.

Smak: Teenage slang for awesome, great, good.

Brakka: A derogatory slang word. (Also means a small, ground-dwelling, pest animal).

Milisti: A small, sweet biscuit, cut into various shapes and iced.

Dask: The equivalent of coffee and the main stimulant drink used on Arcadia.

Salaschar: A whisky-like alcoholic beverage made in the northern foothills of Mountainer country.

Nanoglit: A very small amount.

Fricha: a popular strategy game, the Alliance equivalent of chess.

Measurements

Arcadia uses decimal based, Standard Galactic units for distance, time, mass etc. They have been expressed here in current day terms i.e. second, hour, day etc. However, that is only a current day translation. The Standard Galactic units used throughout the Alliance, irrespective of planetary or deep space location, are based on Natural Units of measurement i.e. on universal physical constants independent of planet or spatial location. On Arcadia, they are roughly equivalent to the following current Earth measurements.

Distance

1 Standard galactic metre is roughly equivalent to 1.5 metres or 5 feet.

Standard galactic kilometre = 1000 SG metres.

Time

Standard second is equivalent to 5 metric seconds.

Standard minute = 10 standard seconds.

Standard hour = 100 standard minutes, and is equivalent in usage to an hour, but in time is almost 1.5 hours

CHAPTER ONE

"My child will be born in this house."

"Not this child," said Anna den Coille to her husband. She set a protective hand on her belly as another of the annoying pre-labour cramps hit her. She had to leave, now, while she could. She sent a signal through her com to her baggage capsule.

Cumchdach grabbed it. "Put that back. You're going nowhere."

"Oh, yes, I am. I'm going home. To *my* home and to family who trust me." She swung around. Or tried to. Making a dramatic exit and storming out with a near-term baby belly wasn't possible, she discovered, tottering toward the table.

"Anna!"

Was that panic in his voice? It ought to be. She grabbed the edge of the table just as Cumchdach's arms caught her. She glared at him and he slowly backed off.

"Stop this. You'll hurt yourself and the baby."

"Oh, yes. Mustn't hurt the precious den Coille heir."

"Or you," he snapped, finally shaken out of his infernal calm. "We've been together too long for that. I'd never want to hurt you and you know it."

She felt like breaking. "Then you didn't lie to me?"

He stopped, face shattered. At least he didn't deny it, even though it wasn't technically true. He hadn't lied—he'd just failed to tell her the truth. The den Coilles were investigating her father for fraud, for diverting Festin, made from the festia pollen that was the heart of the den Coille wealth and on-selling it as a counterfeit product, Restin, undercutting Den Coille.

The worst of it? It was probably true. Anna had always known what her father was. His proper business was import and export. The Falasch were traders, and had been for generations. Why would he put that at risk by undercutting their major customer?

Because at heart her father was both greedy and stupid.

He was still her father.

She shoved a tired hand through her hair, the other cradling her stomach as another cramp tightened it. "I'm going home to my own people."

He released his grasp on her capsule and she slowly turned. She'd given him days to deny it and he'd said nothing. She plodded toward the door.

No, she waddled. That was the only word for how she walked now. There was nothing of grace, nothing of beauty in it. No wonder Cumchdach no longer cared enough to tell her the truth. She paused at the door and looked back at him.

He'd been her world since they were young. Barely in middle school. All those years, to end like this.

"I thought you were my best friend," she said, feeling lost.

"Anna—" he began, then stopped, one hand half lifting to her.

"Don't worry. I'm sure you'll find someone else soon enough. Someone truly beautiful."

"Never," he said, and for an instant she wanted to believe him. Believe that the shock in his dark eyes was real. Then she pulled her capsule close and hit the door panel just as a spasm sliced through her belly, pain like she'd not felt before. Her whole body squeezed tight.

She grabbed at the door and doubled over, gasping.

"Anna!"

Arms grabbed her and a panicked voice yelled into a com, calling the emergency channel.

"It's too early," she gasped as the pain eased off. "He can't come yet, not now." A madwoman cackled somewhere.

That was her last rational thought. For coming now her baby was. Her husband wasn't the only one set on having their baby born in the den Coille house.

Hours later, she sighed and held tight to a sleepy, squirming and very satisfied-looking baby boy. Cumchdach put out just one finger, touching his cheeks as if the little darling might break. The baby's lips twitched.

"He knows his da," the medic whispered with a silly smile on her face that echoed the ones on Anna's and Cumchdach's.

"As long as he doesn't give his mam as much trouble as we did ours," Cumchdach said, and this time his silly smile was directed at Anna. This one last time, she smiled back and leaned tiredly into the haven of his shoulder. It had been a hard few hours. She dimly remembered him yelling at the medic once.

"Give her something. Stop this."

She'd had to tell him it was fine. It was just her muscles working hard, but he hadn't relaxed until the wonder of their son sliding into the world made everything right again.

"Welcome, little man," he said now. She passed him the baby, who squawked in protest, then settled down as Cumchdach took him and cradled him in his big hands. "Welcome, Ser Ruiseart mar Cumchdach an Anna den Coille."

"My little Roo," she echoed, besotted. She reached out her arms and Cumchdach passed the baby back. He immediately relaxed into sleep, his eyes closing and his face turning into her breast. He'd already suckled, a sensation she still didn't know what to make of, but his mouth settled into a half open 'o' as if ready to latch on when he woke up enough. "He's definitely your son," she said to their little miracle's father, who was looking equally besotted. Cumchdach enfolded them both close, and his big fist carefully encompassed the baby's head with the faint sprinkle of dark hair tracing the line of fluff above the high brow. "And yours," he said. "No one else has that curl just there."

He leaned down and kissed her, and for a moment it was the same as that first night so many years ago when he had first kissed her. The only man ever to have kissed her. Their first date was a fumbled teenage affair with him nervous and her trying too hard, but on the walk home they had settled back into their friendship, then into something more as the moonlight touched the tips of the trees and the winds for once calmed. It had been on a bridge between the main retail tree and that holding the school hostel where she lived. Anyone could have seen them, and she'd liked that. Cumchdach mar Bram wasn't a boy to hide what grew between them from anyone.

Only from her. She'd always known he loved her—or assumed he did. Now, she wasn't so sure. A man who loved you didn't keep things this important from you. He *trusted* you.

As for her, she'd fallen in love with Cumchdach the first day she saw him, though she was too young to understand it then, and had never stopped loving him in all the time since.

He was her best friend, and she was his. He'd said that often enough. But friendship wasn't love, not the kind she wanted from him. Nor was desire, though he'd shown that often enough too.

Love needed trust, and Cumchdach didn't trust her. Together, they might have found a way through the mess of the Restin case. A way to protect the people of her home city from the fallout.

He never gave her that chance.

The beautiful halls and passages of the den Coille home had never seemed so long or so empty as when she left a few weeks later. She'd given herself time to recover, she told herself, and it was true enough that her body needed it, but her heart knew the real reason. She wanted to hold onto her illusions while she could. Cumchdach hadn't forgotten. She could see it in the way he watched her when he thought she wasn't looking. The same way he watched the flitterbys he was so fascinated with, careful not to frighten them away by holding still and quiet in a way that shouldn't have been possible in a man as solid and square in build—a man who anchored his family and her.

He was still going to investigate her father and her family's company.

She had a flyer assigned her, a den Coille flyer, but that seemed wrong today. Instead, she hired a standard flyer from the city pool. Once she was home, it would return to Manascraoch.

A piece of her wished she could do the same, come back and slot into the life she'd built here—a very large piece, one so vital it cut into her soul to deny it. But staying here meant waiting for something that wasn't going to happen. The rental flyer would go on to make more trips, more hires at the convenience of whomever chose to use it. The same as her role if she stayed. Cumchdach's wife, mother to the den Coille heir, well mannered supporter of Cumchdach's work, his family's needs, anyone in Manascraoch who thought they had the right to call on the den Coilles.

Was that all she was, all Cumchdach saw in her? Where did Anna the person live within that?

The flyer lifted from the platform and she sent a last farewell to the dense banks of forest below. The fog clung to the mountainside, cold and still, burying her hopes forever. She lifted higher and refused to look back.

Anna's home city, Rubhaicreach, was built on a massive shelf of bedrock jutting out into the wild western sea. Solid to its core, it had withstood everything the planet threw at it for millennia. The geologists said it was formed by the rim of an ancient volcano, extinct since the earliest days of the planet's formation. All that remained was a rocky ring, the largest part forming a flat-roofed peninsula crowning the plunging cliffs surrounding it and holding her home city far above the encroaching seas. Rubhaicreach was unbreachable, but that wasn't why the original settlers had chosen this place to build their city. On the southern edges of the peninsula, safe within the arms of the protruding cliffs, lay the harbour—an almost perfect circle enclosed by the peninsula on one side and on the other, by the curve of a sharp-edged spur of rock jutting high above the waves and stopping the worst of the seas. The smooth, dark waters were serene enough for any boat and deep enough to take the largest vessels. In the early days of settlement, coastal shipping had been the foremost method of carrying bulk cargoes around the continent and it was still a big player in planetary trade.

There had originally been a pocket-sized beach below the city cliffs, but the engineers had long ago sculpted out the harbour sides to remove that slight shelf and build the first of the massive wharves that now dominated the harbour. At first, they'd used shuttles to ferry goods and people from the cliff top to the ships below, but they had long since been replaced by a series of tunnels.

Now those tunnels honeycombed the peninsula. Never enough to damage the integrity of the rock, but unique among mountainer cities, Rubhaicreach was built on and under the land. The natural plant covering of the hilltop was forest at the mainland margin, fading to tough shrubs, grasses, and herbs over the peninsula proper. Her own home was built on the tip of the plateau, facing out in challenge to the wild winds of the sea. The den Falasch family had always been traders, revelling in exploring their world, venturing out to find new places, new peoples, new connections. They were happiest of all when sealing a deal.

Anna hadn't thought she took after her father's people, until she discovered her first new plant species and felt a hunger to do it again. There was more of her father in her than she'd thought. He wanted riches, she wanted knowledge, but the hunger was the same.

Looking down on her home city from her flyer, seeing the brave houses built right on and under the rocks as yet another heavy squall of rain lashed them, her heart slotted back into place for the first time since leaving Cumchdach. She had come to love her husband's home, built within and on the mighty baullnia trees of his home region, but it was not *her* home, not as this city. Her father's house sat on the point of the bluff, big and grandiose, lording it over the cliffs, but her eyes sought another house. Nestled in the protection of a massive boulder and half buried in a natural hillock, this one was softer in lines with native shrubs gambolling over the roofscape.

Her grandmother's house and her target. She landed at the side, on the flyer pad Grandam had ordered built where it wouldn't disturb her peace or her vision for her home. Anna picked up

Ruiseart, cradling him close as she linked to her com to order the shutdown of the flyer and transfer of her luggage to the house.

She'd brought everything most dear to her in it including, nestled beneath layers and protectively cossetted, the first present Cumchdach had ever given her. He'd made this one, a small bowl carved with the awkward scrawls of the child he'd been gouged into its side and a baullnia leaf set into the base.

"Anna, how lovely to see you," said her grandmother, watching her even as she hugged her tight in welcome. "I've been longing to see this wee man."

Her hands reached out for the baby. Ruiseart still slept, blissfully unaware, and his great-grandmother gazed down, drinking in his wee face.

"What a fine young man you have there," said Grandam softly.

"Yes, he is." It still shocked Anna how precious he was. She'd given birth to a miracle.

Then her grandmother looked up. "How long are you staying?"

Anna sucked in a breath. "I don't know."

Grandam settled Roo into his portacot. "As long as you need," she said, "and you can tell me all about it later. Right now, this wee man will need a feed soon and you need a drink and a rest. Come in, come in."

Suddenly, it was that simple. Anna walked into her grandmother's home and took her familiar seat in the main room, while Grandam gestured to the portacot to follow, then set the food prepper to hustling up a veritable feast, all with one wrinkled hand held protectively over Anna's.

Soon the table was set, a feast spread out, and the shutters closed against the storm building outside. Anna leaned into the worn seat she usually took as Grandam took the one beside it. Anna had no more reserves. She reached out her hand and her grandmother took it, then held out her arms. Anna stood and in seconds was wrapped in her grandmother's old embrace.

"Oh, Grandam, I've made such a mess of everything."

"Shush there, little one. It's all right, Grandam's here." The old words, so familiar, so safe. For a short spell, they worked, and everything was good.

But it wasn't, and maybe never would be again.

Cumchdach knew their rooms were empty as soon as he walked in. It didn't need the blank wall, free of her plants, the empty cot, the red warning on the wardrobe, to tell him. The silence said it all. She'd left him, just as she'd promised. His security staff had told him she'd hired a flyer, but a stupid part of him had still hoped.

Had said she'd merely gone for a flight, and his son, her clothes—his wife!—were still here.

She'd made her decision. He had work to do. He took himself to his office, locked himself inside and buried his pain in work.

His mother found him there hours later. He had no memory of what he'd done in the meantime.

"I can't find Anna. I'd planned to take her and Ruiseart to visit with the aunts this morning." His mother spoke the words too carefully. She already knew then, but he said it anyway.

"She's not here. She's gone home."

"For a visit?" said his mother even more carefully, and he lifted a hand to stop her.

"I'm not one of your patients, Mam. No, not for a visit. She's gone."

"She'll be back."

He shook his head. It was the moment he accepted the reality. "No, she won't. We're investigating her father, and she was born den Falasch."

His mother waved that away. "Anna has more good sense and integrity in her big toe than that silly father of hers."

"He's still her father."

A ping sounded on his com. He looked automatically, then dashed it open.

"She's gone to her grandmother's," he said, surprised.

"You've got spies on her?"

He'd had a second security agent assigned to her since the start of this whole mess, and pumped-up surveillance for the rest of her family, but he didn't tell his mother that. "We've had people embedded in Falasch territory since Seolta first warned us. They're all security trained."

"Good," said his mother in that determined voice of hers. "I'm not about to leave my son unprotected."

Thankfully, his mother said nothing to that. She'd known Anna as long as he had and didn't call him on the blatant half lie. The agents weren't just for Roo. Cumchdach wasn't about to let a single strand of Anna's hair be harmed, but saying that out loud only made the pain worse.

"I have work to do," he said.

"Are you all right?"

"Of course."

"Your father and I are here if you need us." His mother touched his hair in that way she'd had since he was tiny, and it did help. But all right? *Nothing* was all right, nor would be until Anna and Ruiseart returned.

The only way for that to happen was to unearth the truth of her father's involvement in selling the fake Restin and swindling Den

Coille. Unfortunately, given what he knew of Eolas den Falasch, he was probably knee deep in this quagmire—and Anna would know it.

His family had warned him not to keep the fraud case from her. Would it have helped?

Of course. She thinks you don't trust her.

Is that better than being the man who brings down her family?

Cumchdach had been in and out of the den Falasch house since he and Anna became friends, and he probably knew her family almost as well as his own. Unfortunately, familiarity hadn't brought liking. There was something untrustworthy in Eolas den Falasch, while Anna's stepmother and half siblings were downright obnoxious as far as Cumchdach was concerned, leaving much of the family's role in Rubhaicreach to Anna while keeping any public adulation to themselves.

Taking the praise for Anna's hard work is what it always looked like to him. Her people weren't fooled though. Anyone with a problem knew to come to Anna.

He liked her maternal grandmother, though. Mother to Anna's long dead mother, Ceana ingh Diomhain bean Eagrai den Guire was a formidable old lady and had read him a round or two in her time. The roots know what she'd say to him about this latest debacle. He slumped down in his chair, staring glumly at the cluttered surface of his desk. This was getting him nowhere.

He needed to talk to his father.

Bram mar Gliocas duine Scathach den Coille had been spinning deals since long before Cumchdach was born, when his formidable grandfather, Gliocas, still held the reins of the Den Coille business. Granda had once said grumpily to Cumchdach that his da had more wheels spinning in his head than the insides of a space freighter. Cumchdach's brother Seolta had inherited their father's wiliness but not yet his cool judgement. Some of his recent actions had prompted hope he was developing it, and his wife was a treasure the family was still stunned had chosen Seolta, but Da still had the soundest head of anyone Cumchdach knew.

He signalled his father and marched down the hallways to the spacious room Da used for his office and meeting space. He had another, smaller room, he called his thinking room, but the family thought of as his version of a cave, deep in a knot in the main trunk of their home tree.

Luckily, he was in the office today. Cumchdach wasn't yet so desperate he'd beard his father in his retreat.

Not far off it though.

His father sat in his favourite place, in the chair on his small balcony, sheltered by a branch of the tree from the worst of Manascraoch's dicey weather but where, as his father said, he could feel the mood of the mountains better than shut in behind walls. His com fields were busy but, as usual he'd set them to private, his fingers leaping nimbly between them. Then they stilled as he looked to the balcony entrance where Cumchdach stood.

"Trouble?" said his too perceptive da.

Cumchdach nodded.

"The Restin case or Anna?"

Something clenched inside Cumchdach. He wasn't ready to talk about Anna, not yet. "The Restin case," he said unconvincingly, even to himself.

Luckily, Da allowed it. "The facts seem clear enough." The whole family were furious with what they saw as betrayal and violation of their territory.

"As we know them." Cumchdach took the seat by the desk. "How far the rot extends is what I'm not sure of."

His father scowled. "This is a simple business attack. No reason yet to think it's anything more."

Not like the political mess hovering over Arcadia thanks to the Alliance Council's threat to empty the planet of its current residents, descendants of the early settlers, unless they stopped destroying its environment. The threat deadline might have been shifted to 'pending', but it wasn't yet gone. Nor would it be while too many refused to believe the damage to Arcadia's environment was real, continually undermining the efforts of his father and others like him to meet the Alliance's demands.

"I want to make sure. I've set a program to trace and analyse all our sales of Festin through Falasch and calibrate it with the known incidences of Restin on the market."

"It's a good start," said his father.

"If only I knew where to go next."

"Talk to the accounts department."

Cumchdach looked up at that. "It's hurting our bottom line?"

His father's scowl was answer enough. "The timing could have been better. It's hard enough with the cutbacks we're making in the festia plantations."

"No chance of easing off our changes?"

"Not after that ruckus with Seolta."

A ruckus that had turned out rather well for Arcadia, all things considered, but Cumchdach knew better than to point that out. His father knew as well as he did that Seolta's actions had stirred up rancour against the Den Coille company on the Council. No need to add to it, not right now.

"And the company? What happens to it with all the changes?"

For once, his father didn't have an answer. "We need your wife back. Now. Anna bean Cumchdach is more than a steady hand on you and a fine addition to this family. She's one of the best tragging botanists on this planet, and we need an alternative planting option, yesterday if possible."

"The chaullnia must be helping, said Cumchdach, hoping to distract his father. Anna wasn't just another resource for Den Coille and Da knew it. But today, those too knowing eyes of his stayed hard and sharp.

"Helping yes, but not nearly as sought after as our Festin. People out there want food, quality food, and Festin turns their worst muck to something palatable and nutritious. That's worth more to a planet than any luxury perfume."

Cumchdach didn't bother arguing. He'd always assumed Festin would provide as long as they needed it. The market wanted more of the rich pollen derivative of the festia trees than the mountains could ever produce.

"What do you think Anna could do? Festia grow well only on our mountain slopes."

"That woman can make plants sit up and sing to whatever tune she calls. Your sister's Survey staff are good, but Anna is better. Who knows what she can make festia do, or what she could discover. Go make your peace with your wife before we end up having to go begging to the bank."

Cumchdach shot up sharply. His father wasn't joking. "We can diversify. Festia can't be the only way to make money, not with our influence and knowledge of this region."

"Your sister has her whole team working to turn our slopes into an environmentally balanced production system. Think you can do better than them?"

Unfortunately no, but Cumchdach wished badly he could say otherwise. Fioruisghe might drive him half-crazy with her demands, but he had learned to respect her intelligence and courage. Not much chance of doing anything else after she'd saved the whole family's lives. If only she didn't keep reminding them all. It wasn't as if he'd go up against her skills without some serious backing behind him.

Like his wife's superior expertise in botanical matters.

Bram said nothing more on the matter, passing a file over instead. "You have all the details available to me. We need an alternative solution, and we need it yesterday. Any ideas you have will be greatly appreciated."

Cumchdach left his father's office soon after, feeling even worse than when he'd arrived, and that was a first. His father always had an answer—in the past.

When he returned to his rooms, they still felt hollowed-out and empty of anything that mattered.

CHAPTER TWO

It was a beautiful morning on the plateau, with only a short shower of rain to wash clean the sky before the sun peered through the clouds. Anna wrapped one of her grandmother's shawls around Ruiseart and carried him outside to finish his feed. No one came to Grandam's side garden without an invitation, and the sound of the gate opening would give her plenty of warning. She settled into the wide chair her grandfather had built against the shelter of the big boulder that formed one wall of the house. Her grandfather had always claimed it was their own special guardian, placed there to keep all who lived in the house safe and well.

A fantasy tale told to a small child, but if ever she needed a buttress against the world, it was now. With the sun for once giving warmth to her small corner of the world, the hardy western plants springing into flower around the small pond at her feet and the critters chirping happily in the nearby shrubbery, she leaned back into the chair as Ruiseart greedily bent to his feed, and she gave in to the easy drowsiness. It was a blessing of early motherhood she had learned to cherish. A precious time when the world must leave her alone and all that was asked of her was to stay still and hold her baby close. She was vaguely aware of a commotion inside the house, but no one bothered her, nor would her grandmother allow it.

Another blessing of this house. Even her father and his wife knew better than to challenge her grandmother. He might be the economic power in this city, but her grandmother held its love, and few would follow if he dared threaten her. He valued his wealth and power too much to risk that.

Eventually, though, all times of refuge must come to an end. Ruiseart finished his feed and fell asleep. She took him inside and placed him with the nursemaid, safe and secure in the warmth of the same bedroom that had sheltered her as a child after her mother's passing. Then she walked through to the main room, where the messenger from her father waited as expected.

But there were two messengers, not one. The second was a face she didn't recognise, and, by the man's rigid stance, she guessed he wasn't pleased at being here. Not while her father's man was also in the room. Maybe she should have checked the calls crowding her com.

"Please, attend to the other Ser first," said the stranger. "If Sera den Guire would show me her famous garden?"

Grandam wasn't about to leave Anna alone with either of the strangers and lifted her hand to her assistant. "Please show the Ser to the potager garden. I'm sure he will be interested. It is most suitable for any feeling hungry."

Not until the man had left did her father's lackey step forward.

"Sera Anna."

"Sera Anna ingh Eolas bean Cumchdach den Coille," she reminded him sharply.

He flushed and repeated her name in full as courtesy demanded. "You haven't answered your father's com calls," he said, and bowed as if she wasn't glaring angrily at him. "The Sera Gria bean Eolas den Falasch hopes you will be free to attend a small family luncheon this afternoon."

She couldn't put off visiting her father's house forever, no matter how she might like to, and she definitely did not want them invading her grandmother's home.

"You can leave the wee one with me, as long as you are not gone long," said her grandmother placidly, and Anna heaved a sigh of relief. She may have run from Cumchdach, but she wasn't about to put his son at risk of being held hostage if her father became desperate.

"Not lunch then," she said with barely feigned regret, "but I will call on the household this afternoon."

She dismissed the man and breathed in deeply. Now to meet the den Coille agent. He could have come from no one else.

The man returned and repeated his deep bow. Nor did he indulge in prevarication, she was relieved to find.

"The family have delegated me to ensure your and the young Ser's safety," the man said after the sketchiest of introductions. He had a name. Ser Ceirden, he said, though she doubted it was his true one, and he flashed her an ID on her most secure com band. One she would have thought unbreakable, but den Coille security were almost as good as the marshals. Not surprising after their past history.

She glanced at it then erased it from her history, to the man's brusque nod of approval.

"This is my home city," she said curtly, "and my grandmother's house is as secure as any place in it."

The man gave a short bow of agreement. "However, the family thought a backup would be best. For both of you," he said, stressing the last sentence. He hadn't just been sent here to keep her baby safe.

"Who gave the order?"

His face became remarkably blank. "The appointment came from the office of Ser Bram mar Gliocas duine Scathach den Coille."

"Not from Ser Cumchdach mar Bram duine Anna den Coille?"

"Who made the request is outside my *need-to-know*, Sera. The message came from my senior."

There was nothing more to say, not when security took that stance. Den Coille security could be as tight faced as any marshal. That he'd been sent here as a spy was clear, and she suspected he wasn't the only one, thanks to her father's stupidity. Den Coille and Marshal security must be crawling all over Rubhaicreach. "My poor city," she murmured softly, and fortunately the man was as good at concealing his reactions as he was at obscuring unpalatable details.

The tragedy of it all was that she understood fully the need for it and was mostly grateful. She had come here for refuge, but it seemed she had work to do as well. Work that could be done only by someone who was of both den Coille and Rubhaicreach.

"And when I'm not with my son? Who do you guard then?"

A slight flicker of his eye was the only sign he recognised the trap, and he honoured her with a regretful smile. "I will stay with the baby, but you will still be safe, Sera."

"Will I have the pleasure of meeting your team?"

That regretful smile again. "I have no team, Sera. But you will be protected always."

The first part may have been a lie—she was sure of it—but the second was solid truth. Anna took the nearest seat. "Grandam, it appears you have a new…"

"Factotum," said the man.

"If you mean generally useful body, young man, be sure you will earn your place here," said her grandmother. "I manage my own affairs and that is not about to change."

The man bowed even lower to Grandam than he had to her. "I wouldn't dream of interfering in your household, honoured Sera."

She peered closely for any sign of patronising an elderly lady but saw none. He'd been here long enough, it seemed, to understand her grandam's place in the city.

What else had he learned? More importantly, how long had he been here?

How long had Cumchdach and the den Coille's known about her father's double dealing?

She set off that afternoon to her father's house, even more reluctant than before. It wasn't far from her grandmother's, a straight line of only twenty minutes' walk, but so many stopped her to say *hello* and *welcome back* and tell her how pleased they were to see her that it took much longer. She wasn't worried about Ruiseart. Her grandmother had hired a lovely nursemaid as soon as she heard Anna was coming, and one synthesised feed wasn't going to hurt him, but she missed the weight of him in her arms as she neared her father's grandiose compound at the head of the peninsula.

It had been a gracious home in her grandfather's day, but since her stepmother's arrival, her father had enlarged it, adding fortified walls and elaborate balustrading inside.

Who the walls were meant to keep out, Anna had no idea. Surely he didn't fear his own city? Then she saw the plantings in front of the wall. A wide swath of tailored, immaculately designed and maintained beds of carefully bred intruders in this wild region. The kind of plants that could survive here only with ongoing and meticulous care, plants meant for urban city streets in kinder climates. She had bred some of them herself.

Rubhaicreach homes were largely built underground, but most had at least a door and window opening to the surface. The two upper levels of the city were for homes, the lower levels for business. When she was last here, this had been a street filled with the kind of gardens native to this wild peninsula. Hardy shrubs with their exquisite flowers tucked securely underneath the canopy of the leathery leaves and thorns. Herbs and vegetables were grown in walled enclosures on the protected side of the house. Homes with children playing in the street and parents gossiping as they wandered home in the evenings or walked out of doors to feel a touch of real air and sun.

A thriving community, now razed and gone to make way for this abomination of a garden. Her stepmother's work. The woman came from Urbis and had never felt at home here, but she had taken to her father's wealth with delight. Not that Anna blamed her for her father's latest folly. That was his shame alone.

He'd been much the same in her own mother's time.

She walked up to the gatehouse, another new affectation, but at least the soldier on duty was someone she recognised.

"Anna ingh Eolas, welcome home."

"Meriac mar Toilich, you've grown somewhat since we last met." Then, he'd been a tow-headed and annoying younger brother of an old school friend, forever wanting to follow his big sister around and get them into trouble.

He grinned at her, then straightened suddenly as another man came into view. One she didn't recognise but who glared at young Meriac. She gave the newcomer a suitably stern look and demanded he open the gates for her.

Her credentials still held, although the newcomer looked put out at the necessity as he opened the gates to let her in. Once inside, they shut with a clang. She risked a short glance back and vowed to one day pay the newcomer back for the scared look on young Meriac's face.

Her father and the whole family stood at the formal front door to meet her, a tableau of a successful family waiting to greet the prodigal returnee, except for the phalanx of guards forming a ceremonial arc around them. Her father stood in the middle, his hair failing to stay in its neat cut, as usual, with curly wisps escaping around his ears. Beside him, her stepmother, taller and rigid. The woman probably thought she looked regal. All Anna could see were the cold grey eyes looking down the too perfect nose. She and Grandam had researched the woman once and unearthed a trove of images of the younger version.

"She's had a lot of work done," said her grandmother.

Beside her stepmother stood Anna's half siblings. Her brother Anton, and the twins Verianna and Charmente. More non-mountain affectations, but the names suited them as far as Anna was concerned. The eldest, Anton, had once been an enchanting toddler who had followed his big sister everywhere, but today he glowered down at her while the girls did their best to copy their mother's supercilious stare.

Anna stared placidly back then walked forward to hug her father, followed by the barest of cheek touches to her stepmother and siblings. They had long since given up any pretence of affection, and Anna saw no reason to try again.

"Da," she said with a smile. He had tried to be a father after her mother's early death, but the gulf had been too great to bridge. She turned to the rest. "Sera Gria, Anton, Varianna, Charmente." A brief nod from the children but her stepmother's face stiffened.

"Anna," chided her father after a look at his wife's face. "I know you were taught better manners than that. It's Sera Gria ingh Ovirisch bean Eolas."

"My mother and grandmother made sure I learned all the nuances of etiquette as appropriate for the occasion," she said evenly. "Shall we go in, Da?" She walked through the door and into the main room of the house. It hadn't changed either. As overdone as ever. She perched on the edge of a brocaded and dark coloured bench seat and waited for the rest to take their places on equally uncomfortable chairs. This used to be the main hall of the house where the den Falasch senior advisors and their families had met in large and rambunctious gatherings, with debate and laughter going long into the night.

Or it had been in her grandfather's day.

She ignored the others and stared at her father. "How could you have been so stupid?" she said.

"How dare you?" squawked her stepmother. "Your father is the head of this family and this city. I will thank you…"

Anna ignored her. "The facts are clear," she said to her father. "With Alliance lawyers and enforcement involved, you're going to lose your case, Father. What I need to know is, do you have a plan to make sure this city and its people aren't taken down with you."

"What do you mean?" he blustered.

"Come to the family room, Anna," said her stepmother, head held high. "Your wild accusations don't need to afford a public spectacle." Rising abruptly, she turned to the guards. "Get back to your posts. This is a family matter."

The rest went to follow her stepmother. Anna rose but did not move, eyeing the guards. Only the faces she knew were moving to leave. The newcomers, the hard-faced strangers, looked ready to follow the family into the private quarters.

"I don't think so, Sera," she said in a voice the equal of her stepmother's. "Troops, hold. I'm returning with you."

For a too long moment, no one moved, and she was forced to wonder if her father's family would actually dare abduct her. The strange guards stood on edge, eyes glittering. All except one, she noticed. Standing rigid, his eyes watched her, but not as rigid the rest. There was a warmth to him that the others lacked.

Could the man be from Den Coille? He bowed, first of all the unknown guards, followed too slowly by the rest, and she was sure of it. A brave man.

Should she tell her father he had a Den Coille spy in his midst?

She dismissed the thought as soon as it formed. A spy, and a protector for her and Ruiseart. Any secrets of the man were safe with her.

"When you come to your senses, Father, I will be at Grandam's, trying to protect the city as best I can from the fallout of your mess. In the meantime, farewell."

She made no attempt to include her stepmother and half-siblings in her farewell, and part of her wept at the torn look on her father's face. But he made no move to stop her or to explain. He'd made his choice and so must she. But first she had to get out of her father's house. She walked briskly past the strange guards and toward the ones she knew. They glanced in her stepmother's direction and, for the first time, fear flickered to life in her. She kept walking, kept hoping, and engaged their eyes, pulling them all back to her.

She had known these faces, known their families since she was a small child. They had all grown up here, so why did she feel her freedom was in the balance?

"Let's go," she said to them briskly, and discovered she'd been holding her breath when the first of them bowed his head.

"As you say, Sera Anna ingh Eolas an Sumhneas den Falasch."

She squashed the urge to correct him. It was the name she'd grown up with, the name they knew her by, the name that said she belonged here as much as them and far more so than the strange troops or her stepmother. But to herself she murmured her true name. *Anna ingh Eolas bean Cumchdach den Coille.*

Her father and his family said nothing, made no attempt to stop her, but Anna still drew in a deep breath when she made it through the gatehouse and heard the clank of the lock engaging behind her. She made some kind of cursory thanks to the guards, hoping none of them suffered for their loyalty even as she asked about their family members and gave a half wave before setting out down the path to her grandam's house.

She kept to the main street where she was visible, trusting in the years binding her to the people of this city, and wasn't surprised when a man joined her, sending her a discreet den Coille signal on her com. One of Ser Ceirden's fictitious non-team. Tomorrow, she would go out and about the city and find out what in roots was going on here. For now, she was glad to make the sanctuary of Grandam's house.

"What's your security like," she asked once she'd picked up Ruiseart and reassured him she hadn't left him, cuddling him close while she fed him.

Grandam didn't look surprised. "I had it increased when I heard about the den Coille's investigation. You're safe."

Anna hoped so. She was now the focus of three security agencies, it seemed. Whether they were willing to cooperate was another question. She left Ruiseart with Grandam the next morning, noting her new factotum working in the gardens surrounding the house, and took a tour of the peninsula, keeping well away from her father's house and ignoring the shadows following her. So far, her new guardians didn't interfere with her actions.

"You're back," said the beaming sera at the main grocery store, reaching up to bring down Anna's favourite biscuits from the top shelf where they'd been stored as long as Anna remembered.

"Sera den Guire well today?" asked the garden shop owner. The old man had been the first to teach Anna how to sort native plants from imported ones. She'd spent many happy hours in the fragrant aisles as a child, helping plant, water and nurture the vibrant stock. She lingered again today, asking about his current favourites, what grew here these days, what no longer seemed to be popular.

"These young folks want something different, something new. Can't see the wonders under their own feet." The old man had been making the same complaint as long as Anna could remember.

"What's selling now," she asked as she always did.

Today the man scowled back at her, a grim look that was new marring his weatherworn face. "Don't matter what they want; it's what will grow that counts," he said. "The airs are changing. You've got all those fine certificates, they tell me. Change them back."

Anna knew what he meant, but still she asked him to explain. Let the old man vent his frustrations.

"The government is working on it," she said soothingly at the end, "but not even they can make it go back to what it was. We all have to make some changes."

"Including that stepmother of yours and your da?"

"Them too."

"Yeah, and who's going to make them?"

She had no answer to that. How could she tell this man in his waning years that the home, the work, the life he'd known since babyhood might be ripped away from him forever if Arcadia failed to comply with the Alliance's demands. Cumchdach's brother might have wrung concessions from the Alliance Council and bought the planet time to fix their errors, but it didn't change the fundamentals. Arcadia was in trouble. The settlers had abused its bounty and now the planet was hitting back.

The seasons the old man took for granted had changed, and unless the settlers took appropriate actions, they would keep changing, and not in ways best suited to its inhabitants.

It had been some months since she'd been home. A violent storm had swept through since, its effect still visible in the black scars on rocks from lightning strikes and the new plantings replacing torn-out shrubs. They were used to that in Rubhaicreach, but this storm had been one for the books. A one in fifty-year outburst from the seas, said the street talk. Only it wasn't. Storms like this would keep coming until den Coille changed its growing patterns and Winter Solaris cut back the swaths of land covered by its old-fashioned solar farms. Both were in progress, but was it fast enough?

And what would replace them? It was a question she'd forced to the back of her mind, refused to examine as it was too tangled up with all those lost dreams lying between her and Cumchdach.

Den Coille was one of the biggest and most powerful corporations on the planet, dominating the entire western slopes of the central ranges. Its Festin was exported throughout the Alliance worlds, its nutritional and taste properties latched onto by spaceships and artificial habitats to enhance the foods they grew. Adding Festin to their food supplies cut the quantities that must be carried by a relished ten percent.

But an excess of festia trees was the heart of the mountains' environmental problems. She stood at the cliff edge on the southern face of the peninsula and looked south to the ranges, south to where Cumchdach lived in his home city of Manascraoch. A magical city built within the mighty baullnia trees but, surrounding it and cloaking the mountains from southernmost tip to nearly here in the north, the original mix of tree and shrub types had been replaced by unbroken vistas of festia plantations—and festia loved boggy feet and constantly swirling mists and rain. Ideally suited to the boggy gullies of the western ranges, now they cloaked every ridge and hollow, helped by water channels and carefully designed weather systems.

Weather changes that clashed at the mountain tops with the hot, dry air rising up from the increasingly desiccated eastern plains making up the bulk of the central portion of the continent of Protos. Cold, wet air meeting hot, dry air was a recipe for disaster, and an invisible line where the two pressure systems met ran unnaturally down the entire length of the ranges in a dangerous collision of battling currents.

Den Coille and Solaris were working to change that, but working fast enough?

Unbidden came an image of Cumchdach as he came to their rooms one evening during her pregnancy, a line carved into his forehead as he entered, to be banished when he saw her with an almost visible exertion of will. She'd rather he'd told her what troubled him, as he'd done so often in their lives. As teenagers, they'd told each other everything.

When had that stopped?

And would the missing him stop when she discovered the answer? He was sunk so deep in her heart, she doubted she would ever get him out. Was that pathetic of her? She'd thought he returned her love, but that was before.

And now? She'd been a part of his life for so long she doubted he'd ever questioned what he felt for her. Like so much about their life together. She was just there, always had been and always would be.

The pain of it squeezed tight, and she stooped to the plants at her feet, needing the feel of growing things to banish it. She plucked at a small yellow flower, tugging restlessly at the petals until they were gone and she looked for another. Then felt guilty. What had the plant done to her?

Then she noticed there were no more flowers at her feet. Strange. The rete flower, commonly known as the *me-too* flower on the peninsula, should be all around her, flourishing in the hard, rocky soils of the exposed headland. But the one she'd torn into nothing was the only one. She pulled up her com and set it to scan down the soil layers with her own botanical program, then pulled up the results.

No wonder there were no other flowers. This solitary plant was a pitiful survivor of what should be a network of roots and affiliated species linked throughout the poor soil of the headland, but only a few wispy rootlets pierced the dirt beneath her feet and few of the usual buddy species and companion microbes registered on her scan. Worse still, the soil composition was already showing the effects, breaking into easily scattered granules that would be easy prey for the winds and rains of the plateau. The folk of the peninsula cherished the churlish native plant with good reason.

Anna's com contained a highly sophisticated botanical program, designed by a top-level scientist in Urbis, with her collaboration. If there were such plants in the vicinity, her system would have registered them.

What had happened to the rest? She marched back to Grandam's house, the remnants of the last pitiful flower clutched in her hand to brandish in her Grandam's gardener's face.

"Where are all the rest?"

He shrugged but his eyes glittered. "Purged, by order of the big house," he said too carefully.

"Whose order?"

But it didn't need his toneless "the Sera" to tell her.

"Why?"

"They have thorns."

Of course they did. They'd always had thorns, and every child on the peninsula knew it. The thorns weren't big, but they carried a nasty toxin that left painful welts on anyone daring to disturb them. Not that any real Rubhaicreach citizen would be so stupid.

"And my father? Did he make no attempt to rescind this insane order?"

She shouldn't have asked the question. She knew as soon as she said it, even without the horrified look on the man's face at the position she'd put him in. "Forget I asked that, Ser. I'll get on to Urbis immediately and have the order rescinded."

The barest trace of relief crossed the man's face.

"Why did she want rid of them?"

The man's face went even blanker. "I understand a younger Sera, one of your sisters, touched them once."

Anna grimaced. "Screeched her head off, did she?"

The man refused to answer that, and she got a bad feeling about what was happening in her home city. Her stepmother had always been overly officious, with little understanding of the rhythms of the city, but it seemed she had grown in conceit since Anna's departure.

"Don't worry, Ser. I'll make sure the Sera is informed of the place of the me-too plant. We cannot afford to lose it, and all efforts will be made to ensure that it is satisfactorily re-established throughout the city."

"And the gardens, Sera."

"Which gardens," Anna had to ask and sighed inwardly. She had fled home for a respite, but people came to her to sort things out no matter where she was. This time, it seemed that her father, prodded no doubt by her stepmother, had commandeered the town's ceremonial gardens, a wild swath of local plants winding through the streets and pathways of the upper surface of the city. Her stepmother had decided the town needed 'tidying up' and was intent on creating a replica of the groomed streets of Urbis' wealthier suburbs.

Did the woman have no idea what it would take to get the species she wanted to import to grow in the harsh salt winds and freezing fluctuations of the plateau? Their street gardens celebrated the peninsula's unique flora, a symbol of the city they had built here. Anna had helped in them since she was a small child, drinking in the lessons of the head gardener, a man lauded throughout the mountains.

But her stepmother had little time for mountain ways. Only mountain money.

"I'll sort it," she promised the gardener and wasn't surprised at the look of relief that washed over his face. Anna had been 'sorting' matters in Rubhaicreach since she was a teenager. Was it any surprise she fell for the staunch eldest son of the den Coille family, who took on the same role in his family.

The rete issue was easily solved. A call through to the Biota Ministry and they soon messaged back to say a biome team was on its way. It wasn't a hollow promise either. Within the hour, the local biome officer was on her com, near to tears as she thanked Anna. News travelled quickly in the city.

"They're arriving tomorrow," the officer gasped disbelievingly. "We've been onto them for months."

Anna felt a fraud accepting the woman's thanks. Whether it was the den Coille name or her own contacts, she didn't know. But at least the problem was being solved. Gria couldn't beat the power of a Ministry investigation. Her next walk around the city brought so many hugs and words of thanks that the shadows following her emerged as a posse of grim-faced men and women surrounding her. She had to glare at them to stop them manhandling the city folk away from her. On her next trip out, two huge men in den Guire uniform hovered at her shoulder. She tried appealing to Ser Ceirden, but he shook his head. Den Guire and den Coille were working together, he said, and warned her not to take risks.

"They just want to thank me. I've known these people forever."

But no hugs were allowed that day. She still got a smile from her favourite garden store owner.

"Well done, young Sera," said the old man gruffly.

She forced a return smile on her face and stumped home, feeling more a fraud than ever. The city expected her to fix things. She couldn't even fix her own life.

CHAPTER THREE

Cumchdach woke yet again to a lonely sleeper and a home echoing with an emptiness he feared was permanent. Even dressing seemed too much effort. It was only pride and the thought of Anna's face if she returned that had him slouching into the cleansing unit. At the end, he left the choice of clothes to his wardrobe. It produced casual trousers and a sloppy tunic. No meeting today, then. The only bright spot in the day.

His father wanted Anna back. To work on an alternative strategy, he said. True enough, but Anna had taken their first grandchild with her, and the whole family felt the loss.

He missed his son, too, but losing Anna... Roots, how he missed her cool, calm view of the problems clogging his desk. Missed her subtle interventions in the volatile mix that was his family.

Missed her beautiful body and her unbridled responses, the hunger that had come into their lives in their teen years and never left. So far, no one had been stupid enough to offer him consolation. He wasn't sure he'd vouch for his actions if they did.

He needed something to occupy his thoughts. No, needed something else to do. A grim smile cut across his face as he ordered up his flyer.

"Where to, Ser," said the head of his security detail. These days, den Coilles never ventured far from home without one, and he didn't have the energy today to argue about it. Nor did he have a reason to, apart from wanting to be alone on his miserable flight.

He was alone too much, his mother said.

He soon made his destination, a sloping ridge line above a deep gulley holding a rushing stream. Deep in the valley, the distinctive green of festia held strong, but up on these exposed slopes, that was changing. He directed his flyer down to a cleared patch on a small plateau where machinery and a mobile shed showed a planting crew working. He landed and marched out, watching the busy team in den Coille gear momentarily slow down, then continue with a brief hand wave to him as the supervisor walked over, accompanied by another man in the uniform he hated, no matter how unfair it was to this particular ser. The uniform of the Ecological Survey held too many memories, too many reminders of the pain and humiliations of his imprisonment.

"Ser Joseph mar Freshet an Sonrai den Braich," he said curtly to the Survey leader, before turning to the head of the Den Coille team working alongside him. "And Dabha mar Tuath. A fine day to you. All going well here, I see."

"The best we can," said Dabha in his usual understated way. He'd known him since first school, and Dabha had never believed in false optimism. Or any kind of optimism at all, really. He was a fine forester though, and Cumchdach trusted him implicitly.

He'd also known Joseph mar Freshet since first school and still wasn't sure how he felt about learning the botanist had been working for the Survey for years, along with the rest of his sister

Fioruisghe's secret team. The man gave him as curt a nod back, but since he was also never given to unnecessary words, Cumchdach ignored it. Anna liked the fellow botanist and worked well with him. A reminder that stung hard today, and he had to fight to keep the edge out of his voice. "What's the Survey doing here."

"Just checking up on you and your teams," said another voice behind him, and he really scowled this time.

"Fioruisghe, I should have known."

"Nice to see you too, brother."

"I thought you were busy with the mud puddle you and Caleb are building out on the plains."

"*Lake* Ben."

"Didn't look much like a lake last time I saw it," he muttered, the weak retort the best he could dredge up in his present mood.

"That was quite some time ago. Since then, we've finished the plantings on the margin and begun establishing the aquatic flora. Anna was helping us with it, and still would be if *someone* hadn't upset her so much she left the city."

Diplomacy might not be Fioruisghe's strong point, but she was capable of it. She'd clearly decided to ditch it today.

"Water plants aren't her area."

"Maybe not," said his sister, her chin jutting forward. "But she does know everybody useful and is an expert on getting plants to work together. Right now, our lake needs her. But no, she's off back home to that pack of predators she calls family and is too busy—translate too miserable and hurt—to help us. Thank you very much, big brother. Next time you decide *not* to tell your wife something, take a deep breath and think again."

He shoved up a hand to stop her but Fioruisghe was like a force of nature and opened her mouth to keep at him.

"That's enough, sister. Look after your own marriage and stay out of mine." He swung around to the Den Coille supervisor. "Dabha, show me what you're up to, then I have to get back to town. I have other *critical* demands on my time."

He half expected Fioruisghe to follow and keep up her tirade, but when he finally risked a glance back, she was comparing records with Joseph. Her eyes stared after him, though, and the frown on her face was too like the ones he caught Samhchair hiding from him ever since Anna had left. Not angry at all. He turned back to his supervisor and concentrated on listening to the man's precise description of the proposed work schedule. Or tried to.

"Good work," he said at the end. "It's coming on well." They were replacing the festia trees on these upper ridge lines with tough shrubs and wide-rooted native grasses to hold the soil until the saplings of the original tree species grew back; along with removing the shelter belts, reticulation, and feed systems the introduced festia had needed to survive on the exposed land.

At this rate, Den Coille would be down to half its former festia plantings within a yearly cycle. No wonder his father was worried. He'd seen the figures, but the bare clearings and felled trees made it real.

He gave Fioruisghe a brief nod as he left. From the look on his older sister's face when he arrived home, Fioruisghe had already updated Samhchair. He slunk off to his quarters and said nothing at dinner that night.

Luckily, he could hide in work the next day, and a series of curt exchanges with a customer tardy in paying took the edge off his mood. He shut down the com feeling better, though knew he ought to feel guilty.

The man had to pay them. They couldn't afford freeloaders, not in this business climate.

Then a ping came through on his com. He checked the caller and swiftly jabbed to accept it. "Ser Ceirden, how is Sera Anna ingh Eolas?

"She is well, Ser, though showing signs of weariness after the baby's birth."

His heart jolted. "Is she all right?"

"Her medics inform her grandmother that Sera Anna is fine. It's normal so soon after birth and with a young baby needing to be fed at all hours."

"Is the baby giving her much chance to rest?"

"As much as young babies do, Ser." Ceirden had family himself and was well aware of the demands of a newborn. It was one of the reasons he'd chosen the man.

"Her grandmother has employed a nursery maid to help," Cumchdach said, as much to reassure himself as anything else.

"I've checked the woman out, Ser Cumchdach," the man said. "She has excellent qualifications and personality. The young Ser likes her. He's happy and growing well."

"That's good."

Such inadequate words. His *son* should be here, should be flourishing under the care of both parents. It was days since he'd felt the precious weight of Ruiseart sleeping in his arms.

"And Sera Anna?" He'd read the report on her aborted visit to her father's house. "Is she safe?"

"She goes nowhere without at least one of us following and is under full surveillance at all times."

There was a *but* in the man's voice. "Where does the Sera go?" he suddenly realised was the right question.

Ceirden's face became too carefully blank. "We may not have understood Sera Anna's full position and status in the city."

She should be home, feeding her baby and catching up on sleep. "What's she up to?"

"The Sera has been pulled into a number of city matters," said Ceirden. "The people of Rubhaicreach trust her and turn to her when there are disputes or problems."

"That's her father's job."

"The Sera Anna…" the man coughed awkwardly. "She has a talent for it, Ser. The Sera knows the people in the city and they trust her. Ser Eolas is not viewed the same way."

"I bet he's not," said Cumchdach sourly. "He's as crooked as we suspect?"

The man nodded. "You've seen my reports."

The agent discussed a few more matters then signed off, leaving Cumchdach staring at the empty com field, a heavy weight lodged deep in his gut.

What are you doing, Anna? You've just had a baby. You need to rest, not run around fixing everyone else's problems.

And you're not on the verge of blazing up there and demanding she come back to solve yours?

Maybe. But first, he needed to protect her. Rubhaicreach may be her birth home, but he couldn't tell himself she was safe there. Not if she was pushing herself right into the middle of whatever trouble her stupid father and stepmother were causing.

"Wardrobe, pack a bag for me. Three days, destination Rubhaicreach. Business and personal."

He got as far as the lobby to the den Coille private landing pad. His father stood there, arms crossed, backed by his mother and eldest sister.

"Where do you think you're going?" said his mother.

"To fetch back my wife."

His father bent a pained look on him. "You're going to fly into Rubhaicreach, throw her and Ruiseart on board and high tail it back here again?"

"This is their home. They should be here."

"And they will be," said Samhchair. "But not like this. Give her time. Maybe even talk to her first before bludgeoning her into submission."

"I wasn't going to," he said, stunned. "I'd never. This is *Anna*."

"Do you even know why she left?" said his mother.

"I hurt her," he admitted. "I should have told her about the fraud case."

"Yes, you should have," said his father, "and now you're going to fix it."

If only it were that easy. By the look on her face, Samhchair thought the same.

"It changes nothing," said Cumchdach belligerently. "She's not safe in Rubhaicreach and I'm bringing her home."

"Not safe in her childhood home city with her grandmother, a whole city who respect and cherish her, and her own father in town?" Samhchair said.

It sounded so reasonable, but that spike of fear niggled him. "Eolas den Falasch is a small man and a coward. I'm not about to trust Anna and Roo's safety to him."

His father lifted an eyebrow at that. "You have a whole team of our best security in Rubhaicreach. What do you think can happen to them?"

It sounded stupid to him too, but it didn't banish his urgent need to bring her home.

"And what do you think will be the outcome of your rampaging in there and stealing away with a cherished daughter of Rubhaicreach, against her wishes—and they will know that," said his father quickly before Cumchdach could deny it. "The situation with the Falasch business is bad enough already. You want to set fire to it?"

Everything they said was true, but none of it helped.

"You're going nowhere, son," said his father gently. "Not yet. Anna is safe, Ruiseart is safe, and she will listen to you in time. Don't make it worse."

His parents' marriage had always been the model he aspired to for him and Anna. Two strong people, they disagreed often enough, but never had any of their children feared they would part. The bond between them was the strong bedrock of his whole family life.

"I'll stay for now," he finally had to agree, "but if there is the slightest hint she or Ruiseart are at risk, I will be going to Rubhaicreach."

"And Den Coille security will go with you," promised his father.

"Ser Cumchdach, we've got a situation."

The message woke Cumchdach from an uneasy doze. He'd gone to sleep early, worn out from weeks of too little sleep and too much worry. Anna had stopped taking his calls, and it was only the regular reports from Den Coille security that kept him half sane. He lifted up on his elbow, peering blurrily at the incoming com message. Then abruptly woke. The message was from Ser Ceirden in Rubhaicreach.

"Cumchdach here. What's happened?"

"The Sera has been taken by Falasch security."

Cumchdach's world crashed. "Where to?"

"She's in the den Falasch homestead. Security forces surrounded her on her evening walk and took her to the main house. She sent a message to say she will be spending the night with her father and his family."

"Ruiseart?"

"Safe in his great-grandmother's house. He's not happy but is accepting synthetics for now."

"Get him out of there. Then find out exactly where in the den Falasch compound they're holding Anna. After which, you can explain exactly how your people let this happen."

Fortunately, Ceirden made no attempt to excuse himself, and right now, they needed to get Anna back safely.

"The message could be genuine, Ser Cumchdach duine Anna."

"And the moons now rise in the west."

A wry grunt from Ceirden. "Her grandmother said something similar, only not as polite."

Cumchdach was moving, calling on his wardrobe for fatigues gear. "Com me as soon as Ruiseart and his nursemaid are safe and you have Anna's position."

He signed off and put a call through to the head of Den Coille security. "We leave as soon as you have your team ready. Make it quick," he finished.

"Shall I notify the Marshals' office?" the security head asked in the toneless voice he used for unwelcome words.

"It's not their business, surely?"

"It would be advisable, given the current state of planetary affairs and the involvement of the Alliance with the Falasch case."

He didn't like it, but nodded curtly. "Keep it as brief as possible. Only what they need to know."

In a thankfully short time, Ceirden came back to him. "We have young Ser Ruiseart and his nursemaid safely away. They're on board a Den Coille flyer and out of Rubhaicreach airspace. He will be home in Manascraoch before morning."

"He's safe?"

"Sleeping peacefully through it all, protected by a full squad of den Coille security. His nursemaid has a cool head."

One part of his heart stopped clenching too tight. "And Anna?"

"Is lodged in her old room in the den Falasch household. The appearance is as the message claimed."

"Why can't I com her then?" He'd been trying to get through to her ever since Ceirden had woken him.

"There is a protective shield around her quarters and a full blackout on her com transmissions. The household have been told it is for her protection."

"But…?" said Cumchdach to the pause in Ceirden's voice.

"Her door is guarded by out-of-town security guards, and all the local guards have been banished."

"Is the city aware of the situation yet?"

"Sera den Guire blocked release of the news until the young Ser was safely away. She has called in the local police, ones she tells me are trustworthy. They are currently being briefed."

Cumchdach forced his team to use maximum flyer speed. They made it to Rubhaicreach airspace before Roo had landed in Manascraoch. His son wasn't his worry right now, though. Not when his flyer was surrounded by a full wing of Den Coille security and with a doting grandmother and aunt waiting impatiently for his arrival.

But a young baby should be with his mother. Over the years, Cumchdach had built up a dossier of grievances against Anna's family, but this latest topped it.

"We're going in shielded," said the security chief. "Den Guire's security are waiting for us."

They landed on the edge of the city, where a tossed-up pile of rocks and shrubs provided good cover for their flyers. One small flyer might have been less likely to be detected, but Cumchdach needed enough people to deal with whatever arose and had also ordered a full medic unit to accompany them, just in case.

He couldn't think about that too much. About what might be happening to Anna even now.

She's in her father's house.

Yes, with a stepmother and siblings who frankly hated her, and a father who had never loved her or her mother as he loved his second wife and children. That had never surprised Cumchdach. Eolas den Falasch's second wife was a fit match for him, while talk said his first marriage had been more a union of the commercial and political leaders of the city. The den Guires had been producing local and planetary politicians for generations and were woven as tightly into the fabric of Rubhaicreach as Falasch was into its economy.

The future head of Falasch marrying the eldest child of den Guire had pleased the whole city. As their only offspring, Anna held a unique place in her hometown.

Once landed, his squad left their flyers and moved silently through the cluster of shrubs and half-concealed walls and streets of the city.

Rubhaicreach was a strange place, unlike any other mountainer city. From the air, it looked like a nearly abandoned minor settlement, the den Falasch home the only substantial building at ground level. The rest showed only as half-submerged houses surrounded by walled gardens and streets that looked more like crooked pathways, with tough vegetation shrouding the low hummocks and rocky outcrops. Beneath the surface, though, lay a warren of tunnels and caverns. Without seeing the busy harbour lying below the cliffs, there was little sign of the city's true size.

Anna had often assured him that geotech engineers signed off every tunnel and underground building, but he never felt truly safe in the place. How could a honeycombed pile of rock withstand the storms that frequently battered the peninsula? The weather here was even harsher than in Manascraoch.

His squad kept to the surface until they met their local contact, a den Guire soldier. He kept com and physical silence, gesturing them to a hatch opening on the landward side of yet another of the ubiquitous piles of rock.

Not until they were all underground and the hatch safely closed did the man signal it was safe to speak.

"Sera Anna? Any word?" said Cumchdach before anyone else could get in a word.

"Still in the den Falasch house. Your man inside tells us she hasn't left her room and is under guard."

"And the city? Word must have got out by now."

"Too many owe their jobs to Falasch. So far, opposition is still at the murmuring stage."

"What if she's not released soon?"

The man scowled. "Murmurs can turn too quickly to shouts and actions. We'd rather that not happen. Not if she can be got away quickly and without fuss."

"Surely her father will see sense and release her?"

"Maybe, but not the Sera Gria. She has no idea how this city works."

They had to get Anna away from this nightmare. "What's the plan?"

The man led them to the rest of his group, a mix of den Guire security and city police. There, they pulled up holos of the city and the talk quickly fell to routes and strategies. Cumchdach listened intently but made little comment. The others were the experts here, and his security knew exactly how important Anna was to him. He had no fear they'd put her at more risk than necessary.

A call came through on his com. He checked it without interest, then saw who it was and cursed as he accepted it.

"Ser an Fallon. This is a surprise." Not for the first time, he wished he could read the police commander's face. The head of the planet's elite Federal police service, Marco an Fallon was as renowned for his inscrutability as he was for his integrity.

"I hear you have a situation there, Ser Cumchdach."

"It's under control," Cumchdach tried.

"A squad of marshals is in transit. Please put me through to the local security."

"There's no need," he tried next.

This time, a slight hint of impatience marked the man's face. "Sera Anna den Coille is an important figure in Arcadia's response to the Alliance's conditions. The Academy has identified her as one of the scientists with whom they've agreed to work."

Yeah, thanks to Cumchdach's newest sister-in-law, who was an Esteemed Scholar of the famed Alliance Academy. He liked Anyara ingh Gevard bean Seolta, but he could have done without her marking out Anna like this.

He lifted a hand to the head of local security and forwarded Marco an Fallon's call through to him and to the head of his own security detail, but kept his own link active and hidden. He wasn't about to let the marshals interfere with Anna's rescue without knowing what they were up to.

"They're sending in their own squad," said his security head at the end, and Cumchdach nodded with a frown. His Anna was no mere object for security to use in their schemes. She was much more than a useful cog in the marshals' and Arcadia's plans, so much more than her expertise and analytical brain.

She was Anna.

When the security heads finalised their plans, telling him they meant to wait until the marshals arrived, with a strong hint that Cumchdach should stay safely in her grandmother's house, he told them exactly what he thought of that. He wasn't about to trust Anna's safety to any cold-minded pack of so-called experts. Anything could be happening to her.

The next hours were a hellish time of waiting for the arrival of the marshals and assembling in a back room off the den Guire offices. It was the only place not at risk of surveillance by Falasch's systems. Cumchdach paced down the utilitarian space, kicking at the odd crate in his way. Not hard enough to damage it or himself, or to satisfy his need for action, but it was better than nothing.

Finally the marshal squad arrived, and the security groups huddled together as they linked in systems and confirmed their plans. They would have shut Cumchdach out if he hadn't muscled his way into the middle. He had to forcibly point out to them that he knew best how Anna would react to get them to agree, although the frowns on the Rubhaicreach troops told what they thought of his claim. Too many had grown up with Anna, and all owed their loyalty to the den Guire family. Whether the den Falasches liked it or not, the den Guires weren't about to desert the city to their questionable control, whatever Anna's benighted stepmother might imagine.

He growled, shaking his head. Getting angry at the woman wasn't doing anything to get Anna back. All it did was remind him of the woman's lack of morals, and that was truly scary. To Gria, Anna was nothing more than a hindrance to her own brats' future prospects.

But even less were the city troops about to leave her safety to a den Coille. Not with that fraud trial hanging over the city. They might work with his security today, but that was necessity and all the troops here were professionals. All except him.

Tough. Anna was his wife, first, last and always.

Finally, the security leaders stopped talking and showed signs of moving out. The marshal squad leader strode over to him and personally did a last check on Cumchdach's gear. He'd brought his full assault kit from home and was sourly pleased when the marshal failed to find any defect.

The man gestured at the weapon on his hip. "You know how to use that?"

"Fully accredited and routinely re-certified." Den Coille didn't have their own well trained security branch for nothing, and after the false Survey's attack on his family, they'd made doubly sure that every single den Coille and their staff were able to defend themselves.

"Keep in the middle of the squad. I want my people around you at all times, Ser den Coille."

"We have that under control," snarled back his own security head. It had no effect on the marshal. The Feds were the best on the planet, and everyone in this room knew it.

"Keep out of trouble," the marshal said again. Then lifted a fist and brought it forward.

They moved out.

Soon they had re-grouped in a line just beyond the den Falasch's grotesquely pristine gardens.

"Do we know exactly where the Sera is at present?" asked the squad leader.

The local security head checked his com and confirmed it with the head of Den Coille security before sending a holo-link to all of them. "In her room, but Ser and Sera den Falasch are heading that way."

That didn't sound good. "We move in now."

No one listened to him. He slapped a hand on both the marshal's and Den Coille security head's shoulders. "Now," he mouthed.

"They're moving," said the Den Coille comms tech suddenly.

"We've been picked up by their security," said the marshals' tech comm almost simultaneously.

"At the back," snapped the squad leader at Cumchdach, and this time he didn't argue, or protest at the man assigned to babysit him. All the troops had suddenly morphed into combat mode and he wasn't stupid enough to claim to be their equal. Even with training, he lacked their swift efficiency of movement or that lethal readiness of hand on their weapon systems.

After that, it was all hand and private com signals only, group comms kept to a minimum. He doubted the den Falasches had the ability to break into a network as secure as the marshals', but these men didn't take chances. Nor did he see when some slipped silently off the main group, finding only when he turned that there were suddenly fewer troopers. His bodyguard grabbed his arm and shook his head, curtly pointing the way ahead.

They know what they are doing.

They'd cut him out of the comms transmissions, so he had no idea what was happening to Anna, but with each silent step forward, moving carefully from stupidly shaped bush to wrongly placed boulder, his heartbeat sped up. Then his guard shoved him down into a hollow and they crouched in front of the wall surrounding the main house.

Why did a local need a wall that looked like the palisades of a fortress? Half the businesses in town relied on the den Falasches for work. Who did they imagine was going to attack them?

Him, tonight, if he got a chance. How dare they upset his Anna?

If only he knew what was going on behind it or where those extra troopers had slithered off to.

Then a sound echoed from the top of the wall and his heart seized to a stop.

"Cumchdach, run," yelled Anna.

He shot up, only to be slammed bodily down again before his head so much as threatened to breach the edge of the dark shadows hiding him. He struggled, desperate to get away from his guard and to Anna. "What are they doing to her?" he demanded in an urgent whisper.

The man sent him a holo on a private link, one that wouldn't show up in the dark. "It's under control, Ser. Stay down."

It didn't look under control, he thought in horror. The man let him up enough to see the top of the wall. Anna stood right on the outer edge, in a thin evening sheath that gave little protection against the vicious night breezes, and held at bay by two burly soldiers pointing weapons straight at her. Both wore full attack armour. He'd seen enough of it when his family had been captured by the mercenaries working for the false Survey bosses and later when they'd been marched off to that hell of a prison.

These men had the same look about them—the type of men who cared nothing for the people or the city they threatened or the woman standing so defiantly on that wall as shivers wracked her body.

One of those mercenaries lifted his wrist and spoke into his com. His voice boomed out across the gardens.

"Ser den Coille. Leave this city now. The Sera is safe and under the protection of her family."

His guard nodded to him. "Keep them talking," he whispered.

Cumchdach went to stand, but the man shoved him back. All he could see was that outline of Anna on the wall.

"Use diffuse mode," messaged his guard, thrusting a finger at the com sliver on his wrist.

Cumchdach nodded and lifted his wrist. "Let her go if you want her to be safe," he yelled and heard his voice echoing over the ground, seemingly coming from everywhere. "The Sera is going home to Manascraoch."

"She's already at home," the man said.

His guard prodded him.

"No she isn't, not any longer," called back Cumchdach. "Her home now is with her family in Manascraoch."

"Then why did she come back here?" said the man in a tone that set Cumchdach's teeth on edge. "Some family your lot turned out to be."

Was the man trying to provoke him?

Yes, he suddenly realised. That's exactly what he wanted.

"Leave her alone," he yelled back, letting all the anguish in him coat his voice. Then he turned to his guard. "What are they up to?" he sent via private com link.

The man shook his head. "We're not sure, but if they keep her out here much longer, the cold will deal with her. She'll fall from that wall and there goes their bargaining chip."

The man sounded as frustrated as Cumchdach felt but couldn't have been as horrified. "Where are your people?" he demanded.

"Wait," the man ordered.

Not an option. Not if it meant leaving Anna vulnerable. He shoved up again, and this time, all the man's efforts couldn't stop him. A flash shot out, and the man shoved up a defensive screen and pulled him back down.

"Now they know exactly where you are."

Cumchdach twisted away from his guard to cradle his arm, but he couldn't hide the smell of burning flesh.

"Where'd he get you?" said the man in a resigned voice.

"Upper right," said Cumchdach. "It'll hold. They just clipped me." He kept in the shadows and used his other hand to clamp the arm to his side.

"We have to move, now," said his guard.

Cumchdach could have groaned. *Move* meant crawl, and that was going to be interesting.

The guard watched his farcical impression of a hopping ganda and grunted once, then gave him a shoulder to lean on. Thankfully, he didn't make any pitiful comment, not even when Cumchdach was reduced to a slither along the ground, teeth biting down hard on his lip to quell any sound each time the injured arm met the ground. Soon, they'd have Anna back and he'd get medical help.

They settled into another hollow in the awful garden. This one had water tinkling through a small stream in the base lined with some kind of stones. They felt too uniform to be anything but artificial. Even the shrub they sheltered behind to get a view of the wall top smelled wrong. Anna must hate this place.

The mercenary's voice rang out again. "Last chance, Ser den Coille. The Sera is waiting for your answer."

All of a sudden, a flurry of bodies erupted into motion on the wall. The two guards vanished with a hard grunt.

Cumchdach shot up in time to see Anna toppling over the edge. He ran forward, faster than he'd ever thought possible. Then stopped as he saw a hidden field grab hold of her. A marshal appeared at the parapet face.

"I'm lowering her down now, Ser. Be ready to catch her. The field won't extend to the ground.

Cumchdach set his legs wide, braced, and looked up, and nodded at the marshal then at Anna.

"You're safe now. I'll catch you, I promise."

He'd said the same to her years ago when they'd been raiding the orchard of a neighbour of hers.

Her eyes caught his.

"I know you will," she said, and he'd never felt more thankful.

Next moment, her body dropped into his arms and he instinctively flexed with it, taking her precious weight and keeping her safe, as he'd promised.

"I have you," he said.

Then Anna leaned on his injured arm and they both crumpled to the ground. He rolled to put himself under her.

"Are you all right?" he demanded in a voice that sounded panicked, even to him.

He heard a choked gasp and twisted up to look suspiciously at her. Was she laughing at him?

"That's what happened the last time you said that to me."

He was about to give her the same answer as last time, a half-baked joke about her weighing too much, then was stopped short. Her eyes loomed deep and dark and that cold shiver still rocked her.

"Roo. I need Roo," she whispered.

"He's safe. Our people got him away to Manascraoch as soon as you were taken."

"But… Good." Her voice sounded as if ready to crack, fragile and breathy. She sat up, clenching her arms around her chest. "Good," she said, and it sounded even less convincing. "I need him," she said in a voice he barely heard.

"You'll be back with him as soon as we can get you there."

"I need him *now*." She burst into a flood of tears that was so unlike his Anna he stared in astonishment. He even let go of her and she rolled away, hugging herself into a tight ball that was even less like his Anna.

She never had to stand alone, not while he was near. He pulled her back into his chest, clamping her to his shoulder with his good arm.

"Shh. He's fine. You'll be with him soon."

"They wanted to use me against you. That woman… She said you'd give up this silly Restin problem if I asked you 'properly'. They were going to hurt you if I didn't."

"Shh. It's over now. You're safe, and she lost."

He gently soothed her, a hand stroking down and down her back, and for a while, it worked. Her gulping tears subsided. Someone offered to help him sit up and he refused. Not until Anna was quiet, with only the occasional betraying gasp. Then he rolled forward and let the hovering medic take her, and another helped him up. Something was happening up on the wall and he had no doubt a lot more somethings were going on inside the den Falasch home, but he ignored it all.

All that mattered was Anna and getting her home. He lifted his com and signalled his head of security.

"The marshals can clean up the rest of the mess here. Get us home."

He didn't relax until they were safe in a Den Coille flyer and back over his own country. The medics still hovered, infusing a concoction into her while another checked Cumchdach's wound.

She'd finally lost that awful, rigid set to her body when they'd commed through to his sister and Samhchair opened it to holoview, showing Roo sound asleep in her arms. His sister had always had a special touch with little ones. A shame she had none of her own, was the frequent comment around the city, and right now she had his and Anna's baby boy tucked up against her chest. His eyes were closed in the blissfully innocent sleep of a newborn, as if nothing had gone wrong in his world.

"He's safe," said Anna.

Then they landed, and waiting in the arrival's hall stood Marco an Fallon, the Senior Commander of the Federal Marshals, the senior police office on the planet.

CHAPTER FOUR

"We're holding the Ser and Sera den Falasch," an Fallon said. "What charges do you want to press."

Anna stared at both marshals. "Charges?"

"Kidnapping, assault, wrongful detention? The list of potential charges is long, depending on what you tell us, Sera," said an Fallon in that misleadingly dry voice of his.

"Anything you can make stick," said Cumchdach.

"No," said Anna, shaking off his hand when he grabbed at her. "You know what it cost your sister to accuse her own family." It was the reason they'd all first landed in prison. "You want the same for me? That one day, I have to tell Roo I'm the reason his grandfather was ruined?"

"He did it to himself."

"No," said Anna again, not fully sure why she did it. Just knew she had to. "For all his faults, he's my father. Watch him, constrain him from doing anything like this again. But I will not do this to my city."

"You could have died up on that wall."

She set her lips and stared him down, seeing the gulf between them yawn ever wider. "It was a misunderstanding," she said.

She repeated it again when another marshal came in to question her, despite all Cumchdach's protests, and when an Fallon told her that her father and Gria were to be released. Without her evidence, the marshals had no grounds to hold them.

The worst of it all; she had a sinking feeling that Marshal an Fallon was pleased at the outcome, though he gave no obvious sign of it.

"They will be watched, Sera," he promised her. She could only hope her father realised it.

"You think he's one of those opposing the Council?" Cumchdach had told her something of the conspiracy intent on stopping the changes demanded of Arcadia by the Alliance. He couldn't keep it from her, not when his own brother was sent into exile for his role in it. But her father? "He's many things, but he's not a traitor." *Please, no.*

"And his wife, the Sera Gria?"

She shook her head, unable to take any more. Gria, yes, that she could believe, but to take her father into it. "I have a baby to see to. It was all a misunderstanding. But my father," she glared at an Fallon, "he's no traitor."

"Not now," agreed an Fallon in that tragging calm voice of his. "Not after all the attention from my marshals."

Only then did they release her to seek her baby.

Later that night, Anna woke, shivering and terrified. She reached for Cumchdach then remembered he was in the spare room. They had fought and she had left him. Now she was back, in their home suite in Manascraoch, but it wasn't the same. She'd told him on that awful flight back that she'd agreed to come only for Roo's sake, and if they kept separate rooms.

Cumchdach had believed her, and that was what hurt the most. He loved his son and was prepared to tolerate this farce to be with him. Didn't he care enough about her to fight to stay with her?

No, this was for the best. They would find a way to make it work. They had to—starting with finding a place of her own, a place for her and Roo to live.

But tonight she needed Cumchdach. She huddled in a miserable ball, wishing she dared go to him.

Wishing she knew what came next.

She'd never liked her stepmother, but this time, the woman had gone too far. Her actions threatened Anna's home city, her family, the future of all she cared about.

She had threatened Anna's baby son.

That was the nightmare that woke her. Anna had been lost in a cold maze of narrow Urbis alleyways, with Roo's terrified cries calling to her. No matter how many corners she turned, how hard she ran, she never got closer. His cries got louder and louder, and an awful cackle of laughter taunted each of her desperate attempts to find him.

She'd never heard Gria cackle with laughter. Brittle titters, yes, but nothing so gauche as a witch-like cackle.

Yet it was Gria's voice laughing in her dream.

She dragged herself out of her sleeper and leaned over Roo in his cot. She'd laughed at Cumchdach when he'd ordered it. Top of the range, not only did it have every soothing device known to paediatric science, it had a truly ridiculous range of security devices.

She was grateful now for every one of them. Her baby slept in the careless abandon of infancy, little fists half clenched as they lay either side of his head, lost in complete relaxation.

His eyes were no longer tear-stained, but never would she forget how he had clung to her when they were reunited or his greedy, desperate slurps as he battened on to her breast.

'You left me,' those gasping slurps said. 'Where were you?'

"I will never abandon you," she promised him in a whisper. She was tempted to pick him up and cradle him tightly into her body, let the weight of him confirm he was back with her and safe. But that might wake him, and he needed his sleep after the upsets of the day. So did she, but that was a futile hope tonight.

She checked all the cot's safeguards to make sure they were on and fully armed to respond with an alarm if he so much as whimpered then slowly backed out of the room and closed the door manually to prevent the sound of it disturbing his sleep.

She needed a drink. Preferably one strong and bracing but that wasn't possible while she was nursing a baby. A big mug of chocostim was her best option. If nothing else, it would give her some of the nutrients and fluids a nursing mother needed, or so she told her inner critic.

Rubbish. You just crave those sugary calories.

And what if she did? She banished all thoughts of what she ought to do and tiptoed into the suite's kitchen unit. She'd had Cumchdach install it some years ago, before they married, so they didn't have to go out to the family kitchen for a snack when she was making a short visit with little time to spare.

A lifetime ago. How innocent they were then. Tonight, everything about the suite brought back memories. Etched in the stray beam of moonlight splashing through the windows on a rare cloudless night, she saw the main room's furnishing too well. There was the lounger they had found in a back-bough Manascraoch store, repository of others' offcasts. It was huge, too big probably for the room, but it was comfortable and large enough for games,

Cumchdach had said with a grin, and she loved the vibrancy of the pattern. It was too big to get through the doors or the corridors so his brothers had manhandled the thing through the outer branches of the family tree and through the balcony windows. Across it draped the throw she had made in her early twenties when she'd been on a craft binge.

She'd had more time then.

That set her off again. Where had time gone? What had happened to her? She had so many calls on her now. Family, her home city, this city, her studies and their impact, her whole planet. First and most urgent was Roo, the one call she would never ignore.

The only one?

She thrust the thought aside. Cumchdach had lost that right. Or that's what conscious thought claimed. The truth, she admitted, was something quite different, and Anna had never been one to lie to herself.

She'd always known the reality of what lay between her and Cumchdach. He was the heart of her, her very core, and now his son had joined him. But…

Where did that leave Anna? It had been the two of them for so many years. Even while at different Higher Schools, following different career paths, she'd always known he was there, a solid core standing at her back when she needed it.

Now, it felt like she'd lost herself. She no longer knew what was real, what assumed. Had she become merely Anna bean Cumchdach, engulfed by den Coille and no longer belonging to her city, her old home family?

To herself?

And who was she to Cumchdach? Loved partner in life, wife, best friend? Or an old habit he was used to having around, used to relying on when needed? Did he even know?

Cumchdach had so many more calls on him than she did. His family, his company, his city and now his planet. When Seolta's treachery was discovered, he'd talked to her of the problems facing Arcadia. Of the enemies facing those who wanted to save their world—misguided fools who ignored the science and thought Alliance Central too far away to bother Arcadians. Fools who put their own profit and comfort over the survivability of their planet.

Now she learned that one of those fools was her own father.

She pulled up the prepper control panel, bashed in the code for chocostim and waited for the steaming mug to appear.

A message came up. 'Enter your required additives.' She stared at it. She'd coded her own preferences into this prepper when Cumchdach had it installed. She tried a few more favourites. The same message. Someone had wiped her details and the machine no longer recognised her.

She was a visitor in her own home.

It was the final betrayal. She slumped to the floor, staring at the bench. What else had he wiped from his life?

She bent over, clutching her stomach, and desperately trying to hold in the pain. She couldn't. Great gulping sobs seized her. She slapped a hand over her mouth, then squeezed both fists against her face to keep in the sound but failed.

Someone touched her head and she jumped, hastily scrubbing at her cheeks. Then turned and saw her humiliation complete.

"Sweetheart," said Cumchdach, crouching down beside her and carefully keeping his hands at his sides. "You're safe now. You're home again. And when I get hold of your father…"

"You can't touch him," she said flatly. "Not you. Not when…" she waved a hand vaguely between them. Not when he'd married her. She'd known it for a mistake as soon as she'd agreed, but she'd found a grey hair that morning and seen one too many of her friends showing off their latest baby.

She wanted Cumchdach's baby. As simple as that. And now he must pay for it.

Cumchdach reached a hand toward her but stopped short of touching her. "What did they do to you?"

She shook her head. "Nothing, not really." Her stepmother wasn't quite that stupid and it wasn't what had made her cry. "They wanted to talk."

It's how she'd escaped. They'd sent up that stupid evening outfit and the fear on the face of the maid they'd sent had Anna agreeing to wear it. Then the maid said they expected her to come to dinner. To act as if nothing was wrong? When she refused, they'd both come to collect her. Gria had stood in the doorway thinking she'd won from the smirk on her face, but Anna had shoved past and simply ran. The guards had followed her, but only after a shouted order from Gria.

"What about?" said Cumchdach now.

She saw the hard set of his shoulders and hunkered back. He jerked as if she'd shot him.

"Just talk," she said quickly.

"No badgering you to stand witness for your father at his trial?"

She shrugged. Of course they had, and worse. Gria had demanded she make Cumchdach stop the court case. Had hinted that if he didn't, Anna would pay. Her father had stood there and said nothing.

"There's definitely to be a trial?" she asked.

"The Alliance trial has already started, though the Arcadian one's not scheduled yet."

"But…?"

"It's unavoidable. He cheated our company and our clients. We can't afford to ignore that."

Once, she would have demanded he tell her everything. Now too much lay between them. Nor did he volunteer more, and that said it all. He no longer trusted her. She thrust up wearily from the floor and turned back to the prepper. "I came out to make a drink. You wiped my preferences.

"I did?"

"Someone has." She automatically went to order a mug of dask for him. Then saw the same message as with hers and stared in confusion. "You wiped all preferences. Why?"

"A technician worked on it the other day. There was a glitch in the system. I haven't checked it since."

"You didn't wipe my details."

"Of course not." He reached over and pulled up the control panel, then entered in her chocostim details. They were correct, exactly correct.

"You haven't forgotten them."

"I will never forget anything about you, *a chiad*. Not from our first meeting until today."

"You can't do that," she wailed. How dare he make her feel guilty.

"What do you mean?"

She shook her head, impossible to explain. "You just can't," she said weakly.

His face closed over and her heart shrivelled. She'd seen him do that to others, shutting himself away and hiding his thoughts when it was necessary, but he'd never done it to her before. She shook her head, forcing away hope, and picked up her drink, lifting it to take a mouthful and hiding behind its protective cover.

"Thank you. I couldn't sleep."

Cumchdach studied her for a moment, then seemed to concede and picked up his own drink. "Roo keeping you awake?"

His voice was so careful, so devoid of anything overly emotional.

She shrugged. "He's unsettled but too exhausted to wake up. He should sleep well tonight and be fine tomorrow."

"Your stepmother deserves to be locked in a deep cell."

She agreed, but Gria wasn't alone. "My father lets her use his authority."

Cumchdach clenched his jaw but said nothing to that. It was too close to the edge. "You're safe now," he repeated as he'd done many times since her rescue. "Get some sleep and you'll feel better in the morning."

He was dismissing her. She was too tired to fight him, too worn out by the weeks of tension. Hating herself for her cowardice, she nodded agreement and said good night in a strained voice that surely failed to hide her misery. Her last view of him as the door closed was him staring after her, refusing to meet her eyes, his face still grim and closed over. She lay awake for long after she had finished her drink but didn't hear the sound of his own door closing. He did that when something troubled him; sat in the outer room and brooded.

When she woke and had finished readying both herself and Roo for the day, he had already left their suite.

She would *not* go hunting him.

What to do instead? Staying in her room was no option. Not after that last day locked in her old childhood room. No sign of that had remained of course. She'd been living with her grandmother for many years, and her stepmother had clearly taken that as a signal she was free to wipe signs of her husband's oldest child from the house. Her room looked like it had been used as a storeroom, and she hated to think where the sleeper they'd hastily shoved in there came from.

It was the only furniture, stuck in the middle of a pile of crates and beneath walls stripped of any decorations.

That room had once been her refuge. The bare shelves where she'd grown cuttings of any new plant found on her rambles remained, but the controls of the walls' landscape images had been smashed, leaving them bare and blank white. Maybe they thought she'd use the wiring to send out a message. What with, she didn't know since they'd taken away her com. She got it back only because the marshals had demanded her father restore it, and her stepmother hadn't yet thought to destroy it.

So unlike these rooms. Here her plants were still on the bench she'd set up in the main room, thriving thanks to her lab assistant, she guessed. Cumchdach had brown thumbs. Otherwise he'd changed nothing. The room still sang with life, filled with the pieces she and he had added over the years. This morning, though, the sight of them hurt even more than the emptiness Gria had made of her childhood room. She waited with uncharacteristic impatience for Roo to finish feeding then bundled him up as his eyes drooped with sleep and nestled him in his cocoon to bring with her.

Where to go was the next problem. All the family had left messages for her to visit as soon as she was free, but most brought too many questions she wasn't ready to answer. Her father-in-law was at the head of the waiting queue, with a request she meet him to discuss the festia problem. It was no doubt true. The whole family had been a mix of happy and relieved when she and Cumchdach had finally married, but Bram had also given her the impression that the shrewd businessman inside was rubbing his hands with glee. He needed her skills.

She'd see him tomorrow.

Nor could she face her mother-in-law. Scathach was one of the nicest people Anna knew, but thanks to years of dealing with recalcitrant patients, she possessed an uncanny ability to see right into a person.

The next message was from Samhchair, Cumchdach's elder sister. The steady pillar of the family, Samhchair was a skilled listener and knew exactly when to keep silent and when to speak up. She had taken over Roo's care yesterday, and thanking her for that was high on Anna's list of priorities.

Samhchair's room it was. She marched down the family corridors of the baullnia tree that was home to the den Coille family. Home, office and fortress, the mighty tree combined all three. When she'd first come here, the faint underfoot bounce of the tree branches flexing with her footsteps had unnerved her and she couldn't look down. Now, it felt normal. When had that happened? When had she changed from a rocky peninsula dweller to a tree person? She hardly ever ventured down to the muddy floor of the Manascraoch forest these days. She'd done it on a regular basis when she first started coming here, returning to her room covered with mud and drenched in the constant mists that cloaked the ranges, a hint of the sea fogs of home that rolled in without warning and smothered everything in its path.

Best of all were the violent mountain storms, so like those of her home peninsula. Cumchdach treated them as mere background to daily life, adjusting his busy schedule without thinking, but Anna loved them, pausing whatever she was doing to peer out the nearest window at the rain battering down on the bark and leaves of the tree, then revelling in the tree's defiance, leaves bending but not breaking under the onslaught. It always fed the courage inside her. These days, she badly needed that boost.

She shook the thought away. *Trouble comes knocking aplenty without asking it in*, was a favourite saying of her grandmother's, and Anna had more than enough already.

Samhchair was home and open to callers, she saw with relief. Mind you, Samhchair's doorpad message always said that unless she was sleeping, and even then, her door would wake her if necessary. Today, the door was wide open, also not unusual, but it gave Anna the confidence she needed. She beat a short rap-tap on the door frame and poked her head in.

"Are you up for visitors?"

Samhchair bustled into the living area from her home office and her face lit up in a smile. Anna often thought that Samhchair's smile would fix any woe, lighting her up inside and out.

"Come in, come in," said the older woman. "It's good to see you. How are you feeling today?" She enveloped Anna in a big hug, one hand gently cupping Roo's head as he slept in his pouch on Anna's front. "And this precious one?"

Anna hugged her before stepping back. "We're both fine," she assured the woman who had come to feel like the big sister she'd never had, and Samhchair didn't fail her today. She asked about Roo, how he was growing, about her grandmother and her friends in Rubhaicreach, then gave her all the latest gossip from here. Of family and the friends Anna had made over the years, the titbits of domestic trivia.

All non-threatening, all peaceful and normal. It was only after Anna had laid Roo down in the portacrib Samhchair kept here and Anna leaned back, replete from what Samhchair termed a tray of light refreshments, that Cumchdach's sister brought up the real reason Anna had come.

"What do you plan to do next?" said Samhchair in the calm voice that had stilled many family eruptions. Cumchdach could do it too, his word taken as law by his brothers and sisters, but not in the quiet way Samhchair managed. Anna often thought the others obeyed her because none of them wanted to hurt her by refusing. She looked down at her tunic, pulled at a barely visible thread in her leggings and glanced over at Roo to make sure he still slept.

She was procrastinating. She lifted her head and looked bleakly at her sister-in-law. "I don't know."

"Ah." Samhchair also glanced at Roo and a twisted smile crossed her face. "You and Cumchdach…?"

Anna shook her head. "I can't. Not with my father…"

"He's no different than he's always been. Den Coille trades with the company, not the man."

"The *company* I'm heir to and still hold shares in. My grandfather started training me to run it as soon as I could walk." Her paternal grandfather may have retired many years ago, but he had retained a firm grip on the Falasch company right up to his death five yearly cycles ago. Nor had he trusted her stepmother.

"Cumchdach knew what your father was when he married you."

"But I didn't, not truly."

Thankfully, Samhchair didn't call her out on that. Anna had always known her father was weak; she'd just never believed it could come to this. He had betrayed not only his company and its integrity. He had betrayed *her* with this latest idiocy.

"How could he think he'd get away with it?" she said, refusing to hear the little girl in her voice.

"How does anyone?"

There was too much truth in that. Only the truly stupid betrayed a powerful and astute family like the den Coilles. "It changes nothing. Cumchdach knew Den Coille was investigating my family's company, and he didn't tell me. He didn't *trust* me enough to tell me."

Samhchair lifted her hands in deprecation. "My brothers may be intelligent, but they've also been known to show a strong streak of stupidity. I do know he regrets what he's done."

Samhchair waited but Anna had nothing else to say, pain slicing through her, and Samhchair sighed.

"I won't say another word on it, except I think you're making a mistake. Almost as big a one as my brother." She lifted the jug of chocostim and Anna shook her head. "What about work plans. I know there's a queue as long as the tree's roots waiting for you to get back into your lab. Anyara sent me a message yesterday asking when she could start nagging you again."

That had Anna smiling. Anyara a Prithand2 never did anything as belligerent as nagging. Roots knew, the whole den Coille family would be relieved if Seolta's new wife relaxed with them enough to do such a crass thing. She was a master of discreet prods, though. After hearing of Anyara's findings on Arcadia's second continent, Deuteron, Anna had begun putting out feelers for a study of its flora with an aim to modifying some of the planet's farming practices. That wasn't Anna's main area of expertise—her studies had been more focussed on the plant life of Mountainer country—but Anyara was an Alliance-wide expert on integration of biomes on artificial habitats and welcomed Anna's more specific expertise in Arcadian plant life. They worked well together, and she enjoyed her new sister-in-law's company. If she hadn't seen the light in the woman's eyes when she looked at her new husband, she'd have wondered what such a sensible woman was doing with a man as slippery as Seolta mar Bram. Her brother-in-law was clever, certainly, but Cumchdach had borne the brunt of too many of his younger brother's quips over the years for Anna to truly like him.

"I'll contact her," promised Anna, and meant it. Anyara and Seolta were far from Arcadia in Alliance Central, the capital city and planet of the Alliance, the encompassing interplanetary authority governing known human worlds. Anyara was divorced enough from the tensions here that Anna could safely talk to her of work and know there would be no hidden questions about her personal life. Besides, she just liked the woman. Anyara challenged Anna to look deeper and further in her work and, right now, that kind of challenge was what she needed.

Anything to stop her mind churning fruitlessly over her failed marriage.

"Then I need to decide where to live."

Samhchair reared back in shock. "You're staying here of course."

"I'm sorry," she said, and meant it, "but that's impossible."

"But you and Cumchdach… This is only temporary, surely." Samhchair stretched out a tentative hand. "You've been together so long. You can't throw that away. You two belong together."

That's what Anna had thought too. "We don't, it seems."

"You can't leave him. Or take away little Ruiseart. It'll be the end of him. He loves you both so much."

"Ruiseart, yes." That, she had never doubted. "Me? I'm someone he'd got used to having around. But now. Too much lies between us. One day, he'll find someone else who matters, someone he can truly love."

"You're wrong!"

Anna shot up, unable to take any more. "I have to pack."

"To go where?" Samhchair looked like Anna felt, eyes wide in shock. "Not back to Rubhaicreach. It's not safe for you."

"I'll find somewhere."

She snatched up Roo and barged out of the room, almost running back to her own rooms and privacy. Inside, she slammed the door and locked it to everyone. Especially to any den Coille, including her husband—most particularly to Cumchdach—then sent out a stream of messages, all with an urgent priority rating. The replies started to come back almost instantly, as if they'd been waiting for her to ask. She signalled her bag to pack and sent a message to her wardrobe, still back at Rubhaicreach. It was the one thing in that last hellish speech that Samhchair was correct about; Anna couldn't go back to her home city.

She opened her com and scrolled through the replies. There, near the top of the list as she'd hoped, one from the Marshals' Office in Urbis. She opened it and breathed a sigh of relief. She called up a channel on her com.

"Please arrange a pickup for me," she said when she got through to the main marshals' office in Urbis. Nor was she surprised to hear how soon they'd be here. After the incident in Rubhaicreah, they'd probably had a flyer on hold over Manascraoch. In no time, she stood on the main platform of the city, watching a flyer settle in to land and the hatch open. She marched toward it and ordered her case to lock into the cargo bay then stepped toward the open hatch as a shout split the air. The marshal beside her stopped and looked to be turning back.'

"It's nothing," she told him hastily. "Just someone I know."

And she hurried into the hatch as Cumchdach ran toward her. She heard the banging on the hatch cover as she took her seat.

"Did you want to wait, Sera?" said the marshal. "He seems very insistent."

"It's nothing," said Anna again. "A minor misunderstanding. Please, take off. I'm needed urgently in Urbis."

The woman looked at her, then lifted her com wrist. Outside, the banging stopped. They must have taken hold of Cumchdach and pulled him back from the flyer. Thank the roots she was on board a marshal vessel. They were the only ones who could refuse a den Coille son in his own city.

Soon the flyer lifted and she dared to look down. A brief glimpse of a dark-haired man staring up at them, and then the ever present clouds closed over and she lost sight of him.

At Urbis, no family awaited her, no confusing turmoil of emotion and tugging ties. Only a stern-faced squad of marshals in their official dress uniform, and one blessedly familiar face.

"Professor Yakashka, it's so good to see you." Short, squat, with twinkling brown eyes, cheek bones so sharp they could slice any lack of proper deference, and soft brown skin worn to the texture of tough leather by years of field studies, the professor had mentored Anna through her senior thesis years. "I have missed you," she said to the small woman with all her heart.

The professor had never been one for fussy language. "It's time you got back here. Your lab bench is waiting, and I have a long list of research chores for you.

"I have to find a place to live first," said Anna with a laugh at the professor's blank look. Life outside her studies had little meaning for Sera Yakashka

"That has been organised," said the terse voice of the marshal sergeant. "You have been assigned an apartment in the Higher School."

She'd fed Roo on the flight and he was sleeping, but roots knew she needed to freshen up. Yet even more, she needed something to focus on other than the debacle of her marriage. She turned to the sergeant.

"Can you please have my bag sent to the apartment and forward me the address? I'll go there after I've seen my lab."

He bowed his head. "Certainly, Sera. Message the office when you are ready to leave and an escort will meet you."

"Oh?"

"You have been marked as a category 1B target. The Marshals' Office has taken over your security arrangements."

"Me? But I'm a nobody."

The marshal smiled in a way Anna suspected he thought kindly. "You have become a strategically important asset, and there are your familial connections."

"Den Coille," she said heavily.

"And the den Falasches and den Guires," he said with a scarily straight face.

"Maybe, but the marshals…? I'm already protected by Den Coille security." Ruiseart alone ensured that was tantamount.

"They are being kept informed of your status."

"And my son?" Anna knew a moment of panic. Den Coille security would put Roo's welfare first. "If you had to choose between saving me or my son?"

The sergeant said nothing and that terrified her more than anything.

"Put Den Coille security back on the list and keep them fully informed."

For a moment, she thought he'd refuse.

"I can't work if I'm worried about my son."

"Do as she says, Sergeant," said the Professor, sounding unusually irritated. "I can't have the sera distracted."

The sergeant looked between them, glancing at Roo, still securely asleep in his carrier on her front. Then he lifted his wrist and put a call through to Urbis Central.

"The child will be fully covered by his own detail of marshals," he said at the end. "They will put him first."

"And Den Coille security?"

"Will be kept informed as needed."

The marshals didn't trust Den Coille, that meant. The marshals rarely trusted anyone, so it shouldn't have shocked her.

She could wring her brother-in-law's neck. *Thank you, Seolta.*

CHAPTER FIVE

Cumchdach stared after the vanishing flyer. She'd done it, left him and taken his son with her. He tried to find his anger, fire it to life, but failed. His son was no prize to be torn between parents. Losing Roo hurt, but that wasn't all that hurt.

Anna had left him—again.

He heard the sound of running steps behind him and cursed. He didn't need anyone seeing him right now. He fought to bring his face under control, thanking the stars for the misty drizzle coating the platform.

Then he turned.

Samhchair stopped in front of him. His big sister came only to his chin but when her arms opened wide, something in him broke. He stepped forward and laid his head on her shoulder.

"She's really gone this time."

"Oh, my dear." Her hand tangled gently in his hair, and she rocked him with the same rhythm she'd used when he was a baby. Only a bit over a year cycle older she may be, but Samhchair had raised him as much as had his mother. There was a nurturing streak in his sister as wide as a baullnia trunk.

A streak it was unfair of him to abuse. He took a deep breath and raised his head, hugged his sister, then stepped back. "Thank you. I needed that."

"You will get her back."

Samhchair always wanted happy endings for everyone, if not for herself. Mostly her family tried not to disappoint her, but this time was different.

"I deceived her, and I can't do anything to fix it. We have to investigate and prosecute Falasch, or every other parasite out there will think we're easy game."

"She understands that. But you should have told her about it right from the start. Now, it's as if you didn't trust her to keep it from her family."

"She shouldn't have to."

"No," said his sensible sister, "but it's her father's fault she's in this position, not yours." She tugged on his arm. "Come on, let's get you out of this mist and put some food in your stomach. Things will seem better then."

She might be right and, at the least, it would make Samhchair feel better. He let her lead him to the family's common room. He almost balked at the doorway on seeing both his parents waiting for him. His two other brothers were absent, and that felt even more ominous. He could have talked in front of Ceart but not Aigherach. Too young, too vulnerable after the appalling abuse during his imprisonment. His leg had healed, finally, but the inner scars remained.

Right now, though, he wished Aigherach was here. It would stop his parents from whatever they had planned.

Dish out sympathy, it turned out. The last thing Cumchdach wanted right now.

He tried to give the appearance of listening, tried really hard to keep his mouth shut and his eyes as near as he could manage to attentive. Then his mother leaned over and laid her hand on his.

"She will come back. Just wait."

"When? After I've had her father tried for fraud and sent his company bankrupt?" He shot up, refusing to hear his father's shout. "I have work to do. Please excuse me."

He rushed out of the room, walking even faster when he heard the footsteps pounding after him.

"Cumchdach, stop right now," said his father. He kept walking. "I can get security to drag you into my office or we can retire in civilised fashion to my lounge area."

It was the slight puff in his father's voice that stopped him. Roots knew, his father was still a fit man for his age, but he couldn't keep up Cumchdach's pace and both of them knew it. He turned back to face him.

"I will not talk about Anna or Roo."

His father lifted a hand. "Accepted, for that is between you two. But Anna is also one of the most highly respected botanists on this world and is involved in Arcadia's response to the Alliance's ultimatums. Den Coille can't ignore that."

No sign of apology touched his father's face. Cumchdach knew when he was beat. He switched direction and headed with his father for his private office suite. Neither of them spoke as they marched along the corridors, past the closed doors to his parents private living area and down to his father's office. His father lifted his hand to unlock the door and walked in, leaving Cumchdach to follow or not as he chose.

He'd come this far; no reason not to enter. His father led him through the main office where he met with the most trusted of his people and into the inner room, the one he used for what he called *musings*. Cumchdach hadn't realised until he was nearly out of Higher School that it was here his father dreamed up his most audacious plans for the company. Da and Seolta used to sit in here for hours. Cumchdach mostly came in here to relax with him; their work talks were in the front office.

Today, he viewed the comfortable chairs warily, nodding carefully when his father lifted the bottle of salaschar. It was one of the best vintages from the northern ranges. His father took it straight, but Cumchdach preferred it with a drop of water. He'd spent a summer once working at a brewery part-owned by the den Guires, Anna's mother's family, and the old factor there had drilled into him that adding a touch of water was the proper way to *address the essence* as the old man put it.

Both knew to take the first taste in silence, letting the liquid fire coat mouth and head in rapture, before speaking. His father leaned back and studied him as the liquor melted down his throat.

"Den Coille needs Anna to get back to work."

"You'll have to talk to her about that."

"This isn't something you can handle and set aside," said his father. "Den Coille is in trouble. You know it. I've told you often enough."

"And you think Anna will listen to me?"

"She has to," was his father's uncompromising reply.

"We have other botanists," he tried.

"Not of her calibre. And not ones whose work has come to the notice of the Academy."

Cumchdach silently cursed his new sister-in-law. "That was family."

His father looked at him. Yes, he was acting like a moron, but he really didn't want this conversation. His father sighed. "As you are well aware in your more capable moments, the connection between Seolta's wife and yours is a welcome gift to Den Coille. They are both at the top of their specialisations. That's why the Alliance and the Academy accept their findings."

Yeah, he knew that. He just didn't feel like acknowledging it at the moment.

"Cumchdach mar Bram duine Anna den Coille, I never thought to tell my eldest son this, but would you kindly get your head out of your self-pitying backside and back to business. Den Coille needs to know what your wife plans to do next, and you must find out."

"Not by harassing her or hunting her down when she clearly doesn't want me anywhere near her."

"Not at this moment," agreed his father, "but given time."

"A lot of time. Maybe forever."

A rare spasm of temper crossed his father's face. "You and Anna have been living in each other's boughs since you were in middle school. That level of connection doesn't vanish overnight."

"I am not chasing her to Urbis. That was a marshals' flyer that took her away. They won't let me near her unless Anna asks them to."

Some chance of that.

But they would give him access to Roo if he demanded it. Family laws overrode everything else on Arcadia.

His father lifted his glass and took a healthy swig of salaschar. Cumchdach copied him, needing the hit of liquor to fill the icy pit in his stomach. Then his father glanced down at his com. Unusual. His father would have blocked inward calls while they talked.

"Take it," he said, gesturing to the com. It had to be urgent to interrupt them.

Then a change crossed his father's face and not even salaschar could warm the icy hole in Cumchdach's gut.

"What is it?" he demanded.

"The marshals. They've taken over Anna and Ruiseart's security. They've told our people Den Coille will be kept informed as necessary."

Cumchdach's shook his head, trying to make sense of it. "Den Guire security?"

"Blocked also."

Cumchdach thrust up, slamming his glass onto the table. "If you want me, I'll be in Urbis."

"And Den Coille?"

"You've been running it for years, Da. You don't need me."

"I do, as it happens. And what about Arcadia? You're supposed to be helping the government figure out what's going on here. You and Ethan made enough noise about what was needed after Seolta reported back."

Cumchdach loved and respected his father, but that was beyond reasonable. "My wife and son are up in Urbis, unprotected by den Coille. You think I'm going to abandon them? The lawyers and detectives have the Falasch situation well in hand. I'm going to Urbis."

"Talk to Marco an Fallon," his father called after him. Cumchdach half lifted a hand in acknowledgement but it was all he could bring himself to do. In no time, he'd stormed into his rooms, set his bags to pull what he needed out of his wardrobe and ordered up his flyer.

When he stalked out onto the landing platform to leave, however, a full security squad waited for him. He glared at the leader. "I don't care what Da ordered. You follow me in a separate flyer and you stay out of sight in Urbis."

He slammed down the hatch before any of them dared try to join him and lifted up fast. Two security flyers followed him. They'd been waiting for him, but he still set a fast course for the north, braving the currents over the highest part of the ranges with no sympathy for the security pilots. If they insisted on following him, they'd better be good enough to keep up.

Despite what he'd told his father, he tried to storm through the security barricade surrounding Anna as soon as he arrived in Urbis. The marshals met him with a stony-faced blockade.

"I'm going to see my wife and you can't stop me."

"The Sera is busy with her research and has requested she not be interrupted—by anyone."

"And my son?" he asked, contrary to what he'd vowed all through that long, hellish flight up. Roo must not become a weapon between his parents.

"Is asleep and well cared for."

"I can at least see him?"

"If you wish, the child will be woken and brought out to you."

Making him the villain in this stupid vidcast drama. "Let him sleep," he said, "but I insist on visiting him as soon as he wakes and has been fed." Anna would still be feeding him herself. He knew that in his deepest bones. She wouldn't give that up unless driven by actual medical need.

The lead marshal agreed, her hand still ominously touching the weapon on her hip.

His father was in the right, curse him. He had to see Marco an Fallon.

Tracking down the man proved another matter. Almost as if the Commander of the Marshals was avoiding him. A downright insult, thought Cumchdach, from a man who'd been repeatedly thrusting his marshals under Cumchdach's nose and into his business.

"The Commander has many calls on his attention," said the huffy clerk guarding the front desk when he'd finally given up tracking an Fallon down by com and went to beard him in his office. "Your request is noted, Ser den Coille, and the Commander will contact you if necessary."

Not even a promise an Fallon would contact him; more a nebulous suggestion he might if he deemed Cumchdach important enough. Clearly to the clerk, Cumchdach ranked somewhere down with the refuse skittering over the streets of Urbis. He'd have to get an Fallon to talk to him by the circular route. Luckily, the Mountainer House Representative was very much in Den Coille's pocket.

"Ser Cumchdach mar Bram duine Anna den Coille, welcome to my humble office. It's always a pleasure to be able to assist one of your estimable family."

"Thank you, Representative Coinneas mar Coille duine Falamh den Cleireach," replied Cumchdach with a formal head bow to match the full formal name. "As it happens, I have a small favour to ask that I hope you can see your way to assisting me with."

The man did manage to keep his face composed when Cumchdach made clear what he wanted, but Cumchdach had no doubt of the man's inner dismay. The representative was one of the more cowardly of the House members. It made him a useful tool but not a reliable ally.

"I will do my best," den Cleireach promised at the end, which made Cumchdach feel no better. He left the building in frustrated gloom but received a call shortly after with a message from the Marshal Commander, promising to be in touch. He was surprised, though, when an Fallon turned up at the den Coille apartment the next morning.

"Marshal, come in," he said warily. He needn't have bothered with the invitation. The man barged through the door and slammed it behind him before Cumchdach had finished speaking.

"What are you up to, den Coille," demanded his visitor, without so much as a pretence at the courtesies.

After that, Cumchdach saw no reason to stand on ceremony. He slouched back into his chair and let the marshal sit or stand as he pleased. The man kept standing, glaring down at him, and Cumchdach discovered he'd made a tactical error. He leaned back in apparent ease but had to look up at the furious policeman.

"I'm trying to get in to see my wife and child, and for some unknown reason, your troops are blocking me. Are the marshals in charge of domestic harmony now?"

"The Sera is more than your wife and the situation more complicated than a simple marital spat. As you are well aware, Ser."

"Maybe, but first and foremost, she's my wife and Ruiseart is my son. Arcadian law gives that priority, whatever your political masters may be plotting for her."

"Arcadian law also guarantees her the right to refuse to see you."

"And my son?"

For once, he wished he knew what an Fallon was thinking. That slow scrutiny of his was a masterwork of intimidation.

"No one will deny you visitation rights."

"I want to *raise* my son."

"Anything beyond visitation," said an Fallon as if he hadn't spoken, "is a matter for the courts and the Department of Child Wellbeing."

Have that pack of wernets get their pincers into Ruiseart? "We don't need the courts involved. This," he waved his hand to cover the whole gigantic mess, "is only temporary."

"I'm glad you think so." For an instant, a slight frown marred the corner of an Fallon's mouth and Cumchdach jerked upright.

"Why do you need Anna so badly? She's not the only botanist on Arcadia."

"She is one of the best, with a specialisation in interspecies plant interactions. The experts tell us that means she knows how to maximise plant cooperation to increase productivity. Combine that with your sister Fioruisghe and her husband's influence in the Survey and the connection to Anyara ingh Gevard bean Seolta, it makes your wife an important player in Arcadia's response to the Alliance demands."

"But Seolta and Anyara got that ultimatum put on hold. You don't need Anna's help right now."

This time, the harsh twist to an Fallon's mouth wasn't wishful thinking.

"They did get it put on hold," he protested. "My brother may be many things, but he makes deals that stick."

"This time, he's dealing with the Alliance and their competing interests."

A cold stone lodged in Cumchdach's gut. "So Arcadia needs to provide real proof we're taking action or all Seolta's conniving will come to nothing?"

It had been more than conniving. The family had seen a copy of that hearing before the Alliance council, handed on by the Arcadian Representative in strictest confidence. His brother had been ready to spend the rest of his life in an Alliance prison to protect his wife.

"Den Coille is doing its best to comply," he said.

"And going broke as a result."

"No," said Cumchdach automatically. The marshal stared at him. "All right, cutting back on festia plantings has been costly." How worried was his father? "It's one reason I need to talk to Anna bean Cumchdach." He only used the *ingh Eolas* of her name now if forced to.

"The only reason?" said an Fallon dryly.

"Of course not. You don't throw away the years we've been together over a misunderstanding."

"Her father isn't crooked and swindling Den Coille?"

Cumchdach sent him a glare. An Fallon had seen the same evidence as he had, and probably more. "Den Coille has to act. You know that."

"You also need to find out if any other groups are involved."

"You're the police. That's your job."

This time, there was no mistaking the frown on an Fallon's face. "We can't do everything, Ser den Coille. We were under the impression that you and Ethan Winter had promised to help. You both have access to groups we can't infiltrate."

"The kind who are fully aware we're proceeding against Falasch."

"Yes. They're also the kind that will be eager to protect their own interests. It should bring a few spealachs crawling out of the bushes—or will do, with your help."

He had promised to do as an Fallon said. At least, he'd been there when Ethan Winter had done so, and had promised to help him out. Unfortunately, an Fallon was right. He and Ethan had free entry to social networks frequented by those refusing the changes Arcadia needed.

"Don't tell me you haven't got your people into every company on Protos, and probably most of those on Deuteron as well now, given what Seolta uncovered there."

An Fallon wasn't crass enough to deny it. "They can't operate at the level of an industry leader like you. The heir to Den Coille is a different matter than simple Jan Smat of the clerical corps."

"Your simple clerics can go anywhere without being noticed."

"Which gives us one kind of valuable information. We need you and Ethan for the other kind, and we need your opinion on what you hear and find."

Cumchdach would like to refuse him on sheer principle—the principle being that he plain didn't feel like helping anyone at the moment, least of all the government politicos who had stood back and said nothing when he and his family were thrown into prison and threatened with execution.

But the threat to his planet was real. He'd been to an Alliance Council meeting once as an aide to Arcadia's representative when he was still learning the business. His father had powerful allies when he chose to tweak his contacts. The interplanetary Council was a vicious place under all the polite posturings. Split between the delegates of Earth Analogue worlds like Arcadia and those of the artificial habitat worlds, the Alliance sat on a knife edge of competing factions and the power of the habitat worlds was growing. Arcadia needed to make sure no one had an excuse to push through the evacuation threat, and to do that, they had to find and deal with the Arcadian enterprises blocking environmental change.

He sighed and leaned forward, staring at his hands as he linked them between his knees. "I did promise," he said then looked up. "But right now, the best argument Den Coille can make is find a way to be financially viable despite the change in Festin production." The food ingredient derived from the pollen of the festia tree was a highly valued nutrient throughout Alliance space, particularly sought after by habitat and space colonies. It could render palatable the driest of ration bars.

"How far off that is Den Coille at present?"

"That's confidential," said Cumchdach. An Fallon probably knew anyway, but the Den Coille heir wasn't going to be the one to enlighten him. The man didn't push further, which confirmed that he knew.

"How long are you staying in Urbis?" was the man's next question. Yet another one Cumchdach couldn't answer. This time because he just didn't know, and that was another thing he didn't want to admit.

"What do you want me to do?" Cumchdach said in defeat. "You must have come here for a particular reason."

The man gestured to a chair and Cumchdach nodded tiredly. He'd had enough of this already, but the man wasn't leaving until he was satisfied.

By the time he shut the door on the marshal, he'd been wrung out and screwed over far more effectively than by any business competitor. He knew exactly what the man expected of him and had some idea how to start it. The only bit he didn't know was how to get his wife back, and an Fallon's failure to press him on that had been the most depressing part of the interview. Clearly the marshal considered it a hopeless case.

He'd had a friend once whose marriage had failed, and he remembered still the eager desperation in the man's face when the visits with his child came up.

Now he was in the same bind, agreeing to anything for the chance to hold his son. It was the reason he'd kept listening to an Fallon. As for talking to Anna…

That wasn't an option yet, it turned out. He sent her message after message. All blocked by her com system. Then he abandoned all pride and asked the marshals for help but not even an Fallon's wiles could get her to agree. She didn't trust Cumchdach. Maybe never would again.

The light was fading over the dull Urbis skies. He stared out his balcony window at the gloomy clouds above and the hurrying traffic below. He hated this city. It rained here as often as it did at home, but here it was a dreary sheet of drizzle and the air had none of the fresh excitement of a Manascraoch lashed by a storm. The Den Coille apartment was in the middle of the business section and handy to the main government offices, a useful location when they needed to use Urbis contacts or for deal making. Seolta had contracted a fashionable designer and it showed, thought Cumchdach sourly. He might love his younger brother, but he very much did not like him some days, and this was one of them. If only Seolta had never discovered the re-branded Festin that Falasch were stealing from Den Coille and peddling as a generic product called Restin.

Typical of Eolas den Falasch. He couldn't even come up with an original name. Instead, he'd abused the brand loyalty Den Coille had built up by using a name similar enough to be seen as cheaper but as good as Festin.

Of course it was as good. It *was* Festin. Stolen Festin. Cumchdach swung around and glared at the room and its tasteful fittings. He picked up the most execrable ornament of all, a small statue claiming to be a baullnia with a stylised house nestled in its branches. The dimensions were so wrong as to be insulting. He flung the thing against the far wall and cursed when nothing happened. Typical. Den Coille had probably paid a fortune for one in genuine plasdam.

He walked slowly back into the room, his legs feeling as if they carried the weight of his home tree on his shoulders.

You're just tired.

He was. Exhausted beyond thinking, but that wasn't what weighed him down. So many depended on him, so many wanted something from him. His father expected him to take over Den Coille one day, though he had none of Bram mar Gliocas' guile; an Fallon appeared to think Cumchdach could untangle the whole mess of conspiracies blocking Arcadia's environmental compliance; Seolta relied on him to uncover the information needed to expose the off-planet forces allied against Arcadia. It felt like his whole tragging planet wanted him to do something.

How could he do any of it without Anna?

You failed her.

When she'd needed him most, he'd deceived her by failing to tell her the truth. She was so sick with the pregnancy; he hadn't wanted to burden her with her father's treachery.

When had he ever known Anna to be weak?

No, be honest with yourself.

The truth was, he'd been scared silly. He'd never known Anna to be ill, not seriously so. The medics said it wasn't unknown in early pregnancy, though Sera Anna was unfortunate to have been hit so badly. They were monitoring her closely and she was in no peril.

They hadn't heard her bringing up any miserable speck in her stomach, time and time again, or watched her vibrant face change to deathly pale, with big staring eyes clouded with misery. She was so strong, his Anna, but this had brought her down, and that had scared him right down to his innermost gut. It was supposed to last only a few weeks, according to all the old aunties, but Anna had been ill for the whole of the first half of the pregnancy. Months of suffering.

She was never having another baby if he had a say in it.

Yeah, some hope of that after what he'd done.

His gaze swung to the drinks panel. He refused to touch it, aware that one swig wouldn't be enough in his trough of self-pity. He didn't have a problem with drink normally, sharing a drink as needed with others and savouring those special ones. A slow sip of salaschar with his father was a treat, or inhaling Anna's favourite wine from the edge of the estuarine plains of upper Protos, where the foothills began to rise toward the northern ranges and the winds were sharp enough in winter to torture the vines into producing fruit of a rare intensity.

One touch of a drink tonight though, and the well inside him would demand filling with rotgut of any kind.

He needed sleep.

But that meant lying down on the sleeper, and that was empty since her departure.

CHAPTER SIX

Anna woke to yet another morning of missing Cumchdach and wondering what to do next. She tucked Ruiseart tight into her body as he had his morning feed, then placed him back in his sleeper to doze off again, making sure it was close beside her. She glanced at her timer. Maybe she could snatch another hour before he woke properly for the day. He was old enough now that he only woke once during the night but getting sleep had become a priority for her.

If only dreams didn't plague her. Or all the competing demands battering the inside of her head. Work, Arcadia, Den Coille, and its changes. Cumchdach and her failures.

All drumming in a cacophony of missed beats and jarring notes.

A ping came through on her com and she switched to answer it with relief. It was Anyara, far off in Alliance Central.

"Did I wake you, Anna? Sorry but I had a thought and forgot to check the time lag. I hate to harass you but how soon before Ruiseart is old enough to travel and you're free to go to Deuteron?"

The delay in transmission between Central and Arcadia blocked an easy reply. Anna had to wait for the system to engage and show the ready-for-reply signal. It gave her unwelcome time to think.

Deuteron. The word teased her with glimpses of a faraway escape. Anyara had told her of the difference in farming methods between Deuteron and the Urbis estuarine plains, and Anna had longed to see it for herself. Her home city depended for survival on the interactions of plants, from the homely rete and its associates holding the soil together to the thorny drach shrub that told of hidden reserves of moisture and were used as hedging to protect their food gardens against the harsh sea winds. She hadn't thought to find the same in a farm, having been bombarded with 'proper' farming science by the so-called experts at the UBS. Cloaked in generations of superiority, they refused to consider any alternative to the monocultural exploitation that passed for agricultural science in the institute.

If Arcadians were to keep their home, everyone had to be prepared to change, including baked-in-mud experts. And if the Arcadian Council wanted to treat Anna as some kind of captive expert, she was perfectly placed to make them change. If the Council didn't like her findings, they only had themselves to blame.

And Deuteron was an ocean away from Cumchdach duine Anna.

When could she leave? Right now, said the irresponsible spark in her head. Fortunately she had Ruiseart beside her. She began her reply.

"Another month," she said into the com message field. It would take that long to organise the details, both with the Deuteron farms and arranging everything needed to take a young baby on a field trip. Maybe the lovely nurse her grandmother had found would agree to come with them. Roo liked her and Anna trusted the quiet woman's steady nature. "I'm sending you my current research outline," she said to Anyara. "Let me know what you think, and add any suggestions from the biome management perspective." She added a few more technical points and hit send.

If only Anyara and Seolta were free to come home for another visit. This would be so much easier without the delay in communication.

And she could do with a friend right now.

Or maybe not Seolta. She hadn't forgiven her brother-in-law for the pain he'd caused Cumchdach. But Anyara wouldn't come without him. The woman was so intelligent otherwise, but she loved her disreputable husband.

"How are you surviving the Academy and Alliance Central?" she sent with a wry chuckle. Anyara had as little time for the politics of academia as did Anna.

Roo had woken for another feed when the reply came back, and he lifted his head momentarily at her snort of laughter. Anyara had sent a particularly acute cartoon doing the rounds of Alliance Central. "The Dean is as ever," she'd added to it, "and the Academy head. My lab is busy and still amazing, and my students have learned discretion in gossip. Otherwise, all is going well. Seolta is learning some interesting street terms, and mostly refrains from using them in my hearing, but I think he is making progress too."

Anyara had been so quiet when they first met and cracked a smile only when her husband teased her. It was nice to see she'd gained enough confidence to release the wicked sense of humour she'd kept hidden inside for too many years.

Anna was friends with Cumchdach's older sister Samhchair, but it was complicated now. Anyara, though, spoke the same language as Anna, that of living organisms. She could relax with her almost as much as she used to with Cumchdach.

She signed off with real regret.

There was a call on her door pad. It must be the professor. She'd promised to call on her this afternoon to talk about Anna's research outline. Anna released the door control.

It wasn't the professor. A Federal marshal entered with a grave look on her face.

"Ser Cumchdach is requesting visitation access to his son, and the Commander has instructed your security to allow it. When would be a suitable time, Sera?"

"Visitation? He wants to see Ruiseart?" She couldn't seem to get her head to work. Of course Cumchdach wanted to see Ruiseart. He badly wanted him back home in the sleeper he'd bought for him and surrounded by all the paraphernalia he'd purchased in the heady days before his birth.

"I can't see him," she said in a panic.

"No, sera, that is understood," said the too sympathetic marshal. "Just the baby. You can monitor it from our office. The Ser doesn't have to know, if that is your wish."

It sounded awful. Did she want to see Cumchdach with his son, watch the love she knew he had for their baby, even if what he felt for her was a mere counterfeit? Want to wallow in *what might be*?

"Yes, I would appreciate that," she heard herself say. "He should wake properly in another hour or so. Please tell the ser you will signal him when Ruiseart is awake and fed again." She wasn't about to land Cumchdach with a fractious, hungry baby. Roo must not be used as a weapon between them. That way lay the loss of any self-esteem she still retained.

Sitting in the office and watching the holovid of Cumchdach cuddling Roo was more painful than she could believe. He'd always had a way with young children. Caring for the vulnerable among den Coille's wide flock came as second nature to him. Being the eldest son wasn't why he was seen as the heir. He enjoyed the business, but not for the credit-gathering that drove Seolta or his father. No, it was the whole interlocking community that drew him. Anna had always known who he was. A leader, a carer. A man to be trusted.

A man who had lied to her.

Roo was smiling up at his father. He'd only just started that, and only with her and a few others. The smile he gave his father lit up his whole face and made a small dimple appear at the edge of his cheek. Exactly the same as the dimple in the myriad images of a baby Cumchdach his mother had shown her when she'd first found out she was expecting.

Something touched her eye. She lifted a finger to move it away and brought it back wet.

Cumchdach was singing to Roo now, silly words. A melody she'd heard the old women of his city sing to their grandchildren as they rocked them in their arms. When Roo gave a small grizzle of tiredness, Cumchdach hoisted him onto his shoulder and walked around the room, keeping up that soft chanting as he did. Soon, Roo's eyes closed and he was gone suddenly into the deep sleep of babies, but still Cumchdach kept walking, singing the same tune over and over.

Only the words changed. Words of regret, of sorrow and pain. Words promising safekeeping for this tiny mite they had made between them.

At the last, words of love that she'd dreamed of hearing. Soon, he beckoned to the door and a woman entered. Carefully, he transferred the sleeping baby into the cocoon she brought in, watching closely to see that Roo was securely fastened in. Then, one kiss on his son's head and the woman took Roo out. Cumchdach stared as the door was closed, his face turned away from her.

"Time to go, Ser," said a marshal entering the room. Cumchdach lifted a hand in acknowledgement.

Only then did he turn and stare straight at the monitor. Straight where he must know she watched him. No smile touched his lips, no words came from his mouth. Just that long look. She thought she knew him inside out, knew every expression on his face.

But this one she couldn't interpret.

The next weeks were both a maelstrom of activity and the most painful in Anna's life. Cumchdach came daily to see his son and, each time, the guilt of it thrust to her heart. At first, he'd cuddle and sing to Roo then leave as soon as her baby fell asleep. But slowly, he stayed longer. To start with, he brought toys and read to him from combooks. Beautiful books with images that made Roo's face light up, and with words that sang to her soul. Some she recognised from her own childhood; some she'd never heard before. Each one exquisite.

Knowing Cumchdach, he would have researched which was the best children's book supplier and gone in person to talk to the staff. He'd done that in Manascraoch. For Cumchdach, it was people that mattered and people he trusted. If the business hadn't claimed him, he would have made a brilliant social advocate, bringing out the self-worth in the least of his people.

Today, when Roo fell asleep, he kept holding him in his arms, staring at his son and talking to the sleeping baby with words spoken too softly for her to hear.

She could have increased the audio volume but his words seemed too personal, words from his heart.

Words she no longer had any right to hear.

"Don't do this to yourself, Sera."

The marshal standing guard was correct, but still Anna came each day, and each day she left with barely controlled tears.

Afterward, she went back to her room and all the problems of the rest of her life. Settling back into her lab routine was easy enough. Too easy, despite the sheer volume of work awaiting her. The professor hadn't exaggerated the number of projects wanting her involvement, even without the proposed expedition to Deuteron. When not busy preparing for that, she was fully occupied in reviewing other proposals, sorting out the trivial from those with potential. A small strand of excitement even began to grow in those weeks.

She was using work as an escape and knew it, but she didn't care. A body could stay in shock only so long and, for Roo's sake, she needed to find a way to live. And if she still kept up a thread of exploration into Den Coille's business problems, what of it? She may have told the den Coilles she no longer worked for them, but she'd been a part of Cumchdach's family too long. She couldn't ignore the people of Manascraoch any more than she could ignore those of Rubhaicreach.

That's what she told herself anyway, and since she worked through Fioruisghe, it was none of Cumchdach's affair what she did.

It might have niggled less at her if she had come up with any bright ideas how to suddenly make Den Coille more profitable. They were losing a fifth of their festia plantations, the most conservative option to allow the central Protos region to restabilise. She glared at the readouts from the Survey and Den Coille technical groups.

"Do all you den Coilles have to be so tragging capable?"

"Pardon, Sera?"

She'd forgotten her lab technician was still in the room.

"Nothing, nothing," Anna muttered. "Just going over an old problem."

"Anything I can help with? I have some room in my schedule."

Which was a lie. Shelda worked as hard as Anna, with too little thanks.

"I was looking at other projects to take my mind off the Deuteron expedition. If only we could set out now."

But Roo was not yet old enough for Anna to take him into the wilds—or what passed for it on Arcadia. Another few weeks, and they'd be free to leave. She gritted her teeth and went back to checking their supplies one more time. Slowly, the days passed as she buried herself in her work and the marshals watched over her. She wasn't sure which had her more on edge.

"Your father sent a message today, Sera," said her protective marshal one day. "Do you wish to send a reply?"

"No, but I'm sure the marshals want me to."

The woman's mouth twisted. "We need his contacts."

"You have people in his house and throughout Rubhaicreach. They must have infiltrated his networks by now."

The marshal made no attempt to deny it, and if her father didn't realise he was under surveillance, her stepmother would. No matter how Anna felt about Gria ingh Ovirisch bean Eolas, she had never underestimated her intelligence—or her greed.

It was the woman's arrogance that failed her. Gria had never once used that intelligence to look below the surface of Rubhaicreach. After so many years of marriage to Eolas den Falasch, she still had no idea how Anna's home city worked.

Then it came to Anna what the look on the marshal's face meant. "Your people can't fool Rubhaicreach."

The woman sighed, as if in relief. "They are some of our best. Their accents, their mannerisms, all studied and worked hard on. They should be undetectable."

Anna's lips quirked up at that. "Have the marshals ever successfully penetrated a Mountainer household?"

The woman's mouth set tight at that. So yes, and no, she guessed, and wondered if Bram den Coille knew which of his people were marshals' agents. But since their false imprisonment, the family always assumed they were being watched and, even if Bram knew, he would do nothing about it. All that would lead to was more spies they didn't know about.

She took pity on the woman. "Your people have no family connections?"

"No."

"Then they will never penetrate Rubhaicreach." She sighed and reached for her comms channel.

It took her father a while to come back to her. She suspected that was deliberate but chose to smile in amusement rather than take umbrage. "You called me earlier," she said when he finally called her back.

"Took you long enough to reply."

"Nice to talk to you, too, Father." His face wore the sour disgruntlement he'd worn for the last few years. Never a happy man, Eolas den Falasch seemed to find less to make him happy with each passing year. "How can I help you today?"

"That would make a change."

She held on to her temper, refusing to remind her father what he'd done to her. Worse, done to her baby. "I will always help my family if I can."

"So *can* you get that husband of yours off my back?"

"Stop the investigation of Falasch's fraudulent appropriation and sale of re-branded Festin?" she said, refusing to tell her father she had no way of making her husband do anything at present. Not when she daren't even talk to Cumchdach. "That isn't possible, as you must realise. Why you ever thought you could get away with it is beyond me."

"They make so many credits, a few diverted our way should have been nothing to them."

Anna knew exactly how important the sale of Festin was to Den Coille, and her father had chosen the worst of possible times to cheat them. "More than a few, is what I heard. How much did you earn from selling this fake Restin compared to the business you've lost with Den Coille. Falasch used to be their main exporter."

"Bah. Falasch can do more than sell other people's stuff."

She'd had this argument with her father before and had no intention of repeating it now. Falasch had been an exporter for generations. Her father had always taken for granted the steady flow of credits into the Falasch business built up by her grandfather and by the ones who had come before. He never understood what it took to ride out the challenges of business cycles, always took for granted the wealth that had cossetted him since birth and made his life easy. He'd married her mother to suit the business, and maybe that was what had made him rebel now. She studied him, saw the softening of his jowls and the growing paunch under his loose-fitting tunic. No longer the fit, athletic body he'd used to entice his second wife.

Not that Gria would care, she thought sourly. "I have things to do, Father."

"Fine. Forget your family. I'll tell your Mama you can't make it."

He said it only to rile her, and that alone kept her from retorting angrily that Gria ingh Overisch would never be her Mama.

"Can't make what?" she said tiredly.

"Your sisters' birthday party. You have remembered it, of course."

As if she could forget. The hullabaloo when Gria found herself huge with twin babies had deafened the ears of the entire household and most of Rubhaicreach. She'd been home then, finishing off a field study of the flora of the peninsula and having one of her periodic stays with her father out of what she now saw as a misguided hope of building a sense of family. The only reason she hadn't fled to her grandmother's home was a warped sense of responsibility for her little brother. Anton was still a toddler then, still adorable.

"Sadly, I cannot see that I will be free to attend," she said stiffly.

She wasn't about to put Roo at risk by taking him into her father's home.

"Your choice," her father said and signed off before she could say any more. Leaving her as the guilty party? Not going to happen, Father *dear*. 'Send me the details,' she messaged him, and left it at that. She'd send the girls a gift.

Roo woke soon after, and she forced away the sour taste of her father's call. She refused to let her baby's childhood be as blighted by her family as her own had been.

No, that was wrong. While her mother lived, hers had been a wonderful childhood. Her father was a barely present sideline, but her mother and the rest of the household had mostly disregarded him so she'd never worried about it. Then her mother fell ill, and all the best medics her grandmother hunted up could do nothing. Years later, Grandam had let drop that her mother had been failing for years but had hidden it from everyone.

Why, Anna still didn't know. All she knew was that the mother she'd trusted to love her and keep her safe was gone. By the time her mother could no longer hide it, the cancer had eaten away too much of her body. Not even the best gene therapy could restore it. She was gone and Anna was left lost and alone. Soon afterward, Gria arrived.

Anna never asked when the Urbis woman had come into her father's life, not wanting to know the answer but, after that, her childhood changed and she increasingly sought refuge with her grandmother. Gone, too, were the secure staff of her childhood. Gria wanted her own people around her, and only those particularly liked by her father survived the purge.

So why was Gria so eager now to have her appear at the twins' birthday? Anna usually tried to put up a façade of family accord by making an appearance, but she always kept it brief, hiding behind the pressure of work.

She could certainly do that this time. Between her lab work, the proposed expedition to Deuteron, and caring for a tiny baby, her days were full already.

She fed Roo, then laid him on his mat on the floor and watched foolishly as he kicked his little legs. He was going to grow up as strong and agile as his father. The marshal in charge of her security came in as she watched him and paused as well.

"They are adorable at this age," the woman said.

Anna looked up in surprise and caught the dreamy look on the woman's face. That a marshal would have a life outside work had stupidly not occurred to her.

"You have children of your own?"

"Two little boys. They're in the tearaway phase at present, keeping us on our toes. My mother says it's not surprising given what I was like as a little one." The marshal chuckled, her stern face softening. "She has no sympathy, she tells me, yet she spoils them something terrible when they visit her."

"My husband's mother is the same. But then, Roo is her first grandchild, so she's allowed to, say the rest of the family."

Something flashed across the woman's face. Her skin was too dark to be sure if it was a blush of embarrassment, but the soft laughter vanished. This woman knew her entire life history so was fully aware Anna had no mother of her own. Her eyes glanced away, but then returned, wearing the harsh face of a professional. Anna wished she dared pick Roo up and hold him for protection.

"What is it?"

"My superiors have asked me to pass on a request." The marshal spoke in the disembodied voice of officialdom that always meant trouble, as if the speaker wanted to be a planet away from what duty forced them to do.

"A request?"

"You and Ruiseart would be kept safe at all times. You will be under constant surveillance and security watch."

"While we do what?"

"It's not much. Just make an appearance at your half-sisters' birthday celebration. You don't have to stay long," she hurried to add.

Anna couldn't believe they'd asked this of her. "Put Ruiseart at risk? Not going to happen."

"We will have the highest level of security on both of you at all times."

"You think that will make me agree? Or Cumchdach?"

He may be a stranger to her at present but he hadn't changed from the boy with whom she'd grown up. Cumchdach would be no more ready than she to have the first den Coille grandchild anywhere near her father's people.

"We're talking to Den Coille security."

"The answer's still *No*. I can't even see what you hope to achieve. I've tried to avoid my half-siblings' birthdays for years."

"And always failed."

Anna felt her teeth grind and had to consciously unlock her jaw. "That was before."

"Why did you fail, Sera?"

Her teeth locked up again. She had a duty to her city and her grandfather and hadn't wanted to cause more tension in the city by turning the stress fractures in her family into full blown chasms. But she wasn't about to discuss her city's problems with a federal marshal.

Not that they didn't know all about it. Her den Falasch grandfather and den Guire grandmother had both separately warned her the marshals had the best spy network on Arcadia.

"Are you still the senior den Falasch heir?" suddenly asked the marshal.

Anna stopped short at that. "It's not relevant," she said.

Only it was.

"Are you?" asked the marshal again, "and who decides?"

"It depends on the charter deeds and my grandfather's will," she said stiffly. "And my father's. Nor is the question pertinent. He's a fit and healthy man.

The woman didn't pursue it. She didn't have to. It was clear from her face that the marshals knew exactly the content of those documents.

Not surprising when her stepmother had been trying for years to get the courts to overturn them.

When her father passed on, the whole of Falasch came to Anna and her heirs, along with the largest share of the den Guire assets. She could delegate duties, but Anna was the next de facto ruler of Rubhaicreach, and no one could change that.

Which made Ruiseart a potentially wealthy and powerful little boy.

"My son is going nowhere near Rubhaicreach," she said flatly.

The woman looked at her in sympathy. It didn't fool Anna. "He stays here," she said again.

Not that Urbis was safe. There was only one thing for it. As soon as the woman left, she put through the call she'd been determined not to make.

Cumchdach arrived within the hour.

Shadows haunted his cheekbones and there was a veil over his eyes she'd never seen before. But he was as handsome as ever, and as dear.

Why couldn't he do her the kindness to change?

CHAPTER SEVEN

She looked as beautiful as ever. Cumchdach wished he could resent that, but Anna would always be the most beautiful woman he knew. Yet her eyes had a haunted look today when he walked into her office, and she moved back, arms hugged tightly around her body. That hurt despite his having expected it. Her choice of her office as meeting place made it clear she'd called only because she'd had to. This was business, and she wanted none of the warring, very personal matters between them. That still meant he had to find out what had forced her hand.

He took the seat she pointed at, one that put the solid bulk of her desk between them. Ruiseart wasn't here but he wasn't far away. A trace of baby odour lingered in the room. As for him, he was in the same room as Anna; anything that made that easier for her was fine by him. He drank her in as she perched on the very edge of her chair, shoulders back and face carefully devoid of expression.

Had she forgotten how long they'd known each other? "What's happened?" he asked, refusing to blunt it.

Her fingers picked up a stylus and twisted it over and over. He doubted she was even aware of doing it. "I've had a request from the marshals," she said.

"To do what?"

"It's my half-sisters' birthday."

He shot up at that. "You're not going anywhere near that pack of wermets." Planting both fists on the desk, he leaned over her, not stopping even when she flinched. She knew he'd never hurt her. "Not you, and definitely not my son."

"Our son," she corrected automatically. She always did that. "Sit down. I've refused them."

"But…" Today was one of those days he wished he didn't know her so well. He sat down slowly but didn't take his eyes off her.

"Their people can't penetrate Ruibhaicreach. Not as well as they need."

"Of course not, but that's not new." The marshals had sent their agents into Manascraoch too. Seolta's people had found them out in no time. Or so he hoped, he'd said. The family still assumed they were under surveillance. "They have to use locals to be effective."

"That shouldn't be impossible, not with the right incentive."

Roots, how he'd missed that dry voice of hers, cutting right to the heart of a matter. "That's how we're working it for den Coille's interest."

"They need my father's contacts. *Arcadia* needs them."

"Others can find them."

"I'm best placed."

"No." Putting her at risk like that was unthinkable. "You wouldn't take Ruiseart there anyway, so why have you even raised this."

She looked away from him then, and he shot up again. "You're not taking him there. That's final."

She shook her head. "Not into the city. The marshals will keep him in their flyer just out of Rubhaicreach airspace."

"You're not seriously considering this. It's impossible."

"Someone has to do it. I want my son to be safe, to be in a world that's safe. I want this over with."

"*Us* over with. Is that what you mean."

She stood this time. "You want me to say it? Yes, I want all this over with. I can't live like this. Not with…" her hand waved in the air between them, "hanging over me."

"And you think letting your father and that nest of vermin he calls family kidnap you and use you to blackmail Den Coille will change that?"

"If I go of my own free will, he can't use me for blackmail. You'd have no cause to rescue me."

"Are you doing this deliberately?" he said furiously. "If you're in danger, I will come. You know that; you've known it since we were in middle school."

"And if it makes this world secure for Ruiseart? You think I won't risk anything to make that real?"

"I know you would." He glared at her, wishing he had an argument to counter her. He pushed off from the desk, marched to the door and back. "Tell the marshals to take the miserly locks off their coffers and pay their stooges more."

"I suggested that. They'd have to get agreement from the House."

"And tell all the traitors in their ranks what they planned." He gave a growl of frustration, stalked once more around the room, then again before he was sure he could speak with some semblance of rationality. "If you go, I'm coming with you."

She flung the chair back at that and marched around the desk to him, her finger poking his chest. "No, you're not."

"Then you're not going." Her unique scent had reached him and, just like that, the fury vanished and hunger reared up in full force. Hunger for her. He throttled it back. Assaulting her for a kiss and more wasn't going to help either of them at present. "I come with you, or I will invoke the family risk clause, with full public declaration by our best panel of lawyers."

Anna stared at him. "You wouldn't."

"Try me."

Her mouth dropped open. "This is not you."

"You married me. That gives each of us rights and responsibilities over the other. You'd do it to me if I was going to be as stupidly foolish. You try to go in there without me and I'll stop you—any way I have to."

He was starting to dislike himself, but in this he was adamant. His beautiful Anna was not going to put herself at risk.

She also had a point, one he hated to admit. Having a baby son had changed something fundamental in him. The environmental risks to Arcadia were real, and he was committed to help fix them, but the Alliance threatened the very survival of settlement on Arcadia, and he didn't trust them one bit. Seolta was doing his best, but Cumchdach had watched the vid of his trials at Alliance Central over and over again and heard his brother's accounts of the back streets of a habitat world. Too many Alliance worlds held people desperate for a better life, and Arcadia was a paradise compared to their home worlds.

If Anna had any hope of hearing anything to help at the twins' birthday, then she ought to go.

But he was going with her.

She glared at him in frustration and, suddenly, he found a spark of hope. Anna arguing with him was better than Anna not speaking to him at all. It may be a poor spark of hope, but he'd take it.

He grinned at her. "The marshals can tell me when you've made your arrangements. Until then, I have a wee boy to cuddle. A good day to you, wife. He leaned over and pecked her on the cheek.

She hadn't expected it. What she had expected he'd try was all too obvious, and keeping her unbalanced suddenly seemed a bonus. He stood back, tilted his head in a Mountainer bow of farewell, turned and left the room.

Outside, the guard's face was suspiciously devoid of expression. He followed the woman down the hall to where Roo lay sleeping and sat with his son for another hour. Anna stayed away, as he'd expected, but after placing the sleeping Ruiseart in his sleeper again, he looked up at the sensor in the corner and gave a cheery wave, followed by a full Mountainer formal bow of leaving. Then gave one grim, glance at the sensor again before walking out.

He would see her again soon. That had to be enough for today.

It would never be enough.

She didn't say a word to him all the way to Rubhaicreach, not until they landed near her grandmother's house and disembarked, flanked by a pair of marshals and three of his own security. Anna glared at them.

"And you think they will encourage people to talk to me?"

He shrugged. He hadn't told her about the squad of Den Coille security who'd already landed or the den Guire people infiltrating the serving staff for the night. The den Falasch local staff would recognise them but he had to hope they were loyal to their city first and would keep quiet. That's what their security head advised they'd do at least.

He hadn't asked the marshals who else they had in place. Not that they'd tell him anyway.

Anna had fed Ruiseart before they landed, and they'd transferred him mid-air to the marshals' flyer under a full security shroud. Now she waited for an answer. When he said nothing, she stomped inside the house, fixing him with a look that should have destroyed any protective gear he might wear.

Not putting you at risk, beautiful. No matter what.

Or at more risk than he had to. This whole trip was a nightmare. He followed after her, privately signalling his team.

'In place, Ser, and liaising with the den Guire team.'

'Anna comes first,' he messaged them.

'We have your orders, Ser.'

Yes, but what had his father ordered them to do? Bram den Coille wasn't going to put a daughter-in-law's life over that of his son. He'd learned that the day of Ruiseart's birth.

For Cumchdach, Anna and Ruiseart came equal first. He would bring them both out safely and refused to consider failure.

Her grandmother greeted them fondly, and he plastered on his company face as Anna gave her all the latest on Ruiseart's progress. Roo was now at the smiling stage and employed his devastating cuteness on any adult foolish enough to come within striking distance. That wide open joy and the sparkle in those little eyes when his father picked him up turned Cumchdach to mush every time.

But tonight, his Anna was entering the folklar's den.

"We have to go," he said curtly.

At their house, the den Falasches formed an entry gauntlet in the form of an old-fashioned receiving line. Gria den Falasch's idea, he was sure. The woman loved pretension. The twins stood immediately after their parents, beaming as one person after another wished them well and offered the latest expensive trinket. Some tasteful; most truly execrable. He wished he dared grimace at Anna as they'd used to at such times. Tonight, he took refuge in his social status and kept every part of him under tight control. Anna's cool smile said she did the same.

When their turn came, both of them gave the Mountainer half nod instead of the more generic Arcadian offering of a hand to press. He wasn't about to soil his skin with the touch of these den Falasches, nor was he stupid enough to offer more than a stilted formal acknowledgement. No one in this room was under any illusion what den Coille thought of Eolas mar Driach duine Gria den Falasch. Anna, as daughter, had to be more demonstrative, but she also kept her hands securely at her side, gesturing her bodyguard behind her to pass over her gifts for the twins.

The girls opened them and their eyes widened. What had they expected? No den Coille would ever offer anything but the best. The complementary bracelets came from the best jeweller in Urbis and were flashy enough to appeal to their youthful tastes, yet simple enough to be worn by teenage girls.

Gria knew exactly where they came from, though, and her smile of thanks looked decidedly skewed. Even more so when both girls forgot all protocol as they pulled on the bracelets and shrieked with glee, flinging their arms about their half-sister.

Take that, Sera, when you think to tangle with my Anna. She could swallow you up for breakfast.

"Girls, please. You have other guests waiting to be welcomed. You can thank your sister fully later. Welcome, Ser and Sera den Coille." She eyed the large men standing behind both Anna and Cumchdach. "There are drinks and food laid out in the lower level for the staff. Your men are welcome to join them."

"That's all right, Sera," said Anna in a voice that brooked no argument, though she did keep it low. "They will stay with us, in light of my last visit to this house."

Gria had the grace to blush but Eolas looked furious. "That was for your own good."

"As you say, Father." She gave the briefest of head dips and moved off.

Cumchdach had his own message to deliver first. "We're not staying long, and the marshals are watching," he said softly to Eolas. "Any harm to Anna and I'll have you locked up in the harshest prison in Urbis."

"You'd know all about that," said Eolas nastily.

"Yes, I do. And so will you."

He could feel the stillness in those waiting behind him. He'd spoken too softly to be overheard, but the others had eyes. Some were there because their children attended the same expensive academy as the girls, but others were there by obligation, like him, and they watched this first meeting between den Coille and den Falasch with the intensity of hunting shalk. The lethal aerial predator of the mountains was ruthless in its hunt, and news of this conversation would hit all the gossip vids and business channels by morning.

As they entered the main salon, the wave of chatter abruptly hushed and as suddenly began again as they passed by. He seized Anna's hand and held it firmly in the crook of his arm. When she made no objection, he didn't know whether to be relieved or terrified. She was as aware as he that their bodyguards weren't for show.

'All quiet?' he messaged to his own people outside. From her abstracted gaze, Anna was doing the same.

"He's sleeping," she murmured moments later, "and safely out of range."

He gave her the smallest of nods back, then steered her purposefully toward what he hoped was a friendly face.

The leader of a northern Mountainer transport company used regularly by Den Coille and Falasch for local freight, the woman had a secure foot in both camps and looked as happy about that as expected.

"Good evening, Sera," he said, keeping his hand firmly by his side.

"Ser Cumchdach duine Anna and Sera Anna bean Cumchdach, a pleasure as always.

The woman had the art of professional lying down to a tab, and her choice of the married-only version of their names sounded deliberate. There was nothing pleased in her at being singled out.

"How's business," he asked as part of polite small talk. "I hope we're keeping you busy enough."

"Oh, yes. As well as expected, what with all that's going on."

Anna plastered a smile on her face and Cumchdach gave a small chuckle. "The lottery of change. It's a balancing act between creating new opportunities and shaking up our smooth regularities."

"There is something to be said for the boringly routine," the businesswoman replied. He'd always appreciated her burnt, dry humour and didn't press her further but added her to the file to be watched.

They circled the room, alighting on one prey after another. That's what it felt like anyway, and he suspected their victims thought the same. Anna included the head of the local police service. She said nothing of importance, but he wasn't fooled. That one was for an Fallon. He wondered if he could stop Anna putting through a more private call to the woman at a later date and getting more involved in her city's affairs. Then stomped on the thought. Not if he ever wanted his wife back.

On another of their passes, Anna had nudged him toward the twins. They looked to be enjoying themselves as much as he and

Anna. He and his siblings had been trained from an early age to give the appearance of enjoyment on such occasions. The den Falasch family were obviously raised differently.

"Mama has organised a party afterward for our *own* friends," Verianna confided in the smug tone that he knew irritated Anna the most. "This is for Pa." She rolled her eyes, making herself look even younger and sillier. Thankfully, they were spared going to that. He could take only so much.

At one end of the room, a small group of musicians played softly, and the side tables held a beautiful array of tasteful offerings. The guests hovered around the tables, talking more than eating, so he gathered the dishes were more for display than for providing tasty treats.

"I wouldn't bother trying them," he murmured to Anna as they approached. She grimaced.

"Gria is in charge of catering, then. All show at minimal cost."

Her grandfather would be horrified at the cheapness. Driach mar Ramach duine Deana den Falasch had been famous for his hospitality. At least it meant none of the guests had a reason to linger, including them. When Anna lifted her arms and clenched them over her breasts, he made their apologies and led her out of the room. In no time, they were back in their flyer with all their nervous retinue and spearing up toward the flyer where Roo waited greedily for his next feed.

Cumchdach kept his comments to himself until Anna was reunited with their baby and mother and child had settled into the tableau that still stunned him. She was so beautiful in that moment, leaning over Roo and holding him tenderly.

He walked out before he said something. Tonight had been the nearest to their old relationship they'd had for weeks.

Roots, how he wanted that back.

He stomped into the control room and discovered the marshals' troop leader standing before an open holo link.

"An Fallon?" he asked sourly.

"The Commander would appreciate a report on the evening."

Cumchdach turned toward the holo field and flicked on his link to the marshals' commander.

"A tragging waste of time, is what it was," he said in a clipped voice. "No one was talking to us. They wouldn't have, even without those hulking watchguards following us everywhere."

"Nothing overt then. About what we expected," said an Fallon with the blank face Cumchdach hated the most. It hid too many secrets, none of which were advantageous for the other party.

Cumchdach shrugged. His da was much the same, with his unerring ability to read the currents in a room. Hiding anything from him in a face-to-face meeting was nigh on impossible.

"We weren't welcome, if that's what you mean. They don't want to be forced to take sides. And I don't mean only in the fraud case. There's a lot of resistance out there to the Council's direction."

"We already knew that." A scowl touched an Fallon's mouth in a rare display of irritation. He supposed he should take some enjoyment from knowing the marshal shared his frustration, but he didn't have the energy.

"I got some names, but you probably have them too."

"Send them anyway, with your reasons."

An Fallon's version of clutching at straws? He pulled up a file and forwarded it. "Here's my preliminary notes from the evening. Nothing is concrete, and I don't want to be publicly outed as the source."

"You're still too valuable," said an Fallon in what felt more like a warning than a comment, then signed off.

Cumchdach glared at the blank space, then slunk back to the main cabin to silently watch Anna as she hovered over Roo for the rest of the trip home. Using their baby to avoid talking to him, was she?

He didn't have the heart to force her to meet his eye. Not when she stiffened if he made the slightest move to come within touching distance.

"How about passing him over to me?" he said when her arms began to droop under the weight of the baby. Roo was fretful, refusing to stay settled in his sleeper if put down, and Anna had been cradling or walking him all the trip.

She looked up briefly, but her eyes fastened on a point just over his shoulder. "It's all right. He's happier with me when he's fractious."

"I'm his father." Cumchdach cursed the snap in his voice when she clutched Roo tighter. "He settles for me too, you know," he still added but forced his voice to soften and was relieved when she gave in and handed Roo over until he fell asleep. She had to face him one day. This distance between them was driving him mad.

That was the only words they exchanged through the whole trip, and when they landed back at Urbis, she took Roo and hurried off the flyer before Cumchdach had a chance to say anything. He slapped open his com and ordered their troops to guard her trip home, then slumped back into his seat.

It wasn't until later that he levered himself out of his seat and made his solitary trip back to the Den Coille company apartment. Solitary, bar the squad of marshals and Den Coille troops mirroring his route. He'd have liked to walk part of the way, but that would have been too much of a farce, him slouching grumpily down the walkways as some of the finest troops on the planet followed him in martial precision.

The next day was worse. The vidcasts must have had reporters at the birthday party. Of course they had; Gria would have made sure of it. The headlines were full of the coolness between Cumchdach and Anna den Coille, heirs to two prominent Mountainer companies. Was this a simple lovers' tiff, or were the rumours of trouble in the corporate world more than rumour?

"Of course they are," he growled at the vidcast. "Don't your reporters check their facts?" Den Coille had made no effort to hide their legal claims against Falasch. It wasn't possible, not after filing the charges in the Alliance Central and Arcadian courts. All the press had to do was look.

It made no difference. The vids were full of it, complete with clips of him and Anna over the years, images that tore open the wounds on his heart, finishing with clips from the party. One vidcaster was too good. They'd caught one of the few times he and Anna had made eye contact all evening and had captured in stunning detail the strain on both their faces. No point either of them trying to deny there was a problem. Not with that image doing the rounds.

An Fallon's appearance at his door was the final blow on the whole disaster. He signalled him to enter but wasn't in the mood to offer any kind of polite greeting. Not that the man seemed to expect one.

"You've seen the vidcasts?" the marshal said as soon as the door shut behind him.

"Anna's report no better than mine?"

The man scowled at him. "The local authorities have agreed to work with us. It's something." But not enough clearly. "The vidcasts," an Fallon prompted.

"Hard to miss them when they're on every station. Haven't they got more important things to waste com space on?"

"Better than scandal in celebrities?"

"That's not us."

"It is now," said an Fallon in a voice that said he better get used to it.

"You're not helping."

"Maybe not you and Sera Anna, but it does help Arcadia, which I understood you are also concerned about."

"You know we are, but how does a simple marital spat help Arcadia?"

An Fallon gave him a disgusted look. "It wouldn't, not normally." He helped himself to a seat in a nearby chair. "When the parties in question are future controllers of most of Mountainer country, it matters a great deal."

"We still hold elections, you know."

An Fallon didn't bother refuting that, and Cumchdach was right, to a degree. Not even his father could change Councillor Seilach ingh Craobh's mind once she'd made it up. The Lower House member often stormed into his office with her latest campaign.

"Regardless," Cumchdach continued, "I've already said I'll help with finding the dissidents. But Anna and my problems are no part of that. Why is the head of the marshals spending so much time on a minor scandal?"

An Fallon gave one of his rare smiles and that scared Cumchdach more than anything. "Whatever it is, the answer's no," he almost yelled.

"I'm not asking you to say anything. Merely to refuse to talk to any gossip vidcaster or journalist."

"You can't be serious. There's no better way of giving the story credence."

"Exactly," said an Fallon.

Cumchdach stared at him, dumbstruck. Then he gave in and threw himself into a chair. "You do know I want very badly to fix the breach with *my wife?*"

"And you will. In time."

"But not yet. By all the roots, why?"

"What it gives us is two vulnerable people, clearly stressed and suffering because of the current problems on Arcadia. Maybe even weakened enough to be open to suggestion."

"No one who knows us will believe that. Neither of us would betray our family company. Anna's father may be a useless wermet, but she adored her grandfather and grew up working in Falasch's warehouses. Falasch is more than Eolas mar Driach."

"Maybe," said an Fallon, "but it's worth a try."

"To do what?"

An Fallon leaned forward, placing his hands on his knees. "All I ask is that you both maintain your silence. And preferably appear unhappy in a discreet way. Any watchers can draw their own conclusions."

Cumchdach scowled. "It's insane."

"We need information, any way we can get it."

"And if it destroys my marriage?"

"We need that information," said an Fallon stubbornly. "You will be under full surveillance at all times."

"And if I refuse? Will the marshals still monitor Anna and Roo?"

An Fallon leaned back again but said nothing more.

Cumchdach had known the man since he was a boy. An Fallon would not leave innocents like Roo and Anna unprotected, yet he dare not call him on it. There was something about the man today he hadn't seen before. If he didn't know the marshal better, he'd have said it was desperation.

"Let me think on it," he said finally.

"You have a day," said an Fallon gruffly, then stood and left.

CHAPTER EIGHT

Anna's com signalled an incoming caller. She didn't even bother to glance at it before snapping back an out-of-contact message. After spending too many hours with Cumchdach, hours of hiding what she felt and walking the tense lines of family, city and business conflicts, and the mess of their marriage, she had no energy left. Her debriefing session with Marco an Fallon had finished her off, not that he'd been particularly grateful. She had managed to get the Rubhaicreach police chief to cooperate with the marshals. What more did he want? She slumped onto the nearest lounger and stared into space.

It had lumps in it. Not quite functional, like everything else in this tragging apartment. The Urbis Higher School of Biota Studies might have a fine sounding name, but it was definitely a second-tier school. Without the funding from the Survey's training section, she suspected it would be flat out broke, like everything else about the biota of the planet.

At least Roo still slept, so she didn't have to dredge up the reserves to see to his needs.

If you were in Manascraoch, you'd be surrounded by help. A huge part of her longed to be home again, to be back with Cumchdach's family and their unbounded joy at Roo's arrival.

The jarring buzz of an urgent call vibrated through her wrist, and her hand automatically pulled up the caller's ID. Can't they leave her alone?

Cumchdach's face stared back at her. She slammed the refuse option and shoved her wrist under the nearest cushion. She really wanted to rip off her com sliver and hide it in the deepest drawer, but she wasn't lost to all sense. Too many out there wanted to use her tiny baby as a weapon in their stupid plots.

The tragging thing buzzed her again, louder and even more insistent. When the face of Marshal an Fallon appeared in the caller screen, she had no choice but to answer.

"Good evening, Marshal."

"I'm sorry to disturb you so late, Sera. I've just come from your husband and I need to talk to you."

Her hand hovered over the *reject caller* option. "What's he said now?"

"Nothing, as yet. But this involves you as well."

That had her really looking at the marshal. The Commander rarely displayed any clue to his emotions, but tonight his face was colder than usual. Her gut clenched. "You want us to do something and Cumchdach refused?"

"He hasn't refused yet, and he mustn't. Not if you want a world safe for Ser Ruiseart to grow up in."

Black anger surged inside her. "Keep my baby out of this."

"We can't, Sera. Not given who he is."

"He doesn't know that yet." Her little man was an innocent. They had to leave him alone. "What's this about?"

He told her, and it was worse than she'd thought. She hadn't known until then how much hope still lingered in her heart, but this would end it.

Pretence came with a price. Her parents' marriage had taught her that, with their false public displays of affection. A child recognised lies, and their smiles at each other had been the cruellest of lies to a young girl.

She never doubted that her mother loved her, loved her city and her den Guire family. But the façade she put up over her marriage ate into Anna's trust. If it hadn't, would Anna have seen the illness stealing away her mother sooner. Would her mother have lived?

Now an Fallon wanted her to do the same to her baby? To lie to her baby? Yes, he was only little, but he already picked up when she was upset, snuffling quietly and wanting to be carried more than usual.

"I will not use Ruiseart for this," she said firmly.

"You have no option."

The marshal's cold words shocked her. The man's integrity was a byword throughout Arcadia. He'd never misuse a child, or so she'd thought.

"I do, Marshal, and so do you."

"Not this time."

Now she was really frightened. "What are you asking? What do you want us to do?"

"No more than you are now." The words might sound as if he was trying to placate her, but there was nothing soft in the man's face. "Stay estranged from your husband and keep your ears and eyes open."

"You want more than that," she said bitterly, suddenly understanding what the man wanted. "You're using us as bait. Using *my son* as bait."

A curt nod confirmed it. "It's the best chance we've had yet."

"What else do you want of me, Marshal. Have you told your government you want me to give up my research duties and turn into yet another wealthy parasite, flitting from party to party in Urbis?"

"Not at all, Sera. Your work is critical. That has been made more than clear to the marshals."

"I'm glad you realise that," she said curtly. Then more understanding hit. "I'm on one of your tragging lists, aren't I?" The lists of people the government requires to be protected or watched. The helpers and the threats. She probably came under both categories, she thought sourly when an Fallon make no attempt to either deny or confirm her accusation.

"There is a reception in three nights. We would appreciate your attendance."

"Is Cumchdach going too?"

"He will be, though he hasn't been told of it yet."

"How can you ask this so soon after today? You saw how it was between us."

"Exactly," said the marshal.

"That's what gave you the idea," she said bitterly. The marshal didn't deny it, waiting for her answer.

What could she say.

"I'm not leaving Ruiseart alone."

"A squad of our best marshals will guard him at all times, and he has a nursemaid he's happy with. We've checked her out and she is fully cleared."

Anna wished she could protest but had nothing to object to. Ruiseart loved Biarsuin, his Rubhaicreach nursemaid, and the marshals were the best security on the planet. "This is so wrong," she muttered.

Three days later, she was dressed in her best gown and lining up to enter the Council's main reception room, a space filled with relics of the first settlers and built of the finest materials available on Arcadia. She scowled at the delicately carved fretwork in the panel closest to her as she slowly made her way up the receiving line, a trio of marshals hovering beside her and no doubt others sprinkled throughout the crowd.

Given the status of the guests, she can't have been their only responsibility for the evening. The heads of both Council houses were in attendance as well as a large number of departmental heads and other representatives mixed with senior corporate names and legendary figures from the arts and sciences sector.

She just felt like it.

After the formal greetings, she plastered on her company manners and began to circulate, reciting all her grandmother's most stringent rules inside her head as she strove to look like she was thoroughly enjoying herself and had not a care in the world.

She knew the exact moment Cumchdach entered the hall. Nor was she the only one. A hum of titillation surged around the room. She waited until he'd had time to complete his courtesies and move into the body of the hall. Then she moved a step away from the crowd and turned toward him.

Nor did she have to look for him. Her body knew where he was as she lifted her eyes to his and met his open stare.

His strong face, that rugged body that had delighted her so often, the sturdy arms that had held her. Still there. But tonight the gentle smile and the laughter lines were gone. She faced the stern presence of the eldest den Coille brother, one sworn to protect his family and his territory. She'd never believed those who thought Cumchdach harsh before.

He'd tried to contact her, but she'd blocked every attempt. The only way to do what the marshals wanted was by making sure their performance was no lie. He wanted to reunite; she couldn't yet forget or forgive that he hadn't trusted her enough to tell her about her father. Had dismissed that she was more than Eolas' daughter; she was the heir to Falasch and a den Guire. If Den Coille made Falasch pay, it hurt Anna's city and her credit balance.

Had he thought she'd ask him to drop it? After so many years together, even her block-headed husband should know her better than that. Know that what she'd expect was that he talk it over with her and, together, find a way through the mess for all the innocents affected by her father's stupidity.

He made to take a step in her direction. She swung away sharply and began to talk brightly to the nearest unfortunate. Behind her, she heard a muffled curse and the stern voice of her bodyguard speaking to someone.

"The Sera has not included you on her list of admitted contacts."

"She doesn't have to," said her furious husband. "We're married, in case she's forgotten. Publicly, in full view of a whole crowd of both our communities."

"Regardless, Ser, she does not want to talk to you this evening."

She held her breath, waiting to see whether Cumchdach would cause a scene, and released it in a cloud of disappointment when the talk stopped, to be replaced by a series of angry grunts receding into the distance.

Had he given up?

'Report,' she ordered her guard. Or more accurately, requested. She had no control over these marshals.

"The Ser den Coille has ceased his attempts to join you, Sera."

And that told her a whole lot of nothing. She daren't turn around to see exactly where Cumchdach had gone. She had to wait until the room stopped buzzing with speculation first. Heading off to the withdrawing rooms, she dared a searching glance about the hall and found him on the very far side, talking to other corporate heads.

She recognised them, and her heart sank. An Fallon hadn't lied. Cumchdach was working tonight too, only more productively than she was.

She was a mere support act tonight. Cement the story of their failed marriage and set Cumchdach up as a disgruntled and angry man, ready for recruitment to whomever promised him satisfaction. Regardless of her protests, an Fallon had succeeded in reducing her to a social butterfly. She had to force herself to remember Ruiseart to stop from storming out of the building.

He was safe in her apartment, sleeping with Biarsuin, and had a full squad of marshals protecting him. What his future held depended on her, on what she did here tonight and on other nights.

She paused behind a pillar to watch Cumchdach, and saw the moment he sensed her. She ducked back into the shadows of the room and hurried off to the withdrawing rooms. There was a crowd in the anteroom, all gossiping, all falling silent when she entered. If only she could back out again, but she plastered on a smile and galloped through to the privacy of the sanitation units. The chatter outside rose up again.

"It's true then? The separation?"

"Certainly looks like it," said the smug voice of an older woman. The voices fell then, too soft to hear clearly, but she had no doubt they were comparing notes, and juicy notes at that. It took long moments to cool the flush on her cheeks before she dared emerge.

She knew she had to go back to the main room, had to be seen. There were even some people she wanted to talk to, scientists from the Survey who had done some of the preliminary work for her upcoming field trip to Deuteron. If only she were flying there right now. A few more weeks and Roo would be old enough. She wasn't taking him away from the medical staff and maternal supporters she trusted. Not yet.

Being a mother was a lot scarier than she'd expected.

She checked her timer, checked again for any messages from home. Nothing. Roo's fine, she told herself firmly and took a deep breath.

A buzz sounded on her com, the tingle of an urgent call. What was wrong? She slapped on the receive link and stood facing her husband, a furious glitter in his eyes.

"Where are you?"

"On the way back from the withdrawing rooms," she said with every speck of outrage she could summon. "Or is that now forbidden too?"

"I couldn't find you."

She might have snapped back if she hadn't seen the shadow of terror in his eyes.

"I'm here," she said, "and you'd better not be where anyone can see you."

Another buzz hit her wrist and Cumchdach glanced down at the incoming signal on his com. He hit it at the same time she snapped onto her new caller.

"An Fallon," said Cumchdach, and this time the panic in his voice was unmistakable.

"We have a situation."

"Roo?" That screech came from her. She reached for the pillar, unable to ask more.

"He's fine. We got him and his nursemaid away safely."

This time, she staggered to her knees, then keeled over and sat with her back propped against the pillar.

"Anna. I'm coming."

"No, you are not, Ser den Coille. Her bodyguards are within touching distance."

Even as the marshal spoke, a big hand touched her shoulder and the oldest of her guards squatted beside her, running a scanner over her body.

"She's fine, Sir."

"Ser Cumchdach, we need you to carry on here as if nothing has happened," said an Fallon. "The guards will cover Sera den Coille's departure. It's soon enough after she gave birth that her leaving early is readily explained."

"My wife takes ill and I stay on partying? I don't think so."

"That's precisely what you do, Ser den Coille. It's your best cover. Or do you want the world to wonder who is after your son and why? Maybe consider copying them?"

She could feel the rage in Cumchdach, and he wasn't anywhere near her. Then his jaws clamped shut in a way she recognised. Agree to the impossible, that said, but only for now.

"Keep me informed of every detail. I'll be with you, Anna, as soon as these heavies release me."

"Thank you, Ser Cumchdach," said an Fallon in a bland voice and his image snapped out.

"I mean it, Anna," said her husband. "Don't you dare shut me out this time. Not when you and Roo are threatened." Then his image snapped out as well. She pushed herself shakily up, helped by her guard.

"There's a side entrance this way, Sera. We have a flyer waiting outside."

"You're taking me straight to Roo."

"Yes, Sera," he promised, and that decided it. She went with him in a haze, out the corridor, through the door and into a flyer marked with the marshals' logo.

Roo was safe.

Cumchdach was safe.

All was well—so far.

She signalled an Fallon as soon as she was safely in her apartment. There was damage, some scuff marks on the walls and furniture askew, but Roo was safe. "Tonight was the last time," she said. "I can't lie well enough. I'm leaving for Deuteron in a few weeks, as soon as it's safe to take Roo there, and until then you can put out that I'm busy with field prep work."

"You did well tonight."

"I collapsed in a pitiful heap. Put out any story you like, but don't ask me to appear in public near Cumchdach again." He hadn't even come to make sure she was all right, as he'd promised. The marshals had told her they were blocking him but he could have found a way. Couldn't he?

She could stand only so much.

An Fallon didn't give up easily of course, and the most bubbly of his marshals appeared at her door the next morning. "I've been assigned to your protection today," the woman said, a cheerful grin on her face and curls bouncing happily. Actually, her whole body looked like it was bouncing. Anna felt very old, despite knowing full well that any marshal an Fallon assigned to her was a highly trained soldier with an education second to none. The woman still looked like an ingenue barely out of Higher School. She even talked like a new student, chatting incessantly as Anna began organising her workload for the coming trip.

"I have work to do," she finally said desperately. "Please excuse me." Then she locked herself in her study. The woman took up a position at the door, but Anna had no doubt she'd barge right into the study if she thought it necessary. For now, though, the door was shut against her and Anna leaned back with a sigh of relief.

Fortunately, her guard the next day was calmer, and kept silent watch on the rooms. An Fallon had got the message. But so had she.

She called in the medics the next morning and set up a field protocol to monitor Roo in Deuteron.

"They do have perfectly respectable medical facilities in Deekin, Sera."

That was the nearest Deuteron had to a city.

"As good as Urbis or Manascraoch?"

The woman's mouth twisted at the hit. "How about we send one of our perinatal medics to Deekin? It's a while since the Health Ministry calibrated their services and we can use that as a cover."

"A team would be better," said Anna. She had a ruthless side she rarely let out, but when Roo's wellbeing was at stake, she'd do whatever was needed. The best she got this time was a promise from the woman to get back to her. When the assigned medic visited to give Roo a final check and he responded with his glowing smile, the softening on the woman's face reassured her more. This woman would always put the welfare of babies first.

"I'll be working in a rural area of Deuteron," Anna told her. "Your team could offer a mobile service to the locals while they're there. Given the spread-out population of the continent, I suspect the Deekin medics find it hard to adequately cover all the country regions."

"True enough, Sera. I'll suggest it to my bosses." Her eyes laughed at Anna. "A well thought-out point."

"My grandmother is Ceana ingh Diomhain bean Eagrai den Guire," she reminded the woman dryly, and the woman's chuckle turned to a snort.

"We're not likely to forget it, Sera."

So her grandmother had been onto the Ministry as well. Good. One less item on her list of worries. Or part of a worry, she amended, staring down at Roo's tiny face as he looked up at her with laughing eyes for an instant before settling back to the serious business of filling his tiny tummy. Cumchdach used to laugh at her with his eyes in just that same way.

She shoved the memory aside. She had too much to do to be melting into a gooey mush of tears.

The next days proved the truth of her list. So many last minute glitches, so many demanding she make a decision. Would she need the prototype seed analyser? How did she know? Not when she wasn't sure what awaited her. She said yes to that one, and to most other requests for top-line equipment unless it was obviously inappropriate. No, she did not need the bulk freeze expansion for the harvester, thank you. She was collecting samples for analysis not setting up a large scale cropping business. Yes, she definitely needed that new amino acid analyser. It gave in seconds results which her lab usually took hours to extract from a sample.

Most definitely yes to taking the full-scale living quarters with every luxury and protection from the elements imaginable. She was taking her baby son with her. Did they imagine she would let him stay in a basic field tent with a mere thin membrane between him and danger?

Next on her list were visits to the Institute of Agrotechnology in a building across the way from her lab. A short walk, but one she had come to dread. Today turned out no better.

Anna had always felt the name branded the place clearly. Tech: that's how they viewed farming systems. Not a community of living plants. Robotic, mechanical farming, driven by rules rather than the soil beneath their feet, the winds and rains above.

"Sera den Coille. We understand you need our assistance?"

She'd suggested a mutual discussion of matters beneficial to both their areas of expertise, but doubted the woman in front of her capable of understanding the concept. She bit down on her pride.

"I am about to set out to do an observational study of a Deuteron farming system…"

"And you're wanting to compare it to more established, intensive methods. We at the Institute are always ready to assist our poorer neighbours."

This time, she had to physically bite her tongue. "I've heard their systems are using some interesting innovations."

The woman raised her brows. "I'm sure that one day they hope to increase their output, but that is many years away. Sadly, the Institute is unable to assist them yet in that. We are fully occupied in maximising the Estuarine fields." She steepled her hands. "It's a matter of economic priorities, Sera. I'm sure your husband's family can explain that to you. The Estuarine fields produce seventy percent of Arcadia's food crops."

"But falling," she said in her most polite voice.

The woman didn't like that one. The rest of the conversation was short and icy, but she did get the name of a suitable farm in the rich Estuarine plains to visit before she set out. The Institute woman had called it a control for her trial; she preferred *comparison*. She set out the next day, wanting it over and done with.

The plains that covered most of the lands between Urbis on the northern coast and the downs at the base of the Northern Ranges separating this part of the continent from her home area in the central zone were the richest agricultural soils on Protos. Most said on the whole planet, but she reserved judgement there. Too little was known about the other main continent, Deuteron.

Fed by a network of rivers coming down from the high ranges and sheltered by the giant peaks of the Northern Ranges that stretched right across the continent, the Estuarine Plains zone was a patchwork of long established and heavily engineered farms.

Too long established, she decided after meeting the farmer. The man actually tried looking down his nose at her when she told him of her planned study.

"This farm is a ten on the production scale. You may not like our methods, Sera, but the city needs to be fed." He sounded like a lower schoolteacher explaining basics to a concerned parent. Putting her in her place, that's what he was doing.

Then she told him what she wanted. The man humphed, his arms crossed.

"Not on my place, you're not. Who knows who you'll give your data to? I've got a business to run here."

"My study has been sanctioned by the Council. They have authorised high-density scans of your farm, Ser." The man looked unimpressed. She opened her com and set the screen to public view. "The official seal of the Dept of Agriculture, as you can see. I'd hoped to avoid this, Ser, but you leave me no choice." She activated her link to her team. "Begin the scan, deep-depth level, all geo and bio substrates. Physical sampling for correlation."

Taking samples wasn't necessary, but she was feeling mean. She took even greater delight in walking away from the farmer when he exploded at the sight of her tests.

"I knew it. Stomping through my premium crops."

"You will be reimbursed," she snapped before marching off, stepping into her flyer and ordering the pilot to take it up to an ostentatious hover, just above the man's precious *premium* crops.

"Over-engineered excuse for food crops," she muttered angrily.

"They are the latest types," said her ag tech mildly, "producing ten times the grain output of the wild origin. Without crops like that, Urbis will starve."

They'd had this argument so many times, and Anna always lost. But she'd also seen the trending surveys on the Estuarine region ecosystems since settlement, and what they were doing here was no longer sustainable. In a few years, farming here was going to hit a production wall. Someone had to turn around their farming methods if Arcadia wasn't to give the Alliance yet one more bad mark against them.

She grumpily pulled up the graphs again. "Their famed productivity is in decline. Explain that."

The tech grinned. "That's your job. You're the plant whiz. Come up with something better."

She scowled. It was always his killing shot. Maybe Deuteron would provide the answer, or at least a chance.

"What they're doing here is too simplistic."

The tech stopped grinning. "So come up with a better way to feed the suburbs."

The time, he unbuckled and marched back into the lab area, slamming the cabin door after him and leaving Anna feeling guilty. The man was a child of the Urbis suburbs. It would be his family, his children, left to starve if these farms failed.

At least he didn't pull out of the trip. The man may not agree with her on the estuarine farms, but in tech matters they worked well together, and he was one of the best around. Practical, sensible, and innovative. She needed his ability. More, that family in Urbis gave the man as much incentive as she had to help this study to succeed.

By the time it came to board the flyer for Deuteron, she was more than ready to shake off the grime of Urbis and its dreary skies and brangling residents. She tucked Roo into the carrier on her front, checked he was secure and sleeping and set foot on the hatch ramp with a relieved sigh.

A shout in the distance. She stopped. Then shook her head. It wouldn't be him. Her guards had told her Cumchdach had left for Manascraoch days ago, and he hadn't been to see Roo since so she believed it.

She went to step forward again.

"Anna. Stop. Wait."

It *was* him. She turned, waited, and tried every relaxation trick she knew to stifle her hammering heart.

Then he had reached her and was putting out an arm for Roo, cradling the baby's sleeping head in his big strong hand as his eyes fastened intently on his son's face. He murmured something, too soft even for her to hear. Then, his hand still tucked over Roo's head, he lifted his head and leaned forward.

He kissed her before she could do anything. "Keep safe, beautiful. If you don't, I'm coming after you."

He'd first said that to her when they were heading off to Higher School. He'd been heading to the exclusive business one in the centre of Urbis, the oldest and most prestigious on Arcadia, while she had forced her father to let her attend UBS. She discovered later that it was her grandmother who paid her fees and blackmailed her father into letting her go.

Tears pricked her eyes at the memory. "Someone will see you."

"I don't care. You're my wife and Roo is my son."

But he stepped back, and she ducked her head to hide from the pain in those dark eyes.

"This is not forever," she heard him say and her head shot up. Then she was caught.

A cough behind her broke the spell Cumchdach had laid on her. "Excuse me Sera, but we need to leave to make our connections in Deuteron."

It was one of the marshals guarding her. She nodded blindly, stretched out a hand to Cumchdach, then remembered and tucked it back again. Then she twisted round and raced up the hatchway, to come to a dead stop just inside. It was as far as she could force herself until the clunk of the hatch closing behind her made it impossible to turn and fly back to him.

She spent the rest of the flight on automatic. She sat, secured Roo in his flight carrier, ate when they served her, and stared down at the grey waves below when they didn't.

Only when the coastline of Deuteron reared up in front did she manage to banish those glittering dark eyes and the promise stark in her husband's face.

This is not forever.

If only that were possible.

Luckily, she was soon busy with all the demands of landing at the border control port on Deuteron, greeting the required officials with her best manners locked firmly in place, and ensuring all their supplies made it to their final base, then she was back in the air. Roo gave her a sour look. For a tiny baby, she was learning he had a wealth of ways to communicate his feelings, and being locked yet again into his travel carrier was not his idea of an acceptable way of passing the day. Fortunately, the next leg didn't take long, and soon they were winging down over tidy fields and the busy paraphernalia of a working farmstead.

They'd settled on the same farm that had so fascinated Anyara on her trip to Deuteron. Gebre of Shiron wasn't a man who trusted easily, she discovered. She'd had to show him every piece of their documentation, all locked under a panoply of impressive seals, to convince him the crazy sounding Protos outsiders were able to deliver the promised credits as payment for his cooperation.

The man himself was as uncommunicative as Anyara had said, but Anna dredged up all her agricultural knowledge, gleaned mostly as a side effect during her field studies, and he grunted some kind of welcome after a while.

"You've got all your own gear?"

"We're completely self-sufficient. We won't have to call on any of your resources, Ser Gebre. Just your occasional input about how best to work without disrupting your operations."

That broke the barriers better. No cost to him, and he'd have a say over what they did here. She found herself respecting this young man. His hands and weather-beaten face told of hard work and the tidy environs of his farmstead told of a well run operation.

He hadn't yet offered to introduce his family, but he had softened at the sight of Roo. "A fine young lad you've got there," he said, confirming his experience with babies. The man had two children of his own, according to his records, though neither had shown their face yet. Feeling the weight of Roo securely held against her, she could understand that too.

"I think this is going to work out very well for both of us," she said at the end. "Thank you, Ser. Now, I'm sure you have work to get back to, and I know we do."

By the time the sun set that night, her face and hands felt as work worn as the farmer's. She mightn't have had to assist with the set-up, but Anna had never been one to stand around while others worked. She slumped into her chair in her new quarters and put her hand on her wrist to signal her com to close the outer door. "I'm done," she murmured to Roo, sleeping contentedly in his new cot. He'd taken to the fresh air and busyness with gusto, smiling madly at anyone who stopped to talk to him and watching everything going on with those intent baby eyes. She breathed in, smelling the scents of wild plants and growing crops seeping through the ventilation system to perfume her rooms with the heady aroma of living plants.

She was right to come. This was just what she needed after the last months. Sleep and work were enough to keep her mind occupied tomorrow.

Sleep. Alone. Without him.

Her hand jerked back.

CHAPTER NINE

His father sat behind the desk in his favourite room, but there was nothing relaxed about him as he stared at Cumchdach through the com link. "You're sure he wasn't simply making stabs in the dark to get information?"

Cumchdach had just come from a working lunch hosted by the head of the Economics Ministry. One that included a too nosy journalist. "Not at that kind of gathering," he said. "They were all vetted business leaders and vidcasters. The man had tracked down our sales figures."

"Commercial espionage?" queried his da.

Cumchdach shook his head. "The figures aren't hard to extract from publicly available data if you know where to look, and Gerrig is one of the best in the business."

Bram nodded curtly. The man's vidcast was required watching for all corporates. He had a finger on the pulse of commerce second to none.

His father's fingers tapped on his chair arm. "I thought you'd gone to Urbis to talk sense into Anna and bring my grandson home."

It wasn't how Cumchdach would have put it but it was near enough, he supposed. "An Fallon got to me while I was there."

Bram's curse said it all. "What did he want?"

Cumchdach told him, and his father's language became truly impressive, though he doubted his mother would agree. "And you agreed to it, of course."

"He had a point—and he used Roo. My son will grow up in Mountainer country, not some cursed and sterile space station."

After Seolta's reports, Den Coille knew exactly what they faced.

"You think that you can make those bone-headed deniers change their minds?" asked Bram.

"No, but maybe I can find which ones are doing more than grouse about it."

"Hmph." Bram pulled up his screen and stared at the contentious figures again. "Den Coille needs new ways to make credits to change those kinds of minds. We need your wife back on board."

"You have Fioruisghe and her team."

His father grunted. "Your sister's good," he conceded. None of them would forget what it cost the whole family before they realised exactly how good she was. "But we need more. Even Fioruisghe says Anna looks at problems differently than the Survey does."

"Anna was trained by Driach mar Ramach duine Deana den Falasch. She remembers companies have to make credits," said Cumchdach dryly.

"I did have a hand in raising your sister," said Da, a man as redoubtable as Anna's grandfather.

A chuckle escaped Cumchdach. "That brat raised herself. The rest of us merely kept her from killing herself while she did it." His father's lips twitched in amusement. "Sometimes I feel sorry for her husband."

The twitch of his father's lips disappeared.

"Winters!" His father shifted grumpily in his chair. "Though I'll admit Ethan Winter's changes are improving their credit balance. An Fallon should have approached them."

Who says he hasn't, thought Cumchdach, but kept it to himself. "We need the whole family in on this one," he said instead.

"And Anna?"

Cumchdach scowled. "She's gone to Deuteron. The marshals have her surrounded and an Fallon wants me to stay away for fear of blowing open the whole charade."

"And…?"

He grinned. His father knew him too well. "She doesn't know it, but she's got a squad of Den Coille and den Guire people there too. The marshals are tolerating them enough to let them monitor her this time. They all know Anna and Roo's safety is their only priority."

"Good," said his father, a smug smile of satisfaction on his face. "Now all you have to do is get her to see sense and we can all get back to normal."

If only it were that easy.

"It will work out, son," said his father's voice softly. "You two are made for each other."

If only.

No more was said that day, but Cumchdach held the memory of it as he set out to follow an Fallon's script, gritting his teeth metaphorically even as he smiled his way through a gauntlet of social obligations and foxllar-packed meetings. Fortunately the queries after *the lovely Sera den Coille* dwindled before he planted a fist in the latest falsely smiling set of teeth. It also helped that his father called an urgent family meeting and his siblings actually managed to agree on a time to be all in one place. The marshals could find no reason to keep him in Urbis, but he still had to shove back his shoulders and force his legs to walk into the private meeting room in their family tree. He was the last to arrive.

They'd all come as promised. Mam and Da at the head of the table; Samhchair, her hair frazzled and her hospital shift showing under her street tunic; Ceart, silent, big, and as deceptively innocent as always; Fioruisghe, perking up in her chair as Cumchdach entered; with her tall husband, Caleb Winter, sitting silent and still beside her; and last of the family, Aigherach, sitting near the bottom, in outdoor gear that too closely matched Fioruisghe's work uniform for comfort. He'd have to have a word with the boy soon. Then he saw there was another pair present. Ethan Winter sat as silent as his older brother, with beside him his red-haired wife, Sarwenna, looking belligerently at them all.

Cumchdach took his seat, nodded to his family, then looked at Ethan. "I didn't expect to see you here."

"An Fallon strongly suggested I join you."

"Know why?"

"No, but I can guess. I owe that man, but he asks a tragging lot some days." Which was Ethan's way of telling him he wasn't here to spy on them. Cumchdach had learned the hard way that Ethan Winter was a man to be trusted; the middle Winter brother had been with them in that hellish prison and put himself on the line for the brothers, especially for the injured Aigherach, too many times for any den Coille to ever refuse him entry.

His father had on one memorable occasions, but Cumchdach had since enlightened him.

"You have the floor, son," said his father. Then Cumchdach told them what an Fallon wanted.

At the end, he had to wait for the angry cries to die down. Only Ceart and the Winters kept silent. Ceart and Caleb out of sheer habit, but Ethan knew Cumchdach too well.

'You okay, Cumber?' he messaged him discreetly, using his old nickname from those prison days.

'As expected, Eshta,' Cumchdach sent back in acknowledgement, with a wry twist of his mouth. He saw his mother and Ceart take in the exchange but neither said anything. Ceart rarely said much at the best of times. Cumchdach had begun to realise, though, that his stolid and staunch middle brother observed and remembered every small detail, though what he thought mostly remained a mystery. All their life, Ceart had been the one to tag along, only shining when put behind the controls of a flyer.

There, Ceart was a madman in the rest of the family's opinion, but he always emerged from his latest trick unscathed and without even a scratch on his flyer. Silence didn't mean nothing happening, though. Today, his face kept its usual bland sameness while the rest of the family raged.

"You going to do it?" Ceart asked.

Silence fell, and all faces turned toward Cumchdach.

"I have no choice," he said.

His father's angry "Hmph" echoed the rest of the family's retorts.

"We have to change, all of the planet. Or do any of you want to watch our children grow up in the habitat back streets Seolta described. Without trees, a Mountainer is nothing."

That wasn't true, said Mam and Da firmly. But they were wrong. To live without trees, without the crackle of ozone skies wracked by storms, without the freedom and bounce of branches beneath their feet? All of them would be mere ghosts of who they were now.

Mam turned to him as the talk slowly died down. "You and Anna? You're happy to go along with this?"

He couldn't hide from his mother. "Am I *happy* to lose my son's first days? I can never get those back." His fists clenched uselessly. "As for Anna and me… She won't even talk to me."

His mother reached out her hand, and he took it, clasped it as he fought for control.

"It will work out," she said. "Give her time, *mo leanadh*."

He squeezed it back but couldn't answer. Couldn't tell his mother she was wrong.

His father had been watching them, said the prickle on his neck, but he gave no sign of it. Instead, he called them to order and leaned forward. "Seems to me the best way we can help Cumchdach is to give him a wall at his back. Change Den Coille as needed and make a profit doing it."

"Do you want us to leave, Ser Bram mar Gliocas?" asked Ethan.

Bram shook his head, thank the roots. "You've earned your seats at this table, Ethan mar Sol. Who knows, maybe a Winter can teach a den Coille something."

Beside Ethan, Caleb Winter hastily choked back a laugh. Fioruisghe of course poked him in the side. "It would be a first," she told him huffily. Her husband quickly wiped the smile from his face.

Cumchdach had to smother a grin. Caleb and Fioruisghe's marriage might have brought out both families with weapons drawn, but maybe Caleb Winter was finally learning he hadn't pulled off such a victory. Then Cumchdach saw the look the two passed between them, and scowled inside. Caleb Winter had won the most important prize in a man's life, and the man knew it.

A prize that seemed to be racing away from Cumchdach. He leaned forward and nodded curtly to his father. "So what's your idea?"

"That's the problem, son. Ideas. We're doing everything the government asked to meet the Alliance demands, and it's sending our profit lines plummeting. We're still above water, but I can't say for how long." No gasps of surprise answered him, and his father's eyes caught each one of them in turn. Den Coille children grew up reading profit margins as their first texts. "I need ideas. New ways to make credits or ways to improve our current lines, and I need them yesterday."

Thankfully, his father refrained from grousing again about their loss of Anna's expertise, though she had worked closely with the botanist on Fioruisghe's team.

Cumchdach turned to his sister. "What's Joseph told you about what he and Anna were working on?"

"Are…" corrected Fioruisghe, and he raised an eyebrow. "It's only Den Coille work she's stopped. Everything else is ongoing." This time it was Caleb who touched her arm—he'd clearly learned the hard way not to poke his volatile wife—and to Cumchdach's surprise, she shut her mouth.

"What Fee means," the whole family scowled at their sister's Survey nickname but Caleb ignored them as always, "is that Anna has left all her notes on festia with Joseph mar Freshet, who forwarded them to Den Coille's own production staff. It was something to do with mutualism, but they had a lot of work to do on it."

In his deadpan Plains voice, it could have been taken as diplomatic. But Cumchdach still buttoned up, as did the rest of his siblings, bringing a glare from Fioruisghe. You could never quite tell when Caleb Winter was reciting facts and when he was taking a chip at his wife's family. That they were all in debt to him didn't help either. Fioruisghe and her husband had saved all their collective lives, and Caleb had never once openly reminded them of it.

It would be better if he did, thought Cumchdach as he turned to meet his father's glare.

Anything to avoid thinking about Den Coille's challenges and how they clashed with the loss of his wife and child.

"As I was saying," said his father, "We need ideas, and we need them now. So please turn on your very expensively educated brains, children, and come up with some."

Cumchdach hastily sat up, feeling like he was back in first school. His father didn't often pull that trick, but when he did, it was tragging effective.

"Fioruisghe, you first. What's the state of play with the Survey projects."

His father was a subtle and powerful man. Unfortunately, it had no effect on his younger daughter. "That is confidential information, as you are well aware, Da."

"We're supposed to be on the same side now," said Da, and Cumchdach held his breath. He'd heard versions of this conversation too many times.

"What Fee meant to say," put in her husband, the bravest man Cumchdach knew, "was that the Survey has a number of trials under way in Mountainer territory, not all of which are related to Den Coille's current issues. However, there are some that may be of interest. Isn't that right, Fee."

"I would have said that if you'd given me enough time."

"And the lake projects are waiting for us to get back."

Suddenly, Fioruisghe broke into a chuckle and Cumchdach stared at her, along with the rest of the family. How did Caleb do that?

"I'm forwarding you the current applicable projects in den Coille territory," she said now. "The only one that looks to be useful in the short term is the one maximising chaullnia production, but you've already said that has its own complications."

"*Cheaper isn't always better,*" they chanted as one. It was one of the first lessons their father had drilled into them, especially when it came to a luxury item like chaullnia extract. Drop the price of the expensive perfume and you made it less desirable. Less desirable made it more prone to fashion changes.

No, increasing chaullnia extract production wasn't the answer.

"Isn't there any way to get more Festin per tree," asked Cumchdach in frustration. They'd been trying to do that for so long. The market for the food ingredient was as big as they could supply. It was in hot demand by habitats and space-going vessels as a compact and tasty way of adding essential nutrients to their rations. "Or there must be another plant that produces something similar."

Anna could answer that. She'd told him often enough why festia produced so much pollen, the raw source of Festin. It was something to do with the cold, wet conditions found in Mountainer territory. The festia trees produced copious quantities of pollen to ensure survival of their major pollinators.

"She may not be working for Den Coille anymore, but couldn't she include that in her studies while over on Deuteron. Anyara claimed that she found some shrubs there that looked to be related to festia." It was Samhchair speaking, the calm voice of reason. Bram looked at her with interest.

"Ask her," Bram said to Cumchdach.

"It would come better from Fioruisghe or via official channels," Cumchdach made himself say. "She couldn't refuse them."

"Will do," said his brother-in-law, pre-empting his wife, and Cumchdach decided yet again that Caleb Winter wasn't so bad.

"We need more options, though," said Cumchdach, and his father nodded in approval. "Ethan, what about your alternative businesses in Sulwith?" Sarwenna Beren Winter's hometown faced economic death until she and Ethan prodded them to expand the town's business base away from the Solaris solar field that used to dominate it. "How are they going?"

"Promising," was Ethan's brief reply. "But Solaris is making a profit now because we're changing our solar hardware, not because of the changes in Sulwith. You can do technology changes quickly. Changing a business based on living organisms, especially something as long lived as a tree, is another matter entirely."

As if they didn't know that already. Cumchdach had a great deal of respect for Ethan, as well as a genuine friendship with the plainsman, but right now he gave him a hard glare. "Thanks," he said caustically.

Ethan shrugged, as if to say, 'You asked'.

"So what we need are alternative streams of income that don't take away from festia production." Cumchdach switched his com to bring up a holo showing an aerial view of the local mountainside. Manascraoch was built on a mid-slope of the dividing ranges, where a long vanished river had laid down a more fertile region, held in place by the hard rock of the outcropping at the base of the mountain and the ridges coming down either side. It created perfect conditions for the deep-rooted baullnia on which the city was built, and gave them protection from the worst of the vicious winds that roared over the mountain slopes.

He pulled up the view and extended the image north and south, bringing up the bulk of their region. Too much of it showed the uniform darkness of festia plantations, but that was changing, with some mountain meadows of local tough shrubs and the long, native grasses to absorb the water pouring down from the stormy skies sheltering the more dry-loving saplings the Survey and Den Coille teams had planted on the less boggy slopes.

But most of it was still festia. Enough that their production shouldn't have been too badly affected, yet.

"By how much is productivity down?" he asked his father. Bram pushed the figures through his own com, overlaying them onto the forest images.

"And actual collection of festia?"

"This year's harvest was nearer to normal, but we lost a full season thanks to those scum Survey usurpers."

Cumchdach knew that, but he also knew that the government had promised compensation. "The funds haven't come through yet?"

"And won't be, if you ask me, no matter what that wermet Coinneas mar Coille says. He may be a relative, but the man couldn't walk a bough line straight."

He'd been telling his da for years the local upper house Representative wasn't reliable. The man might say *Yes* to whatever Bram asked, but he had no backbone when it came to fighting for Mountainers. He turned to Ethan.

"Did Solaris ever get compensation?"

"No, nor did Pa ask for it. Wasn't going to beg from that pack of Urbis scavengers, he said."

"Would he have got it if he'd asked?"

"I doubt it. He was lucky to stay out of prison as it was. And I haven't asked either, if that's your next question. Even if it came through, there'd be too many strings attached."

Sounded like Winters trusted the Council and Urbis bureaucrats about as much as did the den Coilles.

"I know the Restin fraud hurt us, but not badly enough to be noticeable." Which is why they hadn't picked up Eolas den

Falasch's treachery before Seolta found the fraudulent product for sale in Deuteron. "And Festin is still as sought after as ever. On file, we should be able to weather the years needed before alternatives come on line."

"Should, but things have a habit of biting you if you rely on that kind of wishful thinking," said Bram sourly. "The time to act is now, not when we're facing penury. There are too many worrying signs."

No one else countered their father, and Cumchdach nodded in surrender. His da had an instinct for business too well honed to ignore his warning. He switched his gaze back to scanning the holoimage, minimising Bram's depressing figures.

"What are you looking for?" said Fioruisghe, thankfully reverting to the business-like voice of the professional expert she was. He knew his baby sister well enough to pick up the hint of frustration. Survey field staff knew as well as their family did that for the government to succeed, a high profile company like Den Coille had to succeed. Had to not only survive the changes, but thrive—and according to his father, right now they were failing to do that big time.

"I wish I knew," he said, as frustrated as she was.

"You can't change the forest mix any quicker, not even by pouring a stupid amount of resources onto it. We need the new saplings to grow, to moderate the climate, and that takes years, even with some of the quicker growing species we're using."

"What else can we do? And don't tell me tourism. I have no desire to meet gawking outsiders every time I swing by the main retail trees."

They all shuddered. Mountaineers may be hospitable when required, but generally they preferred to keep to their own kind.

"You need to concentrate on your individual strengths," his mother suddenly put in. All heads turned to her, with mouths open in silent squawks, including their father. Mam may run the main Manascraoch hospital and be a power in the city, but she rarely interfered with Den Coille business. "Don't look at me like that. This is hurting you all."

Mam never stood aside when that happened.

"Da, you first," said Cumchdach when no one looked like talking. "You're the public face of Den Coille."

"As are you now," his father reminded him, then sat back. "This is our home and no one is going to take it from us. First, we have to stop all these undercurrents of resistance." He scowled. "You can't fight the Alliance, not head on."

A general scowl rippled around the table, but they all knew the cold truth of that.

"Arcadia has to change. *We* have to change, and we will, if only they give us time."

"They won't. They can't," said Caleb in his cool voice. "The planet is in too much trouble."

Da's hand gripped his chair arm but he said nothing to that. Another truth with which they'd all become uncomfortably familiar, especially since the last landslide which had destroyed much of the city's upper slopes. "Which means we need everyone on Arcadia working toward making the needed changes. Whether it's the techs finding new ways for us, or stomping out these underground mutterings against the Council. Den Coille is already giving our techs all the resources they ask for. Now it's for us to help the marshals find their conspirators." He sighed again. "I've been doing the rounds and keeping my ears open, but few are talking."

"Let it out that Den Coille is worried. Maybe look slightly distracted one day," suggested Caleb.

Their father raised an eyebrow at that, and Fioruisghe stifled a laugh. Da was an expert when it came to closed faces and never let his competitors know what he was thinking. It would have to be a very subtle sign—but his father was a master of that as well, so Cumchdach merely glanced at her and she shrugged back, her lips twitching. Mam was similarly afflicted and Cumchdach refused to look at either of them lest he join them.

His father glanced at his mother before switching his glare to Cumchdach, "If I have to start acting like a mountebank, you can do the schmoozing."

Cumchdach's heart dropped. He generally got on well with others and enjoyed socialising, but the kind of official hand pumping Da talked about was one of his pet hates.

"Ceart can help you," his father added, and his brother gave one of his brief nods.

"Dumb nieten ox," said Ceart softly, and Cumchdach winced. People said things in front of Ceart they didn't in front of others but there was nothing dumb about his brother. An expert mechanical engineer with a co-degree in physics, these days he worked with Den Coille's flyer development team as they modified their flyers to cope with the wild Mountainer skies. But Cumchdach doubted Ceart would ever forgive him for making him keep silent in prison. As it was, a guard had held a blaster right against Ceart's skull whenever they beat up Aigherach, but it was the blaster against Cumchdach's head that had stopped Ceart from beating up their captors.

"You just listen. Don't *do* anything, no matter what they say about you."

Ceart sent him his stoic look. Right, his brother had been hearing slurs on his intelligence all his life. He was idolised by their flyer crew, but to everyone else he was just Ceart, middle den Coille brother.

"Now for the rest of you," Da said, eyeing each one in turn to force them to speak up.

"I'm Survey. Leave me out of this," said Fioruisghe.

"There are areas of mutual interest," put in Caleb firmly, also refusing to look at his wife. "Have your technicians talk to our teams."

They already were, but Cumchdach didn't want to disrupt that and merely nodded.

"I'm often in talks with local and Urbis officials," said Samhchair unexpectedly. "I can put out some feelers."

"How can health workers help?" Cumchdach asked.

Samhchair had started out in the hospital with Mam, but then moved out into the public health field on their release from prison. She'd said something about finding it more fulfilling, and if there was more to it than that, Cumchdach hadn't asked. Prison had affected all of them. If the public health services kept her happy, that was enough for him.

But: "I don't talk *only* to public health officials," she said in that calm voice of hers, as if she wasn't giving him a well deserved slap in the face. "Housing, the economy, environmental changes, all of them affect the health of the city. I also talk to those at the bottom, the ones who make the city work."

"And you think some of those connections might help us?" asked their father, a far better diplomat than he.

Samhchair shrugged. "If Den Coille cuts back, that will cause a lot of problems for the local region."

The most they were going to get by way of explanation, he guessed. "What sort of connections?" he still asked. His big sister had been looking after them all too long for Cumchdach to let her put herself at risk. She raised an eyebrow at him, telling him she knew exactly what he was thinking and wanted none of it.

Tough, big sis. You're too important. "Political or administrative," he said, suddenly suspicious, and saw his father lean forward, his own mouth beginning to frown.

"I've been spending time with Councillor Seilach ingh Craobh," she said, as annoyingly cool as ever, as if she hadn't just dropped a bomb. Seilach ingh Craobh bean Stobach den Bunachan, the lower House representative for this region, was no yes-woman. She may have helped the den Coille family against the usurping Survey bosses but the woman was notoriously independent and was forever arguing with his father.

"Be careful asking for help from that female shalk," their father warned.

Samhchair merely folded her hands in her lap with a placid smile. "I will, Da."

Cumchdach didn't trust that smile, nor did Da by the scowl on his face. Samhchair might complain, but her personal guard was about to get bigger.

They could do no more for now. His father leaned back, looking down to the end of the table. "You have no family obligation here, Ethan mar Sol, but we would appreciate your help."

Cumchdach sat up suddenly and began to reach out a hand to stop his father. Ethan beat him to it.

"If it benefits Arcadia, family has nothing to do with it."

"But thanks to your father's profile…" began Da.

"No," said Cumchdach in horror. "Ethan, we would never ask you to act against your own father. "

Sol Winter may be an execrable piece of weak-willed obsolescence, but he was Ethan's father and Ethan had idolised him as a child. Cumchdach knew what having to seize control of Solaris from his father had cost Ethan. So did his wife, from her furious glares. But Ethan put out a hand to cover hers and she subsided, though still looked at the den Coilles as if they were a pack of foxllars.

"You want me to keep an ear out for any rumours of discontent from Pa's old contacts?" asked Ethan.

"Yes," said Bram baldly.

"My father stays out of it," said Ethan, "but I'll pass on anything I learn."

Caleb reached out his own hand to lay it on his brother's shoulder. "We both will," he said.

The chances of Sol Winter leaking anything to his eldest son were almost zero, but he was glad Ethan wasn't in this alone.

"That's it," said Da. "Thank you, everyone. We'll meet regularly to check up on progress."

Aigherach leapt up from his seat. "You've left me out."

"You're busy enough with your studies," said Da sternly.

"And the cripple is too young and still a kid, so don't expect him to help."

Mam blanched at that, and all the brothers shot to their feet. Even Ceart. They'd all seen how Aigherach earned that injured leg. He was captured late in their imprisonment and served much less time than his brothers, but the guards had made that time a raw hell. He'd been shot in the leg, fracturing the bone, when they'd captured him, and though it was now near mended, it would never be normal. The guards had re-broken it every time it looked like healing, using Aigherach's agony to control his brothers.

No one was ever going to hurt his baby brother again.

But you just have, all of you.

"Leave it to us this time, *mo leanadh*," said their mother gently. "You have more than earned your time to enjoy Higher School."

"And who else do you think studies at that very expensive business school you sent me to? I have access to a gossip channel closed to the rest of you."

Da opened his mouth, and Cumchdach saw he was about to refuse him. He sent his father an urgent message. Aigherach was no child; he'd stopped being that the first day of his imprisonment. Da read it, then looked over at him, and suddenly sat down. The rest of the brothers watched, then slowly subsided as well, and everyone turned to look at Aigherach.

"You listen only," said Da. "Any information, you pass it on straight away. Do not take action yourself. We can ensure nothing is traced back to you."

Aigherach still stood at the other end of the table, studying his father's face.

"You have my word, son," said Da as gently as Mam, "and our thanks."

Aigherach nodded his head briefly. "Good." Then sat back down.

"Right," said Da, taking a deep breath. "That's it, then. Thank you all. Now, get back to work. This company doesn't run itself."

CHAPTER TEN

Cumchdach had never thought he'd be happy to see the murky skies of Urbis, but coming in over the sprawling city and the myriad channels of the Urbis River estuary, all he could think was that soon he would see Roo and Anna again. Or Roo anyway. Anna had promised him access, but their baby's room was near hers, and who knew what might happen.

You're sounding desperate.

Probably because he was.

Too much time and too little that mattered to fill it. After the meeting, his family had begun their own tasks with a busyness that astounded Cumchdach, but it was too early for results, and his own role was the same as ever. Attend inane meetings and listen hard. He wasn't scheduled for anything in the capital for another few days, but Den Coille security told him Anna had come back to the city to meet with her senior professors. She was here for only two days. He came to Urbis now or he'd miss her.

He dropped everything and hustled his staff to make the trip but, striding down the corridors of her UBS apartment block, he still wasn't sure he'd made the right decision in coming. What if he spooked her?

The halls of this building smelled the same as ever, a worn mix of Urbis pollution, too many bodies, and old panelling, overlain with the heady scents of living plants and animals. It was a smell that always reminded him of Anna, of days long ago when they were both students and he would come up with excuse after excuse to disturb her in her lab.

In those days, she'd always welcomed him with that big, wide smile of hers he loved best.

It wasn't on her face when he walked into Roo's nursery.

"What's wrong," he blurted out, and panicked even more when she blushed dark red.

"It's nothing," she mumbled. "I just wanted to make sure…"

"Of what?" He strode forward, grabbed her arms, then dropped them when she flinched.

Anna was never frightened of him.

"What's happened?"

"Nothing." She gulped. "He missed you, that's all. He's been fretting. I wanted to make sure you came."

Cumchdach's jaw dropped. "He's only a tiny baby."

"He knows his father."

That was more like his Anna, and he began to breathe normally again. "He looks well."

Great. Is that the best you can do.

"He likes the outdoors. The farm in Deuteron was everything Anyara described."

"Good. They're looking after you all?"

"Yes, yes. We're quite adequately provided for. And you? Is all well with you?"

"Yes," he said, just as stiffly, just as inanely.

That was the point where he ran out of words. They both stood, staring stupidly at each other like a pair of strangers.

He'd made love to this woman for years. He knew every square of her skin and had mapped all the changes from teenager to young woman, through to her delicious maturing and the astonishing glory of pregnancy, revelling in them all.

But not since. He didn't know what pregnancy had done to her, had been unable to share with her as her body recovered and became something new and equally exciting.

He desired her as much as ever. That would never change.

Nor could he hide it from Anna, and cursed when a flush darkened her cheeks. "I'd better go. The nurse will bring Roo back to me when you're finished."

Roots, she was almost stammering, all her usual self-possession banished by his boorish lack of control. A queen. That's how he always thought of Anna, with her cool self-possession, but he'd thoughtlessly shattered it.

She passed Roo over. "His tummy's full and he should stay awake for a while."

"You have him on monitor. Send the nurse in if you think he needs to rest."

Her hand reached out and traced their son's cheek. "He has your mouth," she said softly. Then snatched it back and hastily turned to scurry out the door, leaving Cumchdach clutching his baby and staring hopelessly after her.

"How do I get her back, *mo leanadh*?" he said softly to his baby. Roo had settled into his arms and peered up at his father's voice.

The monitors were on, but he had faith in Anna. She'd restrict the sensors to the baby's status only. She wouldn't listen in, and he didn't care if anyone else heard him. He walked around the small room, his son nestled into his shoulder, and told the little boy all his heartache, singing him the songs of his childhood, ancient melodies brought to Mountainer country with the first settlers. After a while, he felt the small head relax, and a bit later he held him carefully away to confirm it.

Roo slept, the deep sleep of a well loved baby. Cumchdach carefully nestled his baby's head back into his shoulder and kept walking, this time telling his son all his worries, all his hopes for a future where Roo was a laughing little boy and both parents playfully swung him between them as they walked, with maybe another sister or brother.

A big *maybe*, on that one. He was far from ready to let Anna go through childbirth again.

Then he told Roo of the threat to Arcadia, leaving out the specifics and keeping his voice to a low murmur. He left out the hell of the prison. He was never going to soil his son's ears with that story.

"We have to find a way to make Den Coille pay despite the changes. Then the other companies can't claim the government is out to run the corporations into the ground and take them over, like those false Survey scum tried on us and Solaris."

Not that he blamed them. The fake Survey bosses would never have succeeded without the implicit approval of too many representatives from both Council Houses. The government hadn't protected his family and the Winters then. If it wasn't for the likes of Joe Gibbs, Councillor Seilach ingh Craobh and Marco an Fallon working to save his family, Den Coille may not have come onside with implementing the changes.

Or without the facts Fioruisghe and Caleb had shoved down their collective throats. Their Survey field staff had put their lives on the line to save the Winter and den Coille families. That kind of debt was never forgotten.

His sister might be a pest at times, but she was a very astute pest. Moreover, she and her team had proved the truth of their words when they stepped in to save Manascraoch during the last landslide. Now it was up to him to help save the planet.

To do that, Den Coille must become a shining example of using updated practices to make credits—a company that thrived while making the changes needed to stop the environmental disaster facing their world.

"Do that, and find the folklars trying to stop us," he added in a growl, but moderated it when he felt Roo's body twitch. Not a thought for a baby's ears.

He waited long after the baby's twitches said he'd gone deep into sleep. What did a baby dream of, he wondered.

He knew what he dreamed about.

But Anna didn't come back, and finally he had to put Roo down and return to reality. He took one last look at his baby son.

"Whatever happens, I'm your father. I will not lose your babyhood," he promised. One vow he would keep, no matter what, though right now he had no idea how.

His foul mood followed him into the evening. When he stomped into his favourite watering spot in the capital, his manner was surly enough that one of his oldest associates lifted his hand in mock surrender and said he'd see him again another day. So much for his order to schmooze.

Only the approach of a man he'd always classed as one of the slimy brigade shocked him out of it. Caltan Smierg was a senior executive in a corporate trader. The man had never tried contacting him before, no doubt knowing the kind of reception he'd get from Cumchdach.

Today, he throttled down on his natural reaction and grunted a hello at the man. He wanted something, and Cumchdach supposed he'd better find out what.

"Something annoying you, den Coille?"

The mudbug couldn't even use proper manners. "Not as you'd notice," he replied in his most sarcastic voice.

The man lifted his hand to tap on his com for a drink, and the bot passed over his choice. Not rotgut but a moderate serve of the best salaschar. So he had taste. Didn't make him civilised. Cumchdach threw back his own drink and signalled for another, tossing that back too. This wasn't salaschar, nor was it the rotgut it appeared to be, but the look of the glass seemed to fool the man. Cumchdach switched to a well seasoned wine and turned around.

"You want something?" he said, putting a slight slur into his voice.

"Just your estimable company, Ser den Coille." Like he'd fall for that. "You look like you need an ear to thrash."

That was true enough, but this man's wasn't going to be it. Still… "Why should I do that. You're no friend to Den Coille."

At least the man had the sense not to deny it. He shrugged. "Never needed to be before but strikes me we might have common ground this time."

"Can't say as I see it." Cumchdach wished the man would leave. Caltan Smierg was the last person he felt like dealing with right now.

"Word is that Den Coille's finding these changes they're forcing on us somewhat troublesome."

Cumchdach scowled back at him. Then remembered who the man was married to: the daughter of one of the leading banking families in Urbis. One thing Smierg excelled at—the only thing, as far as Cumchdach was concerned—was making useful connections, and his wife was his greatest success.

"You can tell your in-laws that Den Coille is doing just fine. Our credit's as good as ever, and we're certainly not looking to change banking arrangements."

The wermet put up his hands. "Hadn't even thought about it." Then he paused, and the oily smirk came back again, the one that set Cumchdach's teeth on edge. "If you ever do consider it, I'm more than happy to make the introductions."

"Den Coille doesn't need go-betweens to do our business." He turned back to the bar. "Is that all you had to say, Ser Smierg? If so, I'm planning some serious communing with this drink."

"Hint taken, Ser den Coille." The man laid a hand on his shoulder and chuckled. Cumchdach only just refrained from planting a fist where it was most needed. He'd never thought to resort to violence, but nor had he expected life to lead him to propping up a bar like this. "I'll leave you to it, but don't forget what I said."

Cumchdach raised a glass. "Not likely to."

The man gave another of those false chuckles. He had more nerve than sense—or more greed than sense. But this time he left Cumchdach in peace.

Unfortunately, he wasn't the only one of his kind to approach Cumchdach, and far sooner than he'd hoped, he was forced to throw back a last drink and make his miserable way back to the sterile refuge of his corporate apartment.

Once in, and with the highest security screen in place, he put a call through to Marshal an Fallon.

"Word on Anna's leaving me is flooding the tragging streets. Don't suppose the marshals have anything to do with that?"

An Fallon lifted a hand, as if innocent.

"I got approached today by some of the lowest scum of the Urbis establishment, you'll be pleased to learn."

This time, a slight twitch tugged at the corner of an Fallon's mouth.

Cumchdach cursed. "I may not be able to refuse being bait for your schemes, Marshal, but you go too far."

"Not far enough, Ser Cumchdach mar Bram," said an Fallon with no apology. "Unless you no longer wish to help your planet?"

Cumchdach's curses rocketed into the truly impressive. An Fallon's face showed no change, as he waited for Cumchdach to wind down. He flung himself onto the nearest lounger and shoved a hand through his hair. "You do know I'm said to be the steady tempered one of the family?"

"Your personality profile is on our files, Ser Cumchdach."

"If my family didn't owe you such a big debt…"

An Fallon made no apology for that either. "We must find the disaffected. *Arcadia* needs you to find them."

"I know that. But I will not lose my wife or son over it. That's non-negotiable."

This time there was a downward twist of the marshal's mouth. "Sera Anna bean Cumchdach is a sensible woman and knows you too well, Ser den Coille."

"If only that were true," muttered Cumchdach. He slumped back in his seat. "All right, what do you want me to do now? The sooner we get this over with, the sooner I can get back to my life."

"Thank you for your cooperation, Ser den Coille. It will not go unnoticed."

"Yeah, that's what I'm worried about."

He made no more protests though, and listened to the marshal's instructions. They boiled down to a simple '*keep doing what you are now* and *follow your nose*'. That last bit wasn't a problem. He was good at that. You had to be when you were the oldest brother in a family his size and slated as his father's heir. Reading people was a necessary skill for managing his headstrong siblings and surviving the company hangers-on eager for easy advancement.

He was still inordinately relieved when an Fallon signed off with a reminder that the marshals were keeping him under surveillance.

The man might claim it was for Cumchdach's protection, but he wasn't naïve. Deliver, or else. That's what the upright Commander warned.

The government may have learned from the debacle of the false imprisonment of his family and the Winters, but nothing had really changed. They were still a threat.

He sat, staring into mid-air long after an Fallon signed off, thinking nothing. Letting himself simply feel, and none of it good. Outside, the ragged darkness of a never-sleeping city was splintered by constantly changing spasms of light. He checked the clock on his com. Time to toss on his sleeper for the required number of hours. He slowly struggled up from the lounger. Or maybe he should just stay where he was and down the bottle of salaschar resting in his cabinet.

Or not. Abusing liquid treasure was sacrilegious. Now the wine resting in the kitchen prepper stores… Maybe a bottle or two of those would help. He struggled up from his seat and stumbled into the kitchen area, reaching for the wine stores. He'd started to pull out a bottle, when he caught a glimpse of himself in the shiny prepper surface. Saw the dishevelled hair and the hungry look on his face as he reached for the alcohol. He thrust the bottle back so hard he broke it.

"Tragging roots."

Wine dripped all over him, all the way down to his feet. He reeked of alcohol. The cleaning bot clattered angrily from its cubby and swept up the debacle of broken plasglass and potent liquid.

Was this his future? A sodden drunk, finding solace in a bottle? He stumbled out of the kitchen and toward his sleeper room, signalling his cleansing unit as he walked.

Before he could make its refuge, the door signalled a visitor, then it opened.

Tragging roots alive. Only family had that kind of entry, and in walked the last one of them he wanted to see right now.

"Fioruisghe. A long way from home."

His baby sister's eyes scanned him slowly, from his sodden feet, up the soaked fabric of his trousers and over the stains spattering his upper shift. "I could say the same for you, big brother, but I see why you're hiding out here." Her scowl matched his mood. "Celebrating your freedom? Or is it the deals you're making with the lowest scum of the business world?"

"Come in, why don't you? Except you're already in, I see. Take a seat and wait while I clean up." He glared at her. "I dropped a bottle of wine and, no, I had not drunk a single drop of it."

Her face stiffened. Not surprising. He'd never spoken to her like that, not even when he thought she'd betrayed them all. He was starting to sound like Seolta at his worst.

He waved a tired hand at the lounger. "Take a seat. I'll be back soon."

Despite his fervently hoping otherwise, she was still sitting in the living area when he finished changing. Nor did she look any happier. She scrunched her legs up on the lounger and glowered at him as he took the seat opposite her.

"What are you up to?"

"As diplomatic as ever, Fioruisghe."

"I prefer Fee in Urbis."

"Not going to happen, baby sister."

That turned her frown even darker. "The baby sister who saved your sorry carcass, I might remind you, brother."

Not like he'd ever forget it, but he had no intention of giving his annoying pest of a sister that satisfaction. Not when she was in full brat mode.

"What are you up to, and what have the marshals got to do with it," she demanded.

So maybe not in brat mode. He glared at the Survey logo on her uniform. "You could have at least changed before you came here."

"The Survey isn't those wermet losers who locked you up. It's me, and Caleb, and my team who are working their backsides off to save Mountainer country and this planet."

"By sending Den Coille broke."

Fioruisghe shot up at that. "Den Coille has taken a hit, but the books are still well in the black and we're doing our tragging best to help you with that, as we promised. Don't put that one on me, brother." She marched around the room, almost bouncing in her fury. "You're not Seolta. You are my big brother who always had my back, even when you disagreed with me."

"Yeah, well, your *big brother* has had one tragging day and would very much appreciate being left in peace."

"No can do. Not when the marshals tell me you're making deals with the likes of Caltan Smierg and his ilk."

"Are you hacking into the marshal's feed now?"

She came to a halt at that, her toes tapping madly as she stared at him. "I knew it. This is part of that demon plot of an Fallon's."

He shrugged. "I've talked to him."

"Don't you want your wife and son back?"

This time it was Cumchdach who shot up. "Anna will come home, and my son is my son. Nothing will change that."

Fioruisghe was small, even by Mountainer standards, a glitchit compared to him as he stood over her. It didn't make her back down.

Was this what he was reduced to? A stupid staring contest with his second most annoying sibling. Slowly her eyes softened, changed from glittering black to the dusky welcome of the forest's shade.

"Sit down, brother, and tell me exactly what an Fallon's asking. You gave us the bones of it only at that meeting." She put out a hand and pushed him over to the lounger, and surprisingly he let her. "Undercover work's a sticky bog."

He watched as she slung herself back into the other lounger. Fioruisghe would know. She'd spent years keeping the full scope of her work from her family. He was too tense to talk at first, but she sat and waited, with a stillness he hadn't thought possible in his ever mobile sister. Finally he sighed and leaned forward, staring at the floor instead of her too knowing eyes. Tonight, he sat with the experienced Survey agent, not his bratty baby sister, and the sympathy in her eyes was too much for him.

He was supposed to care for his family, not be the one needing help.

He told her then. All of it. All his resistance, all his fears that if he went along with the marshals, he might lose Anna and Roo forever.

"An Fallon's right," she said sadly. "You'll do it because the marshals can't afford to lose this chance."

He grunted. "If only…"

"…Seolta had never come across that fake Restin? I suspect he thinks the same."

"When he isn't having a thoroughly enjoyable time poking a stick at the Alliance Central judiciary."

They both laughed at that. Too sudden, a short braying, but a laugh.

"You know you're the best one of us for this? Cumchdach mar Bram duine Anna den Coille is a name respected throughout Protos. Possibly not on Deuteron, but they're not too keen on most from Protos, with the exception of your cursed in-laws and Anyara. And what happened between you and Anna is public knowledge."

"Trashy street gossip."

She shrugged. "That, too, but your loyalty to family is unquestioned. No one will be surprised if you put Anna and Den Coille above the planet. The anti-change brigade must be delirious at the possibility of recruiting you."

He shuddered at the thought. "I'm no turncoat."

"No, but few will be surprised to hear of Den Coille in financial difficulties trying to meet the Council's demands. It confirms everything the conspirators fear."

"Roots, we're not having that spread about. Our bankers will have a fit."

Fioruisghe gave him her old grin. The one that said she was contemplating something particularly outrageous. "No one's spreading any rumours. That's the beauty of it. You just have to look cross and worried. The rest will take care of itself."

"Thanks for the vote of confidence. Not sure I share it."

She shook her head. "You really have no idea how unusual it is for you to go around grumpy and frowning. Any business reporter worth the name will be stuck to you like a shadow until they figure it out. You're usually so tragging in *control*."

"And you're married to Caleb Winter."

This time she laughed out loud. "Good point. You were both born thinking you're in charge of everything. Only Caleb believes it." Then she bit her lip and considered. "Well, so do you. But you have sisters to straighten you out."

He sent her a look of disgust. "Samhchair, maybe. She's as sensible as Anna. But you?"

"You were never in charge of me, big brother."

This time, it was his turn to grin. "No, we learned at a very young age not to even try. I'm surprised Mam still has any dark hairs on her head."

Fioruisghe wasn't stupid enough to deny the charge. But the laughing grin slipped and the senior survey agent returned. "You really are going to let yourself act as bait. I hope an Fallon has a full squad of marshals following you."

"I have a squad of Den Coille security watching me."

"The marshals are better. I'll talk to an Fallon."

Cumchdach sat up at that. "You will stay out of this. If not for your own sake, for that poor husband of yours. He has enough to worry about."

Fioruisghe waved a hand at that. "You don't think he's made sure an Fallon has people watching over his family?"

Cumchdach hoped so, after Ethan Winter's adventures, but didn't mention that to Fioruisghe. Her nose was twitching enough already. "Stay out of this. If for no other reason than that the last thing I need is to be seen to be suddenly on best of terms with my brat of a sister who betrayed the family by joining the Survey."

Her mouth opened in shock. "You still think that, after everything that happened."

"No, Fioruisghe ingh Bram," he said gently, "I do not think that. But it would help me if the rest of the world assumed I did."

"And Anna? Are you going to tell her what you're up to?"

He shook his head. "I can't, not if I want to keep her safe."

His sister shot up. "You bog-headed idiot." She marched over and poked him in the shoulder as she used to do when she was a tiny child. "You're going to lose her if you do this. Is that what you want?"

Cumchdach shot up too, all cordiality forgotten. "Of course it's not. But first and foremost, I'm going to keep her and Roo *alive*. Or maybe you think I should sacrifice them to this debacle as well."

Fioruisghe threw up her hands. "That does it. I wash my hands of you." She marched to the door, smacked her hand on the control panel and jigged up and down as she waited for the door to open then slammed through, turning once to yell back at him. "You're a first class nieten dolt, Cumchdach mar Bram an Scathach. Go to the depths your own way, but don't come crying to me when it all turns out wrong."

He could do nothing but watch her go, too conscious of the myriad sensors monitoring the hallway. She reached the down shaft and leapt into the stream, not turning back once, then was lost to sight.

He turned back and banged the door shut on her.

If only he knew how much of that last rant had been real and how much put on for the sensors. His sister was capable of anything, they'd discovered. For all he knew, an Fallon may have sent her here.

But he wished he had his cheeky baby sister back, not the folklar-eyed agent. His baby sister had loved him unconditionally.

CHAPTER ELEVEN

Anna peered through the scanner's magnifying field. A plant lay on the table, carefully sliced open to show the fascinating internal structure of the stem. It was a species new to her, one they'd found hiding in the farm's drainage ditches. Preliminary observations showed this species was able to moderate its transport and storage systems to suit the external environment, a handy attribute in a ditch that was either flushed with stormwater or baked dry between rain spells.

Not an unusual attribute in plants, but it was the how of it that had her currently transfixed. The structures inside this stem were like nothing she'd seen before, varying up and down the stem's length in a way that made no sense to her. She nibbled at her cheek as she turned the plant over, mind busy with possible experiments.

"Seen the latest newscasts?"

Anna turned in irritation, then wiped off the frown. It was her junior lab assistant, Shelda. An astute and capable scientist lurked beneath the primped and puffed-up exterior of the girl, but today it was well buried. She'd changed her hair again, and now the mass of tufts and curls sprouted a clashing mix of pinks, purples, and vibrant greens. Whoever told her the combination was flattering had to be colour blind but Anna said nothing. Shelda looked brave but that shell was whisper thin.

"What's on them that's so important," she asked, with little real interest. But then the girl shone her com feed onto the wall above them and Anna gasped.

"That's my husband."

It was, but a Cumchdach she barely recognised. She knew he was in Urbis still, the marshals gave her that at least, but this was nothing like his usual haunt. Lights flashed in a garish pattern on the wall behind him as he lounged against the too shiny bar. He was dressed in his customary tailored city clothes, as pristine and immaculately in place as ever, but today it looked too careful, too perfect, and he leaned against the bar as if for support. Nor could his city groomer hide the faint trace of shadows under his eyes, not from her.

Worse still, she recognised the brakka leaning beside him. What was Cumchdach mar Bram doing with that kind of scum?

"Have you finished that analysis yet," she said too sharply as she signalled her com to cut the newscast, refusing to feel guilty. She switched her com to a private channel and stared down at her new plants while her eyes saw only the startling newscast images.

The reporter sounded almost gleeful as he described his meeting with the 'eminent member and putative heir to the Den Coille empire'. Cumchdach had given the man short shrift, from the spite in the reporter's voice. Not surprising if the man caught him in this kind of meeting.

What was Cumchdach doing talking to a two bit, underhand dealer like Caltan Smierg. Anna knew the man; she'd actually had to exchange a stilted conversation with him when she first fled to Rubhaicreach and went to one of the mayor's receptions. She still remembered how her skin crawled, and she'd made sure never to attend any more gatherings that included a guest of her stepmother's.

What was Cumchdach up to? This was so much more than an Fallon said he'd asked of him.

She didn't think for a minute that Cumchdach had fallen to doing business with the dregs of Arcadia. Not the man she'd known since she was a teenager. You couldn't be with someone that long and misjudge them so badly.

But then, she had also believed he loved her. But that was before her father's betrayal and Cumchdach's silence. Before he'd shown her how little he trusted her and how much lay between them.

A squawk from the carrier beside her, and she put down her plants hastily. Roo was getting bigger and more active every day. Cumchdach's son had no trouble putting his feelings into sound. Very loud sounds.

"Shh, *mo leanadh*. Mam's here. What do you want, my precious wee man?"

He glared at her, as if horrified she didn't know, then drew his legs up and roared at her.

"I fed you only an hour ago. You can't want more."

But Roo did, and turned his head eagerly toward her as soon as she picked him up.

"He'll be going through a growth spurt. It's common in babies of that age," said Shelda with all the wisdom of the eldest in a very large family. The girl had been helping her mother and aunts with babies since her earliest years and had quickly proven herself a sterling asset to Anna's mothering team. She could even get Roo to settle down and sleep when all his mam's and his nurse's efforts had failed dismally.

"He's just a bit lively. Going to be someone when he grows up," she would pronounce, and who was Anna to say she was wrong.

Unfortunately, right now, Roo was exhibiting all the stubbornness of his father and the quicksilver liveliness of his aunt Fioruisghe. She sighed and gave in to the inevitable.

"Make sure no one touches this dissection, please, Shelda," she said as she carried her son away to the quiet of her quarters. She settled into the comfortable chair her staff had found and nestled him onto her breast. After some loud slurping, the sole point of which was to show his mother how starving he was, she'd long decided, he settled down to business and she leaned back into the chair, letting her mind drift.

She'd thought she knew Cumchdach inside and out. He shouldn't have been able to keep her father's treachery a secret from her.

She shouldn't have been surprised though, the more she thought of it. It was right in character for him. She'd seen the fear lurking in his eyes every time she'd been forced to flee, clutching her stomach, in those early days of her pregnancy.

So she understood him. Forgiving him was a whole other matter. To trust her so little, even thinking it was in her best interest, was no basis for a marriage.

Maybe, but it didn't change reality. They were married in full, public view. It had been the event of the year in Manascraoch, and neither of them had ever contemplated refusing such a grand affair. Not when his city and family had waited so long.

If only she hadn't agreed to the wedding. They'd been happy as they were, hadn't they?

Then she glanced down at his son.

No, she could not regret marrying Cumchdach mar Bram duine Anna den Coille. Given both their families and positions, children were not an option without the formal ties and carefully explicit contracts that came with marriage, and she had so badly wanted to have children with Cumchdach.

Not that she'd told him that. The memory of the shock on his face when she finally said *Yes* to his latest proposal still brought a soft chuckle to her lips, as well as the determined look that came next as he hustled her into a jeweller to choose a ring and opened a link to both their lawyers' offices to start the marital negotiations before she could change her mind. He barely gave her a chance to breathe before they both stood in the ceremonial hall of his home and announced their vows in front of their extended families and anyone else with even the slightest connection to either family or city.

They were married, and every prominent citizen of the central Protos region could attest to it. There was no going back on that.

Had she been right to agree? Another of those hopeless questions, yet whatever came, she did not regret it. Not when she felt the tug of her feeding baby or heard that unique and insistent cry of his, or met those beautiful eyes so filled with love and trust and knew she was the centre of Roo's universe.

How to repay such deep trust was her problem now. That Cumchdach loved his son was never in doubt, nor that he would insist on being part of his life.

But her, Anna? Where did she fit in his life?

Roo drifted off slowly into that wonderful sleep of a baby, his suckling gradually slowing, then coming to an open mouthed stop with the occasional smacking of lips as if still feeding in his dreams. She unlatched him and placed him in his cradle, setting the controls for the soft music he loved best and the rock to the pace of a gentle walk. Biarsuin took her place in the seat near him with her monitor set to alert her if she had to leave his side, and outside her hut, a trio of security guards patrolled. Last of all, she set the alarm and the security sensors, far more than should be needed for an infant only just beginning to show signs of rolling.

But he was no ordinary infant, no matter how much she might wish otherwise. How could one so young have enemies?

He's not a person to them. Just a weapon to be used to manipulate his parents.

She would never forgive them for that. But for now, she had a project needing her attention. She took a moment to breathe in this amazing place she found herself in.

It was nothing like the proud estuarine farms, nor those of her home city. Despite the topography, they had farms in Rubhaicreach. Many of the city's greens came from cleverly lit underground vertical farms. The ocean winds cut through any leaves grown in the open, and few off-world plants could link into the *rete* root network that kept the native peninsular plants intact. Some natives could be cultivated—the tough, ground hugging, fruiting shrubs and the herb-like vegetation clinging stubbornly to the rocks and barren ground. They were valuable sources of essential nutrient elements but couldn't feed a city the size of Rubhaicreach. Anyara had promised to visit her hometown when she and Seolta were next allowed back to Arcadia, and her eyes had popped when Anna sent her through a sim tour of one of the vertical farms.

"I could be on a space station," she'd sent back.

The rest of the food for the city came from the farms of the Protos estuary country. The same ones that had sent her packing when she'd tried to suggest ways to integrate the plants into a more balanced system. As for the professors of the Urbis Agricultural Institute...

Keep your nose out of things you don't understand, they'd as good as said.

But here, all those ideas of hers were old news. "Why do you do it that way?" she'd naïvely asked when she first arrived at the Shirons' farm.

"'Cause it works," the farmer had said, as if stating the obvious. She'd quickly learned to dredge up every speck of humility she possessed, which wasn't much, she had to admit, and keep her eyes, nose, and ears open, and her mouth closed as she observed everything the man did.

Luckily, he'd liked Anyara. Her biome skills, honed in the strict regime of a space station, had thrilled to the farm's systems, and she'd even been able to offer advice for improving production. Anna wasn't yet in a position to do that and wouldn't have dared if she were. Not if it risked her research.

The sun was near its peak and the shadows lingered only under trees, bushes, and by the steep banks protecting the precious new seedlings.

"Soil's good if you respect it. It's the wind's the killer." Another of the farmer's gems. A man of few words, speaking only when he deemed it essential, Gebre of Shiron was younger than she was but already had a growing family. She'd met his wife, but the woman wasn't interested in 'useless gabbing' as she put it. She was busy with all the animals around the homestead and her three little ones, with another on the way, Anna guessed, from the way she'd suddenly blanch and stand still a moment, before carrying on with her work.

Anna rested her hands on her hips and gazed over what the unprepossessing couple had achieved here. The farm was a mix of cropping lands on the fertile river flats near her, a small aquaculture setup in the wide reach of the river bounding one side of their lands, stock grazing the native grasses on a hilly slope rising up the far side, and forestry blocks dotted over it all, serving as both shelter belts and a source of timber. A veritable potpourri of income sources.

The farmer stopped on his way to the nearest forestry block. "I'm taking the first readings."

She'd discovered those short blocks of words were an invitation to join him, and with alacrity she picked up her tools and hurried after him. The man said nothing but did slow his steps to let her keep up. She was making progress.

This time, her chief of security stopped her just before they entered the trees. The carefully blank look on his face had her jerking to a halt. "What's happened?"

"Nothing, Sera. Nothing detectable."

"But…?"

"There has been movement on the edge of the perimeter. It may be locals, but none of the readouts match those registered."

"Increase surveillance and alert levels," she ordered.

"Already done, Sera." He twitched his head at the man following behind him. "The trooper here will accompany you. He is one of our best and fully armed."

Anna wasn't going to argue. "Thank you, Ser."

The farmer had stopped to watch what was going on, then started to move off. At first, he said nothing. Then stopped again before they entered the trees and turned to the trooper.

"Are my family at risk?"

The trooper shook his head.

"Not as far as we know. It's me and my son they're after," said Anna, not so sure. "If you want us gone from here, just say the word."

The farmer looked towards his homestead. "Not yet. Not if what you do here helps us all." A grunt, then he looked back at her. "Your word is what I want. If there's trouble for my little ones, I want your word you or those fancy soldiers of yours will tell me."

"You have it," said Anna. "Trooper, you heard. Please transmit my order."

The farmer gave a nod, then set off again. In the forest, he passed Anna a cutter and showed her what they were doing. She'd taken core samples before and this was similar. He watched her for the first few, then gave that brisk head nod of his again and set to. He didn't even bother telling her which ones to sample, but she watched his pattern and copied it on her own section.

Maybe if she concentrated hard enough, she could ignore her guard's warning. It still took every spark of will power in her body to hold her hand still on the cutter and her legs from swinging her around and running as hard as she could back to check on Roo.

Over the next days, she threw herself into her work, taking to carrying Roo with her whenever possible in his body carrier. It was early summer, and the weather was settled enough most times to let her, only the odd showery day forcing her to leave him behind with his nurse. Whenever that happened, she found work at base camp, letting her technicians take over even the more delicate operations.

By the start of the next week, she was a jangled mess of warring emotions. What she found here, in this simple farmer's operation, excited her as little else had done for months. She'd taken to calling in to visit with his wife most mornings, bringing Roo with her and comparing baby notes and growing hints. Firama of Shiron had grown up in this region as well, and was a source of much unconscious local knowledge now she'd begun to relax with Anna. Her husband would often drop in to check on them too, and in the familiarity of his own home kitchen let down some of his guard and make his own comments on the current subject of discussion, whether it be babies or young seedlings.

After a while, they unbent enough to ask her questions as well as make suggestions.

"What's it all for?" he finally asked her one day. He'd been told the official spiel. A study to compare Deuteron and Protos farming methods and their effects on plant growth.

Anna was looking at something more, though. "Plants are not islands in the soil. What happens to one plant affects others around it. It has to. Plants are subject to the whims of their environment in a way unmatched by animals that can simply move away if given sufficient warning. If they're planted in the wrong place, or with the wrong neighbours, the wrong soils, the wrong sunlight conditions, wind, rain, they will wither and diminish. Only replanting by people can change any of the above, and only if the plant is in a state to allow replanting. Most can't be."

Both their mouths were wide open and Anna blushed. "That's not what you were asking. Sorry, I forget myself when it comes to work and my plants."

"No, dear, just hadn't ever thought of it like that. You're right of course," said the wife. "I guess we expect everyone to know you've got to plant things in the right place."

"You'd be surprised how few know that," said Anna, thinking of some choice targets in the Agricultural Institute and the Protos farmers she'd tried talking to. Their usual response was that if the place wasn't right, you *made* it right. No wonder their output was declining and the planet was in trouble.

She leaned back, enjoying the warm air of the kitchen. For a moment, she let her eyes close over.

"Sera, a drink?"

She sat up in surprise. "I must have dozed off."

"You needed it, Sera," said the farmer's wife with a chuckle, and Anna blushed hard.

"Babies, they tire you out," said the woman with a wry smile. The farmer had gone back to his work, it seemed, and his wife was passing her a mug of dask. She accepted it with thanks, needing the pick-me-up.

"How long was I asleep?"

"Not long, Sera. No worry about your wee one. He'll still be sound asleep, and your Biarsuin is a good nanny."

"I don't usually do this." She lifted the mug and took a deep drink to hide her embarrassment. Yet she made no move to leave. The room felt like a haven, like home in a way she hadn't known since…leaving Cumchdach, she realised with a shock. What was it about this place? Simple farmers, the ordinary bustle of family life, folk close to their land. To the things she understood. That must be it.

"You have a good farm here," she said.

The woman nodded. "We do, and one day, it'll be better."

"Not with all those fertilisers and gear your man thinks will change things. Your production levels already match many Urbis estuary farms."

"That's kind of you to say so, Sera." The woman passed her over a piece of freshly baked bread, made from the sorphlex they grew and slathered with jam from their own fruit. Anna took a greedy bite before continuing.

"Nothing kind about it. Just plain fact. How you do it is what we need to know. So far, it matches no known facts."

The woman shrugged. "Watch the land, do what works best, plant where they like. We did try a few things in our first years here that didn't work, then changed them quick smart. Folk been farming around here a good while now," she reminded Anna. "Can't afford mistakes, so we learn fast."

Good farmers as they were, credits were scarce. The children's clothes were mostly recycled and home stitched, and the cheerful items livening up the friendly kitchen were crafted, likely by the ever capable woman sitting opposite.

Anna liked everything about it. She finished the bread, then rubbed a too full stomach in welcome bliss. "This place reminds me of my grandmother's home. It has the same feeling."

Grandam's house might be filled with precious heirlooms and expensively imported delights, but her own childhood creations took pride of place on the main dresser. This whole farm reminded her of Rubhaicreach. More fertile, with none of the shore-battering storms that marked her childhood home, but there was something in the way it worked. Or had, before her stepmother ordered the rete plants butchered.

The rete…

"I'm an idiot." She stood up so suddenly she sloshed dask over her lap. "Oh, no." She grabbed at the towel hastily passed her by the wife, who was making concerned noises and offering a change of clothing. She dabbed quickly, getting the worst of it off, then thrust the towel aside. "Sorry, can't stop. I have to go. Thank you, Sera. Thank you, for more than I can say."

Her grandmother would be horrified at the rudeness of her departure, but Anna almost ran out of the kitchen and toward her team. Bursting into the main work hut, she pointed at her team leaders. "I want scans, immediately. Soil. Chemical, physical, and biological."

They stared open-mouthed at her. "We've done scans a plenty."

She shook her head, struggling to get the words out. "No, a full one. A complete scan of soil, subsoils, surface, and air, with full integration."

That had their jaws falling even wider open. "You'll have to send a skimmer overhead in a slow sweep for that. The cost…"

She shook her head. "I'll deal with it. Do it. Now."

They still stared. She drew herself up and called on all her ancestors' pride. "Bring me the authorisation form, team leader."

She always used first names with her staff. The use of his title had the team leader shocked into action. He called up the necessary forms. Anna entered the details of her order, then signed it at the bottom, using her fullest of legal names, the one she'd hadn't used since her wedding day. Anna ingh Eolas an Sumhneas o Falasch bean Cumchdach den Coille. The team leader read it, the lines around his eyes tightening, but he said nothing, and appended his own full legal title as witness.

"Get on to it, now," said Anna.

Both of them stood on the highest point of land overlooking the farm as the skimmer began its painstakingly slow sweep, Anna cradling Roo in the pouch in front of her.

"What are you hoping to find?"

She shook her head. "I'll know when I see it. A hunch."

"You're using up ten percent of our total budget on a *hunch*?"

Anna refused to apologise or back down. She strongly suspected her budget was a nominal figure anyway. The marshals and the Council had made it clear enough her work was a priority.

Or so she'd understood and, so far, had no reason to think otherwise. The scan's cost was a fraction of what it must be costing to keep a full squad of marshals hovering over her at all times, let alone the scary level of surveillance she'd been placed under. Den Coille had big pockets, but they weren't paying for this. Or not all of it, fully aware Cumchdach had inserted his own people into her team.

She thrust that thought aside and fixed her eyes intently on the skimmer.

"It'll be hours yet."

Anna nodded, but stayed where she was. "Organise a geotech and a meteorologist to check the results as well."

This time, her team leader merely nodded and added yet another notation to his com file. Not long afterward, and fortunately for her tech chief's sanity, Roo stirred and made his wants clear, and she had to walk back to camp to attend to him. She kept one eye on the sky, but it wasn't until well into the afternoon that the skimmer finished its scan and she could haunt the techs' hut as they decoded and put the results into readable form.

Finally, she walked through and around the holo image showing all the levels of the farm, from the rough native cover and forested slopes all the way down through crops, pasture lands to the banks of the river.

"Highlight native plant cover." There was more of it than she'd expected, natives finding their way into the edges and hollows of the crops as well as spreading randomly through the imported or improved pasture species where stock grazed, forming a thinning but continuous passage from hilltop to stream. "Add in soil biological intensities and chemical flow patterns. Metals and non-metallics." She watched the lines form, the waves of colour surging through the farm. Then looked higher. "Include surface and aerial animal movements, microbial or otherwise."

Slowly, carefully, she walked the patterns, finger reaching out, touching points to further clarify the details, then finally stepped back, and back again. There was a noise behind her. The farmer had come to see as well.

"That my place?"

"It is, Ser."

He peered dubiously at the intermeshing layers and streaks of colour. "Looks busy."

"It is, Ser. It certainly is." She turned to the technicians. "Raise a similar profile for an Urbis estuary farm."

The man smiled. "Up beside it now, Sera."

Anna stared at the contrasting fields. She hadn't imagined it. "Yours is busier," she said to the farmer.

"Huh."

Together, they both stared at the pair of images. The Urbis estuary farm was busy too, but the lines and patterns were more organised, and the colour intensities so much less.

"Not as much going on there," said the farmer.

"No, there's not," said Anna with a satisfied smile on her face. The senior team leader came in and stood beside her.

"What do you think now?" she said to the Team Leader.

He grunted, his face warning he'd concede only so much, yet. "We have some work to do, Sera."

They certainly did.

"What's he talking about," said the farmer suspiciously. "What do all those colours mean. Is something wrong with my farm?"

"Absolutely nothing at all, Ser. Your farm is amazing," Anna said, feeling slightly drunk.

The man looked even more puzzled.

"Remember what I said to you the other day about plants talking to each other. Well, there is a whole cacophony of chatter on your farm, and that's why you grow everything so well. Plants don't merely talk to each other, they cooperate." She walked forward again, as if in a dream, one finger reaching for a sweeping line of purple. "See this, it's a flow of magnesium. Your costa crop needs it, but natives need far less. The soil here is patchy in places for magnesium content, depending on the particle size and make up.

On the higher ridges, the native reticularia take what they need, then release the rest of it when the water content of the soil is high enough to carry it down to the costa seedlings. Now, if you look closer at the seedlings," she pulled up a zoomed image of the costa plants, showing tiny white specks coating the emerging leaves, along with the odd winged critter, to a gasp from the farmer.

"That's the start of a guttabile infection. I'll order a spray first thing."

She put out a hand to stop him. "Wait. Watch." The scan continued, showing other leaves. Many with the same white specks, but others with fewer specks and more of the tiny flying critters, almost too small to see. She pointed at them. "They look just like dust particles to the naked eyes, but they eat the guttabile spores. Now follow the yellow pathways."

Both of them watched as she tracked the yellow up and across the field of young plants to small ridges running alongside, the piled-up sides of furrows from the cultivation machines. The yellow paths dropped down and congregated around clusters of scruffy looking grey leaves and mounds of prickly knobs, the same plants that the purple tracks had started on. The yellow lines all ended on the knobby mounds, then took off again.

"*Scobis volante*. The dust midge, though of course they're not a real midge but an Arcadian aerial critter. They eat the guttabile, it's their favourite food source, then come for the sugars in the reticularia flowers—that's what those knobs are—then fly off again. They're the main pollinator for the reticularia, although they do use other midges and wind transmission. But the *Scobis* are the most productive." Her finger gently traced over the ugly looking knobs. "We have here, Ser, a simple story of mutual gain, and it's repeated again and again over all your fields. Your farm is a living marvel."

The farmer gawked. "You're saying those retic…sticky bids, that's what we call 'em, are thinking plants."

She smiled at that. She did think that, but only in her silliest dreams. "No, Ser, nothing so obvious. We're scientists. We report only what we find. What we think happens is that one plant receives a message of some kind from another plant, probably chemical, maybe in this case from the damage caused by the guttabile spores. The reticularia respond to it by releasing magnesium, and so the cycle starts. Whether it's a learned response or an automated one is a matter for a philosopher, not a simple botanist."

"Nothing simple about it," he muttered, and Anna nodded in pleased agreement.

"Team Leader, please forward these results to the main lab in Urbis, and make a summation suitable for interplanetary transmission. I want to send a copy to my sister-in-law."

"The Sera Anyara?" said the farmer, looking happier for the first time since she'd stunned him silly. "Good. She'll make sense of all this." He waved a grumpy hand at the interconnecting mesh of colours.

"I hope so," said Anna, not at all put off by the man's preference for Anyara's expertise. Seolta's wife was an Esteemed Scholar of the Alliance Academy on Alliance Central, one of the foremost biome specialists in the Alliance. Integrating living systems was second nature to her.

But how plants did it was Anna's special field, and what showed up here was fascinating.

She wandered back to her cabin, not bothering to hide the smile tugging at her lips. The whole camp would know soon enough about the new boost to their study. Foolish dreams of academic glory floated through her head, to be discarded with a chuckle. They might give momentary satisfaction—imagining the contortions on the faces of the stodgy Agriculture professors forced to listen to praise of her was particularly pleasant—but they gained her little.

What did matter was that maybe she now had a chance of fulfilling all those grand hopes in her ability. Her own department and the marshals and Council had put her here, and part of her had been terrified by the responsibility. What if she was wrong?

But now, it looked like she was really getting somewhere. She pulled off her gloves, looking forward to telling Roo all about her imminent success.

"There you are, Sera Anna," said Biarsuin.

"Was I delayed? My apologies," she said. "Hopefully Roo's still sleeping?"

Biarsuin looked confused. "You put him down in your office."

That was when she noticed the strained look on the girl's face. "Roo. Where is he?"

"But… He's with you. She was taking him to you. That's what the security trooper said."

Fear lanced through her. "What trooper?"

"You haven't got him?" asked Biarsuin, her eyes wide with shock. "You must have. She said you'd been held up and asked for Roo to be taken to you for his next feed. I commed you and you confirmed it. You came on my com. It was you… wasn't it?"

Anna slammed her com open and stabbed in her security's code, fingers shaking. "Red alert. Red alert. They've taken Roo."

Immediately, her security chief's image materialised in front of her. She told him everything in a gasping voice. He pulled up his own com and an order rang through the buildings.

"Lockdown. Red alert. The entire site is now on lockdown. No one is to move from their current position." Then he turned to Roo's nanny. "Sera Biarsuin, please describe this trooper. Do you know her?"

Biarsuin shook her head, face bleached. "I haven't seen her before, but I checked. She showed me her com seal."

Her description wasn't much help. Short brown hair, average height and build. Nothing noticeable.

There wouldn't be. Not in an agent infiltrating her site.

"Find my baby," she cried to the chief.

The next hour was the worst of Anna's life. The entire camp took part in the search, first registering with security so they knew exactly where everyone was and had accounted for them all. Biarsuin scanned all the images as they came through, but the mysterious trooper wasn't among them.

"I saw her only briefly. I could be wrong," she said, wringing her hands and looking as miserable as Anna felt. It changed nothing.

"How did an intruder get past your shields, Chief?" She was ready to demand the man's resignation. It was only that he was the best person in camp to head the search that held her off, but his grim-faced mouth said he knew exactly what she was thinking.

"We'll find him, Sera," he said repeatedly, between issuing a stream of orders.

"He could be halfway to Urbis by now."

An exaggeration, she hoped, but the thought of her baby being taken anywhere was too horrific. He must be hungry and frightened. They wouldn't hurt a defenceless baby. Who could be so heartless?

The kind cruel enough to steal him from his mother.

A crackle on her com, on the channel monitoring the search. She switched it to maximum.

"We've found him."

Anna opened the channel, her heart in her mouth. The chief was moving and she ran after him.

The signal took her right to the edge of camp, to a small grove of shrubs.

"Over here, Sera," called a woman. One of the other botanists. Then she saw that the woman held a small bundle in her arms. Better, she heard a tiny cry, an exhausted little bleating.

She ran up and grabbed Roo from the woman, pulling open her shift as she did. It didn't matter who saw, as she perched on the nearest log and set her baby to her breast.

"Shush there, manny. Mam's here. Shush, shush."

His face looked exhausted, his eyes bruised from crying, and fixed on her as if she might disappear again. It took precious moments to soothe him enough to get him to feed. Then she felt the tug of her milk letting down and heard his suckling, broken by half sobs, as if he'd cried himself out and had only the last remnants of voice left to call her.

She rocked him as he fed, hands cradling him close and arms tucked protectively over his head. "Shush, shush, Mam's here," she said, over and over again, and whether she said it to Roo or herself, she couldn't say. "Mam's here."

The security chief coughed gently. She looked up at him.

"Find that woman. Find her—and bring her to me."

"We're trying, Sera."

"Trying isn't good enough."

But her fury gained her nothing. By nightfall, there was still no sign of the intruder. She put Roo down to sleep in their hut, then gave way, her hands and arms trembling.

She stared down at Roo, too frightened to leave him.

"You need dinner and sleep, Sera Anna," said Biarsuin, looking no better than she felt.

Anna shook her head. "I can't. Not yet. You go. I'll be here—in case."

In case he wakes and wants me. Never again would her baby cry for her without anyone to hear. That had been the cruellest part of it. They had taken Roo in his capsule, had enclosed it in a shield to keep his cries from being heard. Then they had abandoned him at the edge of the camp and set the capsule on a timed release. It was the only reason they'd found him. The techs found the residue of a screen in the capsule, blocking her baby from their scanners.

If the capsule had failed to open…

No, don't got there.

"You go," said Anna again. Biarsuin looked at her. Anna stared back. "Go."

The girl reluctantly nodded, her mouth turned down. The door closed after her as she left.

Anna sat there, one hand never leaving Roo's crib.

They might have killed her baby.

Much, much later came the sound of the door opening again. Biarsuin back to try again to persuade her to leave Roo, she guessed. She still turned and stood, putting Roo's crib behind her, and pulled the blaster she'd demanded from security, pointing it straight at the door.

A man walked in. The last person she'd expected.

"Cumchdach." She flung down the blaster and threw herself at him, then clutched the strong muscles of his arms tight.

She lifted her face to his, ignoring everything that still lay between them, seeing only Roo's father.

"They tried to kill our baby."

CHAPTER TWELVE

She looked so raw. Cumchdach held her tight as the sobs wracked her body and cut him to the heart.

"I'm here, *a chiad*. You're safe now."

"They hurt our baby. He thought I'd abandoned him."

The words came out in choking gasps. He could feel the shiver running through her, the aftermath of shock. But he knew his Anna. Under the fury, under the unforgiving rage and distress, she was terrified. Even now, even with her face a blotched, swollen nightmare of suffering, she kept glancing at Roo's crib as if afraid to lose sight of him.

"He's safe. You're safe. We will double his guard."

"Not enough. He stays with me at all times. Always."

He wasn't about to argue with her. "And when you're asleep, I'll make sure there's a full squad of marshals in here, along with the best security shields available. An Fallon owes us."

A grim set to her mouth, she nodded. "Not from den Falasch," she said, with no hint of regret. "Not while that woman holds my father in thrall."

"He loves her, *a chiad*. That doesn't change because she's a monster."

"But I'm his daughter. Roo's his grandson."

This time, Cumchdach kept silent. He'd heard that note of pain in Anna's voice before. Pain she'd buried since she was a child, the daughter of an arranged marriage, and had learned that to her weak-willed fool of a father, she was first and foremost a tool for advancement. The man hadn't even bothered trying to hide it, talking about it openly. He remembered Eolas speaking to his son by Gria.

"Anna will be the heir to den Falasch and den Guire of course, but you will have the money, Anton. What isn't bound up in the Falasch entails. Den Guires have plenty. With both of them, you will have all the wealth you need behind you. Anna will own it, and you, my beloved son, will run it. Isn't that right, Anna?"

She had walked out of the room that time, and Cumchdach had followed her, so tragging proud of her. He suspected it was the first time she'd done that and hated the thought she'd had to listen to such drivel before. They'd been fifteen standards at the time, and she had moved to live full time with her grandmother from that day.

"There will be no one from den Falasch allowed anywhere near him," he promised.

It didn't matter that Anna's grandfather still held the loyalty of much of the wider den Falasch family, despite all Gria's manoeuvrings. As far as he was concerned, while they failed to call out the current head of the family, all den Falasch were enemy to Anna. Taking Roo had been a warning, he'd guess. But from whom? That was the problem.

Anna's sobs slowly stopped, and he watched the courage come back to her. But with courage came self-possession. It was like losing her again when she pulled back from him. He'd have cursed out loud if he didn't think it would scare her off more than she was already.

She hugged her arms tight, cheeks flushed. "Thank you for coming so far. I'm sorry you were bothered with this."

"Ruiseart is *my son.* You think I wouldn't go round the planet and back again for him?" *Or for you?*

"Yes, of course." But her face was turned to the ground. She may have got her courage back, but facing him was a step too far, apparently.

"We have to find out who did this. You and me, both of us together."

She shook her head. "It's my father's fault he's at risk."

Cumchdach's mouth dropped at that. "His last name is den Coille. He's my son and yours. Both of us together. *That's* why he's at risk, not because your father is a gutter dwelling fool of a wermet."

That had her blushing harder than ever.

"*You* are the daughter of Sumhneas ingh Eagrai den Guire and the granddaughter of Driach mar Ramach duine Deana den Falasch. Antecedents to make anyone proud. Where your father got his snivelling genes from is a mystery to me and to everyone who knew his sire."

He'd always refrained from being so blunt about her father, but the day he kidnapped his own daughter, keeping her from her baby, was the day Cumchdach lost all courtesy for him. "We will find who did this. Find them, and stop them."

She gave a short nod but still clung to Roo's crib. He understood. Only the thought he might disturb the baby's sleep stopped him grabbing Roo out of his crib and checking every speck of him to make sure he was unhurt. He'd read the medic's report on the way here. They hadn't physically hurt Roo. He looked down into the crib, studying every visible part of his son.

The baby slept curled into a tight ball, his arms and fists tucked hard into his chest as they had in those first weeks after birth.

He was unhurt, but his son had lost trust in his world. Anna reached out with her hand to stroke his chest and both tiny fists clamped hold of his mother.

Only then did his baby begin to uncurl.

They hadn't hurt him but the brakka had frightened his son. For that, and for what his disappearance had done to Anna, they would pay.

"I have to go and make some calls. There's a guard on every corner of this hut and the marshals have you under surveillance." There was also a marshal sitting quietly outside the door, waiting to come in, but Anna knew that. The woman had withdrawn only when Cumchdach entered.

Anna muttered something, but still wouldn't look at him. Not properly, and that hurt as much as anything. He'd known her proud, he'd known her angry, he'd known her sad and happy. Never had he known her to hide from him, not his best friend in all the world.

"I won't be long," he added, as much for himself as for her. "Com me immediately if you need me."

Then he had to walk out the door and leave her with her face stricken and their baby clutching her hand tightly.

He moved far enough from her building to have privacy then put a call through to an Fallon, demanding an immediate answer. The marshal clerk who answered looked suitably irritated and began to ask a lot of time-wasting questions.

"Put me through to an Fallon. Now. Priority One. Yes, he is waiting for my call and no, I don't care what he's doing at the moment. Not even if he's in conference with the Upper House Chair himself."

An Fallon chose to use Cumchdach for his dirty work, so he could take what came with it.

The Commander of police came online within a thankfully few moments. Before he could say anything, Cumchdach spoke up. "You've put my baby in danger. What are you going to do about it?"

An Fallon didn't deny it or make useless excuses. He listened to Cumchdach's terse description of how he'd found Anna and Roo. At the end, the marshal opened another com window and made a number of his own calls. Cumchdach couldn't see who to or hear what the marshal said, but the man's orders were abruptly short and his face grim.

He looked back to Cumchdach. "A medic is on the way to Sera Anna's camp. The Ser Ruiseart will have a marshal tag inserted and his guard increased. The team there are following all leads, and I've told our intelligence group to put finding who kidnapped your son at the top of their work schedule."

"You've been monitoring Anna since she arrived. That's what I was told. So how did that fake message get through? How can they hack a com when the marshals are watching?"

"It's top of our intel people's list, Ser. We've already pulled her com and are setting in a new shield on all team members' coms."

"Not good enough, Marshal."

His mouth tightened. "We will find who did this, Ser Cumchdach, and we will keep your family safe. In the meantime, I'm sure you have work awaiting you in Urbis."

"Leave Anna, in the middle of all this?"

"Yes, Ser, the sooner the better."

"Not happening, Ser Marshal."

The marshal showed not a speck of apology. "Get back to Urbis before the tongues start wagging and too many start asking questions about why you came out here so suddenly. Or do you want to give Arcadia's enemies a warning? Or let them think they are succeeding? Make them bolder next time they go after your family?"

That last was unanswerable. He growled silently. "In an hour. Anna needs me. She gets that, minimum."

"A cloaked shuttle is on standby. Tell the lead marshal on site when you're ready to leave."

"I have my own flyer."

"It's already enroute back to Urbis. You came, saw all was well with your son, then left. Short, simple and no hint of a reconciliation."

"That'll be believable when I'm not on it at the other end."

"Our double is capable of covering for you from remote scrutiny," said an Fallon curtly, as if he hadn't just revealed a scary insight into the marshals' tech. They must have done a full body scan of him to make the kind of body sim needed to fool a remote scanner. Illegal as trag, and complaining about it would get him precisely nowhere. So how did that com message make it through their tech?

"I have a wife needing me." He slammed out of the com link, sending it a glare holding everything he'd like to do to Marco an Fallon.

The man's only doing his job.

It didn't make what he did any better.

His next call was to the head of den Coille security.

"The marshals are investigating and putting in their own security upgrades, but I want backup by our people. Our safe and verified people."

"We're doing a full scrutiny of all troopers. The Sera Biarsuin has confirmed that the fake trooper is none of our accredited staff."

"A fake wearing our uniform and with our ID seal. To do that, they had to copy our com system security. Check that and trace it, and I don't care whether the marshals are doing the same. Do it."

The chief didn't argue. "Yes, Ser."

"I want an answer before the marshals drag me back to Urbis."

The chief nodded brusquely and signed off. Cumchdach stared into space then clenched his jaw and headed back in to Anna. The nursemaid hovered and a guard stood at attention inside the door, but Anna was still sitting beside the crib, hand clutched tightly by Ruiseart. She'd stay there all night if allowed, he guessed, and there were shadows enough under her eyes. He opened his com and quietly ordered in a sleeper for her, one that had a slot in the side for Ruiseart's crib so she could sleep and still touch him. Then he had a quiet word to the nursemaid, standing stiff and looking shell shocked and guilty.

"It's not your fault, Sera," he said, laying a hand on her shoulder. "Go get something to eat and have a rest. My wife and baby will need you later."

The woman looked torn, glancing at the crib then the door. He held her eye steady and repeated the order. She nodded her head and walked slowly out. Cumchdach ordered up a meal for Anna from the prepper.

She looked up in surprise when he set it beside her, as if she hadn't known he was there. Then glanced at the plate, and shook her head.

"I can't eat. Take it away."

"You can, and will. You need to, for Roo. To keep up your strength."

Her mouth screwed up in a grimace and her eyes looked so tired, but she lifted the spoon and took one mouthful.

"More, beautiful." He put the strength of an order into his voice as with the nursemaid, a tone he never used with her. It worked. She lifted her hand and took more mouthfuls. But soon, she set her hand down again and went back to staring at Roo.

He wanted so badly to take her hand, to give her the support she needed but, too soon, he had to speak.

"I have to go back to Urbis. The marshals have a shuttle waiting for me, and I have to take it."

She lifted her head, and her hand clutched tighter to Roo's as her face closed over. "You have to go," she agreed tonelessly. She pulled back from him, withdrawing into a private shell as if seeking a safe haven.

Roots, it hurt.

Maybe Fioruisghe was right. He still wasn't telling her the full breadth of what the marshals asked of him. An Fallon had told her something of it, from his report. She thought he was being used as bait to identify any suspects, that once seen, his role was finished. But the marshals wanted a lot more than that, and that she mustn't find out. She'd only demand a place in the charade, and that put her at risk. Far better she believed he accepted this tragging separation.

That she thought he wanted to lose her—the one thing he would never want.

It didn't help him to leave the room. "Com me immediately if you need anything." He could only hope she heard the truth in his voice. "Anytime, anywhere."

She nodded again but said nothing and wouldn't meet his eyes, staring intently at the crib where their son lay. The baby they had both looked forward to with such joy. He wrenched himself away and hurried out the door before he made a complete fool of himself by telling her everything.

Keep them safe. That was all that mattered.

Not that the marshals gave him a chance to stay. Two flanked him as soon as he left Anna's hut and marched him to the shuttle parked at the back of the camp.

"My gear?"

"Already transferred to the shuttle."

"Won't it look strange to have me turn up twice in the same day at the Urbis landing field?"

"You won't be seen." What that meant, they refused to say. More of their secret tech, no doubt. His guards escorted him onboard and too soon they were lifting off. All he had left of Anna and Roo was the sight of their hut growing ever smaller and more vulnerable looking in the distance. He slumped into his seat. How would he ever get her back?

The black gloom lasted most of the way across the seas to Protos, and it wasn't until they were nearing Urbis that he managed to throw it off and ask the questions he should have right from the start. "Any word on who and how they hacked Biarsuin's com feed?"

The commander on board shocked him with an actual answer. "They didn't."

"Don't accuse Biarsuin of being part of it. I checked her references."

"She wasn't"

Cumchdach waited, but no more came. "Explain yourself," he finally demanded in exasperation.

"The incoming message was legitimate. It was a very good copy of a security transmission. We have alerted your teams and they have modified the filters to erase the security flaw allowing a copy to be made."

"Our systems should have picked it up."

"Not when it came from inside the Den Coille security com system. You have a traitor in your ranks, Ser Cumchdach mar Bram."

"No." He'd run the crosschecks on Anna's team himself, on top of their best security checks. "Not one of mine."

"Not the false agent, no. But in your com systems team, yes. That message originated from Den Coille space."

Cumchdach felt sick. "In the camp?"

"No, ser," said the man gently. "From the Den Coille tree in Manascraoch. It was well hidden, but our com systems group has its own resources. That message was made in Manascraoch and sent through multiple blinds to this camp site."

"I'll tell my father immediately."

"He has already been notified."

He tried to stand. "Turn back. I'm not leaving Anna unprotected. Not if there's a gap in her security."

"There isn't, Ser. The marshals have taken control of the camp site. Your people are being sent back to Manascraoch, by order of the Council."

"My…" He surged forward, until his safety webbing clamped down and hauled him back. "You can't do that."

He'd been at the mercy of government troops before, troops loyal to the false Survey bosses, and had been saved by the marshals, but ever since, the den Coilles had made sure they always had their own backup security.

"She will be safe, Ser," said the man, his face apologetic. But the shuttle still flew toward Urbis. "The marshals are not false. If we promise to protect, we will. You have no cause for concern."

"Don't ask that of me, Marshal. I left specific orders for my family's welfare, and now you tell me you've sent away the team I trusted to protect them."

"Until the flaws in Den Coille's security and coms teams are identified, you should trust no one in Den Coille, Ser."

"Not even my own family?"

The marshal shrugged. "They are clean, as far as we can ascertain, but best not talk about this too freely with them. We will find your interloper and her sources, and inform you when they are contained."

"We can find our own spies, thank you, Marshal."

If only he could upset this man.

"They will be found, and you will be told," said the marshal. After which, the man stopped talking and pulled up his com. Cumchdach stared down at the grey waves far below feeling worse than useless. He needed to talk to his family, but he wasn't about to try contacting them from a flyer full of Federal troops, no matter how loyal they were to the government.

That's what the guards in prison had claimed, and there was nothing honourable about those brakkas.

As soon as they landed in Urbis, however, he rushed to escape his bevy of marshals. A pity he wasn't successful. One large marshal slid into place beside him and another stood by his shoulder.

"We will accompany you home, ser."

"Not necessary," he tried. He shouldn't have bothered. They escorted him to a town flyer and took him right to his apartment landing pad, then stayed with him all the way to his front door. There, they both came to a halt.

"Not coming inside as well?" he said, sarcastically.

He needn't have bothered speaking. The bigger one put out an arm to block his entry and the other entered his apartment.

"That lock is restricted," he protested.

"Marshals have override of all door locks if appropriate," said his guard stiffly. He supposed he should be flattered to get any kind of explanation.

He wasn't. He was furious.

The other one came out and nodded to his guard.

"You may enter, Ser. The marshals will be monitoring your apartment at all times. Please contact us on the emergency link Marshal an Fallon provided if necessary."

"Monitoring—at all times?"

"As appropriate, Ser," he said straight-faced, and Cumchdach groaned inwardly. Not a moment of privacy.

"I suppose you think you can get away with doing the same at the Den Coille offices. You better have good legal back up for that, marshal. Corporates don't like government control, not when it's so blatant."

"You are to be kept safe, Ser. It comes under planetary security."

Trag it. He'd hoped that wasn't the reason, but the marshals could twist all kinds of violations of his privacy out of that particular statute. He needed to talk to his father, but it would have to be in person. Any com link with him would be scrutinised thoroughly by the marshals. They didn't exactly brandish trust of any from den Coille.

They left him alone as the door closed behind them, or at least physically alone. He wished he knew where they'd placed the sensors inside his apartment. Nor did he bother hiding his irritation as he stared around the room. Give them what they expect, as Seolta had once told him in prison before the brothers tried rushing the thugs beating up on Aigherach.

It hadn't worked then, but there was enough sense in it that he made no attempt to hide what he felt as he slung his bag into his wardrobe for unpacking, pulled off his topcoat and stomped into the prepper area for a drink, pulling out another bottle from the store and being careful this time not to break it. He didn't want to look any more a fool than necessary.

Nor did he intend to touch more than a drop of it. Settling down on the lounger, he pulled up a com link and put through a call to Samhchair. As the most sensible in the family, he had to hope the marshals would consider her no threat.

They didn't know the subtle brain that operated behind that calm façade. Samhchair had been successfully running mitigation on their volatile family for years, and he'd read her reports on hints she'd picked up from her *contacts*. Nothing concrete as yet, but she was making some interesting connections.

She shimmered to life in front of him, a full holo-figure sitting in her favourite chair in her own apartment instead of the usual bland head shot. He clutched the arm of his lounger. How did she know he needed the sight of family so badly?

"Hello little brother. How are Ruiseart and Anna?"

"You've heard then?"

"With the marshals linking into Mam and Da as soon as you set out? Of course we have."

"He's fine. He's safe, and happy to be back with his mother."

"And you? Why are you back in Urbis so soon?"

He shuffled. "The marshals thought it safer," he said as noncommittally as possible.

He saw the instant she realised they were being monitored. One blink only, a slight glance up at his ceiling. His sister may look relaxed but he'd grown up with her and recognised the subtle tension in her. "You're staying in Urbis?"

He nodded. "I have some business here. I'll return to Manascraoch after that."

"And Anna?"

"Has her own projects."

"She's safe on Deuteron?"

"Yes," said Cumchdach. "She has ample protection."

He didn't mention the marshals, but neither did Samhchair, and that alone told him she'd got his message. "Mam and Da look forward to your return," she said. "Sleep well, little brother. All will work out."

She was the only one who called him little, and the familiar farewell settled something in him. He wasn't alone—nor were Anna and Ruiseart. Not that he slept well that night. Not in the empty echoing of his impeccable apartment. The next morning, he took the walkway to his office, hoping the exercise would shift his sour headache. Near the building housing Den Coille's Urbis office, a man brushed up against him. He tensed, stepping back and falling into a defensive posture. The man flashed a marshal link at him.

"A bit obvious, marshal."

The man's face stayed blank. "You need a safer transit to work, Ser. A skimmer will wait at your office when you finish for the day."

"No."

"It will be there, Ser," said the man. Whether he liked it or not, apparently. He was relieved to enter the building and shut the doors of his office to claim an illusion of privacy.

How far did the marshals' tendrils reach?

CHAPTER THIRTEEN

He returned to his thankless mission the next day. Not that his main task, to look miserable, came hard. Thanks to the marshals and his stupidity in handling Anna, he had no smiles inside him. Fortunately, there was enough real Den Coille work to partly distract his mind from its treadmill of obsessions. How to evade the marshals. How to make it right with Anna.

She and Ruiseart were his heart, and he needed them so badly.

The only things keeping him going were the marshals' daily report on their safety and his holovisits to Ruiseart. He might not be able to hold his son, but for a few precious hours he could see, sing to, and talk to his baby. Roo had more control of his fists now, and Cumchdach laughed aloud the first time the baby's hand reached out for his da, only for his mouth to open in shock when his hand passed through the nothingness of a holo.

He had to laugh. Too much of him wanted to break down and cry.

In the evenings, he prowled through the bars and clubs of Urbis most frequented by corporate executives. The kind he'd rarely visited before, and then only out of duty, but now he haunted them. If nothing else, they were at least full of noise instead of the hollow emptiness of his apartment, even if it was just the vacuous bleatings of the anti-change brigade on the bar's vidcast screen. Nor did his grim face put off his targets. A growing queue of *accidental* contacts were all too ready to listen to any woes he cared to drop.

That he didn't want to talk just increased his drawing power, and within a week he had an interesting list of suspects. He returned to his apartment late one evening, bitterly aware he should be pleased with his successes. None had yet put it into words, but enough hints hung in the air that he was left with no illusions about what his new acquaintances wanted from him.

Deliver up Den Coille and all its influence to those set on halting Arcadia's rush to environmental compliance. Keep their profits intact and save them from change, in other words.

A future path that would end their settlement on Arcadia, though none of his new contacts believed that. It would also smear his sister Fioruisghe's crown of heroism, a secondary matter to the marshals, no doubt, but one that mattered to him. His sister would disagree, though she and Caleb were both politically astute enough to realise the threat and negate it. Or would, if only they didn't think Arcadia's survival more important.

She was his baby sister and part of his role in life was to look after her, along with the rest of the family. One day, he might just have a chance of succeeding at that. So far, he'd failed miserably. Fioruisghe and her husband had been hunted all over Arcadia during the rule of the false Survey heads, and his family threatened with execution. He hadn't even managed to stop the torture of Aigherach in prison.

He kicked morosely at the door of his apartment as he laid his palm on the entry pad, then stomped through when it opened.

Then stopped, all senses alert. A light was on in the prepper area and the cushions had changed position. Someone else was here. He quietly pulled the personal blaster he'd taken to carrying and stepped out of his shoes to make sure he made no noise. Trained in the forests of home, he moved soundlessly toward the light, edging into the doorway and carefully checking the shiny surfaces of the far wall for any shadows.

There, a shadow of a man sitting at the table. His table, eating his food.

He set his blaster to full stun, and swung through the door, aiming it directly at the table.

"Ceart!" His younger brother turned calmly toward him with his usual bland expression, and lifted a slice of pie to take a bite. "What are you doing here?"

"Needed tech parts from the flight school."

"You could have ordered them." Cumchdach's heart finally slowed. "I nearly shot you."

Ceart turned his slow gaze on the discarded blaster. "Relieved you didn't."

"Why are you here?" Then his heart sped up again. "Has something happened in Manascraoch?"

Ceart shook his head. "Da thought you might need help with the work, and I had to come to Urbis anyway." He took another bite, and Cumchdach waited impatiently for his brother to stop chewing. "New specs to be checked out," he added by way of explanation. For the new flyers Den Coille were developing, that would mean.

"Help in what way?" Ceart's being here made no sense. Cumchdach tried blinking. No, still here. Then his brother's mouth twisted. Ceart's face was usually a stoical mask, and you had to know him well to pick up his moods. "You could have at least asked Den Coille security to warn me you were coming."

Ceart gave the slightest of shrugs. "They tried."

And were blocked by the marshals keeping watch over him. He huffed in frustration. "They're with you then. That's good."

"Were the last time I contacted them."

Cumchdach refused to ask how long ago that was. The marshals really had surrounded him with a ring of steel. His gut tightened.

"I need a drink and dinner," he said as if exhausted by his day of meetings. "Come out with me, brother?"

Though he'd only just arrived in the capital, Ceart gave no sign of tiredness. He finished off his snack and stood, all in the same steady pace he did everything.

"Jobar's?"

It was the bar they usually visited in the capital, a quiet haven in the city centre near the business district. That was the problem. It was also the favourite place of too many of his targets. Cumchdach shook his head. "I discovered an interesting restaurant down a back alley near here. It's only a short walk."

Ceart's eyes opened but he nodded and pulled on his outer coat. Urbis was as bleak as ever outside.

They took the external walkway to street level. Halfway down, Cumchdach received a harried message from the marshals' duty shift. He replied with their destination. "I'm sure you have sufficient people in the area to keep both of us safe, Team Leader."

The abrupt closing of the link confirmed it. He smiled inwardly. That should make the woman angry enough to make sure they were safe, if only to avoid the embarrassment of losing a target.

He said little to Ceart on the way. Just the occasional comment about family, the kind any listener would expect, while taking note of their watchers: the woman lingering near his apartment building entry, the slowing skimmer crawling along the lower transit levels, and the sudden shadow disappearing into a doorway. His eyes tracked them and Ceart's did the same.

But only Ceart's eyes. His brother plodded along with his usual steady pace, as if walking the branches of home. His hand sat in his tunic pocket, as did Cumchdach's where it rested on his personal blaster. When he turned into the alleyway, though, Ceart stopped at the entrance, eyebrows lifting.

"The security's good here. It's safe," said Cumchdach, and glanced skyward.

A brief dip of his head and Ceart began to walk again. Cumchdach better be right, that quick dip said. There was little enough cover over their heads and few windows opened onto the alley. High overhead, a skimmer came to a hover and he pulled his brother against the nearest wall. It was likely a marshal vehicle, but you could never be sure.

Then they were at the restaurant door, and a strange face welcomed them inside. The man showed them to a table and a waiter he'd seen before quickly bustled up. With an aggrieved look at the strange doorman, he gave them both a cheery greeting and set out the specialities of the evening as he lifted a hand for them to choose a seat.

The restaurant was almost empty, apart from a table near the door and one near the exit to the hygiene units and the kitchen. Trag it, he'd hoped the marshals would leave him the illusion of privacy.

"This place is not as I'd hoped," he muttered.

Ceart took a seat with his back to the wall, adjacent to Cumchdach's. They were in a corner, so both had a plain wall at their back and the rest of the room in full view. Ceart had better sight lines of the rear doors and Cumchdach had full view of the entry.

"Not keen on the company?" said Ceart studying the table by the kitchen door.

Cumchdach grunted. "Their food's good and the service is fast," he told his brother.

Ceart wiped his hands on his pants, then lifted them up and peered at them. "I need to wash first. Something's dirtied my hands."

Cumchdach studied him a minute, then lifted his own hands. "You're right. We must have brushed up against something in that alley."

Blank-faced but with a grin inside him, he stood with Ceart and walked toward the hygiene units. As they passed the kitchen-side table, a man hastily scrabbled up from his seat and began to move toward the units as well.

"Won't be a moment, ser, then it's all yours," said Ceart, surprising Cumchdach. Then smiled inside again. A place this small would have a limited number of units. They pushed through to the back room and now he grinned outright. Just two. He pushed open the door of the first one as Ceart opened the second one. Then they both switched on the hand cleansing unit. It was as antique as the rest of the building and made a thoroughly satisfying racket. Both of them moved to stand close together. Ceart gestured toward the back hatch.

Cumchdach shrugged and turned on the ventilation unit as well.

"Tracker?" mouthed Ceart.

"Don't know, but possible." The marshals had access to a level of tech unsurpassed on Arcadia. Ceart moved closer to him, and they both huddled under the noisiest vent outlet. Ceart held out his wrist and Cumchdach did the same so they could touch coms. He signalled for a full personal link. The marshals may realise they were doing it, but the planetary laws stopped them accessing it, even if they could break his security. An Fallon had stated often enough his marshals must work within the law.

He was still careful about what he said.

'Did Da send you?'

'Samhchair said you were in trouble and needing help.'

'*May* be in trouble.'

'Our friends out there?'

'The marshals. They have me under full surveillance at all times,' confirmed Cumchdach. 'I need a secure way to contact the family, one free of their monitors.'

'They're not blocking your transmissions?'

'Not so far.' He sent an image of him with watchful salks above him, all eagle eyed and talons extended.

'Ahh,' said Ceart. 'I'll contact Seolta. He'll want to be kept in the loop.'

Cumchdach looked across sharply.

'I talked to him after the family meeting. He's linked me into his networks.'

'You're too young.' Seolta's so-called networks were the basis of Den Coille's intelligence branch. Seolta had the kind of street cunning needed for that work, and it had suited him. Not that the family had any say in the matter. Seolta went ahead and set them up, then told the rest of them. It was part of his wide-ranging brief to grow the business, he'd claimed. But Ceart was a different kind of man.

His brother lifted an eyebrow in answer to Cumchdach's frown. 'I hear things and he knows what to do about them,' he simply sent.

They may have asked him to do that at the family meeting, but taking over Seolta's intelligence work was another matter entirely. He opened his mouth, but then took in the almost imperceptible hunching of Ceart's shoulders. Too many outsiders deprecated his brother, the big dolt of the family. Cumchdach wasn't going to join them. He nodded once, then switched off the vents and shut down the cleansing unit as they broke the private com link. "Now, let's go try this place's food. It really is good,"

Ceart peered suspiciously at Cumchdach's waistline, then ruefully at his own. Both were as flat as a Deadlands plain, but he gave that dry smile of his. "You're the expert."

Cumchdach looked twice. His driest brother really had made a joke. He punched him lightly and swung a brotherly arm around his shoulder. "Think I can't take you on in a match, little brother?"

Ceart sent him a look. He'd long been the biggest and canniest fighter of them all and they both knew it. He was good before prison, but since their release, he'd haunted the practice rooms with a new intensity. No one was going to beat up on his family again.

They took their time eating, chatting inconsequentially of family and company matters. Or at least, Cumchdach talked and Ceart mostly grunted. His brother knew the business as well as he did; he was just not fond of talking. It still felt good to have his solid presence. He wasn't alone. Not yet.

"Have you heard from Anna?"

"Not recently," said Cumchdach. A miserable few words to cover the disaster of their marriage. He missed her so badly. Missed her body, the laugh rarely heard except in the privacy of their room. Missed his best friend, the person who understood him better than anyone.

"She's fine," said Ceart, "and so is Roo."

"That's what the marshals say." All they'd say, though he plagued the marshals every day for news. Someone had to give him a better answer.

"It's true," said Ceart. "I'll get Mam to send you some vids. They're both fine."

"And happy?" Then he clamped his lips. That wasn't fair to ask, nor did Ceart answer.

The dessert menu appeared on the table's control panel. He stared at it unseeing. Ceart glanced at him and shook his head, blocking the menu's program and inputting his com to pay. The cheery waiter bustled up again.

"Was something wrong, Sers. Please, tell me and we can make it right immediately."

"No, Ser, your food is as good as I remembered from my last meal here. It's been a busy day and it's time for home."

The man's face showed the strain of the evening. Not surprising. The police marshals hadn't bothered with ordering any food to cover their presence. Must be on a budget, he thought sourly. Between them, they'd cost the man a night's worth of work and only his and Ceart's meals to pay for the inconvenience.

Dining out was off the schedule for now, it seemed, unless it was at a place like Jobar's or other executive haunts. The marshals would do nothing to obstruct his work. He sent them a short glare as they left, but got back only blank faces.

"It's their job," said Ceart as they left the place. "Not their fault."

It was Cumchdach who grunted at that one.

Little more was said before they both took to their rooms. Cumchdach had no more hope of sleeping than on any other night, and the early hours found him slumped on the lounger and aimlessly watching a vidcast. Or he was until he noticed the subject. A gossip channel's frothy item on the 'difficult situation' between a pair of 'well known' celebrities.

He threw a pillow at the holoscreen.

Ceart wandered out yawning, and threw himself down in the opposite chair.

"Sorry. Did I wake you," Cumchdach said.

Ceart shook his head. "You don't sleep when trouble comes."

"You do."

Another yawn. "Not always."

Ceart was right; the brothers had all shared a room as young children. Trouble would have Cumchdach tossing in his sleeper until he gave up and spent the night in a lounge room with a vidcast playing as a background to his churning thoughts. Seolta would occasionally twitch up, then saw who it was who'd made the noise, and groused something at him before burying himself in his cover and falling asleep again, but Ceart had always stayed still in bed, sleeping deeply.

A deception, it seemed.

"Dask or salaschar?"

Ceart didn't answer, walking to the food prepper and ordering up two big mugs of dask and a tray of milisti, the brothers favourite treat as children. Cumchdach had poured himself a glass of salaschar, but it sat untouched in front of him on the table. Ceart picked it up, putting the mug and plate of sweetmeats down in front of him and taking the glass over to the prepper, upending the precious liquid into the waste slot.

"Hey, that's too good to throw out."

"You need dask more," his brother said bluntly. He was probably right.

Cumchdach's hand went first to the milisti. There was something comforting about the taste of them, a reassurance from childhood. Before he knew it, he'd finished the whole plate and looked guiltily across at his brother. "There's more in the prepper," he said.

Ceart waved a hand. "No problem."

Cumchdach took a drink of dask. Another mouthful and he had to admit feeling more capable of coping. "Thanks. You were right."

"Able to sleep yet?"

He had to think about that one. Tiredness dragged at his eyelids, but his brain still felt like it had been kicked into the middle of a spaceship's translation drive. He shook his head carefully.

"Good," said Ceart. He put his hand in his pocket and pulled out a miniscanner. Ceart had always had a knack for gadgets and frequently carried his latest fascination around with him. This one looked as tacked together as the rest, but he'd never been worried about what his creations looked like.

He put this one down beside him and set his com field into action.

Cumchdach felt a moment of brotherly concern. "Is that restricted?"

Ceart shook his head. "Not yet." He stared into his com field. He'd set it to personal so Cumchdach didn't know what he was up to, but seeing it would probably be no help either. Mechanical things were not his territory. Ceart gave a huff of satisfaction and sat back.

"Should be safe now. Most surveillance goes to auto at this time of night, with alarms set for any suspicious movement. Two sleepless brothers eating and drinking isn't that."

Cumchdach lurched upright. "What have you done?"

"Blocked their audio feed."

"This is the marshals we're dealing with."

Ceart shrugged and eased back. "Calm down, brother. You will set off their alarms."

Ceart looked confident enough, but what if he was wrong?

You need to speak with your brother? Then act calm.

He watched Ceart lift his mug and then glanced at the door. No crashing in by the marshals or other guards, not yet.

"And our enemies? There's a reason I have full surveillance by the marshals."

"It's a scanner. It'll hear them and alert the marshals."

"A clever toy that," he said peering at the device. Ceart looked as close to smug as he ever came. "It won't take them long to figure it out though."

Ceart's face fell into its most solemn cast. "Quickly then. Why do you need me?"

"To tell Da what's happening here. The family needs to up their security status." He took another gulp of the dask, welcoming the burn as the hot liquid hit the back of his throat. "Have the marshals told you about the origin of the fake message they used to kidnap Roo?"

Ceart nodded. "Security has prioritised it."

Meaning Da had put a blazing fire under them, but Ceart wasn't given to colourful language.

"The marshals have me under a tight shield." He told his brother of the level of that shield, and at the end, even Ceart gave a soft "Hooo."

"They're not mucking around."

"Can they do all that?" Cumchdach asked.

Ceart shrugged. "Their technical groups don't release information."

"But…"

"If they say they can do it, then they can."

"And the traitor in Manascraoch? It has to be in our security section."

"So the marshals said. Da is onto it."

Cumchdach's gut tightened. "Run another check on the team at Anna's site, in case." He frowned. "Can you contact Seolta without the marshals knowing?"

"They'll pick up a transmission. We can do a content substitution."

"No. They'll know you're talking about this."

Ceart shrugged. "Best we can do. Seolta knows our intel systems."

Not the only brother who did, it seemed, but Ceart was as opaque as ever. Cumchdach threw himself back. "Does anything bother you, brother?"

Then saw the dark glint in Ceart's eyes. "We will find your traitor," said his younger brother. "What does Anna say about it?"

Cumchdach shuffled.

"You haven't told her?"

"She doesn't need to know. She's frightened enough already."

Ceart peered at his face, fleetingly looking too much like Fioruisghe. "And that keeps her safe how? She's not fragile."

"She's just had a baby and is terrified for him. The marshals have it under control."

Ceart actually showed his scepticism.

"It keeps her safe and alive. That's all that matters. I know my own wife," he added defensively.

"I don't know about *your wife*, but I do know Anna ingh Eolas an Sumhneas. Tell her," said Ceart.

Anna woke, stretched, and yelped as her arm protested. All night, she'd clutched tight to Roo until he'd stirred for his early morning feed. She'd cradled him in her sleeper with her afterward, tucking him into the crook of her arm as they both fell asleep.

He was still there, chortling happily up at her as she moved in the sleeper.

"Good morning, little scrumchkin," she whispered with a silly smile on her face.

He was safe, happy, and here. Her arm clenched him tightly. After yesterday, she wasn't letting go of him again.

Roo didn't agree. He wriggled, squirming beside her to escape her hold. He might not be able to crawl yet, but he'd recently discovered how far his wriggling, squirming, body could take him. One of the technicians had built a pen for him with a padded base and soft sides high enough to keep him inside but where he could still see everything going on around him.

Her little boy loved people, she'd discovered.

Or used to, before he was stolen.

No, she wouldn't let them steal that from him. She fed him again, then decided she might as well make a start to the morning. The light was coming up outside, promising another long summer's day. Hot and dry, as the farmer would no doubt grumble, but perfect weather for their study.

Yet today, she had little passion for it. Not compared to Roo's safety. The night had given her too much time for thinking. She dressed quickly then put a call through to the marshals' head office.

"Ser an Fallon has gone home for the evening, Sera," said the stern-faced clerk when she finally made it through the barricade of bots and com systems by shamefacedly using the priority code the marshals had given her.

"Put me through to his home, then. He promised me safety. He needs to deliver on it."

The man appeared to think he could outstare her. She glared back and repeated her priority status. "Do you want to risk a planetary incident, Ser?"

His mouth twisted at that, but he grudgingly complied. "Through now, Sera."

There was another wait at an Fallon's home before the face only of the Commander appeared. He was dressed as far as she could ascertain, but a certain heaviness about his eyes suggested she'd woken him from sleep.

Good. It might be night in Urbis, but if she hadn't got much sleep, why should he?

"How safe are Roo and I here, Marshal?" she demanded without preliminaries.

He carefully dipped his head. "Good evening to you, Sera."

"It's morning here," she said curtly. "Another day. Are we safe here?"

The marshal considered. "We have a full team surrounding you, Sera, and our best intel units are working on the leak that allowed the unfortunate mishap."

Mishap!

"So you can't guarantee our safety. Then I am returning to Urbis, where hopefully you will have sufficient resources to protect us."

"And your project, Sera?"

She lifted a hand. "I've seen the ground and have an understanding of the local bio-systems. The rest is pure data gathering. I can follow that as readily from my Urbis lab as I can here."

That was what she'd spent the night thinking about, when she wasn't checking for the sound of Roo's breathing. She couldn't stay here. The farm was too isolated and Deuteron's allegiance too uncertain. Restin was sold here first.

"I am returning to Urbis. Make your required arrangements, Ser Marshal."

The man said nothing, but his eyes had the look of someone working a com field and he glanced away from time to time. She was tempted to cut the call but knew she had to wait.

Then he smiled at her, or attempted to. It looked like the stretched rictus of a dried corpse.

The marshals aren't the enemy.

If she kept repeating it, she might start to believe it.

"Urbis is not a good option, Sera. We have organised a shuttle to transfer you to your lab in Manascraoch. It is more secure and there are fewer risks there."

Not none, she suddenly realised with a shock. What weren't they telling her. "That isn't an option, Ser" she said stiffly. "Not given the current situation between me and the Ser Cumchdach."

An Fallon ignored her. "The den Coilles' tree has space enough to accommodate your family needs."

Her back stiffened. "My lab is in Urbis."

"And you have a fully equipped lab in Manascraoch. You have used it more than the Urbis one for years."

She could have screamed. Go back to Manascraoch with his family pressuring her to reunite with her lying brakka of a husband?

The same brakka who flew here straight away when Roo was in trouble?

It changed nothing. "I will not go to Manascraoch."

"It is the safest option for the young Ser Ruiseart, Sera," said an Fallon gently, using the tone she hated the most. The Commander trying to cajole her meant he was hiding too much.

Word said that the Commander of the Federal Police never lied; he just didn't tell you the whole truth.

To her, that was a lie. "Why is Manascraoch the best option, Ser Marshal?" she said coldly.

"Your only two other options are Rubhaicreach or Urbis. Your home city is clearly dangerous while your father and his family are under suspicion." An understatement. She'd pick Gria as being right in the heart of the conspiracy. "Urbis has too many factions and too many people. We can confine you to the UBS but it is still a public place with multiple entries day and night."

"UBS houses the Survey's training quarters. You cannot claim it isn't secure, and Manascraoch is a city."

"But they are Mountainers, and Ruiseart is a child of the mountains. He belongs there. Any group working against him is more readily identified."

She took note again of the lack of absolute in his reply, meaning there was also a risk to Roo in his home city. "I cannot stay in the den Coille tree."

"You can, Sera, and must. It is safest."

The tight knot in her gut coiled to an intolerable pain. "Impossible."

"It's not, Sera. I will come back to you as soon as the arrangements have been completed. In the meantime, please do not leave your hut." Then he disconnected and she was left staring fruitlessly into blank space.

He'd left her no choice. If the marshals said Manascraoch was safest, they meant it. One thing she could trust in was their loyalty to the planet, and a successful attack on Roo would set alight all the buried schisms of her world. Arcadia had no hope if that happened. She put a call through to Samhchair. No answer but she left her a message.

Her sister-in-law came back soon. "Your old quarters are ready and waiting for you. The household staff have kept them as if you were all here still."

"No. I can't." She couldn't even say his name, not to his sister.

"Cumchdach is moving to another room. All signs of his presence will be gone by the time you get here," Samhchair said gently. "I've talked to him, and it was the first thing he said."

Who else had Samhchair talked to? Cumchdach's sister had been quietly organising her family for years. Their mother was the heart of them all and Bram the head of the family, but Samhchair was the glue that held all the strands together. It had taken Anna years to see that. The eldest den Coille worked unnoticed, unmarked. It had only been the way she was treated by all her siblings, the deep trust they had in Samhchair to make things right, that made Anna understand.

"Everything else will be as you left it," Samhchair finished.

The decision was made, it seemed.

Her room hadn't changed much. Samhchair had been true to her promise. The only changes were the stripping away of anything personal to Cumchdach. His clothes, his old school awards, the funny shells he'd found on a beach trip once as a child.

She took one look and burst into tears. She was home again; home as nowhere else on the planet could be. But it had been stripped of its heart.

Samhchair stood awkwardly to one side. "What is it? What's wrong? We can fix it."

She shook her head. "No, you can't. Not this time."

"Aah."

Fortunately, Roo chose that moment to give a squawk of protest. He'd been trapped in his carrier for quite long enough, thank you. Anna hastened to release him and pick him up. Then she noticed her sister-in-law's face. Usually Samhchair wore a look of calm control, but now, a hint of hunger shaded the eager eyes. As quickly hidden as seen. She held Roo out to her.

"Would you like to hold him?"

Samhchair reached out her arms before she'd finished and Roo settled happily into his aunt's cuddles. She'd always had a knack for children, beginning her working life in paediatric medicine before moving on to public health, and babies took to her. But now Anna glimpsed the trace of a tear in the corner of an eye.

Do not tell Samhchair she should be settled with her own children. It was one of the first rules of life with the den Coilles. Before now, she'd always assumed it was because no one wanted to lose Samhchair from the heart of the family.

Now she wondered, feeling as if she'd seen a glimpse through a window into a room that Samhchair kept firmly locked against them all.

But the woman was old enough and wise enough to decide what she wanted the world to know, and that included the estranged wife of her younger brother. She left Samhchair with Roo in the sitting room and followed her bags into the sleeper room. Here too, all reminders of Cumchdach had been removed, but nothing could take away the memories they'd made in this sleeper. No one had taken away the quilt on their sleeper or the rug from the floor, and the chair in the corner was still the same overly plump one they'd found in a junk shop and that Anna had had re-covered with a print done by a small craft enterprise in the lower trees of the city.

No one could remove all the years of memories. They may have been married only a short time, but their life together went back so very far. Cutting Cumchdach from her life was nearly impossible.

She forced herself to concentrate on immediate matters. Check off the unpacking, check the cleansing units. Her preferred lotions and cleansers were all fully stocked, along with her favourite perfumes. The room hadn't forgotten.

After too short a time, she stood and looked desperately around for something more to do. There was nothing. From the sitting room, she heard a low-voiced murmur and walked softly to the door. Roo had fallen asleep again in his aunt's arms and she held him close, singing an old song of the mountains—one she could remember her own mother singing to her.

"That was beautiful," she said at the end.

Samhchair looked up, eyes flaring, and this time, there was no mistake. A single tear hovered at the corner of her eye.

"I'm sorry. I didn't mean to startle you."

Cumchdach's contained big sister reached up and dashed away the offending teardrop. "It was nothing. A moment of sentimentality. We have all missed this wee man. Thank you for bringing him home again." She rose with that fluid grace of hers and carefully passed the sleeping baby over. "You are a very lucky woman, Anna bean Cumchdach."

Then she straightened, and the usual Samhchair was back. She gave Anna a small smile. "If there is anything you need, let me know. We would all very much like it if you would join the family for the evening meal. Cumchdach is still in Urbis, so there is nothing to concern you there."

Anna flushed at the reminder. "I'll... I will let you know. I need to check on my lab."

"Of course. Whatever you wish, Anna. We want only the best for you both."

The painful truth was, she meant it, and so did the rest of the family.

"I should be able to come. It depends on Roo."

"Bring him too. I know you have a good nursemaid, but if he won't be too disturbed, we are all longing to see him again."

Samhchair nodded her head. "Until this evening."

Her lab was exactly as she'd left it. Not a particle of dust, her notes still scrawled in the margins of the board she kept on the wall for spare ideas she wanted to write down to clarify them, the clutter of her bench untouched—or looking untouched. Her lab assistant watched her anxiously.

"You've done well, Lucheia. Thank you for keeping it so well."

The woman blushed. Not one to realise her own worth, she had nervously asked Anna for a place here when she was first setting up the lab. Cumchdach vouched for her, and his mother was thrilled to hear Anna was taking her on.

"Her mother is one of my best nurses, but her family have had to live with her earnings alone too much over the years. Lucheia keeps that family together but gets little thanks for it."

Anna refrained from saying, "like Samhchair." It wasn't true, anyway. Her whole family knew exactly who Samhchair was to them. But she took on the girl, and forced her to take the Higher School courses for lab technicians. As she'd expected, Lucheia scored in the top rank of her class and settled into her lab with a minimum of fuss. As if she'd finally found her place in the world, thought Anna, and thanked all the roots for it. With Lucheia in charge, Anna could concentrate on work and leave the daily chores needed to keep a lab functional to her very efficient right-hander. The woman loved plants as much as Anna, worked in well with Shelda in the Urbis lab, and had a rare talent for organising the seemingly chaotic clutter Anna preferred to work in, while keeping the rest of the lab's work away from Anna's area. Only Lucheia understood that Anna put things in a given place for a reason. Shelda was good, but she wasn't from the mountains. Anna had missed Lucheia in Urbis.

She had missed everything from Manascraoch. For many years, the city had been her home as much as or more than Rubhaicreach and, after marriage, she had readily assumed the responsibilities that came with being the wife of the accepted heir to Den Coille's leadership. It was like enough to what she'd been doing at home since birth, and as familiar.

Too familiar, like pulling on an old tunic that fit so well you failed to notice the fraying patches and fading stains of use.

She no longer belonged here.

This was Cumchdach's home and she was keeping him from it. His family had welcomed her home last night, and she couldn't deny their relief and joy at having Roo back. But she was not den Coille, not anymore. She'd escaped to her sleeper early, pleading tiredness. Now, she needed work.

"I'm having the data from Deuteron sent directly here and will message you a list of tasks as soon as I get sorted."

"It's stored in the lab's banks. I have a list of suggested supporting tasks, if you would care to comment," said Lucheia in her quietly competent voice.

"I'm sure it will be exactly what I need. Also we're going to run a full scan of this region. I want to check on something I found at that farm, see if it applies here too."

"Send me the details and I'll make the arrangements."

So simple. Anna sat by her bench and relaxed for the first time in too long. Lucheia didn't demand anything from her, interested only in the work of the lab, and right now, that was the bulwark she needed. She scanned over Lucheia's list. The technician had thought of everything and more. "I leave it in your very capable hands,

Lucheia ingh Neart an Slanach. And thank you. It's marvellous to have you back."

The woman blushed and scurried away, never comfortable with compliments. Anna had long given up trying to make her so. Lucheia was herself, and had more than earned the right to live her life as she pleased.

She settled at her bench and glanced at Roo in his porta-pen beside her. She grinned at his squirming as he turned over to smile up at her. "We're home, scrumchkin."

If she kept saying it, maybe one day she'd believe it.

CHAPTER FOURTEEN

Cumchdach was back at Jobar's and on his own again. Ceart had flown back to Manascraoch but threatened to return as soon as he'd reported in to Da. Cumchdach told him not to bother, refusing to put his younger brother at more risk. Unfortunately, Ceart made it clear he'd make his own decisions, thank you big brother, and that only added to Cumchdach's sour mood.

Of all his haunts, Jobar's had been the most productive. The itch between his shoulder blades said that tonight would be as successful, though why any sensible conspirator would choose such a public place was a puzzle to him. Their ability to stay hidden proved that whoever was in charge of the whole bunch of selfish misfits wasn't stupid.

Another glass appeared beside him.

"Still drowning your sorrows, Ser den Coille?"

It was the unpleasant wermet of his first visit here. "Ser Smierg," he said curtly in his most off-putting voice. It only encouraged the man.

"Your wife's returned to Manascraoch, says word on the street."

"My business," he snapped.

"Word also says your family have moved you to separate quarters."

It was no act as he turned on the man. "What do you want? I came here for a drink, not company."

The man gave a short nod, as if Cumchdach's anger proved something. "There's a meeting on two nights from now. I thought you might be interested."

"What about?"

"A sharing of mutual interests, shall we say. Of a financial nature. Those planning to keep making a profit."

"We all hope for that."

"Some of us do more than hope."

"And if I'm interested?" he growled.

"A contact will collect you."

Cumchdach stared at the man, as if considering it. Then gave a stiff nod of acceptance and turned back to the bar. "Now leave me to my drink."

He received a message with a code before he left but heard nothing more. Two nights later, he waited impatiently in his apartment. An Fallon had almost looked pleased when he'd told him of the contact.

"You'll have to go in unmonitored. They've stayed hidden this long; we have to assume they can detect our probes."

"I'd already realised that," said Cumchdach. An Fallon should be worried, and Cumchdach was more concerned that he wasn't. "Our security gave us all additional defence training."

An Fallon didn't appear convinced it would help, but neither of them had any choice.

It wasn't until well into the night cycle that his door panel was activated. He checked the pad and saw a dark shape waiting on the outside. The door pad sent through the same code he'd received in the message. Nerves finally hit, but he ignored them. Better to get it over with. He signalled the door to open and stood well back. He'd left off his blaster, but his com was stuffed with defence capabilities added by den Coille's own labs, and he kept a small knife hidden on his thigh as back up.

A person entered, shrouded in a full hooded cloak and wearing a mask. He handed a package to him and closed the door behind him. When his visitor said nothing, he opened the package. It was another of the cloaks and a mask. He donned them, feeling decidedly ridiculous, as if a character out of a Higher School role-playing game.

He opened his arms wide. "Ready?"

The visitor touched his com pad and the cloaked shape dissolved into an avatar of a light-bodied messenger. Cloaked and using shrouding com shields? This was getting sillier—or more dangerous.

"Shield, Ser. We allow no identifying data in the meeting." It was a young boy's voice, but his visitor was no callow youth. So complete shielding, including gender and age. That was high level and meant he'd have precious little to go on after the meeting.

"Do you always take this level of precautions?"

"It's necessary, given the stakes at play."

If they meant the fate of the planet and the personal wealth and future of them all, his visitor was correct, though not in the way they meant, he suspected. Did none of them realise the Alliance wasn't bluffing?

He pulled up a shielded avatar. Disliking the level of deception expected of him, he kept to a man of about his own age but changed the racial profile to one of a settler from the upper Urbis plain region, with the unweathered skin and slack muscles of a mid-level clerical worker. Unobtrusive and non-threatening.

No avatar could hide a person's natural gait or mannerisms. Just as his visitor walked with the plodding of a middle-aged man, he couldn't hide his own athletic fluidity from a life lived in moving branches. He wasn't the only one tonight who would be taking note of such clues.

Finally unnerved, he followed the man out.

An equally well shrouded skimmer waited for them in the street. He guessed the building's garage was too well monitored to risk, and the twist in his gut tightened. He followed his escort into the flyer, taking a seat and forcing himself to show no signs of fear.

Inside, the external viewing windows were blanked out. The skimmer followed an erratic path. He soon lost all sense of direction and had to hope the marshals followed him, despite what they'd said. Finally, the skimmer rose into what must be the upper levels of the city, although whether residential or commercial, he couldn't tell. They stopped at an entry hatch that led straight into a non-descript freight corridor. Nor did the odd pile of boxes stored on the floor give him any clues. He'd have to use his com to read the markings and that would only arouse the suspicion of his escort.

He was still convinced it was a middle-aged man but nothing else about his escort gave a clue to his identity. Not a trace of memory was stirred by the man's movements or speech patterns.

Soon they reached a door, and the man gestured for Cumchdach to stand by the door pad.

'Full body scan in progress,' advised his com but without the usual option of accepting or refusing the scan. They must have overridden it, and that had his nerves escalating. He could only hope his extra com programs stayed hidden.

They would expect him to be suspicious. Were they counting on his current anger to make him easy prey?

A mistake, brakka.

Then he was in.

The room was fuller than he'd expected. All were in avatar mode, and when he tried to penetrate their shields, the few his system could pierce wore the same cloak and mask as himself.

This lot were seriously paranoid. That, or those at the top of the conspiracy understood security. After what had happened to Winter Solaris, they must know the marshals were hunting them.

His escort gestured him to a seat near the bottom of the large table dominating the room. A chime rang out and the rest took their seats as well. He told himself it was like any other boardroom. One filled with weird caricatures, admittedly, but he'd been sitting in business meetings since middle school.

It didn't help, not when the tension in the room and the wall of false faces had him verging on an outburst of manic laughter. They had all picked grotesquely heroic figures. A winged nieten stag, a man wearing the sharp-beaked head of the legendary falk aerion, deadliest predator of the plains, even a sharp-toothed hydraseal, giant predator of the seas. His own mundane avatar must be comical by comparison, but he stubbornly kept to it. Did any of them understand the message in his choice?

He hoped not.

At the head of the table, a glowering and hissing foxllar-headed creature with claws for hands and a scaly armour covering his body, banged a gavel and called for attention in a bellow of a voice.

"We have a new member today." He stared directly at Cumchdach. "Any objections, make them to your usual contacts, along with a reason. If valid, the new member will be rejected and appropriate action taken to protect our interests."

It was designed to put Cumchdach in his place and cower him, but the attempt at bullying was too obvious. Cumchdach refused to react, sitting calmly and waiting for the next round on the agenda sent through to his com.

All eyes were fixed on him. Whether they knew his identity, he had no way of telling. He doubted it. From Sol Winter's testimony, when the marshals had forcibly wrested control of Solaris from him and made Ethan take over the company, the model of the conspirators was one where each knew a minimum of others. It was all obsessively secret. Cumchdach was reminded disastrously of childhood games of spies and warriors, with all the exaggerated posturing of schoolboys. He had no doubt he faced a mixed group of genders and ages, but they had watched too many action vids, he reckoned.

No one said anything, not until the chairperson lifted his com and listened to a message. "No objections received yet." He made the pronouncement sound like a threat. Definitely one who'd watched too many vids. "State your reasons for requesting membership."

His escort poked him and Cumchdach rose to his feet. He set his voice to a lighter register and his accent the ubiquitous one of Urbis central. "The government's not seeing straight. It's forgotten that business needs to make a profit to keep this planet working."

He shut up then, slouching back into his chair. Had it been too much? There were a few stares but nothing else. Too many shared the same problems. He kept his own counsel after that. Speak softly and breathe through your nose, his grandsire had told him before his first board meeting. Lips pressed firmly together, he listened as the conspirators began to count down their agenda.

The whole thing felt too eerily like any other board meeting. These people were locked into their existing culture. He wondered if they tried to rule their homes as they ruled their companies. Coming from a large, family-owned corporation had forced the den Coilles into a flexibility that too many here lacked.

Sol Winter had tried to run his business like a fiefdom. All it had achieved was forcing his second son to reject him in a takeover demanded by the Arcadian Council. If any of these were vulnerable to the same, the marshals would have sniffed it out already.

So he had to assume they were either undetected, or the marshals lacked sufficient grounds to act against them.

Don't take the caricatures of their avatars for proof of the identity behind the masks. These came from powerful and astute companies.

He kept to his slouching posture. Sullen but waiting to be convinced. He suspected a healthy dose of scepticism was expected of him anyway. The agenda droned on.

All were variations on the same theme. Complaints by companies of lack of profits, of disaster waiting if they were forced to change, of predicted plunging balance sheets if business as usual was broken. All negative, all self-victimising. They may keep their identities secret, but their complaints labelled them. He took careful note of who said what, listening to the voice patterns and watching the habits of each speaker.

How did these people make their wealth in the first place?

Then the speakers came to an end and all faces turned to him. "And you, our newest member. Do you have anything of note to add?"

He'd known the question might come but had hoped against it. No way was he about to let this pit of wermets into Den Coille's business. He'd discussed it with an Fallon but not his father, and now wished he had Da's sensible voice in his ear. He scowled back at the rest of them.

"Nothing particular. Just a general observation that no matter how much you try to comply with the Council's edicts, it's never enough. Makes me wonder what their real agenda is."

A sudden alertness and much nodding of heads. The last part was his idea but an Fallon had smiled at it in the cold way that reminded Cumchdach of a shalk in full hunt. "An interesting bombshell," he'd said.

He'd been right. The sudden lessening of tension said claims of treachery by the council or its individual members was nothing new to this room of backstabbers. Was any of it based on fact? That was what they had to find out.

And he still had to discover who pulled the strings at the top. Those here were mostly what he'd term middle-of-the-bunch types. Heads or executive members of small or middling companies, along with the second-tier leadership of major corporations, the ones who did the leg work rather than the heads—disgruntled, frustrated, but essentially too lazy or risk-averse to ever make it to the top.

But the odd few… One in particular had him on alert. A banker, he'd wager, by the few words let out. Not from the top tier but close enough to it to have real influence—or be the front person for a bigger problem behind. He or she wore the avatar of a hunting folklar, the sinuous predator of his mountain trees—cunning and vicious, ruthless in its hunt, and brutal when attacking. Was it a deliberate choice of avatar? The person's speech patterns and way of moving had nothing of the mountainer about it, and the avatar was too much like the stereotypes from horror vids. He doubted they had ever seen a real folklar in their lives.

Cumchdach had, and both loved and feared the predator. Most of all, he respected them, and equally this avatar.

At the end of the meeting, he'd learned a bit but not enough.

"You will be advised of the next meeting. Will our newest member be attending?"

Cumchdach nodded his affirmative.

"Any objections to be sent to your usual contact within the next day cycle. That is all."

Cumchdach's escort moved and tugged at his arm. As least trusted member, he was the first to leave.

Once home, he contacted an Fallon on the secure link the marshals had set up for him. It was better than waiting for the man to wake him in the middle of the night. If he was really lucky, he'd be yanking the marshal out of his sleeper.

Not that the marshal showed any sign of it when he came onto his com. Seated at his usual desk, not a hair out of place, the head of the Marshals looked as imperturbable as ever. Cumchdach told him the company names he'd guessed. He didn't know the names of any of the attendees, including the banker, but gave an Fallon what he could of the other participants.

"Few were of the type I'd normally meet. Not heads of major corporations or Den Coille associates."

"As we'd expected. They were sounding you out," said an Fallon. "They need to trust you before they risk revealing their businesses."

"Yeah, I'll have to go back." He'd known it, but the slime of the meeting still clung to him. How much deeper would he need go to find out what was happening. "My father won't be pleased if he finds out what I'm up to."

"He can't. Not yet, Ser."

He knew that too, but he'd never kept anything from his father before. "And Anna. You promise to keep her and Roo safe."

"Of course, Ser."

No *of course* about it. They'd already failed once. "One scratch on either of them and my cooperation ends."

"Better a scratch than a killing blow," was an Fallon's unsympathetic answer. Cumchdach wished he could believe the man was using the words as a threat.

"What do they gain by using Ruiseart to send their warning?" was what he couldn't figure. "It just points us straight to the den Falasches as first suspects."

An Fallon shrugged. "As heir to Falasch and Den Coille, he's a symbol. A reminder of how easy it is for other companies like Falasch to be swallowed up by government friendly businesses like Den Coille. And the den Falasch sera is not as bright as she imagines. She counts too much on her important connections."

"Who would readily sacrifice her and her trio of wermet offspring."

No question about it. Whoever was behind the plotting had no morals. The evidence of the environmental threats to Arcadia had been too well documented, and was accepted by the Alliance council in open session. Seolta's hearings had been widely reported on, including the evidence. These corporations must know the reality, including what could happen to Arcadians if the planet refused to meet the Alliance demands. Or they would if they ever got their heads out of their spreadsheets.

"Whoever is behind it has to have off-planet connections as well."

An Fallon nodded. "The kind to benefit from access to Arcadia's wealth or with potential migrants to replace our people."

The Alliance hadn't rescinded that threat yet. Fix Arcadia or face forcible resettlement of its people off planet and replacement by new settlers who would respect the planet. It was suspended for now, but that could change at any time.

"The connections are the key," added an Fallon.

Cumchdach nodded agreement. "I'll run your names through our databases as well, see if any correlations show up." The marshals didn't have access to Den Coille's business intelligence or linkages. Nor could they risk involving others in their investigations.

Then an Fallon gave him that considering stare Cumchdach had learned to dread. "Data mining machines aren't going to discover what we need here, Ser. Run the names. I want to know anything—anything—that occurs to you. I don't care how unlikely. Tell me."

"And my family?"

"They've gone back to Manascraoch, to the den Coille family home. How much safer do you want them?"

"There's a breach there too."

"The risk is still less than elsewhere.

The man might have a point, but it didn't help any. He commed his father the next day, but Da sounded as frustrated as Cumchdach at their failure to track the spies in Den Coille. Nor could he go back there and do the trace himself, no matter how much he longed to. His old family quarters were the one place barred to Cumchdach. Anna had made that quite clear to his family as her condition for staying there. How could he know they were safe without being there to protect them?

The next conspirator's meeting was no better. The only difference this time was that the other participants came from higher up in the hierarchy. These were managers just below the top tier. He had to hope it meant he'd passed whatever test of trust they'd set. Roots knew he'd made little effort to ingratiate himself with any of them, and he said as little at this meeting as at the previous one, keeping his remarks to the minimum necessary and making them as ambiguous as the first. If they didn't yet trust him, it was mutual.

Nor was he fully certain of the loyalties of those here, not after his time in a Survey prison. Cumchdach trusted no one outside the family and, for all he knew, one of the participants was here as a Council spy. Cumchdach den Coille had no intention of incriminating himself.

"Anything new?" asked an Fallon later.

Cumchdach sent through the latest list of names. He'd made some guesses at the attendees' names as well as their companies this time. He still hadn't met anyone he knew personally from his business dealings, but he had no doubt many in the meeting knew exactly who he was. Den Coille was too prominent a company. After the attempted Survey coup, the whole family had been splashed across the vids for months.

"This is getting us nowhere," he growled at the marshal.

"Information is key to any investigation. Patience, Ser."

He used to be a patient man, prepared to plod through the groundwork to secure a deal, but prison had changed that. Cumchdach had learned too hard the result of failure. "We need results, not more legwork, Marshal."

"You're getting closer, Ser. It's what's needed at present." With which the man signed off, leaving Cumchdach as frustrated as ever. He pulled up his father's latest reports and clicked through to the images his mother sent of Roo. His little boy was growing up too fast, wriggling all over the floor now.

Images weren't the same as reality. He needed so badly to cradle his son in his arms, to hold his wife and never let her go again.

One day, he'd make Eolas den Falasch and every person who had broken them apart pay for it. He thumped down on the lounger and put a call through to Seolta in Alliance Central. In his present mood, putting a spark under his most annoying sibling was exactly what he needed.

"Have you found anything yet?" he started the transmission with. The delay in communications meant a real conversation was nearly impossible, given what he actually wanted to chew over with his brother. But it did mean he could unload a pile of rancour onto the sharp-witted Seolta's shoulders. His younger brother owed his family a long enough debt in cutting remarks and betrayal.

"The trial here is a clear enough case, and Falasch has exposed too many important entities Alliance-wide to risk. Falasch will be found guilty. The same when we go for reparation through the Arcadian courts."

Cumchdach scowled. That was really going to help him get Anna back. "Don't forget my wife is heir to Falasch. We don't need to gut the company, just stop them swindling us and make sure no one else tries it."

He tapped his fingers impatiently as he waited for a reply. When his brother next came on screen, there was no trace of sympathy on the sharp features. If he hadn't seen Seolta with his wife, he'd think his brother had no understanding of what this was going to cost Cumchdach. But Anyara ingh Gevard bean Seolta den Coille held his brother's heart and life, as Anna did Cumchdach's. Which meant his brother knew exactly what he was asking Cumchdach.

"Da has the options worked out. Falasch will survive, but not with their current freedom."

The outlines Seolta sent him horrified Cumchdach even more. Once past the business jargon, it was a straight takeover of Falasch by Den Coille. Anna would never forgive him. "We don't need more power, not in the current climate. You want a revolution in Mountainer country?"

Seolta knew as well as he what the changes in Den Coille had cost individual families. When you looked at your children, few thought of the future if empty bellies threatened them today.

"Don't be dramatic," was Seolta's reply. "We have no choice." His brother's finger tapped on his chair arm, a perfect mirror to Cumchdach's own stress habit, and he quickly flattened his hand on the desktop. "I've forwarded them to the Alliance for final acceptance," added Seolta, "but it's only a matter of form. Falasch takes the fall, leaving the reputation of companies in the wider Alliance clear for now. That's the agreement."

A filthy compromise, as far as Cumchdach could see, and not one that helped Arcadia in the longer term. The glitter in Seolta's eyes said he agreed.

"We're going to get those who are acting against us, but only when we have the full conspiracy exposed. Anything before that risks annihilation for Arcadians."

Seolta was correct, and that made it even more galling. The Alliance companies involved included major banking and transport outfits. That's what Seolta was working on at Alliance Central. Banished from Arcadia for his former treachery, he was redeeming himself by uncovering the conspirators behind the plots against their home world. Falasch lost and was swallowed up by Den Coille, or Arcadia lost and was gobbled up by the predators waiting to grab its fertile lands and rich resources.

"I can't let it happen. Falasch stays separate."

"You don't have a choice. Talk to Da," was Seolta's reply when it finally arrived. Short, ugly, and final. He waited but no more came and he had to accept that his brother had signed off.

"I wish you were here, little brother," he muttered, something he'd never thought to say. Right now, he could do with a healthy dose of Seolta's twisty cunning.

Then his com signalled he had a message from his father. Cumchdach stared at it.

'Security leak uncovered. Perpetrators in custody.'

Too short, too brief, too tragging lacking in anything he needed.

Revenge first, but that wasn't an option. Not in the current situation. Not ever, he suspected. They had stolen his baby and could have killed him.

Cumchdach didn't care who was snooping on him. The marshals knew all the details anyway. He opened a com link to his father.

"Please advise the subject of your call, Ser den Coille."

The woman's disembodied voice was none he'd ever heard before, but the transmission carried the marshal's seal.

"Resend," he said. "This is none of the marshals' business."

"Please hold."

Nothing he tried let him override the block on his com. Nothing going out.

Nothing at all.

Then a vibration signalled an incoming call. He slapped his com to receive and Marshal an Fallon's head shimmered to life in front of him.

"The marshals have been advised of the security situation in Manascraoch. It is under control and being managed acceptably."

"Get off my com, an Fallon."

"It is being managed, Ser," the marshal repeated. An officer will be with you shortly to explain the situation. Please refrain from using your com to discuss the matter." Then he finished the call.

Cumchdach could only stare open mouthed. "No one accesses my com without permission.," he growled at the empty space in front of him.

Except an Fallon clearly had. And if he could... He stalked through the carefully curated space of his apartment, waiting impatiently, until a call sound came from his door. He released his door pad and the door opened.

"What do you have for me?" he demanded of the marshal in the doorway.

The woman walked in, touching her com to close the door, then raising her hand, palm outward, in a brusque order for silence. He fumed as he waited for her to slowly revolve as she scanned the room.

They already had him under surveillance. If they hadn't picked up any foreign sensor in his room, he wasn't being scanned by anyone other than the marshals.

Not that he knew.

At the end, she nodded brusquely, but still kept her silence, passing over an old-fashioned message tablet. Commander an Fallon's personal seal was displayed on top.

'Den Coille security have identified and removed three personnel in your communication section who have passed a number of messages to unknown parties. The dates include that on which your son was taken. The operatives have links, distant ones, to lower bough, unregistered migrants. Mostly from the coaster region. The marshals are liaising with Den Coille security and are satisfied that the matter is being adequately contained.'

He sat heavily. Unregistered migrants. A poor description of the people involved. It meant folk who had been displaced from their homes in Mountainer regions that had been cleared to make way for ever more festia trees to cover the slopes and lower flats. Trees that made more credits for Den Coille than the original settlements, trees that stole the homes of the refugees and left them with nothing, forcing them to leave and find a new place, or stay and struggle on in what was left of their homelands.

Too many flocked to Manascraoch, cobbling together haphazard dwellings perched on the lower boughs of the worst trees. The problem had been festering for a while. Samhchair had brought it up with him a number of times, but so far, the city and Den Coille had held it at bay with a mix of subtle assistance, tolerance of the less harmful intrusions, and keeping it out of the vidcasts, but he'd always known it for a stupid policy.

There had just been so many other problems, and this one hadn't exploded in their faces yet.

Or so they thought.

He stabbed at the tablet to send an Fallon a reply, only to discover it was a message tablet only.

"Your family are safe, Ser. The Commander has advised that the problem is under control and you are not required to take any action," said the marshal in a toneless voice.

"Meaning?"

"Exactly that, Ser," she said, picking up the tablet and marching out. All Cumchdach could do was stare after her. He went to open the door and follow her, only to discover it was locked against him. Nor did his com links work for anyone in Manascraoch.

Not required. Not allowed, more like.

Now, he really needed to talk to Da. "I'm going home," he announced to the dead air and the marshals monitoring him. "Tonight."

Luckily, he didn't need much. Just a small backpack of essentials and his com. Everything he valued was still in Manascraoch. But even packing that and securing the apartment gave the marshals too much time. A squad waited for him at the door when he opened it.

"Where do you think you are going, Ser."

"To Manascraoch. Or arrest, with all the publicity of a trial that will bring. Take your pick." The cuffs they slapped on him made him rethink that threat. "You can't be serious?"

No marshal uttered a word but a blaster poked him in the back and the squad leader gestured to the two hulking troopers either side of him. In seconds, he was being marched down the hall and into a black government skimmer hovering outside his floor's hatchway with no chance of escape at any point.

CHAPTER FIFTEEN

Ceart broke into the peace of the family lunch with all the deftness of a charging bull nieten.

"They've arrested Cumchdach."

Anna's heart seized. She'd been deep in talk with her father-in-law about the scans she was having done of his festia plantations, but now she jumped to her feet.

Bram den Coille got in before her. "Who has and where is he held?"

"The tragging marshals."

"In sentences of more than three words, if you please, Ceart," snapped Bram.

Anna had never seen Ceart so obviously angry, but he clenched his fists and complied. The brother who rarely spoke turned out to be more than capable of sentences with more than three words.

"I came back to the apartment as their flyer was lifting off. They were running shielded but my scanner picked up their backwash. Only the marshals have that level of shield tech." Then he told them everything else he'd learned. Banging on the marshals' front office desk got the information that Cumchdach was being held pending charges, but they refused to say where.

"Charges? What charges? The boy's been going to the boughs and beyond to help the marshals."

Anna had no time to wonder what that meant, filing it for later with a cold lump in her gut. "Did you find out where he's being held?" she demanded over the growing ruckus.

Ceart shook his head. "I tried all the leads I know. No one's talking. We'll be 'informed when the situation is clarified'."

"Clarified? What in tragging depths does that mean," Aigherach wanted to know.

Samhchair alone sat silent, watching her parents take turns to grill Ceart for the little information he could give them.

When it became too obvious Ceart had nothing left, Bram stood up. "I'll be in my study if anyone wants me, calling our lawyers in Urbis. They'll be knocking on the marshals' door within the hour, or they'll be looking for new clients."

Scathach hurried after Bram, leaving Aigherach to grill Ceart between angry rants. Samhchair was still silent. Anna watched her as she stood and began to leave. Something Anna would have thought impossible in a family crisis and with Aigherach so clearly upset. Samhchair was up to something, and if it had to do with Cumchdach, Anna needed to know what. She hurried after her, catching her up halfway down the next hallway.

"Where are you off to?"

Samhchair lips creased for once in a slight twitch of annoyance. "I have a meeting in the lower boughs."

"I'm coming too," said Anna.

"There's no need," said Samhchair.

"I'm still coming."

"Roo needs you."

"I've just fed him and he's happy with Biarsuin. I have time now."

Samhchair studied her with that deep reserve Anna had never been able to penetrate. Then a shrug and a gesture. "I'm taking a skimmer to start with, but after that it's a good walk in the lower city boughs."

Anna was fit after her time in Deuteron, but she'd long ago learned that Samhchair's version of 'a good walk' meant a long hike over less-than-friendly terrain. The lower boughs of the city shouldn't match that; Manascraoch had good standards of civic care and social supports by planet-wide levels, but all cities had their dark corners.

"I'll call for a skimmer if I need it." The marshals and Den Coille security would be following her and Samhchair acknowledged it with an abrupt head nod.

Soon they were sitting in Samhchair's own skimmer and dropping in and out of the interlocking branches and walkways of this complex city. Cumchdach's family took their tree city for granted, but as a newcomer from Rubhaicreach, it had taken her breath away and still managed to stun her. It wasn't only the sheer size and strength of the baullnia trees on which the city was built but also the subtlety and beauty of the locals' enhancements. Buildings, playgrounds, shopping plazas and public parks were built in and on the supportive branches. Sometimes they dug right into the enormous trunks, and Anna had spent hours during her early years at UBS quizzing the local architects on how they managed that without damaging the life force and strength of the trees. They showed her the channels built into all walls and around all entrances to ensure the continued flow of the essential nutrients through the tree's vascular system and the exhaustive calculations and experiments required before any breach of a trunk took place. More calculations were needed to ensure an even weight distribution of all built structures on a tree. No one owned property in a city like

Manascraoch. Rather, homeowners purchased a right of habitation, and the licensing for these included a raft of clauses to ensure the continued wellbeing of the tree.

She had come to a have a huge appreciation for both Manascraoch's scientists and its lawyers. Her own interest in plant integrations had started in those early questions. Beneath the muddy ooze on which much of the city was built—a substrate despised by most of the inhabitants—lived an ecosystem of biological interactions that rivalled even those of her own peninsular home.

Today, fear drove out her usual awe. Cumchdach had been arrested and was being held against his will. Again. She knew what it had done to him the last time.

They had to get him released, and a sharp niggle inside her said Samhchair had a plan for that, despite the path the skimmer took, heading away from any offices of power in the city. Manascraoch was built on the middle slopes of its mountain, below the dark scar that still told of the massive landslip that had wiped out a huge swath of the upper slopes some months previously. The land sloped upward but not so steeply as to be dangerous. Enough that those on the top boughs could look out to all that lay below—a cascade of stunning beauty as trees blanketed the slopes right to the crashing waves of the unruly western seas. The den Coilles' home tree was in the heart of the most favourable region, high enough to clear the lower trees but sheltered by the enfolding escarpments rising either side of the city and cradling it in the hollow between. On the top side, the slopes were still vulnerable to landslides in the increasingly frequent deluges hitting the region, but a series of cunning channels put in place by Cumchdach's youngest sister, the Survey expert, had cut back the risk.

The lower slopes were gentler as the mountainside gave way to the truncated flats that divided the mountains from the stony western beaches. Gentler slopes didn't mean gentler living conditions, though. Here, the trees crowded together and few gave a view from the treetops of anything but more branches and huddled-together homes and workplaces. The trees even looked more ragged, their buildings illegally cobbled together in lopsided trees, despite the city regulations, as the poorer inhabitants fought for scarce space. Habitation licences cost money and few here had much to spare.

Life in the lower boughs of Manascraoch was tough—and would become tougher still if the den Coilles couldn't find a way to maintain the profitability of the business that was the core of the city's wealth.

It was a part of the city Anna never entered without security. Security that must be following her today. For the first time, she wished they weren't so good at hiding from her.

"You're safe. You'll be home again soon," murmured her sister-in-law as if reading her thoughts. But Anna had grown up hiding her fears from too many others, and now, she locked them down hard. Samhchair had a plan, and Anna wanted part of it.

"Are you sure you know where you're going?"

Samhchair gave a curt head tilt as they clipped over a lower branch, barely above ground level and covered from trunk to tip in patched-together homes and shops. This close to ground level, the sun had to fight to penetrate the gloom, and a constant dampness soaked her clothes. She knew Manascraoch had developed dehumidifiers and artificial solar sources to make up for the lack of heat and radiation, but doubted many made it into these houses as she watched a small child run along the thick branch to what looked to be some kind of childcare place, her cough hacking at her small lungs as she ran.

"Why are streets like this allowed?"

Samhchair was settling her skimmer into a small parking space in the side of the largest building on the broad branch. "They aren't." She locked down and set in place what Anna recognised as a high-level security program, the kind Cumchdach had made her use every time they returned to Rubhaicreach. "Believe it or not, Manascraoch is a sought-after home, and we get more incoming mountainers than we can cope with. They either struggle to make a living in small settlements tucked into inhospitable hollows, or they settle for these streets."

Anna knew why they struggled in those villages. Many of them had been bought out for festia plantings. She held her silence, but it didn't fool Samhchair.

"Without festia plantations, there are few other sources of income," said her sister-in-law. "It doesn't mean Den Coille is innocent."

"One of the problems to which your father wants me to find a solution?"

"Yes," said Samhchair bitterly. "The Survey teams are working on it as well."

Anna didn't know what to say next so kept silent, beginning to think she'd made a mistake following Samhchair. The older woman was unloading supplies. Anna gathered up boxes and followed her into the basic-looking building. Inside, a group of people waited. They recognised her and stiffened.

It wasn't surprising. Anna and Cumchdach's faces were known throughout the city and their recent troubles had only added to their fame.

"She's with me," said Samhchair placidly. "I vouch for her silence."

"She'll have security following her," said a gruff-voiced older man.

"As have I. They're only concerned with any threat to our personal safety. Or are you about to try overthrowing the den Coilles and changing the entire balance of the city?"

The man's face flushed, and Anna held her breath. What had Samhchair got her into?

Then an older woman pushed her way to the front. One Anna recognised.

"Councillor!"

Seilach ingh Craobh bean Stobach den Bunachan, the regional Councillor, was a formidable woman, despite her small stature, but what was she doing here? It suddenly felt like the branch had dropped away from under her feet.

"Sera Samhchair ingh Bram—and Sera Anna bean Cumchdach. This is a surprise."

The Councillor didn't look happy. Not a person who liked surprises. Nor was Samhchair usually, but not today. Cumchdach's sister had known the councillor would be here, Anna was sure of it.

"My sister-in-law has many useful skills that may help us," said Samhchair.

If it had to do with why these people were living here against all Manascraoch regulations, it was true, but Samhchair had been too reluctant to bring her for Anna to believe they were the reason for this meeting. Not today.

"I understood the Sera was no long working on Manascraoch projects?"

"On Den Coille projects," Anna corrected. "My current work schedule is full, but it doesn't mean I won't help out elsewhere if needed."

The Councillor looked taken aback, as if Anna had suddenly metamorphosed into an alien entity. But Anna was no longer watching her. Nor was Samhchair. It was the man slipping in to stand behind the Councillor who had her attention, a man with a wooden face and a stance that said he was more than a Councillor's bodyguard.

Recent history had made Anna too familiar with that level of sharpness in a guard.

"Marshal," said Anna.

He showed no embarrassment at being caught out. He gave her the required formal bow of greeting then turned to Samhchair. "Your brother is safe."

"That's good to know. The question is: how long will he stay that way?"

"As long as he cooperates," was the daunting reply. Anna gasped in fear and Samhchair shot her a glance. She quickly schooled her face back to the immobility of disinterest, harder to achieve than she'd have thought. Nor was the Councillor fooled, the woman still grim-faced but watching her with the soft eyes of compassion. Over the years, she had worked with the Councillor on various research projects studying Mountainer food cropping attempts. The constant deluge and cold temperatures generally favoured only those plants bred to the region. The discovery of the nutrient value of the festia pollen, early in the settlement years, had probably saved the original settlements. She didn't bring that up here, though. Not with too many unknowns raised by the presence of this group in the lower branches of the den Coilles' city.

"We'll talk after you've finished your rounds, as per usual," the Councillor said to Samhchair. Her sister-in-law didn't look happy, but nodded agreement.

As per usual? There was nothing usual about today, whatever Samhchair's normal schedule might be.

Samhchair turned to Anna.

"I'm coming too," said Anna in a voice as uncompromising as the Councillor's.

Anna had long ago learned to recognise when she was being manipulated. She'd have thought nothing would make her distrust this sister-in-law, but past feelings now crashed into a big red line squarely in front of her. All Anna's senses were on high alert as she followed the eldest den Coille. Nor was she surprised when the marshal followed them, leaving the Councillor behind. Seilach ingh Craobh's Mountainer guards looked much happier, but Anna's inner warning system was at full strength.

Because of that, she refrained from telling Samhchair she'd seen plenty of Manascraoch's lower branches over the years. They may be less desirable places to live, damp and lacking light making them claustrophobic, but they were also regions critical to the city's wellbeing and the Public Works Department regularly patrolled them to destroy any attacks on a tree's health and integrity.

In a city built on trees, infrastructure and botany were closely intertwined, and Anna had spent many happy days over the years working with the Works' tech and inspection staff. In her opinion, the Works department was one of the miracles of the city.

Not a view shared by the locals, especially of these boughs. But then, the Works department had never taken Anna to city streets like this. These residents were even more wary of outsiders than most lower bough residents. While Samhchair was welcomed warmly, the marshal and she got only dark looks.

No, Samhchair was more than welcomed. She'd warned Anna to be ready to walk and she hadn't been wrong. It was almost as if Samchair was making Anna pay for whatever she got out of today. Along branches they traipsed, up shaky rope walkways owing nothing to the Works staff, hopping over crazily installed pipes that gurgled ominously and showed too much rust to be legal and into makeshift shack after shack.

After nearly tripping over yet another roughly placed bridge entry, Anna tugged Samhchair to a halt.

"How does this bough even stay up. None of these structures are Works compliant." The rest of Manascraoch's homes were as well designed as anywhere, subtle in design, with water and sanitation services constructed in harmony with the tree's living systems.

Samhchair glared at her. "Not so loud, not here." She said no more until they reached a branch grown lopsided out of the main bough, with makeshift steps set against both sides and leaves clustering tightly around them. Anna and the marshal followed Samhchair up to the landing on the top where Samhchair stopped, leaned over as if catching her breath, then straightened and moved over to a small branch set in the middle of the leaf cluster. She sat and beckoned Anna to take the spot next to her. The marshal stayed on the path, watching them as well as the main pathway either side of the steps.

"This street is illegal, these people illegals," said Anna coldly. The growing tide of illegals sneaking into Manascraoch's lower streets was a continual challenge to the survival of the city's trees.

"Yes, every one of them. And we turn a blind eye to it and do the best we can," said Samhchair.

"So what happens if they put the whole tree at risk?" And the hundreds living and working in each of the mighty baullnia.

"They won't. We monitor it."

Anna wasn't convinced. "I've seen multiple violations on our way. If allowed to remain, they'll rot the trees from the base up."

"Which is why Works comes through here frequently. They do a sweep, pick up as many as they can and take them to resettlement villages."

"It's clearly not working."

"They come straight back as soon as they can get transport here. And the violations aren't as bad as they look."

"Yes, they are."

Samhchair shook her head. "See that pipe." She pointed at one of the more disreputable rusty eyesores snaking over this side of the main bough. "It's been routed back to a recycling centre at ground level. An official one, though you have to look closely to find it in the department's records."

"What—"

"There's an unspoken agreement between Works and Lower Boughs. They put in place structures that don't hurt the tree or the city and the Works lets them steal a supply of used equipment and the techs work after hours to help out. Voluntary work. As long as it stays in balance, Works doesn't evict too many settlers or make return too hard."

Anna had been on Works audits of the lower boughs and knew it wasn't quite that benign. She'd also heard too many Works inspectors exclaim in despair. "What can you do?"

"Works also blocks all efforts too near the main trunk," Samhchair added, and Anna nodded, making a decision. Her sister-in-law had brought her here for a reason, one that might help Cumchdach, although she couldn't see it at the moment. This tour was more than a cover for her meeting, but if Anna wanted to help Cumchdach, she had to give something too.

"I've helped with the barriers at the branch collars," she said. Samhchair's eyes widened. "I'm a botanist and trees are plants. The Works department and I are old friends. Some of the security precautions at the branch collars were developed in my lab." It was a bit more than that, but Samhchair looked shocked enough.

"How didn't you know?" Anna said to her. "I know how many responsibilities you take on for the family."

"You've helped with plenty of them."

That was true too. Over the years, they had become the senior women of their generation, long before Anna and Cumchdach had formally married. It was one of the reasons she'd finally given into to his continued stream of proposals.

No, it wasn't. It was the sight of a baby laughing and the hunger on Cumchdach's face—and in your heart.

Anna shoved the thought down deep, into that aching heart.

"I know how much you do, which is why I never bothered you with this. It came through my lab and the research projects there."

"You're an academic. A botanist, not a tech. Not an *applied* scientist."

"I talk to the techs. They had information I needed, and sometimes I had information useful to them. Cumchdach loves this place, so it seemed important I learn about it too."

"And you love this city. Like you love Cumchdach."

Anna refused to answer that. She began to walk on and, after a moment, Samhchair went with her. Not that she'd fooled her sister-in-law.

Was she being spiteful to keep an internal log of the serious issues with sanitation services and branch intrusions she saw along the way? The worst was a long spigot jabbed right into the main bough, a cup below it and the crude tap fitting at the end glaring proof of its use.

"Look there. They've jacked right into the bough's sap system. Who knows what disease they're pouring into the vascular system of the rest of the tree."

"Plant vascular systems can block intrusions. The tree is safe."

"Not necessarily, not for invasive microbes, and below this bough is the base supporting the whole tree and the root system."

"I'll have the techs check it out," said Samhchair, as if that dealt with Anna's concern. She turned back to another small girl with a hacking cough. Nor could Anna deny sympathy with her priorities. The child and mother in this crude shack looked near the end of their endurance.

"Have them admitted to the Maternal Support lodge," Anna said. Manascraoch had an excellent health and social support system for expectant mothers, young children, and their families. There was no reason for these two to be ill.

"They're illegals," said Samhchair. The snap in her eyes was the nearest to angry Anna had ever seen her. "They don't qualify. Since Den Coille has had to cut back festia production, the city's funds for services have been cut. The city is having enough trouble caring for its own."

Anna tried not to feel guilty as she caught the look of defeat on the mother's face. It didn't work. First her home city was being destroyed by her stepmother's greed, now Manascraoch was going the same way.

"What do you expect of me? I can't even fix my own marriage to a man I thought I knew inside out."

She swung round and rushed out of the accusing room, leaving Samhchair to finish caring for the family.

It had been the same in all the makeshift shacks. Check expectant mothers, check the children, dish out advice that may be of no use here, use the medicines she'd brought with her to do what she could for the children, the mothers, the haggard fathers.

The marshal had followed Anna out. "There's no use," she cried out to him. Then Samhchair joined them again, her face closed over. "How do you bear it?" Anna had to ask.

"Someone has to."

"Why don't they just go home?"

"They can't." Samhchair marched to the next makeshift home and disappeared inside, but Anna had reached her limit.

"Why?" she said to the marshal beside her.

"Their homes are gone," said the marshal.

"What happened to them?"

"Most are Coasters, from the narrow strip of lowlands bordering the sea or the small river flats at the base of the mountains."

She knew the region although had never spent much time there. "There's little to live on there," she said, thinking of the festia plantations now covering most of the river flats and the swamps and coastal dunes covering the rest of the land caught between mountains and sea.

"Not now," said the marshal with a strange glitter in his eye that had her staring at him. Then she remembered the whispered voice of the woman in the shack and the rhythms in the speech of this man. "You're from there."

"Was," said the man. "My village was near gone when I was born, and we moved out when I started First School. The local one had closed down. But we went back for visits. The grandparents refused to leave." He stared at the rough house where Samhchair brought what hope she could. "They were the last to leave, and they could stay only because we sent back supplies. The village site was planted over with festia. All that was left was their house by the base of the dunes. When they had to go into care, we had to use a flyer to get them out. GranDa lost the use of his legs and GrandMam had a cough she couldn't throw."

He fell silent, and Anna daren't break it. Finally he thrust back his shoulders and continued in a flat voice. "They never got over leaving their home. Both of them went within a few months. We buried them in the old grave plot—or what we could find of it. Then we planted it with chastne grasses and surrounded it with a thick hedge of drach bushes. Anyone wanting to plant festia over them will pay for it."

She didn't like to point out that Den Coille had heavy duty machinery to clear away the viciously barbed drach bushes. She hoped none had tried but wasn't hopeful.

"I've never seen chastne grass but have heard of it," she said instead. Once, the tough grass had covered much of the river flats, interspersed with the open branches of the fraustin tree, a distant cousin of festia but nothing like it in habitat or form.

"It survives in some smaller flats. Ones the planters hadn't got to, and now the Survey has banned any new plantings of festia on non-natural habitats."

"So they'll restore the flats soon and these people can go back home."

"Eventually. The slopes of the mountains take priority. Fixing the species mix there will repair the climatic imbalance quickest."

She recognised bitterness, no matter how well hidden. This marshal had been hiding it for a long while, she'd guess, and wondered whether his superiors knew.

Then thought of an Fallon. Of course they did. That man knew too much about any of his charges to not be twice as vigilant over his own staff. She wondered at the deliberate cruelty of sending this man here.

"I asked for the assignment," said the marshal. "It was my idea, not the Commander's. He gave me the option of refusing."

As if this man would. "Your leader is a determined man."

"He has to be. All of us will suffer the fate of my family if the Alliance isn't satisfied."

But can they be? Anna kept that thought to herself. This man carried burdens enough.

"One more call and we can head back," said Samhchair, and the marshal fell silent, falling in behind them as if an assigned Den Coille guard. Anna felt a shiver as he settled into place.

Despite Samhchair's lack of invitation, Anna followed her into the last shack. It held three children, one woman who looked old enough to be their grandmother but whose actions said she was their mother, and whose belly showed the swelling of another to come. In a sleeper in a corner lay a man, wheezing badly. Samhchair went straight to him, despite his hand waving her to the children.

"The children will survive better if you recover from your illness, Ser." She fed him some medicine and spent a while checking all his signs. At the end of it, his breathing seemed easier and Samhchair turned to care for the children. The mother shook her head and refused her help. Nor did Samhchair harry her further.

Too soon it was over and they left the shack, turning down a branch pathway that she suspected led them back to the main landing pad. "Will he recover?" Anna asked quietly.

Samhchair shrugged. "With luck."

"And his wife?"

Samhchair shook her head. "She's already doing everything possible for him. She can do no more without killing herself, and she won't do that. Not with the children needing her."

This time the bitterness wasn't hidden. Anna knew this kind, the futility of trying with everything you had and still failing. She'd known enough of it through her childhood as her stepmother and father set out to destroy everything her grandfather and the generations before them had built.

Her den Guire Grandam had stopped the worst of it, as had the resistance of the city, but Anna had never been able to convince herself she'd had any part in slowing down their depredations.

"You can't solve all the city's problems," she said now to Samhchair.

"I can try." Samhchair snapped her mouth closed, saying nothing more until they left the worst of the lower bough streets. Before they did, she stopped beside a small platform on which was built a makeshift playground and, for the first time that day, Anna heard the sound of children laughing.

Samhchair heard it too. Her face muscles tightened as she swung round on their guard. "Marshal, you have a message for me?"

The marshal glanced at Anna.

"She's his wife."

"Estranged," the marshal said as if treading on a barely crusted over sinkhole.

"And the marshals want it to stay that way," said Anna bitterly.

"It would help," he said, speaking to a spot above her head and, suddenly, too much became clear. Not what Cumchdach was doing up in Urbis, but that it was dangerous. Much more so than she'd been told. Cumchdach was still lying to her, still keeping her safe by keeping her in the dark. She fought for control.

Not so Samhchair. "You have no reason to hold him. This is a kidnapping." Usually the voice of calm in the family, right now her sister-in-law was furious and not bothering to hide it.

The marshal stood erect, officialdom personified. "He is being held in safe custody."

"From what threat?"

The marshal held out on her, Anna was surprised to see.

"Put me through to an Fallon," demanded Samhchair. "And that's a formal citizen request if you like. Or do I have to go through the Councillor?"

"She is fully informed of the reasons."

"She is?" said Anna in surprise.

"Right," said Samhchair. "I don't care what her precious *schedule* demands. That meeting of hers stops now." Samhchair began to march forward again. The marshal threw her a harried look then hurried after. So the marshals no longer trusted Den Coille security, she supposed that meant. Interestingly, he stopped to look back at her, pausing as if torn. Anna took pity on him and hurried after them. He didn't relax but looked more comfortable when he stood at both their backs as they all marched on. Like a protective male ganda with his flock, she thought manically.

Soon they were back in the hall Samhchair had first brought her to, only this time a long line of people snaked along the insides, out the door and down the branch.

"It's a constituency clinic." So why the secrecy? This was a normal part of Council duties.

"Sort of," said Samhchair, and marched to the head of the queue.

Then Anna looked at the queue, at the pinched, scared faces watching her and the marshal. So not an ordinary clinic. The people waiting here today were illegals, of no ordered affiliation. None had voting rights in the city, not without sanctioned licenses to live here; none were officially constituents of the Councillor under Mountainer law. Not that Anna was about to point that out to Seilach ingh Craobh bean Stobach den Bunachan. The Councillor took few prisoners when she was bent on a crusade, and this looked to be one of them. She almost felt sorry for her father-in-law, never doubting this clinic would feature in their next discussion.

Samhchair ingh Bram had no such reservations. She marched right up to the Councillor, apologising to those waiting and assuring them they would be seen that day, but not letting that deter her. She despatched the next in the queue with the kind of glare Anna had never suspected lay in her sensible in-law's arsenal, and stood over the Councillor.

"What have they done to my brother?" demanded Samhchair, taking the seat in front of the desk and placing her hands in her lap to wait. She may no longer be steaming in fury but those hands were implacable. She demanded an answer and wasn't moving.

The Councillor had faced many opponents in her political career, but this time Anna was surprised to see her concede to Samhchair's furious accusation.

"Please clear the room," she said quietly to her chief bodyguard, "and assure them we will begin again once I have dealt with an administrative matter."

Not one of the waiting low boughs people argued, silently moving out with the resigned faces of those who knew their concerns always came second to those luckier in life.

"We won't be long," she tried to say to a stoop-shouldered man as he filed past her. He gave no sign he heard her as he plodded out. The marshal behind her touched her arm and shook his head.

"The Councillor will hear them," he said in a low voice. "She is a woman of her word, as is Sera Samhchair ingh Bram."

Fortunately, Seilach den Bunachan had been in enough similar situations to know how far she could push it.

"The marshals have informed me that Ser Cumchdach mar Bram is being held in protective custody pending clarification of a number of matters," she said in that annoyingly reasonable voice of a politician reciting official advice.

"Don't give us that mud fudge," said Anna "Where is he, is he safe, and what will it take to have him released?"

"Always straightforward in your arguments, Sera Anna. It's a pity your father didn't inherit that den Falasch trait."

"We're not talking my birth family today."

"But we are, Sera Anna. As you are aware, the Falasch infractions have placed the Council in a difficult position at a delicate time in our planet's history."

That was one way of putting it. Anna could think of less diplomatic ones. "Given the scale of the opposition to the changes Arcadia must make, someone was bound to get greedy and use the times to add to their own wealth." She glanced at the blank-faced marshal behind them. He'd be recording everything said here for his seniors.

Samhchair saw her glance but kept her attention on the Councillor. "That doesn't answer our questions. Why now? What has changed?"

The Councillor looked to the marshal. He stood at attention, as if this discussion had nothing to do with him.

"Your husband was about to return to Manascraoch," said the councillor to Anna.

"Why would he do that?" asked Anna in surprise. She was getting a very bad feeling.

Her sister-in-law was having none of it. "What game are the marshals playing, or is it the Council?"

It wouldn't be the first time the marshals had been called in to do the government's dirty work. Anna would never forget the horror of Cumchdach's and his family's arrest. She hadn't heard from him for months after it. All that had reached her were terrible rumours.

Rumours she later discovered had nearly come true. She shot up.

"Where is he?"

"Sit down, Sera. You have nothing to fear," said the marshal.

Anna didn't believe that. Nor did Samhchair. Her clenched fist said she was as frightened as Anna. Both of them glared at the marshal.

"He's safe, Sera," the man repeated. "He's being held in an apartment in Marshal Headquarters, pending the outcome of an investigation."

"Arrested and facing unknown charges, you mean. That's what that phrase stands for," said Anna.

Samhchair nodded her head. "What charges?"

"There is a suspicion he may be involved in fiscally disruptive behaviour."

"That's mud scuffle and you know it," said Anna.

The marshal held his wooden stare.

"It's another of your games," Anna suddenly realised. "Hold him in custody, set rumours of anti-government activity, then release him to reel in the guilty." She dragged in a breath, suddenly registering that Samhchair showed no sign of surprise. She felt sick. "It's why you marshals don't want me anywhere near Cumchdach. He's still my *husband*."

"The Marshals are well aware of that, Sera."

"What will it take to get him released," said Samhchair.

Anna held her breath. To no use. The marshal shook his head. "That is a matter for the Commander."

A new glitter appeared in Samhchair's eyes. "Get me an Fallon online. Now."

"He's a busy man, Sera. I'm sure if you make an appointment, the Commander will get back to you as soon as he's free."

Her sister-in-law swung on the Councillor. "I talk to Marco an Fallon today. No later. Or I expose the whole nasty game." She flung out her hand. "Yes, this down here looks bad. The lower boughs are a disgrace and a direct result of Den Coille business practices. But we do try to regulate our effects. The influx of migrants was worse than we expected. You know that."

Anna kept silent. Samhchair had never spoken like this in the family quarters, not openly, though Anna had no doubt she'd pushed her father about it. He'd been one of the few unsurprised when she moved from her paediatrician work into her public health role.

Samhchair wasn't finished. "Our failures don't mean we have to accept whatever schemes the Council dreams up. Not when you're using our family as tools to pacify the Alliance Council."

Anna had seen too many similar situations growing up with her stepmother. She shot to her feet, shoving hard at the table. "Or are the Council and their cronies still trying to steal control of Den Coille?"

The Councillor's hands had shot out to grab the table and stop it colliding into her when Anna shot up. Now, she eased her hands off and sat back tiredly. "I don't know, Sera," she said and, for the first time, Anna saw the shadows of exhaustion tracing the Councillor's face. Then the Councillor sat up again. "Not officially. But…" She grimaced and forced her back straight. Anna was taken aback at the obvious sign of effort needed. "There are still some at the highest levels who don't believe the Alliance is serious or the threats to our world real. Who want to keep making credits the way they've always done it." She lifted a hand. "The problems are so widespread, so diffuse, that it's possible to argue that any one of them is just a minor local matter. That it will take little effort to fix it. But they're wrong. The accumulation of problems is real."

"We know that. Fioruisghe has been fighting it for years, and she told us exactly the scale of the problem after we were released from prison."

Anna would never forget that particular family meeting. Fioruisghe had spared none of them, and her husband had glared at any who tried to interrupt her. But that was past history.

"It changes nothing," said Anna. "Cumchdach is still locked up, and he shouldn't be." Samhchair's own imprisonment had been nothing like that of her brothers. "He mustn't have to endure that again."

"And he won't," said Samhchair. "I was there after they were released the last time." Whether she reminded Anna or the Councillor, Anna couldn't say. That bad feeling was getting worse.

"Why was he coming back home?" she finally thought to ask. Then saw Samhchair's lips tighten while both the Councillor and the marshal refused to meet her eyes. "I know it wasn't for me," she assured them, "and Roo is fine." She didn't have time for these games. Roo needed her and she had to return home soon. "Samhchair, what aren't you telling me?"

"He was worried about a company matter. That's all I know."

"The Commander is online for you, Sera Seilach ingh Craobh," broke in the marshal and Anna sent up a silent sigh of relief. At last, something was happening.

CHAPTER SIXTEEN

Marco an Fallon had always been a hard man to read, which made it more surprising when his eyes shot to Samhchair first before he resumed his normal fixed mask of a face.

"How may I help you today, Seras?"

"You're holding my brother on spurious charges. You need to release him. Now," said Samhchair. Anna had never seen her so blunt but said nothing. Samhchair was speaking the words she wanted to say.

"The charges are not spurious, and the Ser will be released once his dealings are clarified," said the marshal. "A rushed departure of the Den Coille heir from Urbis raises too many questions."

"Meaning?"

This time, an Fallon glanced at the Councillor and Anna saw a slight nod. The marshal looked even more wooden than ever and made absolutely no attempt to engage Anna. That bad feeling got bigger.

"It's the Restin case."

"Yes?" said Samhchair dangerously. Anna could barely breathe.

"The Alliance Central court will impose their own sanctions, and we can do nothing about that. Of more concern is the penalty Den Coille plans to ask for in the Arcadian reparation trial."

"Go on."

This time, an Fallon did spare her a glance, his eyes lingering on her in a way that had her tensing up. "The Council has voiced concern that any move by Den Coille to hold sole control over the western mountains may upset the current fragile situation."

This time Anna had to remind herself to breathe when spots started forming in front of her eyes. *Sole control.* The den Coille family already had the dominant position in Mountainer country. She'd tried to explain so many times to Cumchdach what that felt like from the other side. "We'd never do anything to harm Mountainers," he'd kept saying. But when you were the family who got to define *harm*, it left plenty of loopholes. It was the one thing she'd always agreed on with Councillor Seilach and Fioruisghe. Den Coille and all the other corporates needed opposition and checks for Arcadia to work.

They used to, but now it was all being destroyed.

She glared at Samhchair. "Tell me, and make me believe it, that Den Coille isn't trying to steal my birth family's company."

"They're not," said Samhchair, her hands lifted as if trying to placate her, and her eyes open in horror. "We wouldn't. Da wouldn't."

"He would," said the Councillor drily, "and in this case he has little choice."

Anna swung on Sera Seilach. "It's true then?"

The Councillor nodded. "In a manner of speaking. Den Coille is demanding that a controlling share of Falasch be handed over to them to prevent any more Falasch double crosses. They also demand full entry into the Falash accounting systems to see what else is being done. The Council has suggested an alternative."

Anna waited.

"The Council is to take a controlling share and inspect the systems."

Anna felt as if hit by a falling log. "You, too, had to hide from the false Survey troops when they threw the family into prison."

No one had threatened to arrest Anna at the time, and now she knew why. She'd used that freedom to hunt everywhere for Cumchdach, her despair increasing. And it had been her sister-in-law, the Survey field agent Fioruisghe, who'd found him and his family, not Anna.

Found and rescued them, with the help of the same Commander now staring at them through a holovid and appearing to be once again about to do the Council's dirty work.

"You must be regretting your rescue of the den Coilles and Winters," she said to him bitterly.

"Never, Sera. Their executions would have been murder, and the marshals are not paid assassins, whatever it might look like."

Maybe, but the destruction of the unique culture of the mountains did appear to be their goal. "And the ordinary people of these mountains? Why should they trust you or the Councillor?"

"Are you asking as Anna ingh Eolas or Anna bean Cumchdach?" said Seilach ingh Craoch.

"As me," Anna snapped back. The Councillor nodded, as if confirming something, setting off even more alarms inside Anna. "What's going on?"

The Councillor lifted a hand as if placating her. "Your name is respected from one end of the mountains to another," she said soothingly. "Whether it be den Coille or den Falasch."

"Don't give me platitudes. If you want to use me like you're using Cumchdach, be honest about it."

"We're not," said Samhchair. "You think I would be part of anything that put my brother at risk?"

It sounded good, but Anna had been watching Marco an Fallon's face. He was hard to read but not impossible. That stiffening of his jaw said something was happening he didn't like.

Same as he hadn't liked arresting the den Coilles, but it hadn't stopped him. Not until he was handed evidence of wrongful imprisonment by Fioruisghe. Marco an Fallon followed the law, regardless of whether it hurt or not.

The Council was after a controlling share of Falasch Shipping.

She stood slowly, backing away. "I have to get back to Roo. He'll need feeding."

It was true enough that none of the others could deny it. "The marshal will accompany you," said an Fallon."

"And Sera Samhchair and the Councillor? Who will keep them safe?"

"They have ample security of their own."

"As do I," said Anna, setting her chin.

An Fallon nodded in concession, but when she turned to leave, the marshal was at her back.

"I'll come with you," said Samhchair hastily.

Anna shook her head. "You're needed here. Finish your meeting with the Councillor."

"It will be all right, Sera," said the Councillor in her quietly authoritative voice. "Trust us."

Anna nodded but said nothing, fixing a calm smile on her face. She had stopped trusting anyone the night she found Cumchdach was investigating her family and hadn't told her.

The marshal didn't leave her until she opened her own door. She nodded to him.

"I'm safe here, surely, Marshal. You must have many other duties needing your attention."

He gave her a formal Mountainer bow. "As you say, Sera."

He left, but she didn't fool herself she was unwatched. All his departure meant was that she was back under their normal surveillance.

In her room, Roo was awake and chortled at the sight of her. How he knew she was his mother she sometimes wondered, after all the changing carers in his life, but he kept his widest smiles for her. He had a special one for Cumchdach too, a quiet lift of his lips that she recognised too well. It was the one she used to see in her mirror when Cumchdach's voice announced he was home. Roo knew his father as well as she did.

She picked him up. "Come on, little one, we're going for a walk."

She left everything in her wardrobe except for the essentials and the giant pile of necessities for taking a small baby anywhere. Nothing to arouse suspicion. Then headed for her lab. When she was sure no one followed her, she switched direction to the one leading to her personal flyer.

"Sera Anna, where are you going?" said the launch pad supervisor.

"I'm taking Roo for a trip above the clouds. He needs a dose of real sunshine." It was a common enough practice, bathing a baby in real sunshine instead of the supplemented light found in most Mountainer homes. Her people may love their misty, storm-tossed home but common sense ruled that they needed more sun exposure than was given by the constantly grey skies.

The supervisor still looked at her sideways and she saw him touch his com as she lifted off.

Still, there was nothing to alarm anyone in her early flight. Not until she was above cloud height and judged enough time had passed to ease any fears did she start to head for the mountain tops, singing old melodies to Roo all the while and telling him to wait until he saw the first flowers on the *Daingas piasimo* plants, a hardy plant clinging to the rocky beds above the tree line. "They call them *impossibles* here, 'cause it should be impossible to live there, and they look so fragile, with their pretty flowers and puff ball leaves you want to pick up and cuddle." The silver-grey leaves were actually a marvellous adaption to their environment, but they were also very strokable, their soft fur and round shape better than any toy.

She set the sensors on maximum and the Den Coille flyer that had been tracking her since lift off veered to follow her. So far, it kept its distance. She began to descend, as if looking for plants.

She'd traipsed all over these rock slides many times, Cumchdach tagging behind as she catalogued each species brave enough to face the formidable challenges. Her course so far was nothing to arouse her escort. At least, not unless the marshal with Samhchair had contacted them.

Fortunately, the marshals only did that when they were forced into it by necessity.

You'd never know if the marshals were following you.

The winds cut across the bow of her flyer, trying to slam it into the mountainside.

"Don't try that with a local," she said, laughing, and turned the nose into the winds as if challenging them to do their worst. Roo lay wide-eyed in his safety capsule. "Don't worry, smunchkin, your mam has been flying these slopes since she was first legal."

So had her escort and all the tricks she tried to throw them off failed miserably. But they were from Den Coille. She was a child of the wild skies of Rubhaicreach, and she had one more trick up her sleeve. Ahead, a steep bluff poked out from the mist. She was backtracking over a slope she'd already covered, cutting her speed to hover low as if still searching for plants. Suddenly she dipped down, hugging the ground and picking up speed.

In an instant, she was accelerating up the side of the butte, activating her sensor shields, then over the lip before suddenly cutting power and twisting her flyer down into the narrow gulley at the base. Her flyer groaned in protest.

"You can do this. You were built in Rubhaicreach."

Moments later, she shot out and whooshed through the gulley, rocketing through to safety.

"Done it," she said.

She slipped under a ledge of rock and sat quietly until the flyer above had passed out of sensor range. They'd be turning back soon to find them.

Time to go.

She shot out of the small hollow, riding a roller coaster of up and down as she hugged the ground slopes to make finding her more difficult.

Roots, she'd done nothing like this since her teenage years. Cumchdach acted so staid these days, but when they were youngsters and first in gleeful charge of a flyer, they'd sneak off and challenge each other over the worst terrains in Manascraoch and Rubhaicreach. She'd once challenged Ceart and still prided herself on not losing sight of him, much to his chagrin. Mind you, he wasn't legal then. That hadn't stopped him, and even the Manascraoch patrol had learned to turn a blind eye to his jaunts.

"Keep out of the traffic areas and don't end up in hospital," a grizzled old sergeant had said wearily after catching Ceart for the third time in as many days.

Finally, she judged she was out of Den Coille security range. She shot up to the high stratosphere and set course for Urbis, throwing a grin at Roo.

"We're going to find your da, smunchkin, and no one is stopping us."

But her baby had fallen asleep. He was Cumchdach's son in this. No amount of turbulence bothered him.

She kept a check on her sensors throughout the trip, keeping high enough to set her craft to autopilot when she needed to attend to Roo's needs. No sign of Den Coille security after a distant trace at the edge of Manascraoch airspace and none of the marshals. Not that the latter meant anything. When she landed at the private flyer pad in Urbis kept by her grandmother, a squad of marshals waited for her, with an open link to Marco an Fallon.

"Welcome, Sera den Coille. You made good time," he said with that annoying professional courtesy of his.

She shoved up her chin. "I'm going to see my husband, and you can't stop me. It's allowed under the penal statutes and you always obey the law."

"As is your right," he said with that infuriating calm of his. "The Sera Samhchair has been advised of your safe arrival and destination."

That did surprise her. "Samhchair? Not Ser Bram den Coille or my grandmother?"

"She was the one you were last in contact with," he said, revealing nothing. She gave up. Samhchair was deeper than expected but the mystery of that would have to wait another day. "Take me to Cumchdach."

She was still shocked when they agreed without arguing. Then the troop leader assured her they were covered by a security shield and no outsider could detect her presence.

No outsider? Including no friendly ally, did that mean?

She activated Roo's carry cot and walked in the middle of the squad to the Marshals' flyer, hoping it was taking her to Cumchdach.

No, that was a silly fear. The marshals acted under the law, even when that law seemed idiotic. It was the one constant in this whole mess. They told you if they were arresting or detaining you.

But they would stand aside while the Council stole her company because the Council made the law. Did Cumchdach know?

He must, but talking about it in front of the marshals was no longer an option.

Relief still filled her at the sight of Marshal headquarters. Even better, after landing, they quickly hustled her through the corridors and finally to a room with a locked door.

Inside sat her husband. Her best friend, the man she loved and the father of her child. He took one look at her and swore.

"What are you doing here?"

She shoved up her chin. "I've come to have you released."

The soldiers surrounding him kept a wooden calm that terrified her more than the horror on Cumchdach's face.

"I'm not under arrest," said Cumchdach, despite the soldiers holding firm to their weapons as they surrounded him. "I'm perfectly safe. You can go." Then he drove the knife in. "I don't need you here. Take Roo and go home."

"Don't need me? Next, you'll tell me you're here as a consultant to the marshals."

A strained lift of his lips. "Something like that."

He hadn't even glanced at Roo, although she had no doubt he was aware of his son. Cumchdach always had an unnatural stillness when something mattered badly to him, and his persistent refusal to look at his son reminded her of too many past incidents.

Unfortunately for her *husband*, she was in no mood to let him ignore reality. She picked up Roo from the capsule. The movement woke him and he opened his eyes, giving her his special smile. Then he saw his da and that other smile lit up his face. His arms reached out and Anna walked up to pass him over to Cumchdach.

The soldiers shot to full attention. Both squads, the ones surrounding him and the ones surrounding her.

"Your son wants to say hello," she said.

Cumchdach lifted his hands, something like panic washing over his face. "No, take him out of here. Please."

Anna thrust the baby at him instead, and his arms automatically reached out and he cuddled his son close. Then he lifted him up and smiled back at Roo, whose fists were busily pulling at his father's face and sticking his fingers into his mouth. "Yes, it's good to see you too, bratling, but right now, Mam needs to take you out of here. I'll see you again soon, I promise." His eyes lifted to Anna's. "I promise," he added softly. "Go home. Stay home."

"But I can't. Not until whatever this is," her hands gestured at the troops, "is cleared up and you are free again. I'll never forget the last time you were taken by troops." He'd come too tragging close to being executed without her knowing anything.

That was not happening again.

Last time, it was fake troops who held him.

But it was a legitimate court that had sentenced him and his family to death.

"I'm not leaving," she said.

A bustle at the doorway had them all jumping to attention, the soldiers swinging their weapons up. Cumchdach thrust Roo back at her and pushed her behind him.

Then the soldiers relaxed, though not Cumchdach. Nor did Anna, despite it being only one man entering.

"Marshal an Fallon. Nice to see you in person," she said, pushing her way past Cumchdach, who shuffled sideways as if attempting to keep her where she was.

"Sera Anna," he said in a clipped voice and merely nodded grim-faced at Cumchdach. "As you can see, your husband is safe, and you may return to your research without concern."

"Not as I see it," she said, and glared at Cumchdach when he looked about to open his mouth. "When can my husband return to his duties."

"When he has finished what he came here for."

"What you dragged him here for, you mean."

Cumchdach did jostle her this time in a way that was so familiar she nearly called him on it. But they were no longer teenagers, and this was a far different matter than being caught out when both were supposed to be safely tucked up in their respective sleepers.

"It's fine, Anna. Take Roo to your apartment. I'll let you know when I finish here. It's nothing to worry about."

"I'll decide that when I know what *it* is. Why are you here?"

Cumchdach glanced at the marshal, then met her eyes again, his lower lip caught by his teeth in a way that had her shrivelling up inside.

"Don't," she said. "Not again. You still don't trust me enough to tell me the truth." She swung back on Marshal an Fallon. She may have found out some of it from the meeting with Councillor Seilach, but she needed to hear his confirmation. "Why is Ser Cumchdach mar Bram here and when can he be released?"

"The Ser is assisting the marshals with a security matter. He is quite safe and will be restored to his apartment in the city once we're finished." An Fallon watched her face carefully, then added, "He is not under arrest, Sera. Not this time. But you must go."

"Will it hurt Cumchdach if I refuse?"

"Yes," said Cumchdach forcefully, but an Fallon merely said, "It depends," and that she trusted more.

"On what?"

"That, I am not free to say."

"And is Ser Cumchdach here voluntarily?"

A slight twitch of his lip at that. An Fallon always had a strange sense of humour. "In a manner of speaking," he said.

Cumchdach thrust forward at that. "She has nothing to do with this. Get her and Roo out of here before someone finds out."

The words might have had her looking at him in doubt, but it was the fear in his eyes that got to her.

"What helps Cumchdach the most?" she demanded again.

"The Marshal service would be most obliged if you leave this matter to us and return to Manascraoch and your research work, Sera," an Fallon said in his unnervingly flat voice.

She turned to Cumchdach. "Can I say anything to change your mind?"

His mouth twisted, as if she'd ask him the impossible. "Just— go," he said as if finally losing patience. "This is none of your business."

Her mouth dropped open. "You're still legally my husband. You were seized, nothing voluntary about it. Den Coille security saw it," she snapped to an Fallon. "And you say it's none of my business. What is my *business*, Cumchdach mar Bram? Your son, your people, my work if it helps Den Coille." She gulped in a breath, searching that face she thought she knew so well. "But you? You're not my business?" She grasped Roo tight to her chest. "Is that how you truly feel?" She rocked Roo at his squawk, stroking his back to soothe him and tried hard to keep her voice soft. "You asked me to marry you. Asked me so many times over the years, and when I agree, you say you're not my business." She stepped back as his hand shot out to her. "Oh, no, Cumchdach mar Bram bean Anna den Coille. You do not get to choose what is and isn't *my* business." She snapped back to an Fallon. "I expect to see Ser den Coille released from custody by the end of today. I'll be at my offices in the university if anyone needs me. I'm sure your people will know how to contact me."

Then she tucked Roo back into his carrier, hating his stillness, and set it to follow her as she marched toward the door.

"I'll see you released and share custody of our son, but after this day, Cumchdach, anything else I do is none of *your* business."

Then she slammed out the door and marched down the hall, tears streaming down her face.

Cumchdach had to stand and watch her go. Her face, that was what hurt the most. The blank nothingness after she gave him that last ultimatum, as if clinging desperately to control. His Anna. He'd hurt her so badly.

"I will never forgive you for this, an Fallon."

"You will when she's still alive at the end of it."

He hated that it was true. That was the only thought that had kept him still.

She came for you.

"Make sure someone follows her and keeps her safe. Then you can tell me why you're holding me. Do you want to scare off potential contacts?" They'd had him here for nearly a day and no one had told him anything yet.

An Fallon waved at the other marshals to lower their weapons. "You were about to do something stupid. We had to stop you. This wasn't ideal, but we can make it work. How angry are you, Ser den Coille?"

"At whom?" Right now, the whole world, and those standing between him and Anna in particular. But an Fallon was up to something. "If you mean the Marshals, I haven't forgotten what you did for my family in the past, but the scales are tipping."

"And those wanting to disrupt Arcadia's compliance with the Alliance's demands?"

Cumchdach studied him, thinking about his reply. The problem was, he fully understood the reasons behind the companies' actions. They weren't all greedy profiteers. Most were simply trying to keep their companies going, like he was with Den Coille, and they didn't believe the government's threats. "Not happy with them," was all he said in the end. An Fallon was as complicated a man as any he'd met. He could work out the subtleties. "It changes nothing. I've just kicked my wife in the guts, and all you've told me over the last day is that holding me was *necessary*."

"It is," said an Fallon. Then surprised him by adding, "The entire corporate world has seen you together since you were teenagers, and why you never married until now has been a source of speculation for years."

"Tell me something I don't know."

"No, you tell me. Why did you marry Anna ingh Eolas? What changed?"

Cumchdach felt like he'd been slapped. "She said *Yes*."

"Why did she agree?"

"That's for Anna to say," he said defensively. "It's not a public guessing game."

"Only it is, and it's a legitimate one. When two important corporate figures marry and have a son, that affects the politics of your region and the future of many other companies. Why did you marry, Ser den Coille?"

Cumchdach stepped back, feeling like a cornered nieten. "I don't know. She said she wanted a baby, but I don't *know* why she agreed."

The marshal studied him, his eyes opening as if seeing something clearly at last. "That would explain it," he said. "The Sera is not getting any younger."

"She's not old." She was as beautiful as ever to him.

"She is for a woman wanting a family."

"What, you think Anna ingh Eolas den Falasch would marry me just for that. She could have anyone." Was he only a convenient sperm donor? The thought of it had him feeling sick.

"No, Ser, I don't think that, although it would be a very rational decision to make, considering the combined influence and wealth potentially inherited by your son. The Sera is not one to make a choice like that for coldly logical reasons."

Except Anna *was* a logical person. Practical and pragmatic. All an Fallon's words could apply to her. "I have to talk to her." He could hear the abject begging in his voice and didn't care. He had to see her, had to ask her if… What?

"You need to stay here, Ser Cumchdach, and cement the contacts you have already made with the suspect groups. Running off to Sera Anna now will destroy any progress you have made—or do you want your son growing up in the back streets of a second-hand space station?"

A year ago he would have told an Fallon what he thought of that; but Seolta had been home since, and had described in stark detail those back streets. The threat from the rich Alliance corporates was real, driven by millions of habitat dwellers dreaming of a perfect world to make their home. If only some fool hadn't named this world Arcadia.

It was a paradise, but only for those who respected it and were prepared to work *with* the planet. A stormy day on the mountains was no dream for any who didn't know how to survive it. But he did, and so did all Mountainers. For his people, for all the planet's people, this place was home, and home was always paradise. One Cumchdach had no intention of seeing lost or destroyed.

Goodbye, a chiad. And tears filled his heart.

"What have you in mind?" he said wearily to an Fallon.

"We called you in to question you on the reparation case Den Coille has filed against Falasch. It's believable, and you can say as little or as much as you like about what we wanted to know, depending on the situation. The Marshals will not be releasing any public statement, and you will be returned to your apartment under the same security blackout as you were brought here."

Simple enough, said an Fallon's look. Tragging roots, the marshal's idea of simple was far removed from Cumchdach's.

"And my marriage, my son's love for his father," any chance of Anna loving me, "are they just collateral damage in this battle?"

An Fallon didn't react, but Cumchdach thought he detected a slight rigidity in his jaw. Good. He had no doubt the man had been called on to swallow his pride on many occasions before, but he hoped this was one of the worst.

"Necessity," said an Fallon. "The Sera and your son will be kept safe. That is the only reward I can offer you."

It will have to do, was the firm undertone. Nor was Cumchdach naïve enough to think he was being given a choice. Not with the swift efficiency with which an Fallon had despatched Anna.

Cumchdach let his shoulders slump. "Let's get on with it."

CHAPTER SEVENTEEN

An Fallon kept his word. Cumchdach had never doubted it, but slamming the door of his apartment against the marshals who'd brought him back still felt good. He breathed in the silence, breathed in the scents and airs of a room that wasn't a prison.

Not officially, that is, but he was still watched here. Den Coille security might not be able to find their sensors, but the marshals had their own sources of technology untraceable by private security. He only hoped they watched Anna and Roo as closely, that an Fallon had kept his promise there.

He paced the room, unable to settle. He couldn't even call Anna. It was too risky. Other, unfriendly eyes watched both of them.

An eternity later, a ping on his com finally brought release. She was back in her lab in Urbis under full marshal security measures.

'Her Urbis lab?' he messaged back. 'Not Manascraoch?'

'The sera advised that she preferred to work in her Higher School lab. She would not give her reasons.'

Because they were personal, you idiots. Something had happened in Manascraoch. He put an urgent call through to his mother, but when the answer came back it was his sister Samhchair's holo materialising in his room. She sat at the desk of her home office, a place Samhchair rarely used, preferring the *poky cubicle*, as her family termed it, at the public health offices.

"Where's Mam?" Cumchdach demanded, too strung up for courtesies.

Samhchair looked as placid as ever but her hands hid behind her desk. "She's in a meeting. I said I'd take your call."

Something was wrong. His sister's answer was too pat. "Why?"

"I was the only one available."

"Samhchair, I grew up with you." He didn't imagine that slight blush washing over her cheeks. "What happened with Anna in Manascraoch? Why did she come to Urbis?"

A sudden gulp. "She told you. To free you." The jut of Samhchair's chin said that was true. It also said she didn't want to talk about something.

"What did you do?"

His sister actually squirmed and he blinked. Samhchair was never caught out. Not by him anyway. He stared at her.

Another gulp. "I took her with me to a meeting with the Councillor. It was already scheduled and I'd hoped Sera Seilach could help get you released."

"And…? He was getting a bad feeling.

"I took her on my rounds of the lower boughs first. I always do it that way when I meet the Councillor." Silence, those hands still out of sight.

"Why? She's seen the lower boughs."

"Not this part," said Samhchair, lifting her head. "I just wanted to show Anna she's needed in Manascraoch. That she is part of this city in her own right, not just as your wife."

Cumchdach felt like pulling out his hair. "When I want help solving my private life, I'll *ask* for it."

"All very well if you were better at it. Thanks to your heavy-fisted bungling, Anna bean Cumchdach no longer trusts me, or anyone in our family,"

This time, Cumchdach did pull at his hair. "I want details. Every single tragging thing you two did and said."

"We had a marshal with us."

"Of course you did. You do know I've only just been released from the custody of the marshals."

Samhchair gave him that pointed stare down her nose she'd used since they were children and she wanted to remind him she was the elder. "They are *trying* to save Arcadia, despite what some choose to think."

Cumchdach's jaw dropped. "Did you just take their side against me?"

"No," said Samhchair, looking suddenly flustered. What had his big sister been up to?

"Tell me everything," he said resignedly.

It took his sister longer than expected to regain her poise and tell him of the visit to the lower boughs. She'd mentioned their problems before but not like this. Not in this detail, or with this agony in her voice.

What she said shocked him.

"I'll get the operations team onto it," he promised at the end. "We'll get them better housed at least. Can't promise too much about when we can start restoring their lands." Samhchair nodded. She'd been at enough family dinners to understand the realities of what was involved in making the changes to the region. "Now, what about the visit sent Anna racing off to Urbis?"

"We brought in Marshal an Fallon. He said they were holding you to prevent you rushing back to Manascraoch."

"Yes, and…"

"He brought up the Restin case."

Trag it. "What did he tell her?"

"It was the Councillor. She told her the options being considered; that Den Coille takes control of Falasch, with a full inspection of their accounts, or…"

"There is no *or.*"

Samhchair shook her head. "Not according to the Councillor. The other option is that the Council takes a controlling share of Falasch."

That stopped Cumchdach. He fell into the nearest seat and stared at Samhchair. "Does Da know?"

"He hasn't said so." Not to her, that meant, and if he suspected anything, he hadn't mentioned it to Cumchdach.

But he couldn't. Not when he was surrounded by marshals. Just like Anna was when she walked into that room holding him.

Tragging roots.

"Yet the marshals let her leave Manascraoch?"

Samhchair shook her head. "She didn't tell us. She slipped through security."

"She what? Why?" Then it hit him. "That trip through the lower boughs. All that showing Anna what her role in the city could be. "She thought you'd stop her." The flush on Samhchair's cheeks confirmed it. "Anna reacts badly to being bullied, thanks to that brakka of a stepmother of hers. You *know* that." He glared at her, and Samhchair glared straight back, despite the guilty blush. "What made you think Anna deserved that kind of treatment."

"Necessity," said his sister. "Manascraoch needs her. The marshals are railroading you for a reason. Arcadia is in trouble and we have too few choices left."

Cumchdach shot up, wishing he could deny it. "I'm still here, aren't I, instead of home in Manascraoch salvaging what I can of my marriage?" And Anna was back in her lab, working on the projects wanted by the Council instead of the ones Den Coille needed.

No, that was his pride talking. Anna mattered, whether she worked on projects for Den Coille or the worst of their enemies. She was always his Anna.

He let out a huff, leaning back in his seat. "I'm still not happy with you, Sami," he said using the name he'd called her when he was too young to manage her full name. He'd been Kumma to her then, but not for long. The memory existed only as a whisper from the past, shared by none of their younger siblings. "I'll get onto the resource department first thing tomorrow to look at the problem of the Coasters."

"Thank you. I've talked to them many times, but hopefully having the *heir to everything* do it will work better." She added a small smile. The term had been a joke between them for years. Samhchair had never wanted to be part of the company, taking after their mother. But he was surprised her intervention had been so unsuccessful. She was still the eldest den Coille.

"I'll remind them who you are," he added grimly.

She waved a hand to dismiss the thought. "At least grousing at junior staff will make you feel better."

He shut off the call soon after and sat thinking on the lounger but, at the end, had nothing new. The marshals worked directly under the Council, were answerable only to the law. There had always been a hint of government involvement, but he'd assumed they meant something like the false Survey managers who had abused their position as heads of the department to chase wealth and power.

But now, there was that second option. The Council seizing Falasch.

The Council, or individual members? It would have to be in the upper house for this. Only they had the power, and maybe the sheer gall to try it.

They could change the law, and that would bind the marshals.

Would Marco an Fallon tolerate his squads being abused like that again? The man was angry enough the last time, when they'd had to arrest Cumchdach's family on trumped up charges.

Charges made possible by your actions and that of your brothers. Kidnapping their sister may have been Seolta's idea, but Cumchdach had made it happen.

They had meant it for her own good. It changed nothing.

He was getting nowhere. The law hadn't changed yet. Until the Council openly acted against Arcadia and Den Coille, he would have to continue with the marshals' plots. Would have to stay away from Anna.

If only he could talk to Da. But for that he needed a secure link, and that wasn't on offer. Not yet.

To distract himself, he pulled up the research notes Anna had posted from her trip to Deuteron. Much of it was incomprehensible, despite his general grounding in the sciences, but every figure, every word, sang with Anna's voice, her bright intelligence, and that helped.

His wife, his best friend, his only love. She had to stay safe.

He spent the next days back in the same pursuits as before. To any who asked, he said the marshals had grilled him on the Falasch case in the Alliance courts. The news was well enough known for that to be credible. His surly response to any talk of Falasch and Anna wasn't new, and he heard plenty of sneers at the stupidity of Falasch for such a clumsy fraud. From all of which he gathered that the conspirators had dropped Falasch Shipping as fast as they could. Too dangerous to know, he guessed, and thanks to that, the talk died down quickly. His angry grunts at any mention of the marshals helped as well, and he was soon safe to trawl the nightclubs and gossip mills of the city again.

The tedium and falseness of it grated more than ever. Every part of him yearned to be chasing down his wife and fixing the broken husk of their relationship. Late at night, he clung to the memory of her arriving at Marshal Headquarters.

She'd come for him.

Did it mean anything? Some nights, he could fool himself into believing it. Most nights, he took one look at his sleeper and instead pulled on another slick outfit to hit the late bars of the city, uselessly seeking anything rather than face the dark stretches of the night alone.

The marshals had better be right.

He stuck to the bars patronised by the old businesses refusing to change. The hard-liners and government complainers. The disaffected, fertile ground for conspiracies.

The bars least likely to hold friend or family.

Not once did he seek any to warm his sleeper to make the darkness disappear. He'd been with Anna so long no other could replace her. The very thought of Anna doing that had all the muscles in his body tightening in rejection.

Then one night he saw her. He was in another of the slick bars, walls lined in the latest synth panels with oily patterns churning over the walls in what he supposed was meant to create an air of seductive mystery. Certainly, enough pairs and groups formed around him as he slumped against yet another bar. This one had a person behind it at least, a large, muscular woman with eyes that had seen too much and a patter in sympathy that he was pitifully grateful for. Beside him leaned his first contact in the enemy camp,

Caltan Smierg, a man he trusted less now than he had at the start, and that hadn't been much.

"The next meeting's tomorrow night. Can we expect you?"

Cumchdach nodded brusquely. He no longer bothered with courtesies. The conspirators expected him to be angry at the world, and it was no hardship to give them exactly that. It was why they'd targeted him, and the ruder he became, the more they appeared to accept his cover.

Both parties satisfied, he decided sourly.

A spatter of laughter from the entrance caught his ear. He'd known and loved that laugh since he was a child and hadn't heard it in far too long. It came from the centre of a group milling in the doorway, chatting and cheering, all wearing the drubbed-down clothing of the Higher Schools. Graduates and Masters celebrating some academic success, from the jubilation of their voices. Then they parted a moment and he saw her, right in the middle, a smile such as she hadn't shown him for months shining on her face.

"Anna," he said before he could stop himself, transfixed by the glory of her. Then he noticed the man crowding in beside her, as if shielding her from outsiders. How dare he. He took a step from his seat before he realised what he was doing, and that beautiful joy on her face shattered.

The shock of it blasted him to a stop. He should have walked out before she saw him.

On the next stool, his companion watched him with too much interest, and all those around her glared angrily at him. Did the whole world know of his marriage problems? It was too late to suddenly turn and walk out. He had to say something to her. He forced himself to walk up to her and watched her face as he closed on her. Saw the barriers she crashed up and the blank stare in her eyes as he halted and gave her a short head bow, the least insulting one between acquaintances met unhappily.

"Sera Anna ingh Eolas an Sumhneas," he said, using her single name.

"Ser Cumchdach mar Bram an Scathach den Coille," replied Anna in as stilted a voice.

"Your team has been successful?"

She nodded, short and to the point. "A small academic breakthrough. Of no commercial value," she added with cold eyes.

So many watched them. He couldn't help his glance to the man at her side or seeing how the man pushed himself closer to Anna. *That's my wife,* he wanted to yell. Anna watched him too, and her eyes twitched up at his silence, then fell again and she stepped back. His blasted contact stepped forward then and he saw the shock in Anna's eyes.

"Everything all right, den Coille?" said Smierg.

"Yes, fine." He nodded again to both Anna and the crowd claiming her, then turned back to the man. Behind him, he heard her talking, heard her too even voice, heard the hurt hidden beneath it as she suggested to the others they try another bar.

Then she was gone and the noise in the room was again the empty clatter of the drunk and pitiless.

"Trouble with your ex-wife?"

"Not ex. Not yet," he said. But would be soon if this nightmare lasted too long. He had to work doubly hard to keep that cool smile on his face. "Still under negotiation."

Who was negotiating he failed to mention, but considering the complicated business and legal connections between Anna's family and his, the answer merely brought a knowing "Huh uh," from the other man. Cumchdach wasn't about to tell any conspirator the negotiation was between him, Anna, and the marshals. About when, if ever, he'd have a chance to win her back—and what kind of marriage they could salvage from this mess.

She wasn't his ex-wife yet. *Never* his ex-wife, if Cumchdach had his way.

He must have succeeded in keeping that from his face as the greedy glint of speculation lit the other's face. The man lifted his drink, downed the remainder, and stepped back from the bar. "Until tomorrow night then. I'll message you the meeting location."

Cumchdach managed to hide his relief at that too. "You're trusting me to get there unescorted?" he said in a dry voice as if insulted it hadn't happened sooner. Smierg lifted a shoulder but not in apology.

"Till tomorrow."

At least something was good about tonight. He wandered home, head down and shoulders hunched, and with the occasional lurch to suggest he'd been drinking a lot. When he half tripped, he pulled himself up. All right, not *as if*. He had drunk too much tonight, and probably every night for weeks.

He had good reason. But tomorrow he played with folklars in earnest. If he wanted to survive it, he'd better have a clear head. Unfortunately, sleep came no easier when he arrived home than on all the other nights. When he stopped at his usual breakfast haunt the next morning, he ordered their strongest dask, dark and with a hit that jolted his brain into the nearest possible to functioning.

Tonight he had a meeting to attend. He lurched out of the café and into the city streets. This alleyway took him straight through the fashionable area of town and into the business sector holding Den Coille's offices, without the risk of meeting up with any of the myriad of connections from his old life, the kind he really didn't want to meet this morning.

Nearly at the other end, a short dash would take him through the busy streets until he was safely hidden within the Den Coille building. Then a voice hailed him, a bare whisper but it was a voice he'd never ignore.

"Anna. What in all the roots are you doing here," he whispered at his wife as she stepped from the concealing shade of the back entrance to a shop. "Anyone could have followed you."

He gave a harried glance around. No sign of anyone following him, but she must know he was under surveillance. When she leaned out again and beckoned him urgently inside, he had to obey. She was going to get herself into trouble if he didn't.

Inside, a rubbish compacter and piled-up transporter boxes in a gloomy hallway confirmed his guess that it was the service entrance of one of the upmarket retail stores on the parallel road. He used his com to scan for sensors and to confirm the location.

Anna tugged him farther in and slapped closed his com. "I've already scanned. There's only the standard business security and this is the back entrance of Truffington's."

A name he knew well. The top-level fashion store was favoured by all the women in his family when they visited the city, and Cumchdach had spent a tidy amount of credits with them over the years in presents for Anna. Den Coille credits were more than sufficient to secure Anna privacy with whatever knot-brained story she'd told them to explain her behaviour.

"Where's Roo?" he began.

"What are you doing with the likes of Caltan Smierg?" she said at the same time.

"How do you know a man like that?"

Her lips pursed. "Don't you take that tone with me, Cumchdach duine Anna."

"I'm still your husband. I'll take any tone I like when my wife tells me she knows a brakka like Smierg."

What made him utter such a stupid insult, he had no idea. His only excuse: he was too rattled to think clearly. Her eyes turned glacial in a way he'd seen before but never fixed on him.

"How dare you. I met him, *once*, at a gathering arranged by my stepmother. I do not cavort with wermets that low in the strata, whatever my *husband* cares to imagine. Unlike him, it seems."

"Sorry," he mumbled. "He's bad, not the kind I'd want anywhere near someone I love."

"What's that supposed to mean?"

He watched her fight to regain the cool face of reason she usually showed the world. Those stupid words of his. He needed his private Anna so badly.

He went to speak again, to apologise and tell her what he felt about her, but she shook her head frantically and drew back, deeper into the shade of the inner doorway.

"I came here for a reason, and no, I was not followed by our security. They think I'm in the changing rooms trying on outfits. And it was you and Seolta who taught me how to block privacy sensors."

He had, many year ago when they first changed from friends to lovers. Privacy in either of their homes was a rare luxury and Cumchdach had finally had to resort to asking for help from Seolta, after threatening to disclose a number of Seolta's own undesirable excursions.

"What about the marshals?" was the only attack he had left.

She shrugged. "Unless it affects their plans or threatens my life, they don't interfere with me."

"This might," he said, fighting the urge to follow her into the shadowed doorway and—just hold her. He needed a tragging mess more, but could live with a touch of her skin to keep him going.

He wasn't going to get even that. She folded her arms across her chest, hands holding tight to her upper arms as if protecting herself from him.

What had he said to frighten her that badly?

"What are you and the marshals up to?" she said, her voice barely controlled but her chin up and her eyes hidden by the shadows. "And don't lie to me again. I've already heard too much of it from others. From you, I want the truth."

He had no choice after that, not if he wanted her to stay out of it. So he told her of the conspiracy meetings, in the barest of details and with a voice that almost matched the emotionless tone of hers.

At the end, her arms clutched her body tighter. "Disposable bait. That's what you are to them. Ethan Winter tried the same and it didn't work for him."

"His case wasn't as believable as mine." She stood, waiting. "He hadn't just lost the love of his life."

A choked gasp of horror. "Don't say that. Not when you're about to steal my company."

"We're not," he started to say, then had to stop, and she gave a curt nod.

"Just tell me one thing. The Council. Did you know about their claim?"

"To stop Den Coille and take a controlling share in Falasch? Not until yesterday. Samhchair told me."

She nodded, her arms squeezing her body so tight he wished he could tell her to stop before she hurt herself. "Yet you're working with the marshals."

"They haven't betrayed me, not yet. I have to hope it stays that way."

"But you're still helping them."

"I'll help anyone who keeps Arcadia safe. It's the only sure way to keep you and Roo safe."

"Arcadia, Roo. Not Den Coille?"

"Den Coille has to succeed to show the way for the other companies. We're at the forefront of the changes. Us and Winter Solaris."

"And Ethan Winter is already proving it for his company."

She sounded so defeated. What had he said wrong now. "Den Coille can too."

She heaved in a breath. "Maybe. But can you promise me that Den Coille's take over won't destroy my people? Those working for Falasch and all the others in Rubhaicreach."

Now he knew defeat. He would give this woman the moons, but he couldn't give her this. Not if she was to stay living safely on their home world. "I don't know. I can try, but Arcadia comes first. It has to."

Now she dropped her arms, flinging them out. "Why do you keep saying that? Why do you have to keep sounding like a tragging hero?"

His mouth dropped open. "I'm not."

"And what would you do to keep Roo safe?"

"Roo, and you? Anything I have to, *a chiad.* The both of you are my heart."

That brought her arms tight around her again.

He had to stop himself grabbing her. "What did I say?"

"Don't. Not that. Roo yes, but me?"

What was the problem now? "I love you. I always have. What else should I say?"

The unmistakable sound of swallowed tears. "You're already married to me. You don't need to charm me. Why would you say such a thing?" Then another choked gasp. "I have to go. *Leave me alone.*"

Then she swirled about and ran through the inner door, back into the unreal glitter of the fashion store, and all he could do was watch her leave, grief blocking his throat and coating his mind.

"I can't," he whispered after her lingering scent. "I love you, my Anna. Always have, and always will."

And what if she needed him to let her go? Could he do that?

For the first time, the reality of losing her hit him in a black wave of despair, rooting him to the spot until an annoyed robotic voice ordered him out of the entrance way. The door controls, released from whatever Anna had done, snapped the door half shut and half open as if brushing him outside.

He turned and plodded down the steps and into the alley.

CHAPTER EIGHTEEN

Anna went through the rest of the offered dress choices in a daze, holding desperately to reality.

He claimed to still love her. How could he be so cruel?

She endured all the rites of shopping and somehow exited the shop with two gowns she cordially hated and immediately passed on to her head of security.

"Get rid of them. I don't care where."

"But, Sera, they look charming on you." Her security head had a secret passion for a popular vidcast fashion show and loved nothing more than urging Anna to buy more and more. The woman had a figure honed by years of hard exercise and would look far better than Anna in fashion fripperies, but she stuck to the deep greens and utilitarian uniforms of her calling, living vicariously through Anna. "I must be ready for action," she'd explained as if it was obvious when Anna suggested she wear the stunning outfits she thrust on Anna.

"They look nothing of the sort," Anna said now and insisted again that her security lose the garments. For once, thankfully, her security obeyed her. Anna's headache was reaching astronomical levels.

Why had he said it? He was still going after her home and her family's business, whatever that might cost her. She had grown up with all those people. Didn't he know they expected her to save them?

Her heart crumbled to a soggy, pulped mess. "Get me back to my apartment, now," she whispered to her security through the spikes of pain stabbing into her head.

Once there, she shut her door on the world and shamelessly hid behind Roo for the next night and day. She was dragged out of her self-imposed isolation only by an insistent alarm from her door controls.

"Go away," she snarled at whoever dared to invade her fortress. She was dressed at least, watching Roo play happily at her feet. He was rolling and making crawling attempts with intermittent cheeky grins at her as if to say, 'Look what I can do'. If she weren't so miserable, she'd be entranced.

Or more accurately, she was in a strange state of motherly delight and feminine despair. She was so angry at Cumchdach, or at fate, or life, she didn't truly know which—too angry to shut down, but she wished she could.

Not that Roo would let her. He suddenly banged his head on the edge of a table that shouldn't be there, according to him, and yowled in pain.

The door control yelled at her again at the same time. "Go away!"

It didn't work. The control alarm ricocheted through the room, and Roo stopped his crying to stare, small eyes going wide, but whether at the strange sound from their door or his mother's vicious string of words he was definitely too young to be hearing, she didn't know. She guiltily suspected it was both. He fell silent and stared at the floor, as if scared to meet her eyes. She picked him up, softening her voice and telling him in every way she knew that everything was fine, he was safe and still loved. Would *always* be loved. Not even the now jangling and continuous door alarm stopped her words, but she glared at it and gave in.

Whoever was on the other side really wanted to talk to her. Maybe they had news of Cumchdach? No, the marshals watched him. They would keep him safe.

"I'm coming," she muttered. She slapped the door pad, automatically checking on her caller's image.

Then gasped. What in all the roots was her mother-in-law doing here? Fear had her scrabbling at the controls and kicking the door to open it quicker.

"What's happened. Is he safe?"

Not even having a daughter-in-law shriek at her shook Scathach bean Bram's eternal calm. "Your husband was safe and busy in his office when I commed him a few moments ago."

Her eyebrows quirked, and Anna hastily gestured her inside the room. Scathach held out her arms and Anna passed over Ruiseart, now gurgling cheerily with a full dose of infant charm. His grandmother was a favourite.

"So, my little man, have you been keeping your mam up too many times at night? And what is your latest trick?"

"He's beginning to crawl," said Anna to fill the silence.

"Are you now?" Scathach grinned at Anna as if her daughter-in-law wasn't perched nervously on the edge of her seat. "That can be a good thing and a bad. Den Coille babies are not known for their common sense. Mine needed frequent rescuing from all manner of places—and Cumchdach was no better than the others." Scathach dropped the grin. "He still does, I understand."

"The marshals have him under protective surveillance," said Anna.

"Surveillance, or a loose rein? Their help too often comes with hidden thorns."

Anna nodded and glanced nervously around. She wouldn't trust the marshals not to bug her apartment as well.

Scathach waved a hand. "I had our security sweep this building and your rooms before I entered. The last sensor we found was in your entrance well and we have blocked that."

"This is the marshals," said Anna.

Scathach had shared her family's imprisonment, but it didn't seem to have affected her inherent sense of self as much. Nothing would, thought Anna, not after the hard side of life the woman saw daily in her hospital.

"They are still governed by laws," said Scathach bean Bram. "Anything we say here is about the family only and not theirs to use."

Maybe, but reality lay in the interpretation of the law, and the marshals were past masters of engineering that to their advantage.

She took a deep breath. "How can I help you, Mam-Duine."

Scathach nodded and folded her hands in her lap in a way too well remembered by Anna as her mother-in-law readied for one of 'those talks'. She'd seen Cumchdach's brothers use all manner of ingenious escapes to avoid them, none of which had ever worked. She folded her own hands in her lap, sat as straight as possible and prepared herself to receive it, ignoring the small smile playing at the corner of Scathach's mouth.

"I am not your born daughter, no matter how much I respect and admire you," Anna reminded her, making the first sally.

"No," Scathach agreed, "but you are Cumchdach's pledged wife, and Cumchdach is my born son, first son of my blood. He is currently involved in plots that work against his family's interests and you are doing nothing to stop him. Why?"

Anna's jaw dropped. "Against the family. He'd never." How did Scathach come to think that?

Her mother-in-law's hands stayed still. "Den Coille needs to find new ways to make credits if we are to meet the government and Alliance demands. Instead, he is busy trawling the bars of Urbis and connecting with those companies who spend their time complaining and working against the fixes our world needs." Grey eyes filled with wisdom met and held hers. "My son has loved you since you were both children. Now you reject him, and he reacts as badly as only one who thinks he controls his world can."

"No, no, he doesn't," Anna spluttered.

One of those perfect eyebrows rose delicately. "Doesn't what?"

"Love me. Not anymore."

Scathach's jaw dropped. Anna didn't think anything could disturb the den Coille matriarch's famous calm. "What by all the roots makes you think that? You've been together since you were middle schoolers. You *married* him."

"What else should I think. This Restin case will destroy my family's heritage and my city. And he kept it from me. I *trusted* him." She didn't do that, not after her mother's death, except with Grandam and Cumchdach, and twisted away.

The silence finally forced her head back. Her mother-in-law still looked shocked. "You don't believe Cumchdach still loves you?"

"We always used to talk about our problems." Anna's head felt ready to explode. "We grew up knowing that each of us had responsibilities to our home families and cities. Ones we couldn't ignore."

"It's never been a problem before, not like this. But now it is, and you give up at the first downed branch." A hard look came into Scathach's eyes and she became Sera den Coille, not her beloved mam-duine, the woman second in her affections only to Anna's grandam. Between them, the two women had stood for her through all her troubled teenage years and through all the black days of missing her own mother. "Do you love *him*," demanded her mother-in-law in the voice of one contemplating a new and distasteful reality.

"Yes, of course."

"No '*of course*' about it. Not where I sit."

She shook her head, cheeks hot and refusing to meet those powerful eyes.

"It's complicated," Anna tried.

"No, it's not. That day you marched out on him. What did he say when you demanded to know why he kept the Restin case from you"?

"I didn't. I couldn't."

Scathach's face said it all.

"You think it sounds pathetic," said Anna.

"Tragic more like. Who do you think you are to Cumchdach?"

"The mother of his son. His—" Anna blushed scarlet. This was Cumchdach's mother.

"You've been together almost two thirds of your lives," said Scathach.

"And after so long, people can forget why they're together. Maybe he's just used to having me around and doesn't realise that's all it is for him now."

"How did you two ever conceive a son?" exclaimed Scathach in exasperation.

She blushed harder. "He does want me."

"Because you're his handy piece on the side?"

Even to Anna, that sounded ridiculous.

"That boy of mine thinks the sun shines out of you. Always has, always will," said his mother. "The real question is: what do *you* feel."

"Me—?"

"Yes, young woman. You. Thanks to that family of yours, you've got walls around you higher than anyone I've met." She flung her hands out. "None of the family knows what you feel. Many a time, I've wondered about it. And how someone who's been part of this family as long as you have still hides herself from us, I have never understood." Scathach's eyes snapped. "Or do you imagine we're like that worthless piece of excrement who calls himself your father? Tossing you aside for a greedy upstart like Gria den Falasch."

"No, no." Anna shook her head hastily. "You've always been wonderful to me."

"Nothing wonderful about it. You're family. Have been since the day you and Cumchdach set eyes on each other. You grew up with us as much as that son of mine grew up in your home city."

"I'm still den Falasch, and a daughter of den Guire and Rubhaicreach. They are in my heart as much as Manascraoch, and I can never forget that. I owe them, and they need me."

Scathach nodded her head with a smile. "Of course they do, and of course you are. Your grandfather and grandam would never tolerate less. But you are den Coille too. Your marriage made it official, but it was real many years ago. And family does not make family choose."

Except that was exactly what Cumchdach and the Den Coille company had demanded of her. Her birth family, who had betrayed her, or the second family of her heart, who never had before. Not until that day.

"He lied to me. Not outright, but he should have told me. He should have given me a choice. That's not the action of a man who loves me."

Scathach gave a harsh laugh, short and disgusted. "It was exactly the actions of a man who loves you but doesn't trust you to love him back."

"If I didn't, I'd have good reason."

"No you don't. That boy has put you first your entire life together."

"Not this time."

Scathach raised her eyebrows. "Are you sure?"

Anna felt like squirming. How did Scathach make her feel like a First Schooler again?

"He said something similar. Yet he's going ahead with his plans when he knows what it's doing to us."

Scathach waited, and Anna had to clamp her hands together to stop twisting her fingers. "He was explaining why he was meeting a brakka called Caltan Smierg in an Urbis bar. Apparently, it's fine for him to talk to a man like that, but not for me." She grimaced. "I'd met Smierg once before at one of Gria's parties. The early ones."

"The ones before your grandam explained a few facts of life to her and your father."

Anna nodded confirmation and Scathach threw up her hands. "I know I raised intelligent children. I hadn't thought they were also fools until this past year. First Seolta, now Cumchdach. Who will be next?" Her eyes snapped and her mouth tightened. "Samhchair is making a good fist of it, and that's something I never thought I'd say."

Samhchair, a fool? The wise and dependable eldest of the den Coille brood? "She's the last one to call that."

"That's what I thought too," muttered Samhchair's mother, "until she handled you so badly the other day."

Anna went bright scarlet this time. "The other day?"

Scathach nodded. "Believe it or not, she was trying to help. She said later she'd meant to shock you into action since nothing else was working."

"Action…?"

"Use the lower boughs situation to get you to rush off and demand Cumchdach do something about it. In her defence, it was a plan made on the move after you decided to follow her."

She remembered those children and the despair on their mothers' faces. "Why does he allow it?"

"Because his first priority is to make Den Coille work. There's a whole planet waiting to see what Den Coille does. If we fail, it won't only be the lower boughs in trouble."

"Isn't that his father's job?" said Anna sharply, then smacked her hand over her mouth.

Scathach grinned. "Nice to have you back, Sera Anna bean Cumchdach."

A hot tide of resentment rose up in Anna. "You said all that to make me react. None of it was true."

A grimly straight mouth replaced the grin. "No, it was all true. Despite being in love with you since he first saw you, my son is blundering headlong into something I don't think even he knows he can handle—and putting your marriage at risk in the process. And my eldest daughter is currently vacillating between mortification at her blunder and fury at what's happening to our home. It's the best thing to happen to her in years."

Anna really didn't want to explore the bit about Cumchdach. It was too raw. She fastened on Samhchair instead. "You're happy that Samhchair's unhappy?"

A slight lift of that mobile mouth, but Scathach allowed the change of subject. "Samhchair hasn't been truly happy for years, but that is her story to tell. Better to say she has been content with her lot and a strong arm for the rest of her family. Seeing that calm shaken is the best thing her father and I have seen in too long. It's time that girl got a shaking up."

Since Samhchair was older than Anna, and both had long since passed the new sapling stage of life, the word *girl* was far from fit. Except to a mother, Anna suddenly realised glancing at Roo. Even when he was old and grey and she was white-haired, he would still be her little boy. "Being a parent never ends?"

"Not the worry, nor the delight," agreed the den Coille matriarch. "In many ways, they were easier when they were Roo's age. Less complicated, certainly. Bram and I both burst out laughing when we heard how badly Samhchair had handled you with that trip into the lower boughs."

Anna leapt to her feet. "She had me rushing off to save Cumchdach. Wasn't that her plan?"

"You were going anyway."

Anna gripped her chair. "As if I would leave him locked in a cell. He's my husband."

"A woman who didn't love him might." Anna refused to answer that one. "She just hadn't thought through what came after freeing him. I gather she assumed you'd demand he return home and fix the problems in Manascraoch."

"She should have known better."

"Yes, she should. If whatever he's doing will keep you and Roo safe, nothing will make him stop until he succeeds."

"He has to," whispered Anna and covered her face. This whole bizarre conversation was too much. She felt a hand on her shoulder.

"He won't, and trying to make him will only hurt both of you. Come home, Anna. We miss you and Roo."

"I can't," she said through her hands. Then she dropped them and lifted her face to her mam-duine. "I can't, not to Cumchdach's home. He must be able to return home, and he won't. Not if I'm there."

Scathach stared at her for long moments, as if trying to see through a thick fog. Then she sighed. "You deserve each other, and I mean that in the best way." She stepped back. You will always have a home with us. Roo belongs in Manascraoch, and so do you. You have earned your place there. Come home when you can; we will be waiting."

"Where are you going?" Anna blurted out.

"Calling on the Health Ministry, meeting friends. Then a night with my graceless son."

"Please don't tell him about any of this." Scathach stood in silence, then finally nodded reluctantly. She left soon after, but Anna kept sitting on the lounger and staring at the shut door long after it closed.

Her mother-in-law was a busy woman, one who had little enough time to spare for a trip to Urbis and back. Yet she'd come, and not to see Cumchdach. She'd come to see Anna first.

She guessed that meant something.

The thought had her tossing all night and the next day, settling to work in her lab became impossible. Her assistants began to look at her sideways, to the point where even when she planted a trowel in a pot and dropped a precious and rare seedling into the tool drawer, leaving it mangled, they said nothing. She stared at the bruised remains of the plant in horror, unable to think of the smallest excuse.

"I'm useless today," she finally muttered and grabbed up her things before escaping out the door. Back in her apartment was no better. This place wasn't hers. She didn't belong here.

She had a home, one she loved, but that was barred to her as well. What she'd said to Scathach had been hard fact. She couldn't return to Manascraoch when it might stop Cumchdach going home. Courtesy was engrained in his bones, if nothing else. He would do nothing to upset her.

It was up to her to bridge the gap.

Not yet, her heart whispered. *Coward,* said her head.

She had only one other place to go. She put a call through to marshal headquarters and this time, it was routed directly through to Marco an Fallon's com.

"I have some work here to finish up, then I'm going back to Rubhaicreach," she said. "Can you make it safe for Roo?"

"That would not be our recommendation, Sera," he said in that immeasurably calm voice of his. Did nothing ever unsettle the tragging man? "But if that is what you wish, I will notify your security squad and the assigned marshals. A flyer will collect you when you are ready to leave."

"I have my own," she tried.

"The marshals' one is safer. And to be doubly sure, it will have no identifying markings to alert any troublesome element in Rubhaicreach."

"You're not going to try to make me change my mind? Stay here and keep working on my projects?"

"That would be a more useful option for Arcadia, but this is still a free planet, and the marshals uphold the law. Forcing you to keep working here would only hinder your studies."

She suspected it was the last reason that decided him, but he stopped her challenging him on it by signing out.

"Typical," she huffed.

Cumchdach received the location of the evening's meeting and set out. He probably should feel triumphant, another step gained in his mission. All he could think of, though, was Anna's face as she'd left him.

Half a lifetime together, and he didn't know how to talk to her. How to make her believe him.

The location tonight was through the back door of a major finance house and into their main chamber. How hadn't the marshals tracked down a group so unwilling to sacrifice pride and comfort?

Then he entered the room and understood. He hastily shoved down all thoughts of Anna as everything in him went on high alert. Tonight, identities weren't as well hidden. That didn't mean they trusted him. His own avatar wasn't fooling their com systems either. He needed his wits at full strength against the predators in this room. They included the Finance Officer and three senior executives of one of the top banking houses on the planet. Not a bank Den Coille used. Some of their practices were a shade on the sharp side for the family, but plenty of others used them. As for the rest of the room, he didn't see any corporate heads but recognised plenty of the others, and their behaviours gave away the rest. All came from the senior ranks of major Arcadian corporations asked to modify their business models.

All feeling the pinch unless they discovered a new way of making credits.

"Sers, Seras," he said, taking his seat and keeping his face as neutral as he could make it.

The Finance officer called the room to attention and began the meeting. Cumchdach soon concluded that the man, or his bank, were running this particular group. Whether they were in charge of the whole conspiracy, though, he couldn't say.

The big question of course was how many such cells existed. Did this room represent the resistance to change in Urbis only, or was it the centre of the whole group.

Not likely without the involvement of the corporate heads, although he suspected the bosses attended few meetings. They'd know they were under scrutiny. Nor did he dare scan the room to find if any corporate heads were following by com link.

Why had Anna looked so tense. She'd always told him everything.

Hadn't she?

"Ser. Your thoughts?"

Tragging roots. What was he doing drifting off in the middle of this pit of brakkas?

"On profitability," prompted the other man.

Cumchdach hastily pulled back into his game mode. He gave a scowl to stop any questions, but none would have to work hard to know what—or who—distracted him. An Fallon would be happy at least.

"I'm not about to pass out our private financials," he said.

"Your company is doing fine then?" said the man at the head of the table.

"Up and down," said Cumchdach in his coolest voice. "Much as anyone in these changing times."

A general mutter rippled around the room, but Cumchdach felt the relaxation as well. He'd just confirmed that Den Coille was at risk, like all the rest here.

"I had Council auditors around last week," said a woman near the middle of the table. "They actually want us to cut production. No word of compensation."

A harsh laugh answered that. Of course there wasn't. The real reason, Cumchdach suspected, was that the government didn't have the funds. Not when they had to finance the planet-wide work demanded by the Alliance.

"Lawyers and scientists. An expensive bunch," he commented. "Not sure which are the worst."

"That Survey sure seems to have enough credits. Always sticking their nose in where they're not wanted."

Another man grumbled. "And that was before they *saved the world*, according to them. They're unstoppable now."

Cumchdach felt the expectant looks falling on him and kept his face closed tight. The Survey field staff had saved his and his family's lives. He wasn't about to bad mouth them, even to help an Fallon.

"Change isn't always a bad thing," he said instead. "Not if it creates opportunities." He gave a disgruntled frown. "The trick is to find those opportunities and exploit them before you go under."

A few heads nodded. The banker stared at him as if trying to work out a puzzle.

"Companies with sufficient muscle can always get the government to be flexible and give them extra time to comply."

"You'd think so," said Cumchdach sourly.

"Our lines of influence do seem to have been damaged," said a woman near him. "They must be restored, or new ones created."

"Exactly," said the man at the head of the table. The hairs on Cumchdach's neck lifted.

"What are you suggesting, Ser?" he said as the man continued to stare at him.

"Your company is currently involved in a legal dispute with another."

Cumchdach nodded, waiting to hear where this was going.

"Any chance of that being dropped."

Cumchdach used his coldest voice, the one he kept for enemies, and held the man's eyes as he brought the names into the open. "Den Coille does not tolerate false dealings. No company can allow what Falasch did to us."

Then he waited, as did the man at the head of the table. How many here were linked to Falasch?

He pushed out his chair. "If this whole thing's a set up to stop us going after them, I have more important matters to deal with." He began to rise.

The banker was good, he'd give him that. He waited until Cumchdach was fully out of his chair and ready to walk before he spoke.

"No one expects a well run company to tolerate a threat. Not any company strong enough to be respected."

Silence fell on the rest of the room. They might not be Falasch associates, but enough in the room must be dependent on this man's bank for funding.

Cumchdach stopped. "So why am I here? I thought it was a meeting of like-minded individuals concerned with the current changes being forced on Arcadia. My company's product is highly sought after as a valued nutrient throughout the Alliance. If Den Coille is hurt, many others from Arcadia and the wider Alliance will pay a price." He stared at the man at the top, ignoring the rest in the room. "Or was I mistaken?"

The smile that slid across the man's face set off every alarm in his body.

"No, Ser, you were not. But Den Coille has appeared to support the Council."

Cumchdach shrugged. "A successful business must know when to be flexible or rigid. As I said, change brings opportunities, and Den Coille is concerned about whom those opportunities most benefit. We prefer to control our own destiny."

The man's eyes were cold, evaluating him, and Cumchdach held his eyes in the long moment that followed. Finally, a rap of the man's hands on the desk.

"That will be all for today, Sers. You will be advised of the place and time of the next meeting."

The banker rose. "Thank you, Ser den Coille, for your input."

The others began to file out, with the occasional backward glance. Cumchdach stayed, playing a hunch. When the door closed on the last, the banker leaned forward and placed his hands on the table. "There is a meeting of the coordinating committee coming up. Can I send you word of it?"

There wasn't a hint of supplication in the man's voice, but Cumchdach picked up his tone of celebration, as of a fisherman successfully landing his catch. He shot his shoulders back.

"Send me word and I will consider whether to attend." He gave a short bow, the cool half bow to business associates you didn't trust. "Thank you for your time, Ser."

Then he swung around and marched out before his stomach completely revolted and betrayed him.

An Fallon waited in the agreed meeting place, a bush-surrounded pathway in a small park near his apartment. Cumchdach didn't bother asking the man if he thought it a risk. It was a common enough short cut from the local retailers to his apartment, and the marshals' surveillance was second to none.

He still contemplated asking the question. Just once, he'd like to unsettle one person other than himself in this whole filthy business.

The marshal wasted no time in trivialities. "You think this committee is the top of the tree?"

"I won't know until the meeting."

"But…"

"There's a good chance," conceded Cumchdach. "A bank would fit. They stand to lose big if too many clients are hurt by the current policy changes. They're also stacked with some of the best strategy brains on the planet."

"The kind good enough to fool us?" The marshals had been trying to break open this conspiracy for a long time.

"Exactly." As far as he could tell, the leaders had also kept their identity hidden from the other conspirators. "Their security is as tight as they come."

"Which begs the question—why are they letting you in?"

Cumchdach waved that off.

"The value of the prize is too big to ignore. They lost Solaris thanks to Ethan. They need a mid-Protos company to replace it, and having one of the two targeted by the Survey supports their propaganda. Look what the government did to Den Coille; what will they do to you?"

An Fallon paced. Cumchdach had thought hard about this. It was better than any of the alternatives.

"They want Den Coille badly," he added.

"You're not your brother."

Cumchdach didn't pretend not to know who he was talking about. "Means they won't be expecting a double cross. Seolta was born hiding intrigues but my life has been an open book for years. I deal straight."

"*No one* in your family is an open book, and anyone who thinks otherwise deserves what they get."

Cumchdach looked at him in surprise.

"A blandly genial face is not an open face, Ser den Coille."

Cumchdach shrugged. "That's simply good manners."

"And what happens to the eldest brother in a large family. I would trust you and Samhchair with my life, but I'd never believe you were telling me all of the truth. Either of you," he added darkly.

Cumchdach didn't quite know what to say to that. "Thank you, I think."

"You gave your word and pledged to help us in order to protect your wife and child, despite what it's doing to your marriage. Reading character is a necessity for a marshal. We die if we make mistakes."

Cumchdach shifted uncomfortably. "And the rest of my family?" Defending them was second nature to him.

"Hurt one, hurt all?"

He scowled at their old schoolyard motto, but it still held true. Strong-minded, all of them, and from the wealthiest family in Manascraoch, they'd grown up targets for bullies and learned early to nip it in the bud. "Ceart's solid and Aigherach is still a baby."

An Fallon eased back against a nearby bench. "Your middle brother is as transparent as a muddy bog. The man's a born intelligence agent."

Cumchdach snapped upright and took a step forward. "Leave him alone. He doesn't need you plunging him into danger."

An Fallon lifted his eyebrows and went on. "As for Aigherach, your baby brother hasn't been a little boy for a long time. Not since prison."

Cumchdach couldn't deny that one. "He still deserves the chance to decide what he wants of life."

An Fallon, surprisingly, nodded. "He's more than earned it."

The shock hit. "How much of what went on inside that prison do the marshals know about?"

"Not enough. The false Survey leaders ran it under direct orders from the Justice Ministry."

"And did they know?"

"The audit of all ministries is still ongoing. You would have to discuss it with your Council representatives."

The slippery Coinneas mar Coille duine Falamh den Cleireach, Representative for the Mountainer Region, or Councillor Seilach ingh Craobh, who would demand a point by point, exhaustive analysis of justifications before letting out any information. He'd never decided which was more useful, a conniving Yes-man like the Representative or a stubborn independent like the Councillor. Neither would help this time. He grunted his disgust. "Thanks for nothing."

"Your brother's off-planet associates didn't work alone, but the marshals cannot act without proof."

Cumchdach kicked at the ground, easing back from an Fallon. "Hopefully this meeting helps, and the names. They're not guesses this time. Can you check out the linkages to Gria den Falasch?" He saw an Fallon note the lack of the polite form and didn't care. Anna's stepmother had long since lost Cumchdach's respect.

"My people will be on it immediately."

"Check out her family's banking and commercial linkages," added Cumchdach. "Follow the credits, as Da always preaches to us."

An Fallon nodded curtly, and stood up. "Send us a report on this committee meeting. No contact until then. It's becoming too risky."

"And Anna?" Cumchdach had to ask as the man was about to leave. "Is she safe?"

The marshal stopped, a slight twist marring his mouth. "She is, Ser, and under full marshal watch."

"Why? What's happened?"

"The Sera, your wife, has decided to return to Rubhaicreach. Apparently, your mother visited her."

Cumchdach nodded, barely comprehending. "Mam's at our apartment. She arrived as I was about to leave for the meeting so I couldn't talk. What's Mam got to do with this?"

"You mother's advice is usually impeccable."

Cumchdach's brain raced. "She wouldn't push Anna away."

"Quite the opposite it seems. She tried to persuade her to return to Manascraoch."

A good plan. Having Anna and Roo safely ensconced in their home in the family tree was the safest place Cumchdach knew for them. There might be traitors in the city but, last he heard, Den Coille security had a solid lead on them.

"It seems your wife decided against it. In case it stopped you coming home," the marshal added at Cumchdach's indrawn breath.

Why would Anna think that?

"The Sera apparently felt that it was no longer possible for you two to share an apartment," an Fallon added delicately.

"Oh."

Cumchdach fell back into the bench behind him. Worse still was the look of sympathy on the marshal's face.

"She will be safe. Rubhaicreach is her home, Ser den Coille."

"Home, but not safe," snapped back Cumchdach.

"She is safe, now and wherever she goes," reiterated an Fallon. "That is my pledge," The marshals always kept their pledges.

"You'd better," growled Cumchdach.

"Until your report of the committee meeting," prompted an Fallon.

Cumchdach glared at him.

"Yes." He'd made a promise too. "I'll be there," he added. "Keep her safe."

With that, he swung around and marched up the path.

Keep her safe.

CHAPTER NINETEEN

Nothing had changed by the next morning, and the cheerful voice of his mother at the breakfast table only highlighted that. Especially when she mentioned her visit to Anna before coming to the apartment last night.

"What did you say to her?" His mother had a bad habit of poking her nose into any family dispute. That she usually ended up solving them made no difference, not today, not after an Fallon's report. "Did you upset her?"

His mother gave him that affronted look he was sure she practiced in her mirror. "How long have I known you, Cumchdach mar Bran an Scathach?"

"Since before I was born," he parroted back to her. "And you've known Anna nearly as long," he added before she could get that bit in as well. "This is different."

"From the time you accidentally shoved her into that mud puddle and she thought you'd done it deliberately?"

"We were sixteen then." And after Anna had calmed down, she'd actually listened to his apology. Or maybe it was his frantically running his hands over her to make sure he hadn't hurt her. He'd ended up as muddy as she was. "Not the same thing."

"How so?"

"It just isn't," he said stupidly.

"Oh, yes, you're right. You hadn't *lied* to her then."

"I didn't this time either." He could feel his shoulders hunching in defence, even as his mother's eyes went crystalline grey.

"What do you call not telling her about the Restin case? Not warning her she was about to be caught slap bang in the middle of a major legal battle between her father and her husband's company?"

"She was sick," he tried.

"Morning sickness is not a terminal illness, despite feeling like it."

Cumchdach jumped up from the table. "She was miserable!"

"And you were terrified," his mother said gently, all fire gone from her eyes. She reached out a hand and Cumchdach grabbed at it, feeling the worn lines and the traces of long hours of work pressing into his, telling him that she still stood for him. "You were also an idiot," she added in a soft voice, "and still are. What was that meeting you went to last night?"

He shook his head. "I can't talk about it. I promised, Mam."

She looked sadly at him. "And if you lose your marriage?"

"My family will be safe."

That brought a look of sheer grief to her face. His mother left for home soon after, and Cumchdach felt the weight of it as she touched him on the shoulder. "You're not alone in this, *mo leanadh*."

Then the door closed on her and she was gone.

That night, another call came through on his door panel and Cumchdach tensed. Then looked through the scanner and opened it hurriedly.

"Ester, what are you doing here." He was so glad to see the middle Winter brother he forgot all about the marshals, dragging Ethan in the door and lapsing into the old names they'd fallen into using in prison. The ones they used only in private and when they needed badly to talk to each other.

Then Cumchdach remembered the marshals. He stiffened and Ethan scowled. "No need for that."

Cumchdach shook his head frantically, looking pointedly at the ceiling, though in truth had had no idea where the marshals had hidden their scanners. Ethan rolled his eyes as he lifted his com. Cumchdach slapped a hand over it, but Ethan shook him off.

"Si's as good as the marshals' any day. We've got this covered."

Ethan's younger brother, Silas Winter, was a genius in com systems and possessed a decidedly sneaky streak, but the marshals had access to a whole different level of technology. He slapped his hand back over Ethan's com.

"They'd be rushing in the door right now if they'd broken through Si's block," Ethan said. Cumchdach shook his head, not convinced. "We've got this, Cumber."

"And what do I tell the marshals when they get here?"

"The truth. That not even they have the right to confidential company discussions without presenting a warrant."

"They'll be filing for one as we speak."

Ethan gave a grim smile. "Giving us a good hour. Your family want to talk to you, without their interference."

He walked over to the lounger and plopped down, bringing up a com screen as he did so and setting another sliver down on the table.

"A burner?" asked Cumchdach.

"No one trusts that com of yours. Not if the marshals have been getting their tentacles into it."

A shard of hope lit him. He'd never been cut off from family before, not like this. He sat beside Ethan and picked up the burner com. Moments later, his family's holo images filled the room and it was almost like being back with them.

Almost. But that was still a whole lot better than nothing.

"Cumchdach, what have the marshals done to you?" His father had an ambivalent view of Marco an Fallon and the planet's top police agency. They'd hurt den Coilles as often as they'd helped them, and the marshals always had their own agenda.

"Nothing I can't handle, Da." Or he hoped so, at any rate. "But you need to have our defences on full. I got your message about the security leaks. Do you have them all locked up?"

"The ones we identified. But security have never assumed every Mountainer is on our side, or even halfway to agreeing with us. They're running on the maximum risk protocols."

That relieved some of his worry, but not all. "Have you talked to Councillor den Bunachan recently."

A line gouged his father's forehead and an uneasy stillness fell over the rest of the family. He nodded. "The Council are playing a dangerous game. Our lawyers have been notified of the situation. The Councillor is working with the marshals, she tells me."

"The situation is under control then," said Cumchdach.

"As much as we can hope for," his father agreed, shifting in his chair and bringing his hand flat down on the table.

The subject was closed, that meant. Nor was Cumchdach about to argue, not when Da refused to talk more openly in front of the rest of the family. He can't have told them all yet.

A wise precaution. The courts would find against Falasch, and word was that the Alliance Council would demand a sanction against Falasch, one that stopped them causing more problems. As for the Arcadian Council, they were a threat only at this stage. One he would not forget, and nor would his father. But it increased the risks to his family.

"Maximum security for everyone, then." He looked around at his siblings with the habit of a lifetime. "Make sure you follow it, all of you."

A crack of laughter from Fee. "You're a fine one to talk, big brother."

He glowered at her. "I am not going to apologise for once trying to get you to see sense."

Her eyes glinted in warning. "For kidnapping me, brother."

Thankfully, her husband jostled her side and she subsided. He'd never get used to that, or the way his baby sister leaned into the tall plainsman with that silly smile on her face. Not when his own love flinched away from him.

"Children," put in his mother and they all sat to attention.

"We can't hold this link secure for long," added Ethan, and his family suddenly all sat up. He tensed, waiting.

"Reports," ordered Da, looking at Ceart first, to Cumchdach's surprise. His brother didn't look happy either, leaning back to speak in his usual clipped style. "The leader. He's invisible. Nothing at all about who he is. The conspirators don't know either."

Fioruisghe thrust her nose forward. "How do you know that?"

Cumchdach had the same thought, dread thumping his heart. It might match what the marshals said, but how did Ceart know it? Nor did Ceart's reply help.

"Seolta's networks. He's linked me in. I'm a good listener," he added with squared shoulders, as if waiting to be shut down. Guilt hit Cumchdach.

"You don't need to go putting yourself in—" began Samhchair. Cumchdach quickly pinged her, and her sideways glance said her father had leaned on her foot as well. He'd done that to Cumchdach enough times in meetings when he was about to say the wrong thing.

"Well done, son. Where did the info come from?"

"The clubs. I'm easy to overlook. And Seolta's contacts have been digging." Da nodded for him to continue and Ceart straightened. "None of them can find a name, or anyone who knows a name. Strange though. They all trust whoever it is. Single-minded and highly intelligent, is what they say."

Da grunted in acceptance. "Have to be, to stay hidden this long. Nothing at all on the identity?"

Ceart shook his head. "Only that he's not from the business world. Nor has he ever used intel against any of the conspirators' businesses. Whoever it is, they're keeping their hands squeaky clean."

"Unlike us, I suppose, thanks to that Restin case. They've got to wonder how many other companies we've got in our sights."

Ceart nodded. "Yes."

A scowl washed over Da's face, and Cumchdach felt the same. Den Coille had no choice in what they did about the Restin fraud. Not if they wanted to survive. "Falasch is a good business. Even if we take it over, it doesn't have to go under. That hurts us and too many others."

"Your wife too," said their father. Did he think Cumchdach wasn't all too aware of that. "We need her back here."

"You forget, Anna walked out on me when she found out about the Restin case."

"Told you to tell her," said Fioruisghe. "Now, if only you can get your head in place and apologise properly.

"It's more complicated—"

Samhchair didn't let him finish. "Anna is not the vindictive type. She still works with the Survey, I understand."

Fioruisghe nodded. "She, Joseph and Fridha have their heads together to better map the festia reproductive cycle. Joseph and Fridha have been raving at me about her *unique insights*. Apparently, Anna has some new ideas, despite all Den Coille's work over generations. She 'puts stuff together', is the sum of what they say."

The Survey botanist and zoologist were good, but Cumchdach wasn't surprised Anna still managed to find a new angle. There was a reason the Council were keeping tabs on her. He just wished they would stop looking at her as a resource; she was Anna, not a thing!

"Roo comes first," he reminded his family, more sharply than was wise from the way his sisters and mam stared at him. "It's what Anna wants too," he added wishing he didn't sound so defensive.

"She's a good mother. She can handle it," said Scathach. Cumchdach subsided. He knew when his mother was scolding him. She'd brought up five children while running a hospital department, and none of them had any grounds for complaint.

But Mam had always had Da and the rest of the family behind her. Who did Anna have? He knew she could handle it all; didn't mean it was right to make her.

"She shouldn't *have* to deal with all this stuff," he said.

"Her medical staff are watching her and Roo." Mam's voice had softened. "And she has her Grandam, this family, and those den Falasches not yet lost to idiocy."

Maybe. But her father also had other children. One old enough to start in the business, he suddenly remembered. "Aigherach, what's the word on Anton den Falasch?"

His baby brother's cheeks flushed at being called on and Mam went to rise. Da's hand held her in place as Aigherach coughed then leaned back too obviously.

"Won't talk about his family. Otherwise, he's liked. Someone you can trust to stand at your back, is the talk. Stiffens up any time his family is mentioned though."

"Mmm."

Da lifted an eyebrow in query at Cumchdach.

"An Fallon mentioned that Anna has met up with her brother a couple of times. The marshal says they don't have anything on him, not directly. But he's still Gria's son."

"And Driach mar Ramach duine Deana den Falasch's grandson," said his father, suddenly leaning forward. "His word was solid gold. He'd take a promise to his grave."

Mmm. That matched the other rumour the marshals had heard. That Anton was becoming known as Anton ghar Driach instead of mar Eolas.

"You think he might be trying to cut out Anna and Roo?" asked Da.

"He can't. Not without Anna's agreement and the Falasch board's approval." But it would solve one major problem. He drew in a breath. "And the penalty for Falasch?"

"We have to go for control, son. You know it."

He did. "There is more than one kind of penalty. The courts?"

"Will give us a full takeover if we ask for it," confirmed his father. "Our lawyers have sounded out the board." Falasch's actions threatened the stability of Arcadia's export earnings. Festin was a massive earner for Den Coille, and for the planet. Only the Urbis estuarine farm produce earned more in off-planet credits.

"Can we at least make it conditional? Put a final term on it?"

"And cede the company to Anton mar Eolas under our supervision until he's ready, you mean?"

Cumchdach nodded. It would solve his problems. Anna had too many calls on her as it was. "But only if it's what Anna wants," he added. She already thought he was trying to steal Falasch from her. Telling her what to do with the business was the surest nail in the coffin of his hopes. "They are her people, her city. She is the best judge of what will work for them."

"We'll consider it," was the best his father could promise.

The support from his family helped, but didn't change what he must do. Cumchdach was busy enough during the day, keeping up his Den Coille work, helping his father work out what to do about Falasch when they won the Restin fraud cases, and hassling Den Coille security to make sure Anna and Roo were protected. He also followed up on the Coasters in the lower boughs for Samhchair, but the options were pitifully few in the short term. Not when they had no other home to go to. He put their strategy team onto it, hoping someone could find a way through.

But the conspirators were never far from his mind. Then the call he'd been waiting for came through.

That night, Cumchdach sat a table filled with the kind of business predators he'd spent a lifetime avoiding. The banker from the last meeting was here, but this time he sat next to Cumchdach near the bottom of the table. Ranged alongside him sat the head of the man's bank; an official from the Justice Ministry; and another from the Trades Ministry, the junior and much maligned partner to the Galactic Ministry—the Ministry charged with mopping up the fallout in trading arrangements from the Falasch disaster.

On the other side of the table sat the head of an Urbis export business, which also happened to be Falasch's major competitor, although not as well connected in Den Coille's estimation; the head of the planet's Corporate Association, a lobbying group to which most major planetary corporates belonged, including Den Coille;

the head of another bank, one avoided by Den Coille; and a senior executive from one of the leading vidcast companies known best for providing highly sensationalised news reports backed by a minimal level of fact-checking. A gossip mill, in other words.

The chair at the head of the table sat empty. Nor was there much chatter around the table. Trust was in short supply, the group united by one thing only. The greed for power stank the place out. He fixed on his coolest business face and upped the blocking on all his com interfaces.

A holo appeared at the head of the table. A faceless avatar using a generic headshot, the non-differentiated kind used when the sender wanted to stay anonymous. The voice was equally robotic.

"The Senior will be unable to make today's meeting and expresses apologies but will follow by com. Please continue, Sers and Seras. You have all been sent the agenda."

A ping on his com and a list appeared on Cumchdach's com screen. Top of the order: introduction of new member, Den Coille.

Actually, it was the only item on his agenda. There were other, numbered entries but all the contents were blank on his version. He was still being evaluated, he guessed that meant. A wise move on their part. Roots knew Cumchdach had no desire to be here.

"What can I tell you, sers?" he said after the introduction. His first contact, the banking executive Smierg, was the only one to show any warmth in his welcome, which simply meant the man wanted something. The rest stayed cool. They were all taking a risk in revealing themselves and their dark glances said they knew it.

The only ones unknown to him were the Justice and Trade Ministry officials. Their titles might sound impressive, but they were very much from the middle ranks. Frustrated at failing to gain promotion or overly ambitious? He couldn't decide yet.

After that, the talk drifted to general financial matters. Seemingly innocuous, but Cumchdach had attended enough corporate gatherings to be wary of social chitchat. This was an interrogation, and he must not forget it. Within a few exchanges, the room had established his financial wellbeing, his views on the risks brought to that financial ease by the current government actions, whether he supported the government, and to what extent he'd be prepared to act against Den Coille's current positions.

Nothing that would endanger his family; none that would make Den Coille poorer.

Did they believe him? He was used to covering his real feelings in a business dealings, used to putting forward a negotiating position rather than raw truth, but so was everyone here. No banker, in particular, would survive long if they accepted at face value what their clients told them. They'd be broke in a year.

"What can you do for us? That is the fundamental question at issue," said a robotic voice from the chair at the head. The leader, Cumchdach had to assume from the lack of surprise from the others.

Cumchdach put on his most rigid face. "What is it you want me to do?" he said, his whole body alert.

There was silence for a moment, and that contained look in the others' eyes told Cumchdach another discussion was raging all around him.

Then the robotic voice answered him. "Nothing that will damage your company or make your family too suspicious."

"I cannot halt the Falasch case," Cumchdach said, with no hint of apology in his voice. "The company attacked our profit line. We do not tolerate that."

"Nor do we tolerate fools," said the other voice. "Falasch acted on their own. We do not risk exposure to save such." A warning and a reassurance in one.

"Thank you. and noted," said Cumchdach.

"You will be advised of the assistance that most benefits all of us," said the voice again. "A courier is waiting outside to escort you back to your apartment.

He was dismissed. Cumchdach rose, bowed to the room, then a deeper one to the empty chair at the head. He walked out and found a man waiting for him. Large, muscled, and with that withdrawn look of the best of security people. The look that said he might die for you but wasn't about to treat you as other than an object to be protected.

No chat allowed, said that look. Mouth firmly shut, Cumchdach glanced at the man, then walked where the pointing arm ordered. A confusing time and numerous detours later, he was back in his apartment. When an Fallon contacted him, he told him the location of the meeting but wasn't surprised when the marshals found no sign of anything. His guide had given the others plenty of time to get away with his tortuous route.

"I hope you were discreet," he said grumpily. The marshals weren't the only ones watching him.

"We're not fools, Ser den Coille," said the Commander.

"Maybe, but these conspirators have stayed hidden from you up until now."

Was that a trace of irritation on an Fallon's face? Yes, a definite twitch, quickly controlled. Good. If he had to stick his head out and deal with a pack of greedy, short-sighted wermets and betray everything his family stood for, an Fallon could squirm too.

"We are using the latest in our surveillance systems," said an Fallon.

"Let's hope they don't have similar," Cumchdach shot back.

"If they do, we will track the leak, and that will help too."

They were in a quiet back corner of a busy store and were using a personal link to cut out any chance of being overheard while both browsed the shelves with heads down.

"Send word as soon as they notify you of the next meeting."

"There's one more item." This one Cumchdach liked the least. "Smierg wants me to attend a reception for the capital banking fraternity. If I do, it's like making a public declaration that Den Coille is reconsidering its current banking arrangements. We don't need that."

An Fallon frowned. "An unusual request. The man must realise that will bring public attention onto you. What's he up to?" He was silent a moment. "Nothing for it. You'll have to attend."

"Check that guest list for me. If our own bank isn't going, nor am I."

An Fallon grimaced, but there was no choice. The marshal switched to his private channel then came back. "It will be arranged."

"And Anna?" Cumchdach had to add before the marshal broke their link.

"She leaves for Rubhaicreach in a few days. We have people in place there, and she will travel in a marshal shuttle. She is safe, Ser, and fully protected. As is your son."

Cumchdach thanked him but made no apology. Not even Anna's cursed stepmother should be stupid enough to try to hurt them again, but he still hated Anna going back to that nest of wermets.

The night of the reception, Cumchdach paced his apartment, cursing the whole affair. He loved the gatherings in Manascraoch, filled with family, friends, and laughter. He'd even enjoyed the social extravaganza that was his and Anna's wedding. But this kind of occasion was his worst nightmare. A minefield of manners, closely watched all the time by most in the room. It was days like this he wished he was born at the tail end of his family, instead of sharing Samhchair's leadership as the eldest. Samhchair handled it with ease no matter what life threw at her.

Like the way she botched handling Anna?

A rare mistake. He couldn't regret Anna rushing up to save him, but he did her precipitate retreat to Rubhaicreach. She and Roo belonged at home in Manascraoch.

The door gave a signal just before a man opened it.

"Your skimmer, Ser."

The man was no chauffeur, not with that unmistakable air of a trained security agent, but Cumchdach nodded curtly to retain the illusion. His scanner drew a blank on weapons on the man, but he hadn't expected to detect one either. Not on a marshal. No amount of deference hid the man's alertness. Den Coille was known to pay for top level security. He'd have to hope the guests at the reception assumed the man was one of theirs.

He'd needn't have worried. Security was rife at the reception, many of the guests with hulking figures mirroring their steps and more spread through the crowd at the side tables. Bankers were a singularly untrusting bunch, it seemed. He'd been to many receptions in Urbis, but security wasn't usually so visible. Too much was going on, and Urbis was becoming nervous.

The crowd included the senior staff of all the important banks, as well as a rich helping of highly valued clients. The credit balances attached to this guest list must leave their finance hosts slobbering in anticipation. He met up with the Den Coille bank's representatives shortly after arriving, putting on his most genial air to reassure the dismay on their faces. He had probably received a form invitation to the gathering, but members of the family rarely attended such occasions. They didn't need to advertise their wealth and were satisfied with their bankers.

Unlike others here. The frenetic desperation hidden on too many faces only confirmed what he'd suspected. The evening may be touted as the annual celebration of the banking profession; it was also a trading market. Banks touted for new business and clients assessed the opposition. It was why his family rarely attended such nights. Den Coille's wealth and financial arrangements were the company's affair, not the rest of the banking world's.

The same was true for all the stable corporates, or those without problems. The interesting thing about the evening was the number of guests here from corporates he would have thought as stable as Den Coille.

Or as Den Coille touted itself as being. Until the eldest son of the family turned up at this predators' gala.

He broke off from his bankers and began to circulate, watching the interactions in the room. There was also a different kind of guest here tonight, he soon realised. Political back-room types, the policy and polling managers, quietly talking and making connections. No politicians. Too blatant a sign of concern, he guessed. But their minions filtered through the room and inserted themselves into multiple conversations.

Before he could delve into what was going on, Smierg hustled up and he had to pretend pleasure at the man's company. A woman also hurried up beside him, much younger than the banker. Then he saw the colour of her eyes and the beak of the older man's nose. It didn't take Smierg's introduction to confirm the young woman was the man's daughter.

So that was the reason for his invitation. Smierg was looking to the future and saw an opportunity.

The man had decided his daughter would be Cumchdach's next wife.

Cumchdach had to fight not to show his fury. That any man should think this over-decorated woman could replace Anna…

But he needed Smierg for now and had to endure a dance with the woman. Every time she opened her mouth in that leer of a smile, he had to grit his teeth to return it. At the end, he gave her a short head bow and what passed for courtesy in Urbis. Any Mountainer would have immediately recognised the insult of it, but the woman tilted her head and tried to press closer.

"Thank you for the pleasure of your company, Sera, but I'm afraid duty calls. I must make my salutations to a number of others here tonight. Please excuse me."

Then he slid away from her as fast as he could and wove through the crowd as if making a beeline for someone on the far side of the room. Fortunately, he found an old school acquaintance to drag into a deep and unnerving discussion, judging by the man's reaction. They had been friendly but not close at school and had seen each other only occasionally since. By the look on his face, the man was seeing a plot in Cumchdach's attention.

"How's business?" Cumchdach asked after a while, and swore he saw the man gulp.

"Fine, fine, much as ever," he said and suddenly lifted his head as if answering a com call. "Excuse me, I have to go. I see an associate I must catch."

Cumchdach could only stare after his departing back. Nor was the man the only one suddenly avoiding him when he started asking after their businesses. By the end of the evening, the presence of all those political flunkies made a lot more sense. Den Coille was far from the only company caught in the planet's current dilemma, but they at least had some buffering.

Did fixing their world need the destruction of all the work of the settlers over the hundreds of years since landing? He even began to wonder if the conspirators had a point.

He then remembered the men and women at those meetings. None were prepared to make the smallest move to adjust. These companies here were trying, if not yet successfully.

Suddenly his father's words about finding a way for Den Coille to make a profit sounded a whole lot more ominous. He almost welcomed the sight of Smierg's rapacious daughter though was in no mood to pander to the she-folklar's greed.

"Thank you but no, Sera. I already have my transport home organised and have an important report to finish tonight. I must go now."

He might as well have saved his breath. Thankfully, his pet marshal hadn't taken his eyes off Cumchdach all night long and appeared at his side immediately. The man took his arm and together they marched from the room leaving the Sera no chance to follow.

Later that night, he slipped into a small office Caleb kept on the far side of Urbis to report to an Fallon. "The evening was a front. Just a greedy banker hungry for advancement."

"Nothing gained?"

"Not quite." Cumchdach brought to mind the anxious air of desperation in the room. "The situation is more complicated than I thought." He told an Fallon of his observations. At the end, the man looked as serious as Cumchdach felt.

"It matches what we're hearing across the planet," said an Fallon. "But we didn't think it had become a real problem yet."

"These banking markets aren't new. We don't usually attend but send along our engagement staff to keep an eye on the gossip level. In the past, the main reason for looking for new banks was dissatisfaction with the current bankers or looking for a better deal. No company will survive long if it doesn't get what it's paying for."

"And tonight?"

"They weren't simply disgruntled customers. They were companies scared their own bank would close on them. They were hunting a safe haven."

"Companies with their debt over-extended?"

Cumchdach grunted in agreement. "Way over-extended," he added, remembering that glitter in the eyes of too many he'd met last night, "and we're not talking marginal dream chasers. A big chunk were long established companies with good banking histories. The kind that should be safe."

An Fallon fell silent, then shifted and opened another channel. "I'm linking into our finance sector chief. This is more his area of expertise."

Cumchdach jumped up. "You promised confidentiality."

"I'm making our link private."

Cumchdach wasn't convinced. "I'm taking enough risks already."

"He's a marshal. Our systems haven't been broken yet."

True enough, and Cumchdach had no doubt that everything he'd told an Fallon had been disseminated to other parts of the Marshal's service. But he knew an Fallon; he didn't know this person.

"Talk to them after I've gone." He was being ridiculously over-cautious, but he didn't care.

"As you wish," said an Fallon after a long silence. "And Smierg's daughter? What are you going to do about her?"

"Make sure I stay well away from her," snapped Cumchdach.

A look that might almost be one of sympathy crossed an Fallon's face. "We'll up the security around Sera Anna and your son," he said.

Cumchdach was about to cut the link but that had him come to a sudden stop.

"She may not be the only one," said an Fallon in that dry voice of his.

"Surely not? I may be the supposed heir to Den Coille, but I won't inherit any more than the others. I'm no guaranteed path to wealth."

An Fallon waved a hand as if discarding that. "You will have the deciding say after your father retires."

"He's not that old." Cumchdach thought of the spirited man who ran Den Coille, "and mentally no one can challenge him. Not yet."

"And may that long continue," said an Fallon. "Your father's influence is far reaching."

A nasty thought suddenly struck Cumchdach. "He's not at risk too?"

The marshal shook his head. "Not that we've heard. But we haven't found who heads this conspiracy yet."

Cumchdach stood and began to pace. An Fallon still sat at his desk, but one hand tapped against the top of it.

"Whoever it is has to be linked to Malgrave and Hilmar," Cumchdach said slowly, speaking of the two off-worlders who had used his brother Seolta to steal Arcadian assets. "Maybe even to the false Survey heads"—the conniving past heads of the Survey who had nearly succeeded in having both the den Coille and the Winter families executed to steal their assets. Den Coille was still recovering from the effects of their greedy management.

The more he thought about it, the more he began to wonder. Sol Winter had been tangled up with the conspiracy but only on the margins. It had taken his imprisonment and the near death of his son Ethan at Hilmar's hands to wake him up to the dangers facing Arcadia. Even after that, the man still didn't accept there was an environmental crisis, only that the Alliance was bullying Arcadia into giving up their wealth.

"We've looked at all the obvious suspects," he said, jaw tensed in frustration. "Who else is there?"

An Fallon's mouth tightened. "Not a corporate highflyer. Not a traditional power in that world."

It matched what Ceart had said. "Hilmar?"

"We've followed all his lines of association. Seolta's discovery of the fake Restin and Hilmar a Kevand3's intrusions into the Deuteron continent helped, but we've salted our people all through the place and nothing comes up."

"The head isn't from Deuteron." Cumchdach knew his world too well, including its prejudices. "A hint of an accent from there destroys any credibility the person would have with the Protos corporate types I've met so far."

"No, it's someone or a group from Protos, most likely in Urbis. That's where the power is, and where the decisions are made."

"Someone to do with Malgrave?"—the former Alliance Deputy Attache to the Alliance representative on Arcadia. "You've kept very quiet on her."

A tapping of the marshal's foot this time. "It's not us keeping quiet. It's Alliance Central. The Galactic Ministry has pulled a blank on her so far."

Cumchdach frowned. "She's the key, but untouchable?"

"Mmm. My guess is that's she's the front for an Alliance group, one that includes the companies your brother has identified."

As well as seeing through the Restin case, Seolta was using all his skills to delve into groups in the Alliance with their sights on acquiring Arcadian assets. He'd already had a run-in with some, companies too closely linked to attempts on his life. Those were now lying low, thankfully, as the full weight of the Alliance Council was turned on dissenters. But no one believed those companies were alone. And the secrecy around Malgrave suggested they were very high-powered groups in the Alliance. But that was Seolta's concern. Cumchdach had to find out what was going on at home.

"Run the lists of everyone possibly connected to Malgrave while she was the Deputy attaché here," he suggested, "including the Survey. Everyone in headquarters when the old bosses were in charge." The fake bosses must have had help to take over a department made vulnerable by its pathological drive for secrecy.

An Fallon grimaced. They'd had this argument too many times. Cumchdach hadn't yet accused the Commander of risking the same with their own secretiveness, but he'd come tragging close to it. He opened his mouth then shut it again at a glance from the marshal.

"We are not that Survey."

"You sure? You've interfered plenty in my family's affairs since you rescued us."

"Should I apologise for saving your life?"

Cumchdach welcomed the spark in the other man's eyes. Right now, he needed a good old-fashioned fist fight. Failing that—even he wasn't stupid enough to tangle with a marshal—a verbal slanging match would do.

"You're charging a tragging high price for your services."

"Maybe we should have left you for the executioner."

"You nearly did." Was that a growl from the marshal? His cheeks showed a faint flush. "Without Fioruisghe's intervention, you would have left us all to die," said Cumchdach.

The man gritted his teeth. "Our legal department was in constant touch with the Prosecutions Service, looking for any way to overturn the cases. No one, no person in real power, wanted those sentences carried out."

"Then they should have cancelled them. That's what real governments do."

"A bit harsh when your family handed them the charges on a plate. No one asked you to kidnap a government official or attack her wedding."

"That official was my sister, and it was a family matter."

"No, it wasn't, and you should've known it. And you got your parents and Samhchair dragged into it."

Suddenly it became serious. "Leave them out of this. And," he added, too many small instances coalescing into a new whole, "my big sister is not for you. Samhchair doesn't need the baggage you bring with you."

"You think I don't know that? Don't know that someone hurt her badly once?"

"You know nothing of it."

"Nor do you," the marshal spat back, his face as sick-looking as Cumchdach felt.

Worse, the man was right. Something had happened to Samhchair at Higher School. Something she refused to talk about. Not to him, not to his parents. And not to this man, he hoped. He pointed a hand at the door.

"Out, now. I'll attend one more meeting and send you a report, then I'm off to try to repair my marriage."

CHAPTER TWENTY

Landing at Rubhaicreach, Anna felt like a whipped gandy matriarch scurrying back to her home hole to lick her wounds. Unfortunately, no one else thought the same.

"Sera Anna, so good to see you again," was her greeting at the landing pad's reception counter.

"Sera, you're back. You're staying?" said the hopeful-sounding baggage supervisor as he disgorged her carrier unit, scanning the codes and sending it on to her grandam's. Her direction reassured him, from the grin on his face. Outside, a veritable fleet of skimmers jockeyed for her business, all loudly offering their services.

She was used to the hustle for business at the landing but had commed Grandam on her way here, and her skimmer stood waiting for her. Her security looked horrified by the scuffle, but Anna knew her people.

"You're back," was whispered so often and in such a relieved tone, she had to say *something* to them. She stood up on a nearby box.

"I'm off to my grandmother's. Tomorrow, if they're available, I will be meeting with the city and company officials. For now, my wee boy has had a long trip and needs quiet rest in a familiar place."

"But you're staying?" yelled a woman at the back.

"For now," was all she would answer, all she could promise. Beyond the *now*, she had no idea what her future held. Only that it was bleak and grey. Her son was her first focus.

And now, her city too.

It was nice that someone wanted her.

She slept that night as she hadn't since this whole nightmare began. Roo woke only once, and she relished the midnight peace of feeding her baby in a home and place where she felt safe, felt she belonged.

The next morning, she got back to work again. Not the studies that were her delight. This was the work she'd been trained for since birth. First on her agenda, a meeting with town officials.

"No, I don't know exactly what Den Coille is threatening. As you have heard, my husband and I are currently estranged. I know no more than is publicly available." She had put a call through to her father-in-law, but Bram den Coille was a man of scarce words.

"That's for your husband to tell you," was all he would say.

What was publicly available was bad enough. Everything pointed to Falasch losing the Alliance Central case, and Den Coille had filed a claim of damages against Falasch in the Arcadian courts that would bankrupt her family's company if they won.

"And will they?" asked the town's finance head when she suggested that to the meeting.

It hurt to answer, so badly that it shocked her. "Yes, they will win. Falasch has deliberately defrauded Den Coille and broken generations of contracts. Den Coille can't afford to lose, nor can the courts let them. It would shatter all the principles underlying the planet's trade."

Stony faces met her. None condemned her, not outright, but she saw a flicker in too many eyes. *Why didn't you know this was happening? Why didn't you stop it?*

Because I was busy loving my husband and having his baby. Since the wedding, she'd lived in a fantasy of hope. Cumchdach had been so thrilled with the baby, so gentle and caring.

He was always like that with you.

He was also the man fully involved with breaking her family's company and who had kept it from her. Whatever he felt for her, it wasn't love as she needed it. The kind she'd seen in his parents.

How do you know?

Another thought she thrust aside.

"So how do we survive this?" said the mayor at the end to the whole room. A pragmatist to the core, the mayor held his office because the city trusted him to get the work done, and he would. She answered with her honest hope.

"Trade still happens, Falasch has the routes, the contacts and the knowledge we always had. The ownership may change, but the work continues. The city will survive as it always has."

"Den Coille will want their own people in here."

"Yes." She couldn't deny that. "They've been hurt by Falasch; they won't let it happen again. But their people will take time to learn the business, and it's questionable whether they can afford to release too many of their best to do that. They have enough other problems at the moment, as do all the major Arcadian companies."

She may be a scientist, but Anna had grown up at her grandfather's knee and been a friend to Cumchdach too many years. The ins and outs of the business world were as familiar to her as the nitrogen pathways in soil.

"They're going to get rid of us all. Push out locals and replace them with their own."

Anna had grown up with the man shoving out his chin and glaring at her. Paolu was the head of the dockers, his family here as long as hers. "Who told you that?"

"It's the talk. Everyone says it."

"Gria," she said in disgust and saw the truth of it in the man's quickly shuttered eyes. "You'd trust an upstart import from Urbis over my word? My grandfather worked with yours all their lives, and you put a woman like Gria above them."

A flush coated the man's cheeks but he didn't lower his head. "It's the talk, and you married a den Coille."

"You've known for years that would happen one day," said the man beside him. "Cumchdach mar Bram grew up in this city as much as Anna den Falasch did in his."

"But Anna ingh Eolas moved to Manascraoch after marrying him. Her name has more of there than here now."

Anna studied the docker. Names mattered in Mountainer country, the form used mattered even more. She was her father's daughter to this man, a woman who had betrayed family, while to the other beside him, owner of one of the city's major retailers, she was of the family Falasch, a family with a proud history before her father gutted it.

"My name is as it has ever been. I have a number of loyalties, as has everyone here. This city is one of them, Manascraoch another," it always paid to be upfront in talking to Mountainers, "but my first loyalties are to my son, my husband, and my planet. Gria and my father's actions threaten Arcadia, and this city. I will not help them." She caught the eye of every person sitting at that table, and was depressed at how many narrowed their eyes back in defiance. How many supported her father.

No, were afraid of change.

"Rubhaicreach has a future, a good future. Arcadia needs trade as much as ever, but they need to be in products and services that help Arcadia in our fight to heal our world and stop the Alliance."

She fought back the despair threatening to overwhelm her and looked to the head of the table where a woman nearly as old as Grandam sat silently. She headed Rubhaicreach's Science Institute.

"Sera, how real is the environmental threat to our world."

"Real, and imminent," said the woman in the measured tones she used for everything, from a simple greeting to a complicated dissertation on an obscure process. "Even if the Alliance doesn't evacuate the planet, the accumulated planetary challenges will make life here unsustainable for our present population within this generation."

Dead silence fell on the room. Had no one here asked the question before?

"You're lying," finally shouted the docker and two others, and a shocked gasp went around the table.

"The Sera never lies," said the head of the teacher's union.

"How dare you," chimed in the city's engineer and head of the infrastructure unit, sitting straight up with puffed out cheeks and an angry flush overwhelming his face. She remembered the man proudly explaining to her, as a child, the city's water system, a complex interaction of reservoirs, water flows through the underlying bedrock, rainfall and seawater collection, with subtle monitors tracking everything from flow rates to non-potable intrusions. A system that increasingly must manage the ever-worsening storm surges hitting the peninsula, thanks to the clash of weather systems along the Western Ranges. The Sera was the man's aunt and an early mentor.

"Only a fool insults one of the most respected members of our community, and on matters about which she has proved herself above and beyond," said the mayor firmly, saving Anna from being in the firing line again.

"In this city," pointed out the docker. "But there's others…"

"Up in Urbis?" said the city engineer scathingly.

The docker's face mottled, but he stuck steadfastly to his line. "Yes, up in Urbis, where there's whole Higher Schools looking into these claims. Not everyone agrees with this crisis palaver."

"And you got that from my stepmother, I assume."

The docker glared at her. "At least she lives here. And her last name is now den Falasch."

And hers wasn't. Not any longer.

The meeting limped on after that. She said more, but didn't fool herself she'd made much difference. When it broke up, a sullen group hastily left and she stood with the mayor watching them go.

"How did we get here," he murmured sadly.

She glared at the sullen group, and a surge of anger filled her. Grandfather and Grandam had brought her up better than to accept this. "Greed and deliberate blindness," she said, feeling the tension in her neck muscles, "combined with stupidity and laziness. It stops, now. We meet again tomorrow, without the naysayers, and start working."

Then she marched away before the mayor could say anything. She had a night to come up with a plan and no time to waste.

When she told Grandam about the meeting, her beloved but stern face cracked open and the old woman leaned forward, gasping in laughter and tears. "What I'd have given to see that tired old man's face," she got out at the end. "About time someone made him do his job."

"He's been trying, Grandam."

"Huh. The man believes a den Falasch says jump and we all ask how high. "

"My family is the main employer in Rubhaicreach."

Her grandam stuck out a bony finger and thrust it straight at Anna. "And Falasch needs the city as much as the city needs them. Who trains their workers, provides homes and supplies for them, makes this city a place where folks want to live? About time they remembered that."

"Yes, Grandam," Anna said with staged meekness, and got another laugh and a finger wagging for her efforts.

"Go feed your baby. And while you do it, turn that expensively trained brain of yours on. You haven't yet told me how you plan to save us all."

As if she needed the reminder. Late that night as she tossed in her sleeper and prayed heartily that Roo would give her one night of uninterrupted sleep, she turned over one idea after another. All hit the same unshakeable barrier; Den Coille was going to take over Falasch, no matter what she or the city said. They had no choice. Not after her father had so publicly cheated them.

She opened her com and looked up the Alliance trial. Then gasped. It had been going for days already. Far off in Alliance Central, the fate of her family and her city was being decided, even as she lay here, and she could do nothing about it.

Worse, when she finally pulled herself blearily from her sleeper in response to Roo's determined squawk, she glanced at her com and discovered the trial was already over. The results had been sent on a fast-track home and, as Cumchdach's wife, she was among the few given access to the secured stream.

Falasch had lost. She'd known it would, but seeing the outcome in cold hard text made it too real. Cut and dried, the judges said. The evidence was clear enough, and no appeal was likely to succeed.

The Falasch lawyers would try anyway, but they'd fail. Her father had lost all his alternatives. Arcadia couldn't afford to ignore an

Alliance Central ruling, not in this political climate, even if Eolas had any support in the government sector.

Not from his old allies. No one backed a fool, no one put their businesses and lives on the line to help one either. Eolas and Gria were going down, no matter what. But how to save Falasch and her city? Rubhaicreach was too different from the rest of Mountainer country, too long used to doing things its own way. They weren't about to tolerate becoming a dependency of the den Coilles, no matter how benign.

"What a mess," she murmured to her baby. Roo barely glanced up, saw the slightly twisted smile on her face and settled back to his suckling, reassured his mother was going nowhere.

Anna chuckled. "Thank you for the reminder, my little smunchkin. Priorities: food and home first, politics a very long second, eh?"

But food and home were exactly what was at stake here. The trial was over, Falasch had lost, but how badly? What punishment would the courts impose? What was the price of her father's stupidity?

The second trial, the one in Arcadia for reparations would be decided by politics as much as law.

Who had won most support in the court of public opinion: Falasch or Den Coille? No, whose demise threatened most among the business community. Falasch was the exporter for many companies, not just Den Coille. But Den Coille was wealthier, and the actions of Falasch threatened the established order in the business community.

By the end of all her tossing, turning and plotting, one thing only stood clear in her head. She'd have to talk to Cumchdach and negotiate a compromise.

Grandam wore that annoying grin when she told her. "About time you two sat down and talked."

Anna flushed, but didn't answer that and, luckily, Grandam didn't push it. "I won't agree to leaving Father or the children creditless. They are still my family."

"And Gria?"

"Father will provide for her." It was true enough to be an adequate defence. "She must have other funds as well."

"She'll be furious."

Something snapped tight inside Anna. "So she should be."

At least the Rubhaicreach citizens at the meeting later that day refrained from displaying anything like Grandam's glee, but they did look happier when she informed them she was placing a call to her husband to negotiate the future of the city. She shouldn't have been surprised, not after their glowers at the start of the meeting. The outcome of the Alliance Central trial had spread like wildfire through the city, and her security was already doubled and extra twitchy.

"I can't promise anything," she warned them.

"Ser Cumchdach mar Bram has been running at your fingertips since you were a child. He'll sort this mess."

Did none of these worthy leaders understand Den Coille's position. They couldn't afford to let Falasch go untouched.

"Den Coille isn't like Falasch Shipping. It's held in a family trust. All the siblings hold an equal share, along with many extended family members. Cumchdach can't act alone."

A snort from the city's Finance head, but none of the rest seemed to understand. "The young Ser and his father have the say, everyone knows that."

Had none of these people met Bram den Coille? Her father-in-law didn't tell anyone other than his wife all that was on in his mind.

At the end of the meeting, she was more frustrated than ever, though the townspeople looked less anxious. Nice to know she could still do that.

She spent the rest of the day wandering through the tunnels and rocky slopes of the city, down to the vast caverns holding the city stores and trade goods and out to the docks, talking, watching, chatting. Putting off the moment when she must call Cumchdach, said the cowardly side of her. She left the Falasch warehouses until last. Huge echoing caverns equal in size to all the rest combined, the entry chambers still showed the bare rock walls of the peninsula. "To remind us of where we started," had said her grandfather to her once. "Have to be tough to beat rock, and Falasch is tough."

"No longer, Grandfather," she murmured to herself, one hand touching the smoothly worn knob he'd touched every time he entered the warehouse. Inside lingered the same smells she'd known all her life, an infusion of dried Festin, fabrics, dehydrated plants, metals, and machinery that made up the vast repository of goods exported by Falasch.

A man blocked her. "This area is secured."

She looked up in shock. "Not from me."

The man glared down at her. "ID," he snapped.

She held out her com, her family registration shining. "That's enough. Let me through."

He spent a long time examining it before grudgingly stepping to one side. "Don't touch anything."

"I'll touch whatever I like," she said and shoved past him. He didn't move, jostling her arrogantly and shoving back at her, causing her to stumble. A shocked gasp alone gave her back her pride. This was her home, hers by birth to enter whenever she pleased.

"Sera Anna, are you all right," said a man hurrying up and reaching out to help her.

"Yes, fine," she said, ignoring the stinging pain in her knee. She'd probably grazed it but wasn't about to let the brute on the door see she was hurt.

"Don't you know who this is?" her saviour was saying to the guard. But he kept a distance from the man, as if unsure of the bigger man's response.

Scorn laced the thug's voice. "The elder daughter. The one who left here."

"The heir, the one who will one day rule here," replied the other man, but with no force to his voice. No one in the city knew who would rule Falasch next.

"Not yet, and not going to, according to Her Ladyship."

Since when did Mountainers use that kind of wording? "The Sera Gria has no say in that. It depends on the courts, and any Council orders.

The guard looked at her, as if he thought her an idiot.

The shoe's on the other foot, Ser.

"Council and the courts will do as they should," the man said. "Don't touch anything without permission." Then he turned deliberately back to face the front and dismissed her with a slap of his hand on his weapon.

"Come along, Sera. Let me show you our latest changes," said her rescuer. She remembered him. A junior supervisor when she was here last, assistant to old Waghin, the warehouse Controller.

"No. I'm sure you have plenty to do. I'll call in to say hello to Ser Waghin then have a wander through. Don't worry, I know my way."

The man flushed scarlet. "The Ser retired a while back. I will escort you."

"Retired? No one told me."

"You haven't been here much during the last year, Sera. Understandable, given everything in your life."

And the city had thought she'd forgotten them. "A shame. He's a good man. I'll call on him at home on my way back."

The flush deepened. "The Ser left Rubhaicreach not long after, Sera."

"He did?" Shock held her in thrall. She began to ask for his new address, but something in the man's face had her falling silent. As if he didn't want her to ask.

What was going on here?

Her walk through the rest of the warehouses left her feeling even more shaken than when she'd arrived. So many empty bays, echoing in warning. Home was meant to be a refuge; her city felt more like a battleground. Her only safe ally was Grandam, and Falasch wasn't hers to run. Grandfather had never spoken a negative word of his son, but one day not long before he died, Anna had sat with him, and they both watched her father and his new family strolling through the old gardens a long past ancestor had established in the inner courtyard of the house. Gria had since 'modernised' it and the inner courtyard was now a regimented showpiece. Then, it had been a rare botanical wonder, home to the most precious of the mountains' small flowers and shrubs. Only the rare chaullnia now survived, and that only because not even Gria had the gall to remove it. Or maybe she dreamed of selling the flowers to a parfumier, undercutting the Den Coilles. The woman was arrogant enough.

That day, Anna had watched her stepmother pace off the far walk with a look on her face she distrusted.

"She'll change it, of course," said her grandfather. "Don't let it bother you. It's the heart of a place that matters, not the outward look. The heart will be there when it's your turn."

Anna turned to stare at him. Her grandfather shook his head. "Manascraoch is your home for now," he said, though she hadn't yet married Cumchdach. "Rubhaicreach is always here, and Falasch is strong. The peninsula is used to batterings by storms."

He said no more that day, but his hand reached for hers and gave it a squeeze. She'd squeezed his back, a promise. More, a vow. She'd keep the heart of the peninsula and, when her turn came, she'd bring Falasch back to life.

She swung abruptly about and set out for the entrance way. She'd had enough of the warehouses for today, the problems crowding in the back of her head almost as vast as the empty, echoing chambers where once had rested towers of containers carrying goods for all parts of Alliance space.

What were her father and his family living on these days? Some of the caverns still held stock, but too few. How did he meet the wage bill alone? Depleted the staff numbers might be, but Anna had grown up helping her grandfather as he tallied up everything, and knew there were enough staff still in the building, let alone the cost of Gria's bought-in security, to make a serious ongoing cost. He had to be paying that with something. That new guard's attitude was too ugly for a man awaiting payment from his new employers.

As she neared the entry to the caverns, a shadowed figure stepped from the side office. For a moment, she could have sworn it was her grandfather come back to life, the head held in the self-same tilt she'd seen on Grandfather so often. She shook her head to make the shade disappear, but it stayed. The outer doors opened and the shadow sharpened, the dream resemblance disappearing. Or fading beneath the force of reality.

"Anton," she said coldly. "What are you doing down here?" She'd thought none of Gria's offspring even knew the way to the caverns that paid for their lifestyle.

"I work here."

Something about the way he said it made her look harder. Beneath the usual sulky petulance lay more, a defensiveness that surprised her.

"You do?" Then could have cursed as a flash of anger darkened the boy's eyes. No, *young man*. Anton had recently finished Higher School and was in his early standard twenties. She could no longer call him boy, although he would always be one to her.

"My name's den Falasch too," he reminded her.

Then she saw a trio of new guards hovering at his shoulder, all with weapons in their hands.

"I know that. I'm your sister, remember," she said, though she hadn't called him that to his face since he was the small boy who used to come running to play with her as soon as his nursemaid turned her back. They had been family then, no matter what Anna thought of his mother, bound by her father's shared blood. But it had been a long time since those days, and Gria had done her poisonous work on her children since.

"It's what *you're* doing down here I'm wondering about," her brother said now. This time, the set of his chin reminded her of Roo when she'd taken away a dangerous toy. Blood will out, they said, but she wished it didn't have to out now. She'd always managed to compartmentalise her half siblings into *Gria's children*. They shared a father but, so far, she'd managed to ignore the physical reality of that.

Why did Anton have to remind her of those she loved?

She lifted an eyebrow and stared back at him. "I usually walk through the caverns when I visit. I've been busy this past yearly cycle so it's been a while, but I grew up in these warehouses. Grandfather liked to talk when he walked here and he liked me to join him."

A definite scowl crossed Anton's face and she saw she'd made another mistake.

"He never asked *me*."

She sensibly refrained from pointing out that Anton had never shown her grandfather any interest in coming, not in front of Anna anyway. Then the men behind her brother slapped their weapons up to *Ready*.

"Hey, no need for that," said her naïve brother.

"The Sera has seen everything she needs to," said the middle of the men, his finger hovering over the trigger panel. She was versed enough in military gear to know these blasters had com controls. That hovering finger was a warning and a threat.

She quelled her nerves and wished she had her own fingers near her com patch. Hiding the slight distancing of a direct brain to com link was impossible from trained troops. That's what her trainer had always told her. "Only do it in an emergency if you have no other option," she'd said.

Anna was beginning to think this may be such a situation.

"As it happens, I was leaving," she said in the coolest voice she could summon. "But maybe I should stay. Is there something here I missed?"

"Nothing of concern, Sera," said the very stupid but very dangerous man in the middle.

Anton turned and went to shove at the man's weapon, but one of the others took hold of his wrist and, from the blanching of Anton's face, it wasn't a light hold.

"That's good, then," she said. "Anton, would you like to come and visit with your nephew? Roo hasn't spent time with his Rubhaicreach family yet."

Her brother's mouth dropped open and he blinked at her.

"I know he's not civilised yet, but he does love attention and you need to get used to handling him if you're staying in Rubhaicreach."

"Staying? Of course I am." Then his brows drew together. "You're not getting rid of us, not my mother nor the twins and me."

She shook her head quickly. "Of course not. This is your home."

"Yes, it is," and he glowered at her.

"I never said it wasn't."

The guard's hand had relaxed on Anton's wrist, and dropped when Anna took a step away and toward the entrance door. She took another step, praying desperately that Anton would follow.

Then the guards' weapons slapped hard into position again and they swung sharply around, as more shadows darkened the door.

"Drop them," said a hard voice, and a man dressed in a black uniform that not even these idiots dared threaten stepped into the doorway, followed by five others. A marshal patrol, in full combat gear and carrying fully armed blasters that had a power cell far above anything available to civilian security forces. One of them was the man who'd broken the tension the first time she visited her father and made sure she got out safely. She'd thought him a Den Coille agent. She'd been wrong, it seemed.

She also recognised the leader, but gave no sign of it, not here. It was the same marshal she'd met with Samhchair in the lower boughs, now transferred here, it seemed.

The very air of the cavern held still, as if waiting for a thunder burst.

"Sera, can we escort you somewhere?"

"Home, to Grandam's. I was going home. My brother too."

The senior marshal studied Anton, his eyes momentarily pausing on his wrist. The one the guard had grabbed. "If the Ser wishes," he said, with little enthusiasm. The patrol stepped forward, the guards around Anton holding their position.

Anna had been in enough situations before. She stepped into the breach, walking quickly into the shelter of the marshals. "Thank you for your escort, Sers." She turned back to her brother. "Anton?"

But Gria's son stayed where he was. "I have work to do here," he said gruffly, "and no, I don't need help with it," he added quickly when she opened her mouth.

Right. She snapped her mouth closed. "Marshals?"

The leader nodded, and the patrol fell into place around her, the leader beside her in the middle and the rest staged about them, like in the adventure vidcasts Cumchdach and his brothers favoured when they had what they liked to call a testosterone day, all gathering in a beat-up lounge in the bowels of the den Coille home, complete with big squashy loungers and a bar. She'd ventured in one day, just to prove she could breach the bastion, but stayed only a brief time, bored silly by their choice of vid and too aware she was stopping the brothers talking freely.

Her breathing didn't return to normal until they were safely back within the outer walls of Grandam's home. She marched through the door, head held high, offering no invitation. But of course the leader followed her, the rest standing outside at full attention.

"What was that about?" she demanded as soon as the door shut behind the man and while he was still checking out the room.

"Your scans showed physical damage," he said in a flat tone.

"My scans?" Then gasped. "Medical scans, you mean? Bruising from that idiot. You've got me under that level of surveillance?"

"Of course, Sera. You are listed as planetary critical."

"I'm what?"

"An essential person in the current Arcadian situation with the Alliance. Your particular abilities as a botanist are critical to finding a solution to the Alliance's ultimatum."

"I have some ideas to help restore the balance of our world, yes," she said, "but that doesn't make me some kind of critical resource."

He stared at a spot over her head. "Yes, it does, Sera. Or so we have been advised."

She let out a breath. "Next you'll be telling me you'll be escorting me full time."

The man stared straight ahead. "Those are our orders, Sera, while you remain in Rubhaicreach."

Her mouth dropped open again. "This is my home city. What do you imagine will happen to me here? And I have work to do. My family needs me."

Her brother needed her, today said, something she'd never thought possible.

"Our responsibility is to the planet, Sera."

"And family comes second? I don't think so. I'm *needed*."

"Yes, Sera. By Arcadia."

With which he gave her a salute and click of his heels, and went back to his men outside. She could only stare after him, stunned. She shook her head to clear it then hurried to her room and was relieved to be greeted by a wide-awake Roo, happily playing with Biarsuin. He saw her and his special smile spread over his face as he chortled his own version of hello. She grabbed him up and hugged him tight.

"It is so good to see you, little man."

CHAPTER TWENTY-ONE

The marshal found her again soon enough. He didn't barge right on into Roo's room, but when she carried her son out to the family room, he was waiting. He said nothing as she settled Roo onto the rug and played blocks with him, clapping enthusiastically as his little fist swept out and tumbled each pile over, barely giving her time to stack them again before he thrust at them, laughing loudly each time.

In the way of babies, he could play the game for hours, but Anna was too conscious of the man standing quietly in the corner. Roo had glanced at him but taken his cue from his mother's outward lack of concern.

She was getting too good at fooling her son. A mother should be more honest. She gave Roo a bit longer, then distracted him with his favourite clacky toy and nodded to Biarsuin to take over. She moved over to the table where he could still see her and waited for her approving smile before continuing his new game with his nursemaid. Then she pointed to the other chair and the marshal sat down, sitting rigidly against the high back of it and with not a trace of anything but formal duty showing on his face.

"We meet again, marshal. I can't say it's a pleasure."

"It's necessary, Sera."

She wished badly he wasn't right. She took her seat. "Your name, marshal? We were never introduced properly but you seem to know everything about me. It's only fair I have a name for you."

He flushed. "Dunan, Sera."

"Thank you, Marshal Dunan. But I need more."

He stiffened further, though she'd not thought it possible. She put her hands in her lap and simply waited, a tactic she'd learned many years ago and was rarely beaten. Something about his accent niggled at her today, something more than his Coaster origin.

"My mother's family were from Deuteron," he finally said. "Da met her when he worked on a fishing boat one summer" he said, as if sensing her unease. She nodded. The same was unusual, but not unknown, for seafarers from Rubhaicreach. "I spent my Higher School years in Urbis," he added.

A marshal scholarship, she'd bet. He had that look of mixed pride and embarrassment she'd seen in too many top-level students from lower income backgrounds. The marshals set a high bar to their scholarships. This man was both intelligent and sensible. A man she could trust.

"It is good to meet you properly, Marshal Dunan."

He rubbed the back of his neck. At least she could fluster him, a fitting payment for her tension. "Thank you, Sera," he finally settled on.

"And now you can explain to me exactly what you're doing here. Why are the Marshals monitoring me so closely, in a way that violates every privacy law on this planet?"

He shook his head at that. "Not under the regulations. The privacy statutes can be set aside if your life is at risk, or you are a critical resource for the planet."

"You need a warrant for that."

"Yes, Sera, we do."

That left her gasping in a way that nothing else in this insane day had. "Which is it: life at risk or critical resource?"

"Both."

The flatness of his voice left her floundering.

"And Roo?" she asked, latching onto her most important worry.

"Life at risk, possibly. And can be used as a threat."

"You mean, take him hostage to force me or Cumchdach to obey them?"

The marshal nodded. Once only, short and abrupt, but it scared her more than anything else today.

"He has security already. Everything Den Coille and Rubhaicreach can throw at him." That's what she'd ordered, anyway.

"He's under Marshal security too," the man said.

Anna breathed out. "Thank you."

"You will follow our orders, Sera."

She nodded, all resistance gone. If it kept Roo safe, she'd dance in the streets. "What do you need from me," she said simply. "A platoon of marshals in full uniform following me around the city will cause talk."

"Yes, Sera."

"You're betting they're too scared to take on the marshals?" Any sane group would be.

"We'll see."

Anna fell back in her chair. "Just who do you think you're up against?"

"We'll see," said the man again, his face totally closed to her.

What did the marshals know? How bad was it here?

"Anton is only a boy."

"A boy with armed security ready to threaten you, Sera, in a city on edge with uncertainty."

She swallowed. She was sure Anton had been as surprised as she was when the guards pulled up their weapons, but that didn't make him innocent. "He resents my position, but that doesn't mean he'd kill for it."

Not a baby, surely. Not his half-nephew?

But how well did she know her stepmother and siblings? She'd first fled the family home to Grandam's when the twins were babies and Anton barely at nursery school, and only returned intermittently afterward. Her brother had only patchy memories of the big sister he'd worshipped as a little boy to offset the stream of poison from his mother.

And that hint of Grandfather?

She hastily pushed the thought aside.

"You trust your family?" asked the marshal, eerily echoing her thoughts.

She half shook her head, too ashamed to put it into words. "My grandfather was an honourable man," she said defensively.

"And tried to bring his son up to be the same. Yes, Sera, but Falasch is—or was–a heady prize."

"Roo is den Coille. Harm him, and you take on the whole family and all of Manascraoch."

That Falasch already had didn't need to be said. Not after the Restin case, and this marshal would have identified every single Den Coille operative Cumchdach had sent to Rubhaicreach.

The marshal was silent for a long, tense moment. Then he looked up and caught her eyes. "You need to think of yourself, Sera. Your son isn't the prime target yet."

"I'm a mother, Ser Marshal. He is what matters most to me."

"But you matter to Arcadia."

Was that meant to make her feel better? It left her deflated instead, as if all her work was nothing but the output of a machine.

"No one else has achieved what you have in understanding how the botany of our world works, and how we can live with it better," said the marshal gently now, revealing the smallest of upward tweaks of his lips. The hard eyes still watched her, but there was a softer light touching them. "Your studies on Deuteron have brought pride to my mother's home region and protected it. Arcadia needs you, Sera. Not just its plants, but its people too."

"And my son needs me. I cannot work unless I know he is safe."

The marshal held her eyes a moment longer. Then slowly bowed his head in a formal acknowledgement that would satisfy the sternest of Mountainer critics. "He will be, Sera."

That night, she put the call through to Cumchdach. He looked as bad as she felt, his eyes bleary with exhaustion as he held himself rigid.

"Anna? Is something wrong. Roo?"

"No, no." He thought she'd need an emergency to call on him?

"He's fine. Nothing's happened."

He waited, saying nothing. She wished she could see all of him. He'd kept his holo view to his head only, his arms, hands, body hidden.

"It's about the Restin case," she finally made herself say. "The city—Rubhaicreach—needs to know what Den Coille intends."

"That's the reason, the only reason for this call?"

"Yes," she said, and watched all the lines on his face slump. "I have to ask for the city."

"Nothing is decided yet."

She gulped in a breath. "And when it is? What happens to my city, to the other businesses here."

"It's not yet decided," he repeated, as if driven. Then he disappeared, as if blocking her, before appearing again. His hair stuck up on one side, as if he'd dragged a hand through it. "We have to do this. You know that. We let Falasch get away with this; it makes Den Coille a target for every scammer out there."

"My father, yes. You have to act against him. But he's not Falasch, not all of it."

"He's the head of it. But a change of controlling owner doesn't mean the end of Falasch. No one wants that."

"You won't succeed without the good will of the city. Falasch is too deeply embedded in Rubhaicreach."

This time, she saw his hand come up and tug at his hair. "You think I don't know that. Your grandfather taught me as well."

They'd both spent many happy hours walking through the warehouse with him in their teen years, listening to the old man's wisdom.

"Can you at least promise to talk it over with me when the case is decided?"

"It's not just up to me, Anna."

She knew that too. "Please, just talk to me." Like he should have done right from the start. "Maybe we can come up with something." Though at this stage, she had nothing.

"Whatever happens, you'll be safe. You and Roo."

She nodded jerkily. She'd never doubted that. Not given the security shadowing her every step. "My city matters. It's Roo's heritage too."

Then she wished the words back, at the sharp flinch from him. "It's yours too. Your family and your rock," he said in a strangled voice. "You matter to me."

Suddenly, she couldn't be here. "Please, just talk to me," she said and signalled her com to close.

"Anna!" she heard as the link dropped. She jumped up, slapped a ban on incoming calls, and ran out the door, stopping only when she was outside and the stormy night winds of the peninsula swirled around her.

Why did he have to say that?

A strange time followed, when everything seemed to hold its breath. She spent the first part of each day in her lab, working on her plants and trying out new and different connections. Then lunch and play time with Roo before touring the city, followed always by her new entourage of uniformed and fully armed marshals. After a while, the city got used to the sight of her in everyday gear with a military patrol stomping around with her and ignored the marshals to a greater or lesser extent when she stopped to talk, or shop, or took part in a meeting. But they didn't forget them, and none ever spoke to her as freely as they once had, not even her closest supporters.

Nor could she forget that call with Cumchdach, despite all her attempts to bury it right to the back of her brain.

He had looked so tired. What were the marshals doing to him?

"I don't know whether I'm doing more harm than good," she said one afternoon to Grandam, both of them trying not to notice the whiplash-fit marshal stationed at her shoulder and the second pair of hefty muscle-bound troopers standing by the door. Roo played at her feet. Today, he had a piece of felted material that she recognised with shock came from a troopers' torn uniform. The metallic glint in the dark material as it caught the sunlight, delighted him and he waved it about triumphantly.

"You're trying, love, and that is more than anyone else in your family," said Grandam.

"Maybe."

Her grandam looked at her sharply.

"Anton," she explained. "I've never met up with him, not again, but he's before me everywhere I go. I catch sight of him sometimes, or a suggestion of mine is countered by what Anton is putting in place, or they mention he's been there or is coming." She clasped her hands. "He's making himself a power in the city."

"He's a den Falasch, just like you."

"Are you saying I don't belong here?"

"Nothing of the sort. Rubhaicreach is your home."

"And it's Anton's too. Is that what you're saying?"

Grandam gave her the same look as when they'd had these kind of discussions during Anna's teen years. When Anna was in what Grandam had called 'grown-up training'. "You need to ask him. What of the effect of his interventions here? Is he resented? He's young enough, but is he helping or hurting the city?"

Anna grimaced. "That's just it. Some of what he does is good, is what the city has needed. But some— He resents me, and lets it rule his words, and that's not good for the city. Not with the Restin case hanging over it."

"Resents you, or wants what you have?"

Anna sighed. "Both," she admitted. "But it's the 'why he wants it' that's leaving me flummoxed. He's not just *Gria's son.*"

She'd underestimated her half-brother, was the problem, branding him as no more than to be expected from Gria's offspring. A spoiled and greedy brat. But the boy—no, man, she reminded herself—worked hard, spending hours in the warehouses helping load the shuttles and more in the offices, learning all the ways of the business her grandfather had taught her in the years of her growing up but from which he'd been excluded. "He might make a good leader of Falasch, when he's older—and if he can bind the city to him."

"Which he won't do while he resents you so much—and Den Coille won't permit it. The other question, of course, is what do you want? Falasch, and all that comes with the leadership, your studies—or your baby and husband?"

Something clenched inside Anna. "It's more a matter of what's possible."

"Once on a time, a girl sat in that chair who never set herself limits."

"That girl grew up a long time ago and learned that wishing can't make others do.

"The Restin case? Pshaw," said Grandam with a flick of her hand. "You think that changes anything for that boy? He worships the ground you walk on."

There was no point reminding Grandam that Cumchdach had left boyhood years ago. To Grandam, he would always be *that boy* who had roamed in and out of this house as freely as his own. "I had hoped," she admitted now, "but reality has a habit of getting in the way."

"Sometimes, Anna, I swear you're as blind to what's in front of your face as that father of yours."

Anna flushed, really not wanting to continue this conversation. "You let my mother marry him."

To her shock, it was her grandam's turn to blush and look uncomfortable. "It looked a good match. They grew up together. Your mother went in with open eyes."

"Like me and Cumchdach." Anna couldn't keep the bitterness out of her voice.

"No, nothing like," snapped her grandmother. "We should have stopped it, but we told ourselves he just had to grow up some—and your mother looked happy enough with her choice, at first."

"She was good at hiding her thoughts from those who loved her," Anna said sadly. "She was a good mother."

"She loved you dearly," confirmed Grandam. "You were her delight. But we let her down. She thought we wanted the match and knew it was good for Rubhaicreach." Her eyes went distant, as if looking into the past, then blinked back. "I should have realised what was going on when she stopped coming over, and then she was gone and the piece of nothing she married had installed that woman in her place before my Sumhneas was cold in her grave."

A knife cut through her innards. "You mean—"

"No, no," said Grandam hastily. "Your father did nothing to hurry your mother's decline. But he didn't notice when she was so ill and she… She made sure to hide it, determined to be the wife of the head of Falasch at least, having failed at being the wife of Eolas. That's how she saw it," said Grandam sadly. "I found her journal after she'd gone." Then a sharp frown cut across her face. "And now that woman's son thinks to steal your birthright from you."

"He's my father's son too." The words were out before Anna realised. She shut her mouth with a snap and Grandam stared at her.

"Anton grew up here too," said Anna in defence. "He was a gorgeous wee boy."

"Don't count on that still being there," said Grandam.

Anna lay in her sleeper that night remembering the conversation and mulling over her confrontation with her brother. The next morning, she called Marshal Dunan into the room she'd co-opted as a study. On the wall behind her glowed the results from her Deuteron farm study, green lines and notations overlaying the holo of the farm.

The marshal lifted his eyes to it when he walked in and came to what must be attention in front of her desk. He tilted his head toward the holo. "Is that the Shiron farm?"

"Gebre and Firama of Shiron's farm? Yes. You know them."

"A bit," he said, noncommittally. "Firama is a second cousin of my mother's uncle by marriage."

Anna's mouth dropped open, then she dragged it shut again. "Deuteronians are worse than Mountainers with family connections," she said faintly.

The marshal lifted his shoulders a fraction. "Don't know about the rest of Deuteron. But the farming folk in the central downs are. Not enough people there not to know who everyone is. My mother took us there for holidays."

She watched in fascination as his eyes tracked her flow lines. "You can understand it," she suddenly realised.

That small lift of shoulders again. "A cousin told me that Gebre talked about it at the last gathering, and news spread through the downs."

"Oh." That could be a problem.

The marshal looked down at her and offered the merest lift of his lips. "Gebre was right proud of it. Said you'd told him Deuteron could give those fancy farmers up in the Protos estuary plains a lesson or two."

"No one told the estuary farmers that, I hope."

"Don't worry, Sera. Even if those estuary farmers would listen to an outlander Deuteron farmer, they don't talk much. Not to outsiders."

"Oh," she said again. "I found them very helpful," she went on, hoping it hadn't all been fake and her theories nothing but dreams. "They also helped Seolta and his wife."

"They trusted you and Sera Anyara. You understand the land," the marshal said simply.

"So?"

"Anything they said to you, you can trust, Sera," said the marshal. "This planet is their home too, and Deuteronians would be first on those eviction shuttles the Alliance is threatening."

"You know about that too? And accept it as true?"

"Deuteronians been coming second place on this world a long time. They learned early to have their own lines of information. Some of the Sera Anyara's questions got them wondering, and the Survey had been working there too. Not as much as on Protos, but enough. The Survey has always used locals."

"Who else are you related to?" Anna suddenly thought to ask.

The marshal's face stilled again. "Enough to know who's important to Arcadia. I read all the briefing notes before coming here, and made sure every one of my troop read them. Your work is important, Sera, and the marshals mean to make sure you are free to continue it."

"You sound like Marco an Fallon," said Anna on an outward breath.

At the mention of his Commander's name, the marshal snapped into what even she realised was parade ground attention. The official side was back. "You wished to see me, Sera?"

Anna took in a deep breath and threw back her shoulders. Later, she'd go over his words, but for now, she had other concerns. "I intend to visit my father and stepmother this afternoon."

"No."

"Yes, marshal. I'm going. You will have to arrest me to stop me, and you have no grounds for that. Nor, I think, do you want to antagonise the people of this city, not that way and not yet."

The marshal's mouth tightened, all trace of that incipient smile vanished, and his head snapped back. He stared at a spot over her head. "Very well, Sera. A patrol will be readied to accompany you— and no, Sera," he added, bringing down his head and looking her straight in the eyes, "there is no discussion on that. A patrol will accompany you."

She argued, but the next morning found her heading out for her father's home, surrounded by a patrol in full combat gear, Roo safely ensconced back in Grandam's home.

She eyed them up and down then turned to Marshal Dunan. "Just where do you think I'm visiting?"

"The house at which you were held involuntarily on your last visit," he said, staring over her head, all trace of that relaxed rural speech gone from his clipped voice. Not a farm boy any longer, it said to her.

"Is this necessary?"

"Yes, Sera. Another patrol is remaining on guard at Sera den Guire's, half with young Ser Ruiseart and the rest surrounding the house."

"Well, thank you." She faced toward her family home to hide the shock of that, although she should have expected it. A step forward brought a surge from the patrol. They kept a tight formation all the way along the meandering surface pathway, and it was a marshal patroller who knocked on the main house door to request entry.

The man who answered was a stranger but, by the sneer on his face, he recognised her. She was probably on his security risk list. Then he saw the patrol surrounding her and his face blanked out.

"You got no business here," he said to Marshal Dunan. The marshal ignored him, waiting with the rest of the patrol for one of the family.

Finally, the senior housekeeper appeared. "Sera Anna, a pleasure to see you again." This time, Anna believed the woman. She'd been here since Anna was a tiny girl. Grey-haired now, and with tired lines bracketing her mouth, the Sera ran the house staff and bots with a rod of steel. She was good at her job, which was the only reason Gria hadn't got rid of her years ago. Her stepmother had never mastered how to run a great house like the den Falasch home, only how to change it from its past grandeur to the current crass fortress. Her grandfather had warned her but that had made it no better,

"I'm here to see my father," said Anna in her most commanding voice.

"I'll see if he's busy."

"He's not, not today," said Anna as firmly. "Are the family still at breakfast?" Last she was here, none of them were early risers, lingering over the breakfast table set in a room facing the inner courtyard.

"They are, Sera. Would you like to wait in the front room until they are ready to meet visitors?"

This was her family in name, the house the traditional den Falasch home. "No, I'll see them now." She pushed past the housekeeper and marched along the hallways and to the back of the house, passages she'd played in as a child that now rang with an unfamiliar rattle of hard floors and echoing walls decorated in holos of life in Urbis. As if the woman wanted to remind everyone she didn't belong here.

Soon, she came to a pleasant room in soft colours looking out over what remained of her grandmother's charming courtyard. Her father had always loved this room the best, the only reason she could find that Gria hadn't got her claws into it. As she'd expected, the whole family still lounged at breakfast, her father reading over work notes as usual and Gria catching up with the latest missives from Urbis. The woman had a network of what she called friends there who kept her up to date with the trivia of the social life of the capital, all the latest scandals and gossipy titbits.

Or at least that's what Anna had always thought. Now, she wondered if she hadn't underestimated her stepmother. The twins picked over their breakfast, taking a bite then guiltily putting the rest of the morsel back. They must be on another of their diet kicks. Anton had sat up when she walked in and watched her warily. The twins and Gria saw his face and turned quickly, faces paling, but no one said anything. Just waited. Her father was the last to pick up the tension in the room.

As usual.

Don't think that.

That was fear sharpening his eyes.

"Anna, what is the meaning of this? You were taught better manners than to barge in on a family this early."

"*My* family, Father, or so my birth records and the den Falasch deeds state." She knew Gria had checked Anna's DNA during her childhood, and her lack of action spoke for itself.

"A double reason for respect, not this harum-scarum behaviour." Her father always fell into bluster when he was unsure of his ground. "And why do you have a troop of armed guards with you if we are family?"

"The marshals," she said, although no one in this room needed telling who wore that uniform, "insisted on it. Apparently, my home city is no longer considered a safe place for me."

"What do you expect," shoved in Gria, "when you let your husband cause such a ruckus here?"

"I don't control my husband," said Anna pointedly and watched the slight flush darken Gria's cheeks.

"So why are you here?" said her stepmother.

Anna glanced at Anton. He was holding quiet yet. She turned back to her father. "When I visited the Falasch warehouses the other day, your new security ring-ins acted as if unaware of the ranking structure in Falasch."

Her father opened his mouth again, and Anna couldn't bear to hear what flummery he'd come up with.

"You run Falasch now, Father, but you don't own it. Not outright. Under the deed you are the majority shareholder, but your leadership of the company is dependent on the other shareholders' agreement. You put the company at risk by, say, illegally defrauding a major customer, and you risk defaulting your shares and your position."

Gria looked about to open her mouth as well. A marshal moved to stand over her.

"You default to me, Father. So, tell me again, who are those guards and what in all the roots are they doing threatening me in our own warehouses?"

Her father began to talk again, more flummery, and she shut him down. "Get rid of them or make it plain who's really in charge here," she ordered. "And reinstate the original supervisory staff. People who can haul Falasch out of the mess you've got it into."

She swung around to leave then stopped a moment.

"Anton, next time I go to the warehouses, you'd better be working somewhere else. You and your thugs—"

Her brother finally shot to his feet. "You'd like that. Steal my share in the company from me, like you and your husband are stealing everything else. This is our home too."

He's only a boy.

No, he's not. He's now a man, and he just proved it.

"Then start acting like it," she snapped. "Meet me in the warehouses tomorrow without your thugs and show me what you know about the business."

This time she did swing around. She marched out, surrounded by her patrol of marshals, boots rapping on the floor, leaving an empty silence behind her.

He brought his guards of course—she doubted he had the authority to keep them away—but he did turn up. Sour-faced, a sullen downward turn to his mouth and his body tensed as if ready to run at the first hint of trouble, her brother marched in the doorway at the time he'd told her, wearing dusty work gear with stains on the knees confirming what she'd been told. He'd spent the morning working down on the docks with the loading teams. They hadn't said it, the dockers were a closed-mouth bunch at best, but they also let it be known they approved and accepted him.

"The young ser can work all the machines now and does his share." High praise from the tough forewoman of the docks. Another Anna had known since she was a child, the big woman still treated her as the youngster she'd spent days teaching every part of the business. It took real work and effort to win the woman's approval.

"You brought your guards too," said her brother, with a jerk of his head at the marshals surrounding her.

"They're needed."

The marshals still outnumbered his guards, who were carefully keeping their hands well away from their weapons. This could all go wrong so quickly.

"You have a problem with me?" she said to Anton.

"You're not interested. You've made that plain."

She pulled in a breath. Roo needed the calm, mature Anna right now, not the hurt girl facing the brother set up to replace her. *Remember that long ago little boy who followed you everywhere.*

"I have no intention of forcing you to leave your home, you or any of the family."

"What about your husband's family? They've filed for control of our company."

"They have to." She let some of her exasperation show. "Falasch stole from them and put their business at risk. If they let Falasch get away with it, who else will come after them next?"

"And Den Coille is so squeaky clean?"

Anna ignored the sarcastic tone. "As much as any major company can be. They recognise reality and have better sources of information than most."

"Are in the government's pockets."

"What's that supposed to mean?"

One of the guards suddenly hustled Anton, and her brother clapped shut his mouth. "Nothing."

Anna studied him. "You've heard something."

His guards suddenly closed in.

"Just talk," he said angrily. "Everyone knows Den Coille's too rich for words."

Now the guards did hustle, shoving at her brother. He blanched as one of them grabbed his arm.

"Anton, talk, now."

"We have a meeting with the bankers, Ser," said his lead guard. "They will be waiting in the com room."

Anton muttered at her, and his guards began to move, hands hovering over their weapons. Anna wished she dared stop him, but her marshals closed in, stiff-faced and hands hovering over their own weapons.

She folded her hands calmly in front of her. "Goodbye for now, brother. And take care," she added softly.

"That was not wise," said Marshal Dunan after Anton and his minders disappeared.

"Maybe, but it was necessary."

She'd almost got Anton to talk. That crack about Den Coille. It had to be about the conspiracy. He was angry, but so would she be if she faced losing her home.

And you haven't?

She shoved the thought away. She had two homes.

And was safe in neither of them. The threats here were real. She could no longer ignore them, not with the murmurs she heard on her travels through the city, or fail to notice the new people in positions replacing old and valued Falasch employees like the warehouse supervisor. New people with jobs and positions to lose if Den Coille won. No, they didn't see Den Coille. They saw her, the den Falasch who had married into den Coille.

They lost out if she prevailed over her father.

Had it come to that?

She broached it at dinner with Grandam. Anna hadn't told her of the murmurs, but Grandam kept her finger on the pulse of the city.

"Has it come to that?" she said, her shock echoing Anna's. Then her eyes shuttered and Anna could almost see her mind ticking over, calling up memories and feelings. "There's talk. Too many worried about what comes next after Den Coille won their case."

"You think it's past hope?"

Grandam's lips curled. "If so, it's thanks to that father of yours. How a man like Driach den Falasch could produce a son like Eolas is beyond me. Your grandfather was as astute as they come and hardworking to boot. He'd never have got the city into such a mess."

"There are other businesses in Rubhaicreach."

"Agreed. But Falasch is the biggest, oldest, and the one with the transport routes. Too many of the rest are in support services. Falasch hurts; the whole city hurts."

Anna lifted her shoulders helplessly, unable to deny it. Cumchdach claims Den Coille has no choice. Not after what Falasch did."

Grandam nodded. "He's right. Doesn't make it any easier to take. We've always been a bit different from the rest of Mountainer country. Now, they're going to come in here and tell us how to run our affairs."

Anna's fingers twisted together. She noticed and forced them to lie still. "Not necessarily. And Cumchdach would never."

"He won't have a choice," said Grandam dryly. "You said it yourself."

She looked up. "What do I do, Grandam? Grandfather expected me to keep Father in check."

Her grandmother reached out a hand. "No one blames you for what that man and his silly wife have done. But plenty are blaming Den Coille, and will do more than just talk if they seize control of Rubhaicreach holdings."

Anna clutched at her grandmother's hand "I tried talking to Cumchdach. I don't know what they will do. I asked him to talk to me first."

Her grandmother nodded. "First sensible thing I've heard from you in days. And what will you say to him when he does."

Anna sighed. "I don't know."

"You need a solution, one that works for both companies."

"Yes. He did say no one wants the end of Falasch."

"Of course not. You don't build trading routes like theirs overnight. So what can you offer Den Coille?"

If only she knew the answer. She'd been out of the company too long. Hiding in her labs.

What you do there matters. The marshals told you that.

Didn't make her feel any better. "I need to talk to Anton," she said. "Properly, without interfering guards. It's possible he's not just Gria's son.".

"Good bones there," agreed Grandam, to her surprise. "A pity much of it's been spoiled. He reminds me of your grandfather."

"And of Roo sometimes." Anna stared down at her son as he slept in his blissful innocence at her feet. "They're family, Grandam. I can't abandon them."

Her grandmother nodded slowly. "No, you can't. But when this is over, it's past time to think of what you really want, my girl. Whether that's spending the rest of your life running Falasch."

Anna stared in shock at her grandmother. "It's my job. Grandfather trusted me to see it right."

"For now, yes. But would you give up your plants, your labs, your research for it?"

Anna opened her mouth, then snapped it shut again as a vice seized her. A thousand times, *No,* said too much of her. But her city needed her.

Grandam watched her with a sad smile on her face. "Do what you must for now, but after… Just take time to think." Grandam's hand seized the arms of her chair. "Duty isn't always enough for a life. Your mother learned that the hard way. Don't make me watch you learn the same."

Anna felt as if slapped. "I have no choice, Grandam. Not yet. Yes, Anton may be a possibility, but he's too young."

"Even with help?" said Grandam.

"Maybe. I don't know." She sat, watching the dark of night fill the spaces of the window outside. Would her brother even listen to her or accept any offer of help from her. Anna sighed unhappily. "Ask your staff to find out when Anton is likely to be alone, without those tragging guards of his breathing down on him."

It took some days, but word came at last. At the end of the morning shift, he takes a short cut home through the tunnels, said her informants. She knew those old tunnels like the backs of her hands, but the guards wouldn't. In there, Anton would be isolated and she could talk to her brother without listeners.

She hoped.

She didn't tell Grandam the next part of her plan.

"Biarsuin, can you get me a burner com?" she asked the nursemaid while she changed Roo. "My backup one's not working for some reason and I won't have time to pick up one today."

The nursemaid didn't turn a hair. With the increasing storms hitting the rugged Rubhaicreach peninsula and so much of the city built underground, everyone carried a backup burner com. It also helped that the marshal patrol on duty today were all young and male enough to step back when Roo was being changed. None had yet acquired the hardy stomachs of their older teammates.

"Leave it with Roo's things and I'll pick it up in the morning."

Anna had asked Biarsuin to do similar errands before when she was too busy to pick up something. The nursemaid nodded and went on to tell Anna of all Roo's latest triumphs. He was growing up fast now and guilt stirred in her. Cumchdach was missing out on so much.

The day was as busy as she'd predicted, torn between meetings with the town leaders and spending time in her lab, catching up with her team's findings at the Deuteron farm study. The latest results had just come in, and she happily buried herself in them.

Hid in them, was closer to the truth, but she needed to hide somewhere.

They were learning so much. She'd have to call most of the team back soon, but she already had arranged to leave a small group on site for a longer trans-seasonal study. Then wondered if she could do a similar study on the Den Coille lands.

But that meant working with Cumchdach again. She didn't even know whether that was possible.

He'd looked so tired.

No. Not today. Don't think about it. She'd go through Fioruisghe and the Survey. Then the field work would be done with Joseph mar Freshet. The Survey botanist was as fixated on plants as she was, and rarely noticed the doings of people outside his studies, making him a welcome haven of peace from her worries.

She spent the rest of the day formulating a proposal, and then sent it through Joseph to request approval.

He could take it to Fioruisghe.

That night, she made sure to spend time with Roo, just her and her son. She cherished these short evenings hours before his bedtime, when she was alone with her son and no one was interrupting her with all their competing demands. She giggled with him as they played tug with his latest favourite toy—an old spoon from the kitchen that he used for everything, from chewing to relieve his teething gums, to banging it as loudly as he could on any hard surface. She spent the next hours happily just being a mother, and refused to give any more thought to the mess facing Falasch.

Tomorrow, she told herself when she snuggled into her sleeper, having finally managed to persuade Roo that nighttime was sleep time. There's nothing urgent.

Now she was telling herself lies.

She'd know more after she talked to her brother. She hoped. When she had something concrete to propose, then she could talk to Cumchdach again.

Coward.

She ignored the niggling voice.

The burner com was there the next morning, innocently nestled in with all the paraphernalia Biarsuin deemed essential to manage one small baby's hygiene. His bottom wrap might collect everything up and reduce it to a small packet of sterile dust that Anna had found ideal for her collection of Terran flowering plants, leaving his bottom clean and smooth, but Biarsuin still insisted on cleaning him and slathering on sweet-smelling creams. Since they appeared to do no actual harm to Roo, Anna said nothing, and today, the pots and bottles nicely hid the small sliver of the spare com. She picked it up with the waste packet and popped both into her carryall to take to the lab, as was her usual practice—it made wonderful fertiliser for the non-food plants—giving Roo a big smarmy kiss before handing him over to Biarsuin.

Once in the lab, she set the packet down beside her system's jack point and opened her own com as if about to check the previous day's tests and data, concealing the new com sliver in the palm of her hand. Then began downloading the lab data on her com from the previous day into the system, bypassing some into the burner sliver along with all her personal and contact details she'd need, keeping her hand hovering over the jack point to confuse any scanning by the marshals.

The marshals knew not to interfere with her lab data and should assume the second destination to be a routine hard backup. She was still tense as she continued her usual wander around the plants in the lab and checked the latest results. Two marshals stood by the door and another followed her around the room, as was their custom. She waited for a shout or any sign they'd picked up on her activity.

They kept standing as they were, not relaxed but showing no signs of alarm as their eyes continuously scanned the room.

She'd counted on their being on the lookout only for a threat from outside and, so far, her gamble was paying off. They didn't expect Anna to be the threat.

Finished, she headed to the nearest personal amenity bank. The woman marshal followed her in, but even the marshals had some respect for privacy and left her to go into the cubicle on her own.

She had no doubt they had in their ranks some born in Rubhaicreach, who'd know of the old tunnels, but did that include all of them? The long-abandoned ones, narrow and hard to access by any but nimble children? She waited a suitable time, then set the sanitation cycle in progress, hoping the noise of it would cover her actions.

The brief moments it gave her were enough to use a handprint to open the concealed panel at the rear, strip off her old com and slip into the black cavity behind the panel and sneak away wearing only the burner com.

Closing the panel wall plunged her into complete darkness, one she dared not break. Not this close to the marshals' surveillance. Her hands touched the walls as she crept quietly along the tunnel.

When she was a child, the tunnels had felt dangerous in a safe kind of way. Equipped with a tuned backup com and giggling excitedly with her cousin, it had been an adventure. Together, they had explored the rough-walled passages and peered into abandoned rooms, shrieking dramatically when a tunnel ganda ran across their feet. The small, furry animals were herbivores, keeping the tunnels clear of moss buildup. No risk to people, but that made no difference to the children.

Today, the danger felt all too real.

She had about five minutes before the marshals became suspicious. She put a hand to the wall and walked as fast as possible in the darkness. She had run in these tunnels as a child.

She walked quicker. Where was it? Then her hand fell into emptiness and she stumbled, putting out her other hand to right herself as she turned the corner into a side tunnel. A few more steps and she came to a wall. Her hand reached up, feeling for the control pad. Nothing.

You were a tweenie when you last went through here.

She pulled her hand lower, feeling for the slight bump of the pad, conscious of the seconds ticking away on a clock in her head.

There! Her fingers flattened against it and a faint hiss told of a door opening. Then she was blinking in the sudden flush of light and she stepped into the janitor's cupboard, picking her way between the cleaning bots, hopefully all properly powered down as required at this time of day.

Wishful thinking. A sudden clacking from under her foot had her stumbling sideways. "Power down," she hissed at the stupid thing. Then saw the telltale flash of the sensor in the upper corner. She rushed for the opposite wall with the rack of hanging coveralls, shoved between them, and banged on the door pad hidden in the panel of hooks. The wait for the door to open was endless and she expected any second the shouts of marshals coming to catch her. Then it opened and she was through to another tunnel, manually slamming the door panel shut behind her and setting off at a run. This section ran straight for long enough but her hand trailed on the walls for directions. She took the second opening she came to. She kept running, her hand flat on the wall. One more opening, then another and she ducked inside, brushing away a wisp of something sticky.

It's only a tunnel weaver's web. Small critters harmless to anything as big as her, but swift to eliminate any pesky wernets finding their way in here. "Sorry," she whispered to the weaver. She slowed to a walk and soon came to the place she wanted, a small side tunnel, almost concealed by a long-ago fall of rocks. It had been her favourite refuge when she lost her mother.

She palmed the burner, opening up a faint light but leaving everything else shut down for now. She needed to see where she put her feet here. Carefully she stepped over the dusty rubble and bent down low to squeeze through the narrow gap. It had seemed a lot bigger the last time she was here.

Inside, it was exactly as she'd left it, all those years ago. A small, dust-caked blanket draped over the pile of cushions she'd so carefully brought in one by one so as not to be noticed. She looked at them but decided not to risk it. Their fluffy interior offered too tempting a nest for tunnel critters. Instead she perched on the small table beside it, pulling it well away from the cushions and blanket. It held her weight, just, but she needed to sit down a minute. She breathed in deeply and opened up the rest of the burner to scan for anyone tracking her.

The surrounding passages were still empty. Good. Now to wait. She'd checked Anton's schedule and knew exactly the one spot in the tunnels where she could catch him out of sight of his guards for a moment. Just long enough to persuade him to talk to her privately.

He'd agree. She was sure of it. She hoped.

The waiting was the worst of it. She hadn't dared put off her escape into the tunnels, the quiet of the lab a thing of the morning only, but all the time she expected a marshal or one of her local security to barge into her hideout. The only thought keeping her sane was that only the den Falasch knew of this place, and they were unlikely to talk. Gria wouldn't allow it.

Then it was time to go. She stood up and clambered back over the pile of rocks.

CHAPTER TWENTY-TWO

Cumchdach paced the floor of his stupidly luxurious apartment. Who decided anyone needed so much stuff? He kicked at the glossy table in his way, then cursed when the tragging thing turned out to be heavier than expected.

Anna would have laughed then told him to get over himself.

She'd called him. Reached out to make contact. Was that a start? All she'd been interested in was the fate of Falasch. What he could do for her. But she hadn't said Den Coille was wrong in taking action against her father's company. She'd asked him to talk to her first. That had to be a start.

She was still in Rubhaicreach.

One more meeting. That's what he'd promised an Fallon, but he hadn't expected to wait so long. Days it had been, and he'd snatched at the invitation when it landed discreetly on his com through a multiple blind route. It was for lunchtime today, and he had his flyer loaded and ready for him afterward. He was off to Rubhaicreach and, whether she liked it or not, Anna and Roo were coming back with him to Manascraoch.

Not that he'd figured out how to make her agree. Without that, he had no hope of taking her anywhere. She wouldn't allow it.

His chrono beeped at him. Time to go.

He switched his com to full security mode, blocking all incoming or outgoing traffic, unless he manually accepted the link, and armed his body alarms. Heading into this lot of brakkas, he needed all the protection his systems could give him. He suspected the marshals had hacked into it and added their own tweaks, but until he could get Seolta or Ethan's brother Si to check it out, he had to hope the marshals had good intentions.

Hope, but not trust. The marshals worked to their own priorities and Cumchdach had no illusions about his disposability.

The location for this meeting was much as the last. A routine city hotel conference room, the kind used for any business seminar. That's what the hotel's site had the meeting down as. A seminar on Opportunities and Challenges in Business. Suitably generic and covering the types attending today. Many still chose to enter by a hidden back door regardless, Cumchdach included.

The room was bigger today than for the last meeting, the faces of those at the last one present again, as well as others from similar companies. They included some of those he'd been surprised to see at the reception, staff from companies that should be in good heart and others like Den Coille which were already working to meet the new regulations. He was relieved to see their own bankers were absent, as were most of their critical connections.

Did the politicians know of the level of unease in the business community? No, more like panic, given the past actions of this conspiracy.

Some did, if Councillor Seilach ingh Craobh was right.

The back of his neck prickled. If this pack of folklars sniffed even a hint of his role with the marshals, his life wouldn't be worth a drop of mud.

His seat today was near the bottom of the left side of the table. Not prominent, not important. A stupid attempt at a power play. Den Coille's Festin was too sought after throughout Alliance space for a den Coille to ever be considered unimportant in a gathering like this.

He said nothing, though, and took his seat, watching the rest of the room as carefully as they watched him behind their false smiles and head nods.

It started much as usual. The Chair attended by anonymous avatar, just as the last time. Cumchdach would dearly like to know the person's identity. Even thinking of him as a man was only thanks to the avatar's image and voice tone. For all he knew, it could be Malgrave herself, despite the Alliance's statement that she was under their control and away from Arcadia.

No, they could trust that she was being kept away from Arcadia, and the lack of delay in the avatar's responses said the person behind it was definitely on-planet. But whoever it was could still be taking orders from her, and that kind of traitorous wermet was as unreliable as all roots.

The marshals' comms section must be working furiously if they monitored him as closely as he suspected. Tragging roots, he hoped they did. He needed backup here.

The discussions moved on to reports from the various attendees on their troubles and what they needed to solve them. None of them sounded like being anywhere near taking action, but he didn't count on that either. They all amounted to the same demand. The government must ensure Arcadian businesses kept making credits at the same level as before all this nonsense started.

See how they like it when the Alliance shipped them out and they ended up as nobodies on some failing space station.

"And you, den Coille? How's your company managing?" the chair suddenly asked and all heads turned in Cumchdach's direction.

He hadn't expected such a blunt attack, and the sudden silence from all parts of the table said his face showed it. He mentally breathed in, then forced his body to relax. He stared straight at the avatar at the head of the table. "We manage. Our reserves are still intact."

Did they really imagine he'd gossip about Den Coille's affairs in a mixed group like this? The talk may have been loose, but only a foolish few were too honest. The rest may be worried, but were not about to give their rivals any chance to add to the threats to their companies, and Cumchdach had stupidly assumed the table would expect him to be the same. No serious business the size of Den Coille laid themselves open to risk. Cumchdach's presence here was bad enough, with its hint of concern.

"So why are you here?" asked the chair again.

He wished he could see the man's real face. "A watching brief," he said, putting on the kind of severe face that should have warned anyone not to quiz him. "My company shares the general concern at the current direction. No one likes anything that interrupts trade, and Den Coille is not in the practice of allowing interference."

He tightened his mouth and glanced at the Falasch bank's representative, hoping the rest of the room took the hint. *Don't play games with us; we fight back.*

The shuffling across the table and around the banker said they did. But enough others still watched him, and the tension in the room held taut.

Then his com buzzed, and a message popped up in his private field. The incoming code identified it as from the marshals.

He dropped all interest in his surrounds.

'Anna is missing,' said the message. He rapped mentally at the com and waited for the rest. She'd vanished into some old tunnels in the rocky labyrinth. Worse, she had ditched her com.

What in tragging roots was she thinking?

He thrust up from his seat. "I have urgent business elsewhere," he said and began to turn. But suddenly the sound of a security lock echoed through the room and two hulking guards appeared behind him.

"What in— This is a family emergency."

"This room has monitored sensors, and you just received a Federal Marshal-secured com message. You are working for them, den Coille."

"What? No. I don't have time for this. My wife's in danger."

A weapon dug into his back.

"The wife from whom you've been at pains to show you are separated? That your marriage is over? You seem overly concerned about an ex-partner, Ser den Coille."

It was Smierg, the Falasch banker whose daughter he had rejected.

Too many others were on their feet now and glaring at him with unfriendly eyes. They all knew the danger of being found at a meeting like this.

"He knows too much," said one.

"Deal with him."

"He's too prominent." One voice of reason at least.

"An accident," shrieked another. "One no one can suspect. Your guards are good, Ser Chair. You promised us."

Now the men behind him had grabbed hold of his arms and, worse, locked him in with a security field. He was going nowhere.

The bland avatar in the top of the table turned grim, the cartoonish face leering at him with a mouth gouged down.

"Take him out and secure him until we can decide his fate. The meeting will vote on it. We cannot afford any dissent on such a matter."

"Plenty have already tried to kill den Coilles," he shouted back as the men tugged at him. "They didn't succeed then either."

Some recoiled at the blatant accusation, but too few, and none he could see with the courage to make a difference in this scared room. The guards began to drag him and he dug his heels in, fighting to buy as much time as possible.

An Fallon, you'd better be listening in to this.

They had him at the door. He tried to put out a hand, hold off the inevitable and give the room enough time to come to their senses.

"Murderers, that's what they'll call you."

But the room had gone too far, the hint of violence firing up the scared and squashing the honourable.

One man tried to speak up for him but was quickly jumped on by the rest.

"You want to go down with him?" said the Chair avatar. The man still struggled to talk, and Cumchdach noted him. If he got out of here, one man would be safe.

But the rest…

If he got out of here.

Now they had the door open, and one of the guards moved behind him, pulling his arm up behind his back and shoving him forward. Cumchdach wasn't small by mountain standards, but Mountainers weren't big, and this guard towered over him. His muscles strained to break the locking field, but the chasm of the door loomed closer, drew him in.

Crash! An explosion ripped the far wall open, and a troop of black-clad soldiers suddenly appeared in the opening. The guards stopped their shove for a vital instant, and he flung himself against the wall to stop them pushing him through.

Then the leader of the troop stepped through the hole in the wall, hand on his com and surrounded by other marshals with weapons aimed squarely at the room.

"Stay seated, Sers and Seras, if you value your lives. My officers are short on patience and long on accuracy."

Two ran to Cumchdach, grabbing the guards and breaking the holding field. He slumped to the ground as the marshals locked the guards into restraints.

The leader looked across at him. "Ser Cumchdach, your attendance at this meeting is over. The service requires you to accompany us. Troopers." Two more came and took him by each arm, frog marching him toward their leader. "Take him out," the man ordered.

"And the rest, sir?"

"Secure the room, then process them here. Transport is on its way."

The avatar had winked out at the first explosion, but a voice came from the back of the room. "You're marked, traitor."

Then the marshals had dragged Cumchdach out the door and slammed it shut on more insults.

They eased up on him around the first corner, but he didn't fool himself that meant he could escape their hold. The blood was nearly blocked to his hands. He twisted in their hold and they eased up, taking turns. He still wasn't escaping. Bundled into a dark skimmer with blacked out windows, he had no chance of following his route until the doors opened and it disgorged all of them into a depressingly familiar courtyard—the internal entry to the grey barrack of Marshal headquarters.

He was taken to a small, cell-like room inside and pushed into a seat with the two troopers on guard behind him. He tried to stand up once, but they quickly thrust him into the chair again.

"Am I under arrest?" he demanded, twisting his head to challenge them.

Neither replied. Just stared at the wall over his shoulder with the cold, disengaged look of a professional soldier. He'd seen it often enough on his guards in prison, when they weren't grinning gleefully at the treatment being dished out to one of his brothers or Ethan Winter.

They're on your side. If he repeated it often enough, he might believe it.

"My wife is missing. I can't wait here."

"The local marshals are attending to it, Ser."

As if that was going to stop him worrying. "You don't even know if she's escaped you or been kidnapped."

"The local marshals have it under control."

No, they didn't. Not if they commed him about it.

He was on the point of forcing his way out through these highly trained and muscled troopers when the door opened again and a familiar face finally arrived.

"An Fallon, what in tragging roots is going on? Where are Anna and Roo?"

The Commander's face stayed as uninformative as ever. "Your son is safe and under full Marshal surveillance."

"In Rubhaicreach?"

"Your wife's grandmother's home. It is secure, and no one there is likely to attack it."

Maybe, but why were they so worried? "You commed me. You haven't found Anna yet."

The marshal gave a clipped nod of his head.

"How did it happen?" How did the best security police force on the planet lose one woman? Anna was a botanist, not a trained agent.

An Fallon stood, legs apart and hands behind his back. It looked too military. Cumchdach wished the man would sit down.

"The Sera was working in her lab. She went for a routine break to the lab amenities, and… disappeared. We have one possible trace of her after that, in a nearby cleaner's room."

Cumchdach was standing now too, and this time, no one told him to sit. "Her lab. The one off the main tunnels down to the docks?"

"You know something, Ser?"

Cumchdach was thinking hard, remembering back to the first holiday he'd spent at Anna's home. Both their parents were still wary of the new friendship then. Anna's grandam had insisted on having her followed everywhere by an older girl, who also happened to be the eldest daughter of the head of Grandam's security. Anna had taken him to those same amenities, distracting her friend and running out with a grin on her face, grabbing Cumchdach's hand and pulling him into a cleaning cupboard. Inside, she accessed a hidden door he would never have guessed at and pulled him into a dark, dusty passage. When they lit up their coms, he saw it was an old tunnel, something like the hidden passages in the Den Coille home that his youngest brother had used to escape their captors when the family was arrested.

"Do all old families have secret hideaways?" he'd said, laughing silently with her as she tugged him onward.

He still didn't know the answer to that, but Anna had a secret place.

"Get me to Rubhaicreach and show me where she disappeared."

An Fallon studied him. "You go looking for your wife and you blow your cover completely, putting your life on notice to the conspirators. Most may be ordinary business types, but the core is another matter."

"Like those who tried to have my family executed?"

"They may be linked," said an Fallon.

Cumchdach wasn't surprised. The arrogance and stupidity were too similar. "You blew my cover when you busted through that wall. I assume all the others are now under arrest?"

The marshal shrugged. "They made their choice; now they face the consequences."

"And Arcadia, if you destroy the heads of our major companies and banks?"

That very closed look came over an Fallon's face. "The Council has it under consideration."

"There was one man stood up for me," Cumchdach felt honour driven to add. An Fallon nodded.

"We noted it."

"And the Chair. The one there by avatar only?"

An Fallon's mouth twisted down. "Our people are following the links."

"You've lost him," said Cumchdach. "He won't forgive what happened today."

"We can protect you, Ser den Coille."

"Use me as bait, you mean. It doesn't matter. Maybe he'll decide the risk of coming after me is too great."

An Fallon said nothing. Cumchdach was still nothing more than a pawn in the man's schemes. A pulse of anger shot through him.

"I may or may not be at risk; my wife is definitely in danger now." What in tragging roots was Anna up to? He headed for the doorway and this time the troopers followed him. "Brief me fully on the way to Rubhaicreach."

"Who else knows of these secret passages?" was an Fallon's first question after Cumchdach told him the full story in the flyer.

"I don't know. Not many. Anna was shown them by her grandfather den Falasch."

The marshal next commed Sera den Guire. Anna's grandmother knew about some of the older tunnels and sent a man to lead the local marshals through them. None they explored sounded familiar to Cumchdach. "My guess is the den Falasch family held the secret of the ones they built. Anna only ever showed me the way to her hiding place, no more. Not without her grandfather's permission, she said."

"Her father? Would he know?"

Cumchdach shrugged. "Anna's grandfather never trusted his son. He told Eolas only what he needed to know to run Falasch." Cumchdach had always thought that a mistake, given the resulting mishmash of Eolas mar Driach's leadership.

He lost count of how many times an Fallon made him repeat, word for word, the details of that long-ago trip with Anna. "It doesn't matter," he said, "I don't know the access codes to the tunnels."

The marshals soon discovered the entry panel Cumchdach had described, but nothing they tried unlocked it and they were reluctant to try blowing it open. "We don't know what's on the other side or whether it could injure the Sera."

"Her father has siblings, and a brother of her grandfather is still alive. Maybe one of them knows the codes and the passages."

The marshals were onto that one already. None of the codes the siblings gave them opened this doorway, and the granduncle was a notorious recluse, keeping the secret of his refuge known to very few. He had no more time for the siblings than he did for Eolas, it turned out, and none were privy to his home.

Was there anything else Cumchdach remembered to help them?

"You told us of the passages, Ser Cumchdach. A good marshal doesn't need much to solve a problem, but we do need something."

Cumchdach looked up at the Commander, his face as cold and ungiving as ever. But the words helped. "Thank you."

"We will find her," the man added in his clipped tone.

Commander Marco an Fallon rarely made promises, but those he did, he kept. Cumchdach had to hope this time wasn't the exception.

The marshal would find Anna, but he hadn't promised she'd be alive or unhurt.

"Worry muddies thinking. I need you sharp-witted and ready."

"You reading my mind now?"

A trace of what might almost be sympathy crossed the marshal's face. "I've been leading a department of strong-willed hellions for years. Learning how to read what troubles them is a necessary survival skill."

Cumchdach choked. An Fallon had nearly made a joke. Dry, cynical as all roots, but Cumchdach's lips lifted involuntarily in response. "Not sure if even your marshals are as tough headed as my Anna," he replied as dryly.

He took the man's words to heart though, and spent the rest of the trip staring out the window at the rigidly groomed stretches of the Urbis Estuarine zone below as he tried to remember everything he could of that long-ago adventure. It did nothing to stop the panic eating at him, its grip easing only when the flyer began to lift up to cross the crags of the Northern Ranges.

Nearly to Rubhaicreach.

The rocky peninsula stood aloof in the stormy seas, jutting out on its own from the northernmost slopes of the Western Ranges. A creek cut across the base of it, a trickle now but he'd seen it turn into a raging, angry torrent that separated the peninsula from the rest of Mountainer country. It tumbled down from an outcropping of the mountains then turned sharply north to cut off the hard-edged rocks of the peninsula.

Maybe that's why Rubhaicreach never quite trusted the rest of Mountainer country—even their accent showing its own quirks. When the creek raged, all access to the peninsula was gone. On the mainland side, the Western ranges fell into the sea in an impossible-to-cross, jumble of steep rock faces.

Was that difference what lay between him and Anna? Why he couldn't reach her?

No, they'd grown up together. Anna *knew* him.

He concentrated on the land below. On the bleak, scrub-covered plain sitting between the creek and the city. Not that it was clear where the city started. A few rooflines, the trace of vehicle paths and tracks, coloured to blend in with the surrounding vegetation, and the tossed heads of the few shrubs brave enough to reach for the sky. The buffeting of the flyer was proof of the strength of the winds that made the peninsula home.

Rubhaicreach built down because you couldn't stand straight at ground level, said an old Mountainer truism. He leaned forward, peering out the window at the ground looming up far too quickly. It looked forbidding but, at the last moment, a black tunnel appeared and they whooshed inside, settling gently on a pad in a wide hall.

"I swear one day these tragging stiff necks are going to refuse to open that door and we crash into it," grumbled his pilot.

Cumchdach let out his breath, in full agreement. Not even the Rubhaicreach controllers would refuse entry to a marshal's flyer, or so he'd told himself as they hurtled into land, but they did like to play hard and fast with outsiders.

He'd never heard of an actual crash. Didn't mean it hadn't happened.

Things got no better after they stepped out. "Falasch is closing ranks," reported the dour-faced local marshal. The hint of an accent broke through the standard Urbis voice.

"You're not from Urbis?"

The man stared back, cold-eyed. "Marshal Dunan, at your service, and that of the Marshals and Arcadia."

Cumchdach flushed. "My family are grateful for all you've done."

The man gave a stiff-necked excuse for a bow, but Cumchdach said nothing. The marshals on duty in Rubhaicreach had saved Anna, and he would never forget that.

"Have you tried the senior Ser den Falasch?" he asked instead. "Ser Eolas den Falasch's uncle."

"He's not been found."

"Falasch is hiding him?"

The man shook his head. "He may be the last of his generation but the ser has a reputation for not caring what Falasch wants. They looked as frustrated as we are. He's hiding, and will come out when he's ready." Marshal Dunan turned to an Fallon. "That's what the talk is in Rubhaicreach. They don't want us hunting him either."

"Too many secrets of their own?"

The man lifted his shoulder. "That, or they've grown wary of outsiders. Ser Cumchdach den Coille's presence doesn't help. You need to be careful here, Ser."

"The rumours are flying," guessed Cumchdach. "My wife's safety is at issue here. Tell them that. She's still of Rubhaicreach."

The man shifted on his feet, as uncomfortable looking as a marshal could be, with their tragging habit of hiding what they thought.

"She was born here," said Cumchdach sharply.

"Problem is, no one's quite sure of her loyalties. Not after the legal strife, or that's what their attitude says. The Alliance Central outcome is already hurting the city financially."

Marshals were also particularly good at reading people. Another part of their tragging training.

"She's loyal to Rubhaicreach. It's her family that's betrayed the city, not Anna."

Marshal Dunan lifted his shoulder, and Cumchdach felt as if he'd been slapped. "Do not blame it on my marriage. We'd have mended things long ago if the marshals hadn't interfered." There was enough truth in that to slap the marshals into a fraught silence, faces tight and with that abominable fixed look that said they were in a private comms link. Then salutes all round and Marshal an Fallon gave him a grim nod and marched back into the flyer without another word. It lifted off, leaving Cumchdach surrounded by the local squad. He wasn't sure whether to be relieved or annoyed at the sense of being a package passed on by the marshals.

So far, the locals had held back, keeping a healthy distance between themselves and these dangerous outsiders. But the rigid looks of the marshals at Cumchdach had a few twitching their lips as if muffling laughter. Good to know he was some use, even if just as a source of amusement to landing workers.

Enough. Arguing with marshals wasn't getting him anywhere.

He slapped his com to signal his luggage to follow him to Anna's grandam's house, then stepped away from the patrol. "I'll meet you once I've seen Sera den Guire and made sure my son is safe," he said.

"Ser den Coille," called the squad leader, but Cumchdach ignored him. The tramp of boots followed him anyway, making him look ridiculous as he tromped through the caverns with a troop of marshals trailing after him, but he no longer cared. He put a spurt on to give him a moment's respite as a corner approached.

"Ser Cumchdach duine Anna," said a voice from the dark shadows and his hand went immediately to the small blaster he'd taken to wearing hidden in his tunic. The shadows coalesced but the man—no, youth, he saw now—made no move to show himself.

The boots behind him sped up. The marshals didn't like losing sight of their target.

"Who are you? Quickly."

"Follow me," said the voice. "The old uncle sent me."

It was stupid, foolish beyond measure, but Cumchdach had no choice. Not if he wanted to find Anna. He stepped into the shadows, and the boy bundled him through a concealed doorway, sliding it closed behind him even as the marshals' running boots rounded the corner.

It was pitch black, but the boy's finger touched Cumchdach's mouth as if warning him. He also suffered the boy's hand taking his arm to lead him on and kept his steps as silent as possible. Manascraoch folk were known for their skill at that, thanks to growing up in moving branches, but this boy was a master at it and they both hurried down the dark passageways with only the taste of stirred up dust to betray their passage.

The boy led him down a sloping tunnel, deep into the peninsular rocks. He lost all sense of direction, the feeling of the weight of rock above him and a faint hint of salty dankness alone telling him they'd gone well below dock level. He hadn't realised Rubhaicreach delved so deep.

The boy finally came to a stop, tapped on a doorway in the darkness, and a panel slid open. The light beyond was dim but still had him blinking furiously and struggling to see. Then his eyes adjusted and he saw an old man sitting in a chair and watching him curiously.

"So you're the husband of my Anna. I remember you as a boy, but you've grown a bit since then."

The light breathlessness of the man's voice told its own story, but otherwise his long years sat lightly. The spareness of his bony frame and his white hair betrayed his age, but it was the old and laughing eyes that caught the attention. The man may be one of the oldest in the city, but he wasn't giving in easily.

"Ser Aonar mar Ramach an Cinna den Falasch, this is an honour," said Cumchdach, giving him the most formal bow of young relative to older and revered senior.

The man let out a dry cackle of laughter. "Your parents taught you well, boy. I remember them too. Your father was ever a slippery rogue, even as a youngster."

"Thank you on his behalf, Ser. He will take that as a compliment."

Another laugh at that one. "Slippery too, I see."

Cumchdach wisely said nothing to that. "You sent your boy for me, Ser."

"Huh. The other way round, I'd say. You were hunting me."

"And you let me find you, Ser. I assume there was a reason."

"Anna. Too good a girl for their games. You've lost her."

Cumchdach hung on to his patience by too thin a thread. "I would much appreciate your help in finding her, Ser."

"Decided to hide, did she?"

"Yes, Ser. I think she's in the place she took me once."

The man nodded slowly. "It's a place to start."

"But?"

"Talk still comes to me, young man. There are outsiders in the rock. We tolerate problems within families; bringing in outsiders to solve it is another matter entirely."

Cumchdach took a careful breath. "You support Sera Gria ingh Ovirisch bean Eolas's actions?"

"That silly madam. Of course not. But she is the wife of my nephew, and he is the current head of Falasch Shipping. Driach was the business brains in our family. But his son…"

"And his grandchildren?"

"Anna is the hope of Falasch, and you've known that for years, young man. Don't try telling me otherwise."

Right now, he'd like to tell the man to get on with what he knew about Anna's location, but he knew better than to hurry the old. They tended to go slower in revenge. "And the other children?"

A breathless huff that could be a chuckle or a sigh. "The twins are as silly a pair as you'd find. Their mother's daughters. The boy… potential there, if he's not been ruined already."

Cumchdach held tight to his control. "Anton den Falasch is behind Anna's disappearance?"

"In a way. He's the one put out the call for her."

"But…"

"He's got himself a catch on a line that's running wild. The boy hasn't a hope of landing the monster, and doesn't know it yet."

"If you tell me where she is, I'll find her, Ser. Just tell me."

For the first time, the old man's self-assurance slipped. "There's the problem. I don't know where she is. Not at present."

"Then why…?" Cumchdach bit down hard on the fury boiling up. "If I describe her past hideout, can you tell me how to find it again."

"Why do you think I brought you here, boy? You know Anna as well as anyone living, including that silly father of hers."

Cumchdach coiled his fists together and described the old hole in the passageways, setting it out in terse and precise words that brought that unreliable twitch back to the old man's lips.

"Do you know the spot?" he said at the end.

"Of course I do, boy," the old man said in a tone he was sure was intended to aggravate. "It's nice to know it's still keeping young dreams safe. I spent many a misbegotten hour there a long time ago." Cumchdach's couldn't stop the lift of his lips. "Books, boy. Books and old reader files, of the kind long discarded by my credit-grubbing relatives. Get your mind out of the gutter. I had plenty of that in my time too, but none were my passion. Not as Anna is yours," he added in a serious tone that crashed into Cumchdach's badly shredded nerves. "I never found my match, but you did, boy. And you took her for granted."

He'd taken a step forward before he realised it and brought himself to a grinding halt before he could do worse. "Anna is everything to me, and always has been. She *knows* that."

The twitch was worse than ever. "The young. So blind," the old man murmured with a lift of his shoulders. "Perhaps you should remind her of it when you find her. She doesn't appear to remember it as well as you do."

"You can be sure I will—*when* I find her, Ser."

The old man nodded. "The boy will take you there."

"About time," Cumchdach muttered, and this time didn't care that the old man heard him.

"And when you find her, Ser," the man added, in that scarily serious voice, "take her away from here. She's paid her dues to Falasch. It's time for others to pick up the burden."

Cumchdach couldn't agree more. He gave the man another formal bow but followed the boy out of the room with more than a touch of relief. He led them back into the old, dusty passages through yet another of the hidden panels, but this time the tunnel went uphill.

Was the whole rocky peninsula honeycombed with hidden passageways to add to the warren of homes, shops and business caverns already burrowing through it? He was surprised, though, how quickly the boy brought him to the hiding place he remembered from all those years ago.

Nothing much had changed, except for the air of neglect from years of abandonment and the dust coating everything, clogging his throat already irritated from the dank, cold passageways.

He then thanked the roots for the dust. Clear as the stars in a cloudless sky were the footprints dotting the room. The small ones he knew immediately. Anna had been here.

But the others filled him with dread. Larger, mingled in with her prints, and clustered most around her shelf where the childhood treasures once took pride of place. Now, they lay smashed or mangled on the floor, and a flurry of footprints and streaks on the walls told of a swarm of activity.

Anna's prints entered and left the worst area. Had she been here? Had the intruders taken her, had they hurt her?

He pointed the boy to the smallest prints, leading out the door. "Anna's. We follow them."

He had to peer closely to see Anna's prints among all the scuffs and tromps of the rest, but together they managed to follow her track. The occasional scuffing of her feet, or swipe, had his heart pause, but he gritted his teeth and kept looking. Occasionally they lost her in the flurry of disturbed dust, but then one or other found her again. Mostly it was the youth, and Cumchdach thanked the uncle for sending him. Not that the boy was here for him. The youngster made it quite clear from the start he was here to help Sera Anna.

"She helped out me mam in a tough time," he said, then shut his mouth again and bent to check the tracks. "They're heading for the Falasch warehouses."

Cumchdach increased the pace. "What in tragging roots is she up to?"

The boy hurried on, his eyes following the same story on the ground as Cumchdach's. Did he also see the occasional slip as if Anna had tripped?

There were no drag marks.

He held tight to his sanity. *She's fine. She's safe.*

If only the repeated litany could make it real.

Suddenly the boy stopped, pointed urgently at Cumchdach to douse his com light. Cumchdach did so and plunged them back into darkness. He heard a slight scrabbling and a thin slit of weak light appeared.

"Where—"

A hand slapped over his mouth and he kept the rest of the question unsaid. The outline of the boy's head peered around an open door and then held up a hand in command.

Wait.

He beckoned, pointing low, and Cumchdach crouched as he followed the boy through the door and back into the public passageways.

Not a well-used one, by the lack of people and empty silence. A row of cleaners' coveralls hung from a nearby wall.

The boy straightened and put on a swagger. Cumchdach copied him, as he'd done all during this journey. Nothing to see here; merely the husband of a den Falasch using a guide to explore the city.

He'd been coming here too many years for that to be believed. Once they got back to the main tunnels he knew well, Cumchdach would need no guide. Only the boy didn't take him to the main tunnels, and there was no longer any dust on the floor to show him those precious small footprints.

"Why are you taking us this way?" Cumchdach hissed.

The boy scowled back. "It's the way we go when we don't want to be seen. Quiet."

Cumchdach usually gave the orders. He didn't take them from nobody striplings. Today, he was too worried to see the funny side of it. He nodded his compliance.

More cleaning supplies and storage cupboards. They had breached the realms of the night cleaners, he guessed, feeling like an intruder. Then they rounded a bend and saw a body crumpled on the floor. Cumchdach broke into a run.

It wasn't Anna. His heart started to beat again. He rolled the young man over. Anton den Falasch. Still breathing, but too lightly and shallowly, and a nasty gash split the side of his head and cheek.

The kind made by an armoured fist.

He wanted to shake the boy into consciousness. He lifted his com and called the emergency medics instead. Shaking the boy achieved nothing and might end up getting him a police charge.

He had to stay free to find Anna.

"Get water," he ordered his guide. He brought back a bottle, and Cumchdach sloshed it over the young man's face.

"Wha—?" A flicker of life touched Anton's eyes.

"Anna. Where is she?"

"They took her. Guards." Then he fell silent again, and no amount of cold water brought him back.

The medics arrived as he was about to throw the last of the water at the boy.

"That's enough, Ser Cumchdach. You trying to drown him?"

The medic grabbed the bottle and threw it at his second. He bent to check Anton. Then saw the blood. Dark eyes blazed at him.

"You did this?"

Cumchdach quickly shook his head. "I found him like it."

"And what are you doing down here, Ser den Coille?"

"My wife is missing and her brother is involved."

"So you decide to finish off your peoples' work and drown Ser Anton? You'll have this city soon enough, den Coille, without eliminating a boy."

The marshals had warned him that rumours about the Restin compensation trial were rife in the city. "Nothing is decided yet," he tried to say.

The second medic elbowed him aside and bent to help his colleague. They settled a pallet under Anton and carefully loaded him into their unit.

"The city will find Sera Anna, Ser. Please return to your hotel. Word will be sent when she is discovered if she wishes to advise you."

"I'm staying at Sera den Guire's, not a hotel," he snapped, and was pleased to see he'd startled them. "Let the marshals and city security know the instant Ser Anton wakes."

Suddenly the boy on the stretcher came to life. "The docks," whispered Anna's half-brother. "Lock down the docks." Then he collapsed again.

Cumchdach slapped his com. "Marshal Dunan. Priority one."

"Ser," came back a furious voice. "Nice of you to link in again."

"Lock down the docks, now." He sent through the record of the last few minutes and waited impatiently.

"Done," finally came back from the marshal. "Wait there. Do not move. A troop is on its way to you."

"Track my com. I'll be at the docks—and get my son to Manascraoch immediately." He slapped off the link. "Boy," he turned to his youthful guide. "Where do the smugglers dock?"

CHAPTER TWENTY-THREE

Anna cursed as her captor dragged her too fast and she stumbled. "Either kill me now or ease up before you do it anyway."

The troop's headlong rush didn't stop. She cursed again, this time in her head and at herself. She'd been so sure she could evade Anton's guards and persuade him to help her. She may have been right about her brother, but she'd been dead wrong about the guards.

Her brother, now a crumpled heap on the tunnel floor, so small, too small. The back tunnel from the docks marched mostly straight, but this stretch bent and twisted around old diggings, with one blind spot where Anton was out of sight of his trailing guards. It should have been a safe place to waylay him. She hadn't counted on them putting a tracker on him, or the guards that had followed her without her picking them up. With guards ahead and behind, her brother's cry when she suddenly leaped out at him on the bend had brought both squads down on them.

Anton had tried to defend her. All it had gained him was a shot from a guard running in from the rear. He went down so suddenly. Too suddenly for a paralysing shot.

No, they can't have killed him. Not the next in line to the control of Falasch. They needed her family's company. Gria's troops wouldn't kill her son.

If Gria controlled them. The hard faces and strange accents of the troopers dragging her along made that unlikely. They weren't from Urbis, nor from the central Protos region or the parts of Deuteron she'd visited.

Who had sent them?

They were nearly at the docks. Someone must see her and put a stop to this madness. She was born here. Rubhaicreach was her home, its people hers. Despite the angry murmurs she'd met over the last few days, none of them would allow her to be kidnapped like this.

Then they turned left when they should have turned right and into the dark pit of an old tunnel. It led to one place only.

The smugglers dock.

A back cavern that opened through a concealed tunnel into the open sea on the opposite side of the peninsula from the main harbour. You had to be a good captain to navigate that entrance with its sudden buffeting and treacherous currents as the waves crashing on the rock cliffs clashed with the running tides of the tunnel. Only the most experienced or the most desperate attempted that opening.

That peril limited its use enough that Rubhaicreach turned a blind eye to the few ships daring the passage. Pirates all, but smuggling was going to happen whatever you did. So said the official line, and this way they knew and could track every user of the passage.

Or to put it more bluntly, Rubhaicreach was in no position to refuse the percentage the canny pirates paid to port officials to look the other way.

But stealing away a daughter of den Falasch and den Guire was another matter entirely, and no sensible port official would put his job at risk to be a party to it. Pirates were in it for the credits, not politics. Meaning these troopers were no pirates. Nor were they stupid. The smugglers' dock was empty when her captors dragged her kicking and screaming to the quayside.

She must not let them put her on that ship. She dug in her heels, grabbing at anything passing.

It made no difference. Black and blue with bruises and scrapes, she was inexorably pushed toward the boarding chute. Then she was on it. She grabbed for the sides, holding on tight. All that brought her was manhandling to unlock her clinging fingers. One by painful one, each finger was levered off the chute sides as they pushed her from behind.

"Hey."

The voice came from the dock entry. A local coming on the scene and recognising her?

The tugging on her fingers increased and she clung harder, turning her head to see the newcomer.

Then shock made her release her grasp.

"No. Go back," she cried.

"Never," said her husband.

Cumchdach began to run. All colour washed out of Anna's face when she saw him, but her captors still shoved at her. She tumbled to the floor. Her cry of pain had him spurring faster, pulling his small blaster out and firing at the man holding her.

He ducked but caught enough of the paralysing ray to stumble. Only he fell right on top of Anna.

Cumchdach raced up and thrust him off, seeing only Anna lying in pain on the deck. Before he could pull her up, multiple hands piled onto him, dragging him back and the unmistakable sound of restraints locked his hands hard to his sides.

"Leave her alone," he yelled furiously. Anna pulled herself painfully up, and crouched staring at him with wide eyes.

"What are you doing here?" she whispered.

"You're in trouble. Where do you think I'd be?"

"You were in Urbis."

One of the men beside him laughed in a way that made Anna flinch. Cumchdach lurched sideways and relished the crunch of his shoulder into the man's gut. It felt good, despite paying for it with a fist to the face.

Another man grabbed Anna and held his blaster to her head. Cumchdach froze.

"That's enough, den Coille. Unless you want an end to your wife, right here and now."

Sickening reality hit him. "She's more valuable to you than I am. The government will pay to have her back."

Then a new figure strode down the chute, and Cumchdach's heart dropped. He'd seen this man at one of the conspiracy meetings, standing behind a woman seated near the top of the table. He tried to surge forward, but the hands and restraints tightened painfully.

The newcomer marched up and spat straight in his face. "We have no argument with Sera den Coille o Falasch. She made no agreement with us."

"Then let her go."

"Not yet, Ser den Coille, or should I say, Ser Traitor. There are worthy people sitting in prison tonight, thanks to you. Once they are free, the Sera will be safely returned to her family here in Rubhaicreach."

"And Ser den Coille," called Anna from behind the man.

"Shush, my heart."

The man laughed again. "The Ser owes us. Once we are paid, he will be released."

Cumchdach noted he made no promise on the state Cumchdach would be in. "Sera Anna will be released free from harm," he said.

The man stared him straight in the eye. "The Sera stays alive—if you cooperate fully with us, Ser Turncoat."

It wasn't nearly enough but was all they were getting. Cumchdach looked at Anna and hoped she read the message in his eyes. She opened her mouth instead.

"And Ser Cumchdach. You harm him, and you lose every Mountainer's support."

"It's better than losing everything we've built. When the planet realises the folly of this government's nonsense, they will thank us for our actions."

Cumchdach stared. Did the man truly believe that? He'd thought he was dealing with greedy corporates, not raving idealists. Anna's guard dug that blaster harder into her head and another shot at her legs. He surged forward but not before she slumped to one side, her paralysed legs giving way under her, and banged her head on the hard deck. She lay ominously still. Her guard ran a scanner over her.

"Unconscious only. She'll do."

The man went to pick her up. Cumchdach thrust forward. "I'll carry her. She's my wife."

"One false move and we kill her, Ser."

Cumchdach nodded curtly. "Understood."

They removed his restraints and he hurried to Anna, with blasters tracking his every move. She was in his arms and alive, for now. He carefully picked her up, carrying her gently as the guards bustled them down into a room deep in the ship's hold. A door clanged shut behind him, and they were shut in with the sound of the sea shivering through the sides of the room.

He couldn't see much from the pale light glimmering through the one small gap high above the entrance door. There was little enough in the room. Only a crude bench, marginally cleaner than the floor, where he laid Anna down. There wasn't even a hygiene closet. He opened his com and shone its light on Anna, his temper rising with each new bruise and scrape he discovered. Bloody scratches covered her fingers. She'd fought hard against her captors.

"That's my *a chiad.*"

They had to get out of here. He tried raising a link on his com. Nothing. Their captors must be blocking him. But a den Coille always had more than one track to follow. He opened up his hidden files and called up an emergency link he'd sworn never to use. One an Fallon had warned was for emergency use only, if his life was at risk. The unspoken condition was, if his life was at risk and he fully agreed to follow the marshals' orders, whatever they asked. Do that, and he surrendered completely to the marshals. He set his com to a mind-to-mind link and within seconds, the link came back.

'Den Coille. What have you got yourself into this time?' said Marco an Fallon.

'Anna and I have been captured by the conspiracists. They're holding her hostage for my help. Follow the link to locate us.'

An Fallon didn't sound surprised, but then little ruffled the man's calm. 'A team is being despatched. Give me the details then shut down this link. We can only hold the shielding for a limited time.'

'It will be good to get out of here.'

After that, a worrying silence fell, as if an Fallon was consulting with someone else. *Come on, Marshal.* Then the marshal came back to him.

"Our team will monitor you at all times. You will be safe, Ser, along with your wife. But you must follow the conspiracists' orders as if submitting to them. It's our best chance yet to expose their core."

'No.' Cumchdach couldn't believe it. 'Anna's safety comes first.'

'She will be safe, Ser. But this is too important.'

Then the link broke and Cumchdach was on his own. An Fallon had left him no choice. Go along with the marshals and keep fooling the conspiracists, or lose their protection and put Anna at risk. The policeman was cold-blooded enough to enforce it.

"One day, you'll pay for this, Marshal," he swore to himself. He wiped the exchange and deactivated his comms function to stop their captors finding it, cursing out loud. "We'll get out of this, Anna. Don't ask me how yet, but I promise you will be safe."

A cold chuckle sounded through the door. Their guards were listening. He glared at the door, then bent to check Anna again. A slight fluttering of her eyelids said she was recovering, but it was a tragging hard wait until she opened her beautiful eyes fully.

"Cumchdach. *Mo stochri.*" Then her lips pursed and full consciousness returned. "Where are we," she asked, struggling to sit up. He stilled her with a hand on her shoulder.

"Wait. You've been hurt."

He sent a look to the wall opposite the door, the one through which Cumchdach could hear the sea surging. It had changed. "We're sailing," his Rubhaicreach wife said with horror in her dark eyes.

He couldn't tell her of the marshals' surveillance. Not with the guard listening at the door and monitoring their com signals. Nor did he trust a personal link. The marshals had shielded his call to them, but he had stopped counting on them for anything else the moment an Fallon had set out their brutal condition for helping to save Anna.

"You will be safe. I promise it."

Anna gave him the same twisted smile as when he'd first brought her to Manascraoch and promised her she wouldn't fall from any of the constantly moving branches. He'd delivered that day, though afterward she set herself to learn everything she could about the security features built into the city to stop accidents. They weren't foolproof, she'd pointed out.

Nor was his promise today, but he'd do everything in his power to keep it. "You will be safe and return to Roo."

"And our baby?"

"I ordered him taken to Manascraoch. I'm sorry, but it seemed safest with you missing."

"Good," she said with satisfaction, and one of the weights on his shoulders eased. Now was not the time to talk about their future, but soon, very soon. When they were all safe again.

Which would happen only if he betrayed his company, his region and his family and went along with their mad captors as the marshals ordered.

The sounds of the sea rose. "We're out in open water," said Anna.

"Someone will see this ship and ask where it's going." It was a vain hope, but it might ease her fear.

She cocked her head again. "They're keeping close to the cliffs." She fell silent, looking at the wall. "Her captain's a mad one."

Cumchdach was listening hard now too, but he lacked Anna's knowledge of the sea. "Can they make it?"

She nodded slowly, staring at the wall as if trying to see the land beyond. "It's the smugglers' route. There's a narrow channel with a driving current. If you stick precisely to it, the current takes you through a gap in the waves to open water. If he knows of it, he's a smuggler proper and we're safe." She waved a hand to shush him and bent her head to the wall again. He sat, watching her, seeing the intelligence hiding behind those calm, dark eyes charging into life. Watching her lost in her work had always fascinated him; now his heart pulsed too fast as he waited.

Then she gave a sharp nod. "He's caught it, the change in the currents when you reach the end of it. He knows what he's doing." She kept listening as he felt the ship keeling to one side.

"They're turning."

Anna nodded, her face grim. "Heading out to sea. They'll make for the open seas, beyond our zone of control, then we'll find out where they're going."

"The marshals will be looking for us." It was the nearest he could come to telling her the truth. Her eyes suddenly lifted to his and searched his face in a searing wide-eyed scrutiny. He nodded, then pointed to the door.

Her mouth dropped and a worried crease crossed her forehead.

"That's good," she said in a cross voice. "As long as there's no price to pay. The marshals play a long game."

And those eyes studied her again, but this time he straightened his mouth, keeping it firmly closed and refused to give her any hint. His bargain with the marshals was his business. She pointed at him, then put her hand on her chest, and peered at him, eyebrows raised.

He couldn't lie to her. Not again. Not even to make her feel safe. Look where it had got him last time. He pointed at her and nodded.

She shot up, her head shaking furiously. Her hand thrust at him, then at her, then circled. *Both of us, together. We're both in this.*

He wanted to refuse, to tell her she came first with him and always would, but then saw her bite her lip, and jerk back as if denying it. He'd done that to her, made her doubt his faith in her.

He nodded and put out his hand in the way of a business deal being sealed. She changed it to an arm-to-arm clasp as in a vow of honour, one he had to return. We're equals in this, together in whatever comes, that clasp said. Her lips lifted in the nearest he'd seen in months to her smiling properly at him.

Keeping to the agreement was sorely tested a few hours later when the lack of a service unit became too uncomfortable. He banged on the door and demanded attention.

"Put us in a cabin somewhere."

The guard peered in the door slot. "Orders are, you stay here."

"Then provide us with water and a service closet."

The guard grinned unreliably. "Orders include that, but one at a time. The woman first."

Cumchdach surged forward. "No. I stay with her at all times. You want my cooperation; that's the price."

"You're in no position to make demands Ser. One at a time, or not at all."

He wished he could agree to that, but Anna shook her head, gripping her mouth. "I'll be fine," she said.

"You'd better be."

He moved back from the door at the guard's order and scowled furiously at the mag-sized blaster the man pointed at him when he entered the room. Another man stood near the doorway. Apart from that, all he could see was a blank wall. Some kind of passageway, he guessed.

"She'd better return safe and untouched."

Anna touched his hand as she passed, then walked out with head held high and that contained look of hers on her face. A woman in charge of her surrounds, it said, a look that had worked miracles more times than he remembered.

He hoped it helped now.

Not when she returned with red flags on her cheeks. Her hasty scurry behind him drove his temper to a dangerous edge. He touched her arm.

She flinched, pulling away from him, and scuttled over to the rough bench. "I'm fine."

But she wouldn't meet his eyes.

"Your turn, Ser," said the guard with the surly face, leaving him no time to find out what she'd endured. Anna was staring past him at the man standing behind the guard.

"You keep my wife safe. I'll go with the other," Cumchdach said to the surly one, refusing to move until the man gave a curt nod.

"Be quick, Ser."

Cumchdach marched out, wishing he could stay. "I won't be long," he called hopefully to Anna.

He was as quick as he could manage and kept the service door slightly ajar to make sure the guard he distrusted stayed in sight.

The guard slammed it shut. Cumchdach swiftly finished up and shoved it open again. The man leered at him. "You're not as attractive as your wife."

Then he gave him a totally unnecessary full body search, hands lingering where they'd most embarrass him. But Cumchdach had endured the same from the prison guards. He'd mastered the skill of dissociating himself. All he gave the guard was a stony silence, and at the end the man shoved him and slapped restraints tight on his arms and legs, so he had to shuffle painfully back to his cell.

At least he took them off before shoving him back inside, making him stumble painfully to the hard floor as the door slammed shut on him.

He picked himself up and straightened before he frightened Anna. "Are you all ri—"

A sudden chop of her hand waved him quiet, and she put a finger to her ear.

He stopped talking and listened. Then felt the ship lurch sideways. He caught hold of the wall to steady himself and saw her automatically lean with the swelling motion. Finally it stopped.

"Where are we going?"

"Back." She listened again, her mouth open in concentration as she touched a hand to the wall as if trying to feel the sea outside. "We're going back to Rubhaicreach."

This time, he heard the changing noise. The ship's engines on full propulsion. Anna sat up and grabbed for a hand hold. "Must be a storm coming. They're running fast for the docks. It's the only safe place on this coast if a big one is blowing up."

"Will we make it?"

"I don't know." She clamped her mouth shut, as if shutting inside any fear plaguing her.

To Anna, it seemed to take a long time to get back to port. She listened intently all the way. At least it gave her an excuse to stop Cumchdach's questions. She was not telling him of the awful moments in that service cubicle. The guard had insisted on keeping the door open and afterward, made her stand while he thrust his fingers all over her. At one stage, she saw his hand go to his trouser fastening, then a glance at the ceiling and he stopped. She'd have liked to say something cutting. The thump would be worth it, but that wasn't what stopped her.

Cumchdach had been on a knife edge when she was marched out. It wouldn't take much to make him erupt. Violence was usually a last resort for him. He had to be pushed hard.

Danger to her did it, she discovered today.

If he tried anything, these men would kill him, that was all too clear. They needed him, but only if he cooperated.

Back in her cell, she latched onto the changing sea sounds to stop Cumchdach talking. Not yet. Not till they were free. She had reason enough to shush Cumchdach. The storm's sounds soon began to smash onto the hull. Just on the other side of the wall she leaned against. The waves rocked against the ship, a wash of sound at first but growing louder and more insistent with each beat of the engines.

"How close?" asked Cumchdach. Will we make it, he meant.

"It'll be tight."

The city guards locked the port gates before a storm arrived. Massive metal plates reaching up to the cliff top to keep the angry waves from smashing into the sheltered cover of the harbour. They wouldn't keep out the winds; only ships anchored in the inner caverns were safe from that. But it was the giant waves that upended ships.

That could kill all on board.

The captain was running fast and straight. A prison cell was better than a watery grave. That's what one smuggler had said to her grandfather years ago when caught with a haul of vicious drugs after running for port in a storm.

A storm like the one now beating against the hull of this ship.

Then she finally heard another sound. A graunching, scraping of metal on rock. It was coming from the front of the boat.

"They're raising the port gates," she said in horror.

Cumchdach had always been able to read her face. "Will we make it in time?"

She couldn't answer, could only cling to the side of the bench.

He hadn't touched her, not since she flinched from him, but he'd taken a seat beside her, close by if she needed him. She put out a hand and dug it into his thigh, needing the feel of those solid muscles. His arm shot around her and he dragged her into the shelter of his body.

"Together. Always." The old promise renewed. Today, his murmured words cut through everything that still lay between them and had her snuggling in as close as she could.

"Always," she mouthed softly, but he heard and his lips closed on hers.

It was like a coming home.

They had kissed so many times over the years. Fraught and frantic, laughing with the delight of passion roused, soft with desire and need. Today was different, a long, slow kiss, mouth to mouth and body to body, rich with promise and gentle with the ease of it.

He lifted his mouth and stared at her in the dim shadow of their com lights. "Not here, not in this place. But I need you so badly, *a chiad*. When we get free, when we have Roo safe with us again and we're a proper family, in our own sleeper and our own home."

"Manascraoch is a long way from here," she tried saying with a watery chuckle. The thought of it was too enticing in this dark place. She daren't think of it, not if she wanted to endure the present.

"We will get out of here."

The chuckle wasn't so forced this time. "Because Cumchdach den Coille says we will." She'd teased him so many times at his assumption that whatever he ordered would happen. That it was too often true made it funnier between them, when he knew so well not to order her. Together, always. A vow they'd first made as young lovers, and that they'd kept for so many years.

Until her father betrayed his contract with the den Coilles and stole from them. No, until Cumchdach didn't trust her enough to tell her about it in case it *upset* her. Had made her so much less than she was, just because she carried his child.

Not that she hadn't understood him. She'd been as nervous about this new adventure of pregnancy and parenthood as he. Had understood he'd never before faced something so important that he couldn't control.

But it was no excuse.

So how to find a way back?

He gave her the look he'd always done when they'd hit trouble, a pained grimace. But it wasn't followed by the usual cocksure grin. "No, *a chiad.* Because together, we are unbeatable. These wermets don't know what they're up against. You're not alone, not this time."

He'd glanced at the door at that last one. As if about to say something else then stopped in case they were heard. She touched his com. They couldn't risk a personal link, not with these captors. If their backers were as powerful as she guessed, they could break even a personal link, but could Cumchdach have warned the marshals? The Council troops had resources they kept very secure, and it made them unbeatable by private troops. She touched the sliver on his wrist and looked up. He gave a slight nod, then leaned down and touched his lips to hers again.

A scraping outside the door, as if a guard had stumbled in his footing, had him pulling back. Then a surging sea tossed them both hard against the wall and she banged her shoulder.

"Anna."

She angled herself back, holding on tight to him. "I'm fine. Just a bruise."

He braced his feet against the floor and locked his arms around her. "I have you, *a chiad.*"

The ship bobbed madly. The waves must be starting to break against the rising gates. The engines shrieked in loud peals, complaining vociferously at their treatment. A high-pitched vibration threatened to shake the ship apart if the waves failed to destroy it. Both of them clung tightly to the bench, Cumchdach keeping one arm hard around Anna's shoulders. The boat lurched back and forth, bouncing up the waves. Then a graunching sounded under them, as if the prow had hit metal.

She held her breath. The gates, grazing the bottom of the hull as the ship raced for safety. Images of hull breaches poured into her head. They were deep in the bowels of the ship here.

Then the movement slowed, the waves eased, and the engines throttled gratefully back. Behind them, the slapping sounds of water against a barrier. They had made it through the gates.

She breathed again.

"We're safe, for now."

CHAPTER TWENTY-FOUR

Cumchdach glanced at Anna, then at the door. Once they docked, this ship daren't let them be found onboard. Not when their faces were so well known in the city. They had to get out of here.

"I saw only two guards outside," said Anna. She'd always been able to read his thoughts.

"There'll be others." No kidnapper with a spark of brain matter would use only two trained troopers. The one thing the government accepted about the conspirators was that a sharp brain drove their actions. How else had they stayed hidden so long? He checked the door again. Nothing in the way of a catch or lock on this side, not even a concealed door pad.

Why would you need one in a simple cargo store?

He returned to the bench, bending his head close to Anna's. "Nothing," he said in a voice barely above silent. The sounds of the ship slowing and the docking chains beginning to clank should cover what they said from eavesdropping guards, but he didn't put it past them having a sensor in here as well. Anna angled her head into his to cover both their mouths.

"We'll have to make our break when they come to get us."

"I'm putting a call through to an Fallon. It's risky, but we haven't any choice."

That broke her calm. "They'll pick it up."

"Not on this link." Her gasp said she understood the grim set of his mouth. He angled in tighter, taking her hand and crossing it with his, using the movement to cover his activation of his com. He opened up a mind link again and waited.

And waited.

All he got was an annoying static, then a standard systems message. 'Environmental conditions preventing transmission. Please try again later.'

He'd always hated that machine-added courtesy at the end. Empty and meaningless.

"The storm interfering?"

He nodded.

"It happens," she said. "Especially with these big storms we're getting now."

"How long?" he mouthed.

She gave the slightest of shrugs. "For external links? Until the storm passes."

They were on their own. Just when he actually needed the marshals and their tragging intrusive surveillance. "We will get out of here."

Was he trying to convince himself or her? He hoped it sounded better to her than it did to him. Soon afterward, a sharp jolt announced their docking. He grabbed hold of Anna.

"This captain's in a tragging hurry," she muttered. "That's no way to approach a dock."

Then a scurry of sounds told of the ship locking into its berth. Anna listened intently. "We're at the far end of the dock. That scraping is other ships nearby. They're cramming them in."

Lots of thuds and noise followed, none of which he could follow. Cumchdach walked over to the door and listened for the sounds of the guard on the other side.

He shook his head in annoyance. "I can't hear anything out there. Either the guard's skived off, or its too noisy outside."

Suddenly, an eerie whistle echoed through the hull, shivering in a vibration right down to his bones, and Anna shot up, face stark.

"That's the breach siren. The gates aren't holding."

He looked at her blankly.

"The sea is coming in here any moment."

Outside, the racket increased.

"We have to get out of here," she said. "Anything dockside will be destroyed if the sea makes it in."

Cumchdach stared in shock. "And the city? Where's safe?"

"We have backup shields on all the dock exits, and they'll be evacuating everyone to the upper levels."

He began to bang on the door. "Hey, let us out."

No answer, not even a bang back. "We're on our own," he said grimly. He looked around the room, searching for anything to break down that door. Nothing loose, nothing lying discarded. Trust a pirate captain to run a tidy ship.

Anna came over to push against the door with him. But it was built too well, the framing too strong to yield and the door a flat panel of plasmetal. Unbreakable by even the strongest person. There had to be something else here to use.

"The bench. It's the only thing. Help me break it up."

It was as well made as the rest of the room. Tugging at the joins did nothing. He levered it with his feet, with Anna pulling from behind and stopping him toppling over.

Finally, the slightest creak and the metal started to give way. He kicked and tugged both ways to stress it.

Then one end broke free. After that, it was easier to lever the other end free as well, twisting the beam back and forth.

All the while that eerie whistle echoed through his bones and the lines on Anna's face deepened. She was listening to the outside sounds.

"I know it sounds bad out there, *a chiad*, but we will make it. Concentrate on getting out of this room and ignore the outside until we're in it." Deal with the problem in front of you when you get too many. That had always been his father's advice and had kept Cumchdach's head straight in many difficult times.

Luckily the far end had snapped clean. It would be a bit weaker thanks to the bending of the metal but was the best end to slip into the crack of the door. He pushed on the rod, wedging it into the small space.

"Now lean on it with me," he said.

Anna grasped the middle and he used the far end, hoping the spread weight might keep the rod intact. How strong was this door?

Push, push, his muscles straining as hard as they could. He saw a bead of sweat start to trickle down Anna's beautiful face but didn't tell her to ease off. Not if they wanted to live. Anna was pushing as hard as he was, but nothing moved. What was the mechanism of this door made of? He looked over at her, not ready to give up. She looked back. Raised her eyebrows in that way she had. The one that said, 'Let's see who gives up first'.

The one that sent him right back to their teens and trying to scale a cliff too high and too hard for their young bodies.

They'd scaled that cliff—and they would open this door. He wasn't letting Anna die and they had a little boy waiting for their return.

A sudden slosh on the outer hull warned him they had no other option. He bent to the bar again. He could feel it beginning to give way under the pressure. He slammed it sideways, shoving it harder into the small crack of the doorway.

Was that the smallest hint of movement? He braced his feet, pushing harder. Suddenly, the door gave way. He crashed forward, shoving the bar aside before it slammed into Anna, and they both sprawled onto the ground. The door slid smoothly to one side as if innocent of any obstruction. They scrambled up and he peered around the corner.

Nothing. No guards, no running feet at the sound of their breakout.

"They've left us to it," said Anna in disgust. "This captain's never berthing on this coast again." Then she cocked her head. "Time to go."

He heard the same as her. The slap of water above them. He grabbed her hand and began to run. He had some memory of the twists in their passage down here, but it was Anna who found the emergency stair. Up they scurried, Cumchdach going first to counter any threat and Anna breathing close on his heels.

He was dragging her up the stairs as they finally reached a level above the sound of the sea. They came to another locked door. This time, it answered to Cumchdach's hand. They opened it and stepped into a slosh of water, waves splashing over their feet and spreading across the deck.

"It's still rising," he said, staring at the water thrashing the boats around them.

He knew she could swim. They both could. But the maelstrom surrounding them was a different matter.

"Dockside," she gasped, pointing. He followed her as they hurried around the deck, stepping over and pushing around the hatches, projections, side walls and equipment blocking their path, and squeezing through a narrow gap between the cabin and outer rail, with the sea dragging relentlessly at their calves.

Cumchdach twisted around to help her over a loose box skittering in the wash. "How high will the water go?"

Anna hauled in a fraught breath before answering. "Near the cliff top. As high as the gate. The top city level is all refuge."

"They let the lower caverns flood?"

Silence as they pushed on again. A too long silence. They'd reached the end of the narrow passage and he turned to pull her through to the next open part of the deck. "Anna?"

"All the dock doors are shut and locked down."

"We're locked out?"

She shook her head. "There are emergency airlocks."

"Where?"

They were around the ship and dockside now. It looked nothing like his past visits to the Rubhaicreach docks. The ship had floated up with their mooring links, the dock floor was hidden in a swirling mess of grey water, and all the other boats bobbed on the surging waves, crashing against each other in a cacophony of badly tuned metal plates.

"Look for rope," said Anna. "We'll have to swim for it." Her hand pointed upward to where an external stair tottered against the dock wall. At the top, the rising waters hurled sprays of foam against a large, heavy door. "There'll be another lower down, but that will be well under water by now. That one's our best hope."

A slim one, at best. Right now, it looked an impossible distance away.

"All ships have powered emergency floats. They'll be in a box marked with a red cross. They usually put them mid, fore, and aft, against the outside walls."

A rectangular box was still showing above water level where the deck started sloping toward the prow. As he watched, it disappeared under water.

"That look about right?"

She peered at it, then nodded.

"Hold tight to that railing. This shouldn't take long."

"No. You'll get swept away."

She took a step to follow him and he put out a hand to stop her.

"Hold tight," he ordered, hoping she'd obey. To make sure, he clamped both of her hands onto the railing, then surged into the waves.

The water tried hard to pluck him off the ship. He gripped any hand hold available and finally reached where the box had disappeared. A painful bang on his shins said he'd found it. He felt around for an opening. His fingers met a pad. He pressed against it.

Nothing happened. He turned back to Anna. "How do I get in?"

But she couldn't hear him over the noise of sea and boats. Thankfully, she hadn't taken her eyes off him. He lifted a shoulder, one hand pointing to the box, then splayed his palm wide.

She lifted a fisted hand, then raised one finger, closed it, then raised it again.

One-zero-one. The universal emergency code. He'd have to hope this pirate vessel stuck to essential regs. He felt again, and this time found the faint indentations of a numerical pad. He entered the code.

The box clicked open. He ducked under the waves, eyes and mouth firmly shut against the filthy water, feeling inside the box. His hand met a squishy belt. That must be the float. He pulled it up, wrapped it around his neck and waist and felt it lock into place. Then he reached down and felt for another, and pulled that up too, draping it over his neck and letting it lock down.

Was there anything else useful? The waves splashed up and he got a mouthful of salty water. He choked, bending over to cough up the liquid and lifting a hand to stop Anna's step toward him. He stood up again, shaking his head. "I'm fine," he yelled. He doubted she heard him, but she seemed to understand and stayed where she was, looking sick with worry. He shut his mouth firmly before ducking down to feel in the box again. A rope. Yes.

He bundled it up. Beyond that, he found some tubes that must be alarm flares, and various other, unknown boxes. They might need them, but he had no way of carrying them. He grabbed tight to the rope, wrapping it securely around his body to leave both hands free, then walked fist over fist, clinging to anything he found, as he fought his way through the water back to Anna.

By the time he'd battled through to the prow, the water was up to her waist. He shoved the second float at her, not breathing easily until it was locked in place around her.

She had a chance now.

Then he lashed the rope around her waist and his, with enough slack between them to give both of them some movement.

"Time to get out of here." He braced against the rocking deck, sighted for the spot where she'd said the airlock waited. The top of the door was all that was visible now. He took firm hold of Anna's hand, then climbed up to crouch unsteadily on the railing, and pulled her beside him.

"I love you," he said, staring into her beautiful dark eyes. "I always have and I always will. And we are not dying today." Then he banged the pad to activate his float and watched as she did the same. With a leap, they both plunged into the churning waters.

Anna coughed in a mouthful as she sank under the waters. No, the floats were faulty. She mustn't die, not today when Cumchdach would go with her and they had a baby waiting for them. She kicked out strongly, felt the tug of the rope on her waist.

Upward. It tugged upward. Then she felt a surge of power from the float as its small engine kicked in. She roared to the surface and gulped in precious air. She thought frantically. There was something else about these floats she must remember. She'd done so many emergency drills as a child.

Oxygen, that was it. The floats all carried an oxygen reserve. Not much but enough to get them across this gap and to the airlock. Where was it?

She shut her eyes and let the rope and float tug her. Then patted the centre of the front fastener. There. A small, hard indentation. Tap once, count one, then tap again. The pad opened and a small mask fell out. She grabbed at it before it could be torn away in the water and clamped it over her mouth. Clean air, sealing her mouth from the killing waters.

Cumchdach needed to know too. She grabbed at the rope, tugged hard at it, barely making any movement against the tension between them.

Her husband barely slowed. He'd made her a promise and was going to bring her safely to that airlock if it killed him. But Cumchdach was a man of the forests. He hadn't been raised with the sea like a child of Rubhaicreach.

She grabbed hold of the rope and used it and the float's power pack to haul herself painfully up to her husband. It had seemed such a short rope on deck, now her hands burned with the effort of fighting the water and his float's power. Hers was as strong, but he had more muscle power to add to it.

Finally, she felt him. His arm reached out to grab her, then his head bobbed up and gasped for air, before she felt him sinking beneath the next wave.

She hauled herself closer, wrapping herself around him and reaching for the pack. No point telling him. He tried to push her up, toward the surface as they both sank slowly. She had to slap his hand away.

There. The same hard patch as hers. She quickly entered the code, grabbed at the mask and slapped it on his face before he could try another heroic trick.

Breathe, *mo stochri*. For Roo, for you.

For me.

Then he gasped, gave a kick and surged up again, working with the float and swimming strongly. He grabbed her hand as they both fought the waves, and they powered together through the stormy waters.

Even with the push of the float and Cumchdach's assistance, Anna felt herself tiring. The constant buffeting of the waves and the fear galloping inside her fed her exhaustion. Debris littered the waters, from the small to the dangerously large. Ships were supposed to secure and stow all dockside equipment before taking to the caverns, but this storm had come up too quickly and was too big. Cumchdach swerved away from a large box, kicking it away from her, and she batted off a tangle of ropes and gear. The sea level was well above the ships' tether height now, but the docks had auto release in a storm situation and they had to steer through a careening mass of large and small craft.

Soon, she tugged on Cumchdach's hand again and pointed down. The only way through the maze of obstacles was under it. There was another dock airlock at the bottom level. Cumchdach led the way down and she was happy to follow him. Even with the float's power, he could pull her better.

It was quiet below the storm, but it was also dark. She felt for her com, praying it worked in the storm. Then she felt a vibration and heard a familiar tone in her head as the mind link locked in.

'Anna,' said the mental message from Cumchdach with his unmistakable calm assurance.

'Receiving.' She sent back in huge relief. 'Is your sonar function working?'

'Just. Not reliable, but enough.'

Anna checked her own com, sending out a scan of the path ahead and looking for the dockside lock. She grabbed harder onto Cumchdach as she searched.

There, a few metres below them, but the current was pulling them away from it. She checked her float's energy and oxygen levels.

Getting low, thanks to the huge resistance from the turbulent waters, but should be enough.

It had to be.

They had one more problem. She contacted Cumchdach again. "Do you have comms function to the port officials?"

'Been trying all the way but nothing.'

'Once we get back inside, we'll be safe,' she sent.

He squeezed her hand harder. 'Together, we'll beat this. I can see the side of the dock. How far was that airlock?'

'The lower one's closer.' She sent him an image of the lock, with a downward hand signal, gave him a second, then dived sharply.

It was black as night as she swam down, deeper and deeper into the forbidding waters. Her com sent her a series of pings, keeping her on track to the door. Ahead of her, she felt the steady pull of Cumchdach's hand. She kept checking the image on her com, kept focussing on the airlock door.

Nearly there. Her muscles were protesting loudly, and her float signalled automatic energy-save mode. Cumchdach's must be doing the same. The tug from him lessened as the current strove to claim them, tugging them away from the door even as her hand reached for it.

Only a few metres more. Her engines went down another notch.

'I'm nearly out of power,' sent Cumchdach. Worse, she heard the slight wavering in his link that spelled low oxygen.

'Kick harder. We make that door, or nothing,' she ordered him, and the trace of a laugh came through the link.

'That's my Anna.'

It warmed her, strengthened her as so often before when the boy Cumchdach had dared her on to some secret challenge their families never knew about. They had lived so much of their lives together. Today must not see the end of that.

She kicked, grabbed in a breath of the last of her oxygen, sucking it up hard and holding it in tight. Around her waist, the rope tightened as Cumchdach pulled it up and knotted her close to him.

They went together—saved or lost. She felt the surge from his kicking and reached deep into her resources to force her legs to go harder, feeding on every last speck of strength left in her body.

A shape began to materialise in front of her. Then she saw it. The lock.

Her fingers touched cold metal, and she clung tight to the edge of the door, too tired to do more.

'I've found the pad. It won't respond to me,' came Cumchdach's link.

'Pull me over. It reads your identity as well.'

He tugged her into his body, felt for her arm, then pulled her hand into where his own touched a pad on the door. Later, she'd remember the feel of him, the hard muscles and gloriously familiar shape.

Now, they must live. Her fingers found the pad, entered the code.

Then she waited. Listened hard.

Nothing?

No, there it was, the first sounds of a door lock opening and hinges clanking. The sound of water pouring into the lock to equilibrate with the outside.

Hurry, hurry, she urged, feeling the need to breathe overwhelming her.

Finally, a click and the door opened. Cumchdach pulled hard, yanked it open and shot in, towing her with him. Then turned and slammed it shut behind him and she heard the glorious sound of the pumps sucking water out of the space and air pouring in.

Up, up to the ceiling. They thrust together against the floor of the lock and pushed up hard. Then they shot above the water and into an open gap. She pulled off her mask and opened her mouth. Breathed in deep. Breathed in real air, fresh air.

Lifesaving air.

They were safe. For now, at least.

The water still tried to drag them with it as it poured out of the lock, but the makers had prepared for that, covering the drains with mesh and keeping the outward flow to a strength easy to resist. Or it would have been, if they weren't exhausted.

"Handholds," she gasped, and locked the tether strap of her float belt to a nearby hoop. Cumchdach copied her, clinging to the wall and watching the water slither away down their bodies and out the holes, leaving them dripping and hanging against the wall. She leaned over tiredly, touched the clip and dropped in a clang of metal and bumps to the floor. She didn't care, lying there as Cumchdach dropped down beside her, hitting the ground with a thump that had her lifting her head.

It was all she could move for now. She lay, gasping in air and urging her muscles to respond. Then lifted herself painfully up to check him as his head rose and he groaned.

"I hurt all over," he said, glaring at the outer door. "Someone is going to pay for this."

She had to chuckle. It sounded weak to her, a whimper of laughter, but the attempt made her feel better. "First, we have to find out who's behind this."

Cumchdach levered himself up to sitting. "Are you hurt, *a chiad?*"

That brought on another huff of a laugh. "Every part of me hurts to move. But nothing's broken or torn, if that's what you mean."

He shuffled over and pulled her up to sit beside him. She clung tight, burrowing into his sturdy body and needing to feel his muscles holding her, telling her they were both still alive.

His head came down and his mouth claimed hers. The power of his kisses. She had never forgotten them, no matter how hard she tried. Then she stopped thinking, opening her mouth to his and flattening her hand against his chest, fingers digging in to claim him back.

Only the need to breathe had them lifting their heads. Cumchdach rested his forehead against hers. "Never again. You are not to leave me ever again."

She lifted her arms to latch them around his neck and pulled his mouth back to hers.

"Never again," she murmured, before claiming him back.

After a while, reality intruded and she began to shiver. Cumchdach looked as cold as she was, his lips blue and his cheeks pale.

"We need to get out of here and get warm," he said, pulling her in close as if to muffle both their shaking bodies. "Can you stand up?"

"If you can, I can."

He laughed at that. She'd said it to him many times before. He pulled at her hand, his other hand anchored to the hold on the wall, as she levered herself up. It wasn't elegant, but it worked. She rolled upward and clung to the wall with him, gasping for breath and feeling the air slowly bringing strength back into her body.

But not enough. They needed help.

First, though, they had to get out of here. They clung together and limped slowly over to the exit door. He helped her lift her hand to the door pad and enter the code again, then waited with her for the interminable time it took the door to activate and roll back.

On the other side was a black vault. They limped through the door but no lights came on.

"They've turned them off."

"Air?"

She shook her head, then said, "No. There's always an auxiliary backup in rock passages that comes on if any life-form registers."

You didn't need light, not when everyone had coms, but you did need air. Only the bare essentials were kept running in emergencies, as the city's resources turned to keeping its people alive and its goods intact. All the warehouses would be locked and sealed tight against water incursion.

But using their coms carried too much risk of discovery. They'd been forced to use them in the sea, but to keep using them unnecessarily was foolish. Someone had arranged for their kidnapping and knew they were still alive. Probably someone in Rubhaicreach.

No, someone in your own family.

Gria. It had to be.

Please don't let it be Anton. Don't let him have betrayed her. Not the first in her family in whom she'd sensed anything like the core force of her grandfather. The first to give her a hint of hope.

But hope was nothing if they didn't make it out of here. She drove her mind back to reality. "There should be torches in a locker near the door." She risked using her com light to look around the passage. "There, on the left of the doorway."

Cumchdach slapped a hand over her com. "Turn it off. Now." She pointed to the locker she wanted, but he ignored her. "I mean it, Anna. Turn off your com. We'll use mine when we have to. I don't want anyone locking onto your com to find you."

"And they won't be locking onto yours?"

"Yes, and if they come looking for us, I'm bigger and trained in defence."

"Your security put me through the same training after you were all released from prison." Then she saw the tension lines gouging the side of his mouth and gave way. She waved her hand over her com, switching off the light and the other functions. "I'm turning it back on if we need my Rubhaicreach maps."

He nodded tersely at that. The power surge if they tried to transfer them to Cumchdach's com was too easy to lock onto. He let go her wrist and stomped over to the locker, barely visible in the minimal light he was using from his com. She stayed still, letting him grab out the torches and something else.

Energy bars, she discovered when he came back and thrust one at her along with the torch. The kind that gave a rapid boost to depleted reserves, which certainly described both their states. It was a pity they didn't have a change of clothing in there too, she thought, shaking uselessly at the fabric clinging to her arms and legs. She bit down hard on the energy bar, taking the largest bite she could manage, chewing rapidly and swallowing it down.

The simple act of eating helped, her body feeling marginally less like collapsing in a pathetic heap on the floor.

"Time to go," said her husband. "Best direction?"

"The emergency stairs are to the left of the airlocks."

"They may be guarded too," said Cumchdach.

"We have to get above this level if we want to survive." They needed warmth, a change of clothing, and proper food. The ration bars might give them a boost but wouldn't keep them going long or help them stave off the insidious cold of their swim. Cumchdach didn't argue. He'd already started walking and soon discovered the doorway to the stairs. A manual door this time, the only sign of their passing the creak of its opening. He held it for her to pass through then let it close again as gently as possible.

"I go first," he said as they began to climb.

"I don't want to lose you either," she said. "Together always, remember."

"Please, Anna. Don't. You nearly died out there."

So did you, she wanted to say, but the strain in his voice was too obvious. She was beginning to think his talk of love might be real.

As real as the love inside her.

They began to climb.

CHAPTER TWENTY-FIVE

Cumchdach stepped carefully around the twist of the stairs, ears and eyes straining for any hint of pursuit. It was too silent, the only sounds coming to him the faint mechanical hum of the ventilation system. This was too easy.

Not that he believed their captors brave enough to risk the seas, but they had to have been well paid to kidnap people with profiles as high as his and Anna's. Which meant powerful backers, the kind who didn't forgive failure. The kind to have others in their pay.

First, he wanted Anna safe, warm, and fed. He could feel her shivers through the hand he grasped. Using two hands might be more efficient in climbing these interminable stairs, but he wasn't about to let go of her and was relieved she showed no sign of wanting him to either. He needed to feel she was still here, still alive.

That moment of knowing they were locked inside a flooding ship and he was going to watch her drown would never leave him. He didn't care if she didn't love him as much as he loved her; he was going to spend the rest of his life keeping her safe and happy.

And if that means letting her go?

Once she was safe. Right now, she was far from that. He heard a puff as she climbed the stair behind him.

"How much farther?" he asked softly, turning back so his voice wouldn't echo up the stairwell.

"Level two. The refuges are all on level one. It will be crowded there, but level two has back-up safe places. Offices and other rooms with full services still on. There are retail shops as well, for a change of clothes."

He shook his head. "That means com credit transfers. Too easy to track. Look for workers' lockers. They'll have serviceable clothing."

"We don't steal from each other here."

"And you don't usually try to kill each other."

The shock of that resonated through her dark eyes, but she said nothing. He began to climb again and she followed him.

Soon, he heard her breaths coming shorter. He could feel himself tiring as well, but Anna was still a nursing mother who'd given birth less than a year ago. Her breasts must be aching, and her legs tiring. He tugged harder. "We'll take a break on the next level."

Anna only nodded, hunching her shoulders and lifting another foot. She looked like she was reaching the end of her reserves. He paused, waited for her to step up beside him, then put an arm around her waist.

She looked up, eyes flaring wide. "You're tired too."

"Physiology. Bigger and stronger muscles, remember."

She scowled at him. "A simple trick of birth." Another old joke between them. Anna never let him get away with anything.

"It's no good me making it out if you can't. Roo needs us both."

The pain in her eyes almost made him regret the low tactic. He doubted she'd stopped thinking of their baby. Anna might hide her worry as she concentrated on enduring the present. It didn't make it less real.

"Just a few steps more. You can do it."

She didn't reply, leaning into him. That had him really worried. He didn't have much left himself, but she'd reached her end if she wasn't arguing. Her shivers were worse now and he was nearly dragging her up each step.

He was as relieved as possible to reach the landing. Luckily, all the stair doors had viewing panes. He peered through, seeing no sign of anyone. The passages here were as black as the ones below. Cautiously, he pushed open the door, listening hard, before letting Anna through. He lifted his torch, looking for any kind of map or signboard.

"Offices to the left. The preppers in them will have food," Anna whispered.

"Cleaner's supplies?"

"Between the office hubs."

They crept down the corridor, trying door after door.

"Why did they all have to decide to follow the rules today," cursed Anna.

He was too pleased at the fight in her voice to say anything. They kept trying doors, until finally they found one where the locks hadn't quite engaged. Opening the doors, he saw why. This company had kept working until the last possible moment, chairs askew as if they'd left in haste.

Anna glanced at the door and read the signage. "A Falasch subsidiary. They'll be in trouble if Falasch goes under."

"It won't." No matter what the courts came back with, Falasch was too important for Den Coille. Cumchdach had no intention of letting the company go under.

Anna said nothing. She kept looking.

"Take a seat. I'll look."

Cumchdach scowled at her until she slumped down in the nearest chair. "Happy?"

"Not yet, but it's a start."

He kept hunting, one ear open for any sign of movement from her. Finally, in another room he found the cleaner's cupboard. There was also a snack prepper, but he daren't open his com to operate it. He opened the cupboard and pulled out the overalls there. One pair only, and far too big for Anna.

She'd just have to roll up the sleeves and legs.

When he came back, he saw her slumped against the desk and his heart jolted. She heard him and jerked up, eyes flaring, then saw him and relaxed again.

He held out the overalls. "These are the best I can do. Get those wet things off."

"What about you?" she said, predictably.

"Roo needs you more at this age. Strip, now—unless you'd like me to do it for you?" He squelched the disappointment as she began to hastily tear off her sopping wet tunic. Both of them were leaving drips on the floor, but they couldn't do anything about that.

He couldn't have looked away if his life had depended on it. Anna had always been the most beautiful woman he'd ever seen, and she'd become more so with every passing year. He had a glimpse of full, swollen breasts before she turned away from him, but that only gave him an unimpeded view of her gorgeous backside, the curve of her spine and that luscious long line of leg, ending in the graceful arch of her feet. Nothing could stop his moment of enjoyment, watching as she lifted each foot and slid it inside the overall, then gave a shimmy of her hips that had him groaning as she tugged it up. Her face was flushed when she turned back to him, and he had to grin.

"I'm a mature woman now," she protested.

"Yes, matured nicely."

She yanked up the fastener with a huff that had him laughing.

"Spoilsport."

She didn't answer that one either but did turn and run her eyes up his body in the way she had that set every cell in him on fire. She then flushed, and looked away as if remembering they were no longer together, and the pain of that cut deep.

"I still want you, *a chiad*, and nothing is going to change that," he said softly. "But I'd never force any woman. Especially not you."

Her eyes shot to his, wide with shock. "I'd never accuse you of that. I *know* you, Cumchdach duine Anna."

"I wonder," he murmured even softer, and she flushed but made as if she hadn't heard. Then another shiver overcame her.

"Food next," he said briskly, as if the strange interval had never been. The priority now was to make sure she lived. Finding out what she really thought of him must come later. "Try the office drawers and caches. There must be someone in this room hiding a snack habit."

At the end of their hunt, rifling through every hidden nook in the room, and poking under some truly disgusting drawer contents, Cumchdach wasn't sure if he really wanted to eat anything from this sloppily run outfit. They stared at their haul.

A half-eaten cereal bar, an opened pack of candy, a sealed bag of cookies, and three bars of chocostim.

"They're carbohydrates and fat. They'll give us energy," said Anna staunchly.

"It's what else they'll give us that worries me."

"See the medics for a shot as soon as we're out of this mess."

They both still decided to leave the half-eaten bar and candy, and shared the rest out. Cumchdach tried to make Anna take more but she refused.

"I need you fit and on form. If we meet anyone, you're better able to take them on than I am."

It was too true to deny. Both of them had fight training, but Cumchdach had done more than she had and was stronger—despite his still hollow stomach when they'd finished and the sapping cold of his slick wet clothes.

"We need to find another cleaner's locker," said Anna, catching the shiver he tried to suppress. Her shivers had improved, but her face still looked pinched with cold and fatigue.

"We'll stop on the next level."

He wanted Anna back above a possible flood level as soon as possible. Both their bodies showed the cost of battling the power of the sea. The break had given her strength, but she still slowed as they neared the next level. He pulled her up the last stair.

"You sit while I hunt."

He checked the corridor first before opening the door. It was as dark as the floor below. He found a chair in an alcove not far from the stairway and led her to it. "Wait here, don't move, and com me immediately if anything goes wrong." Leaving her brought a nasty feeling to his gut, but he had no choice. She needed rest. "I mean it. *Anything* that sounds, feels or looks suspect, you com me."

He glanced back once and saw her outlined in the dim shine of her torch before he rounded the corner.

He soon found another office left badly locked, and this one held treasure. A pile of coats left behind in the rush, as well as larger overalls that would fit him. He also found more carbs in the office drawers. This time, he left the half-eaten or frankly disgusting behind. He pulled on the dry overalls, happily leaving his wet clothes in the nearest rubbish chute, then hurried back to Anna.

"Look what I've found," he said, rounding the last corner, then stopped abruptly. Anna was no longer alone. Three people stood over her, and she had scrunched right back into her chair.

He plastered his coolest smile on his face and stomped loudly as he approached them. "More who missed the alarm siren?"

The tallest swivelled on him and Cumchdach noted the lump of a weapon under his outer coat. "Arms out to your side, Ser den Coille. Unless you'd like to watch your wife greeting us properly."

"You have the advantage of me. I didn't catch your names."

"It's who we work for that counts. And none of them are happy with you, Ser. Not after that trick with the marshals you pulled."

Two turned toward him. He needed one more. He kept his gaze off Anna, but never lost sight of her. He drew out his arms, waving them as he did, and hoped she'd caught his meaning. Then hoped like crazy she'd obey.

"Don't see that's any of your business," he said, drawling it out to make it as offensive as possible.

This time, they drew their weapons, and all three turned to him with pleased grins on their faces.

"That's just what this is, Ser. Our employers aren't too happy with your interference in their business. Now, if you'd turn around and put your arms behind your back, we can get on with our *business.*"

He waited, holding his arms out. "Can't see why I'd do that."

He wished he dared use his com. *Move, Anna. Now.* Then saw her shake her head. "You folks do know the marshals are on their way?" he said, hoping she'd get the message.

Two of them looked to the first speaker. "He's bluffing," said the man.

"They have me under surveillance," said Cumchdach.

"Don't mean they see everything."

The right-hand one looked like he was turning back to Anna.

Cumchdach took a step forward and those weapons shot up again.

Come on, Anna. She'd spent enough years in the trees of Manascraoch to have the same flexibility as his.

"What does your boss want with me? Den Coilles stick together." He took another step forward and brought up his fists. This time, a burn zapped his lower leg. He had to smother a yelp. He stopped short, glaring angrily. Keeping all those eyes fixed on him.

Finally, Anna began to move, slithering off her chair. He'd apologise to her later. Right now, she needed to remember all the tricks he and his family had taught her. The ones that let her move as silently as any Manascraoch Mountainer.

He sneered at the three men, balling his fists tighter and leaning forward.

His leg hurt, but he ignored it. "You tell your bosses I don't frighten easily. They want me to do something, all they have to do is ask."

"Oh, they will," jeered the middle man.

Anna was nearly at the corner.

"They coming here, or you have something else planned?" He took another step, and this time his arm copped the blaster shot. He clapped a hand over it and held it tight to his body, glaring at them angrily.

That's it, boys. Keep watching me.

"How about you drop those weapons and take me on fairly."

"Now, why would we do that?"

He kept his fists clenched, kept looking as threatening as possible. Anna had vanished. Now, to give her as much time as possible to get away, he kept taunting them, daring them to frighten him.

Kept taking the hits.

"We can keep this up all day, Ser."

"So can I," he shot back, gritting his teeth,

"Your wife doesn't even care. Hasn't uttered a peep," said another after a while. He went to turn and Cumchdach stepped forward again. Too late.

"Hey, she's gone."

He rushed them all and a searing beam caught him head on. He collapsed to the ground.

"Bind him—and find the woman. The bosses want them both."

They were the last words he heard.

Anna kept running, her fingers trailing along the passage walls to keep her on track.

Get help, had been Cumchdach's message. Find the marshals.

But the last she'd heard had been a yell from the men, a zip of blaster fire, and a barely smothered gasp.

Please let him be safe.

If they were going to kill him, they'd have done it at the start.

She kept repeating the thought all the way up the dark passage, keeping her torch off, hoping by all the roots to be heading in the right direction.

She was still exhausted but an image of Cumchdach's body crumpled on the ground kept her moving.

She found another stairway. A service one this time. She traipsed up and refused to stop. The levels seemed endless.

Where were the marshals?

Did she dare use her com yet? If only she knew who held Cumchdach. She looked for a number.

Three more flights to go. She *would* make them. Then she heard a clatter of steps above her. She stopped, huddling back against the wall and hoping against hope they'd stop at the flight above her.

But the clatter came on, loud and carefree.

A couple of young workers rushed around the corner, saw her and stopped.

"You had enough of hiding too?" said the youngest, a girl barely out of her teens but with a face that had been given a full treatment by one of the cheaper brands of cosmetic systems.

"What? No. Has the all clear siren sounded?"

They both giggled. "Nah, but it's just a hyped-up thing anyway. We've got a party tonight. Not about to miss it 'cause some stupid rule says we can't finish work in time. Get our stuff finished, then home to get ready."

"Then we going to paaa-ar-tay," chimed in the slightly older but just as silly one.

"The rules are there for a reason," she heard herself saying in her grandam's voice. "You should stay up in the safe levels until the storm is over."

"It can't get in here. Anyway, we're not the only ones."

"Yeah, tons of others are coming back down."

"All these drills. Just a lot of stuffed-up doomsters."

"The risk is real," she tried to say, but they both ignored her and carried on their way. She could hear their giggles and chatter all the way down.

Roots, she hoped those outer doors held. It would be long before she forgot the power of that cold sea outside. She trudged up to the next floor, pushing herself up each step.

Then heard a sound drilled into her since childhood but never heard before. The storm siren. The second one, the one used only when the door locks were leaking.

She was on the last stair and burst into a rush. Cumchdach was still down there. She broke through the door, broadcasting on her com for a marshal. She ran for the refuge caverns and was horrified at the crowd blocking her, all swirling and confused and going in any direction but the right one.

"Go back. Lockdown. Lower level breach in progress."

"It's just a drill," said too many.

But the odd one looked as terrified as she felt. My son, cousin, best friend, were back down there, they shouted, as if pleading for her to rescue them.

"Com them to get out now," she shouted as she pushed through the crowd. Panic was spreading, and now the cries of those being trampled joined the general riot of sound.

A voice came over the intercoms. "Form orderly lines and make your way to the caverns. This is not a drill. Repeat, this is not a drill."

"Nah, the water won't come this far up," said a girl nearby.

"Repeat, this is not a drill. All citizens to take shelter in the refuge caverns," the inexorable voice of the intercom answered her.

Anna ought to stay and help. But Cumchdach was down there. Then a woman wearing the uniform of the marshals blocked her way, grabbing her arm and pulling her to one side. Anna clung to her in relief.

"My husband. Cumchdach. He's still down there."

"I'm sure Ser Cumchdach will make his way up to the caverns in time. We are contacting him now."

"You don't understand. They've got him. They don't know it's real."

"Got him?"

"Captive. We were captured. They'll kill him."

The woman pulled her into a side passage and began running, dragging Anna with her. The marshal slapped on her com. "Emergency call. Ser den Coille is held captive. Override local com security. Federal priority in force."

Then Anna heard a welcome voice. Marshal Dunan, the man who'd saved her life once already.

"Tracking activated. He's alive but still below the safe level. Get Sera Anna out of there."

"No, save Cumchdach. Please, save him first."

"We'll do both, Sera," said the woman beside her. "You must get to safety. We can't keep you secure here if it goes bad."

Anna kept pleading. They didn't know how much he mattered. She couldn't lose Cumchdach, not again.

"Come, Sera. Your little boy needs his mother. We *will* save the ser, but you have to reach safety. Otherwise we tie up resources keeping you secure that we need to find your husband."

It was the only argument that could defeat her panic. Then they were in a refuge cavern and the noise dropped. This was a high priority cavern, filled with the leaders of the city and their families. In a corner on her own, Anna found her grandam and flung herself into her arms sobbing out all the pent up terror of the past hours.

"He's going to die, Grandam. The sea will take him."

"There, there, my girl. It won't. Not that stubborn man."

If only Anna could believe that. She watched the marshals, peering at them as they huddled in a corner, scanning the crowd. They checked her location, then Dunan counted off two men to monitor the cavern and the rest left. He came over to her.

"We are getting the situation in hand here, Sera. Our monitors have Ser Cumchdach under lock. He is still alive and above the breached levels."

How long would he stay there; that was the question that ricocheted through Anna's head.

Cumchdach woke to the heavy weight of a restraint field locking him in place and an empty place on his wrist where they'd stripped off his com. Every part of him hurt, and he fought to hide the pain from his captors.

"Call in the others," one said.

It had to be the conspirators. He knew many of their names now, men and women he'd encountered through business over the years. It did nothing to comfort him. And he didn't yet know the names at the top.

Then he heard a new sound. A trickle, a splashing, faint and deep down, but one that set every nerve in his body on edge.

How strong were those door locks?

"I hope you're planning on taking me out of here soon," he said, as laidback as he could manage.

"In good time, Ser. All in good time. I wouldn't be in such a hurry if I was you."

He shrugged. "All the same to me. Die here by drowning or whatever unpleasant method your bosses are planning. But you might like to save yourselves."

"Don't listen to him. He's bluffing."

One of the sidekicks. The stupid one.

"Don't you hear the water? Smell it?"

"So? We're below sea level here. Always smells like water and black damp. This city's built strong. That's what we were told," said the other sidekick, marginally less stupid but not so it made a difference.

"And you heard that sound when you first came down here?"

"Don't listen to him. He's trying to trick us," said the first man sullenly.

The main one, the one supposedly in charge of the trio, scowled and said nothing, but did tilt his head as if listening.

"You hear it?" said Cumchdach. "That's water, and it's inside the building." The man glared at him. "I'm not playing you."

"Doesn't matter. That door behind you is solid. We're in a chiller, air- and water-tight. You're going nowhere, den Coille."

The man grinned as if he'd won some stupendous prize.

"Air in a room this size will run out. Or do you imagine it's eternal?"

"We'll be long gone by then," said the leader. He gestured to the other two. "Time to move."

Cumchdach shouldn't fight back, but he still didn't know what had happened to Anna. "Let me go. You're safer without me."

One of the sidekicks gave a harsh chuckle. "He don't know the bosses."

No, but clearly he was going to find out. They tightened the restraints on his hands and ankles, gave him a cuff that had him falling to his knees before painfully pulling himself back, then grabbed him roughly and shoved him toward the door.

"No—"

The water began to seep in at the first crack of the door opening, and they desperately shoved against it, barely managing to close it in time. Cold, filthy water sloshed around his feet. The leader finally discovered his brain and lifted his com to scan the surrounding spaces from the way he stared at each wall then shook his head.

At last he pointed to the rear wall. "Up higher. There's a passage leading from there that's still dry." The second man lifted his blaster and sent a splatter of charges against the wall and Cumchdach dived for the floor.

Just in time, his leader slapped it down. "Not that setting, you fool."

The man snatched the blaster, touched his com and sent a focussed beam to the wall, using a shield around it. One of them at least had proper training. Soon, they'd blasted a man-sized hole at the top of the back wall, exposing a dark cavity behind it. A dark and *dry* space. Now they only had to figure out a way to get up to it.

By clambering over him, it turned out. They forced him to his knees and the first two men climbed on top of him, each one punching a hole right through his kidneys in the process. Or that's what it felt like.

The leader pointed his blaster at Cumchdach.

"Up," he ordered.

Cumchdach played dumb.

"Don't try that with me," the man growled. "Up, now, before I decide you're not worth the price they're paying."

"Has to be high?"

"High enough." He shoved the blaster right under Cumchdach's jaw and used a faint burn on his skin. He couldn't help his jump. That burn stung. He clambered up and stared at the hole in the wall.

The man shot at the wall again, and Cumchdach tried to jump back. The man grabbed his arm.

"No one's letting that water in."

Then Cumchdach saw what he'd done. The blast had been carefully calibrated, far more so than Cumchdach would have expected. Each one had made a small hollow in the metal, melting it enough to cause a slight pooling.

The man did something else with his blaster, and the metal hardened. It had a cooling function? That was high level, the kind of weapon needing serious credits.

"Climb, Ser," said the man.

He had no choice, not with that blaster now dug into his temple and no other way out of the room. He put his foot in the depression, nervously waiting for it to collapse or burn him.

Neither happened. His captors weren't as inept as he'd first thought. He'd better revise his escape plans. He only hoped the marshals would find him. That Anna had made it out.

They'd have dragged her back here and shoved her failure in his face if she hadn't. He clung to the thought. His Anna was the most resourceful woman he'd met, a match for his mother and sisters. She would make it and she'd send the marshals back.

He was getting out of this. But first he had to find out who was in charge of the whole pack of idiots, and from what the men holding him said, that was exactly what they planned.

Yeah, and after that, they're going to kill you.

The marshals would come through.

They'd tragging better.

The leader pointed that blaster at his hands and, above him, the others waited. He lifted his arms up and the men at the top dragged him up the wall and through the gap. They didn't bother making it gentle, and he picked up more scrapes and bruises, falling into a heap on the floor of the tunnel as they whooshed him through the gap. One pulled out his own blaster and trained it on him as the other helped their boss up. The leader came over the tunnel entrance a lot more evenly than Cumchdach had and stood up immediately. Cursing under his breath, Cumchdach levered himself up to stand when they poked him with multiple blasters.

It looked like they were in one of the older tunnels, maybe even the back ones that Anna had brought him through earlier. That meant Falasch help, or someone planted here at the least.

His bets were on Gria den Falasch and her imports.

"Move, Ser." The man slammed his weapon into Cumchdach's back, and he bent over in agony, fighting for breath.

"Do that again and you won't leave your bosses much to interrogate," he managed to snarl after a while.

"There'll be enough. Then they're going to take care of you, once and forever, Ser mighty den Coille. You and that too clever wife of yours."

"You've lost her. She's safely on her way to Manascraoch."

Or he hoped she was. The man grinned. "That won't help her."

Cumchdach went cold. More traitors in his home city? Den Coille security had told him the last ones were safely contained. These had to be still active, still dangerous. He had to get away from these men. Had to keep Anna safe. Forget her finding the marshals and going home to Roo. Not if she was walking into a trap. The marshals too thought Manascraoch safe.

"Where are these bosses of yours hiding?" he said.

"You'll find out."

He made another show of resistance, and grimaced when they hauled him upright and jabbed their blasters into his back to make him move. It was all show. Painful, but these men had their orders. Cumchdach must be delivered in a state fit to answer questions. They might hurt him, but they weren't going to kill him.

He had to escape and warn Anna. Then he was going to find the safest place possible and drag her there with Roo if he had to. He'd had enough of this constant churn in his guts of fear for them.

If only he knew where he was. The passage they stumbled down was dry, but how long would that hold? And worse, were the other passages around them flooded? The dank smell of invading water was getting stronger, not weaker.

The tunnel was also clearly unused. They all stumbled from time to time on the rough surface and piles of fallen stones. It looked to be cut into the raw rock and any sealant had long since worn away. When he put out a hand to stop tripping, his fingers came away caked in sticky dirt.

"I hope you lot know where you're going. This old wall is crumbling away already."

"Keep walking, den Coille." Another jab to his back reinforced the order. At this rate, he'd be a mass of black and blue by the time he met the bosses.

He scanned the walls as they walked, searching desperately for any way out. They now constantly seeped, and even the men behind him began to look worried.

A split in the corridor loomed ahead of them. The leader checked his com and pointed to the right branch. They all broke into a run. Cumchdach didn't need their prodding to join them. At the junction, he glanced sideways at the dark hole of the left branch and saw the tell-tale seep of water at the base. Not a safe route.

Not that his captors gave him any chance to try it. They surrounded him and hustled him down the right. Soon they were all splashing through water.

"Nearly there," said the leader.

The lights were out now, and the water up past their ankles. They ran in the deceptive dark of their coms' wayward lights. Cumchdach wished badly for his own com back. They came to an old-fashioned metal ladder tacked onto the side of the wall and he was forced up it. Going first to try it out, said the leader with a sneer and a grunt.

"We'll have weapons on you at all times, and there's nothing above but an empty tunnel and water on all sides," he warned. "Don't try anything foolish."

Cumchdach nodded curtly, as if surrendering. He had no doubt they'd shoot if he tried to run. But he was a Mountainer, unlike these men. Fast and flexible. He took it slow up the steps, as if labouring and puffed from the run and all the beatings, grunting audibly as he used his arms to pull himself up. Then he flopped over the top and lay panting. The first of the men began to climb, the other two standing with blasters trained on him.

Two shooters against his speed. Fair enough odds. He flipped sideways, jumped up, and began to run, trailing one hand on the wall to keep his direction. Running blind in an unknown maze, but it was the only chance he had. All he knew was he must go up.

There were no more ladders, but he did meet doors. Each had the telltale chill and seepage warning of the sea churning behind them. He kept running, his footsteps as light as possible. But even a Mountainer couldn't keep completely silent in this water-soaked tunnel, not with the speed he needed, and the light splashes of his passing betrayed him to his captors. He soon heard their shouts and heavy boots chasing after him.

He had to break their expected pattern somehow. The leader had been right. This tunnel gave him no options. All they had to do was keep after him.

So time to leave it. He stopped a moment, holding his breath and lifting his head. Reaching for the feel of the currents wafting through it.

Since he was breathing, the ventilation was still on to this section. And that meant the ventilation tubes were free of water. So he must be near the top of the water level here. All he had to do was go up a level and he'd be safe for a time.

A very short time, but that was all he needed.

All ventilation systems needed servicing; the reason all main tubes were big enough for a serviceman to enter. Cumchdach was big by Mountainer standards, but not by the rest of the planet. He should be able to fit, just.

He lifted his damp palm, listening and concentrating.

Then turned his head and began to move again, softly and slower this time. The other men's splashings came closer, but he should have time. He hoped.

There. The air currents dipped upward. Above him was an outlet. A large one, by the feel of the suction. He jumped, his fingers touching on empty air. Tragging high ceiling. He needed rope.

Yeah, some's about to jump into your hands.

What else to use.

He touched his belt. It was a long shot, the digital lock the only protuberance in its length, but he opened it anyway, and flung the square end upward.

And heard a solid clunk.

His brother, Seolta, had delved into plenty of questionable areas in his childhood as he came up with diabolical trick after trick. One had been the mechanics of basic items such as belt locks. He once managed to momentarily blind Cumchdach by setting off his belt as he was getting undressed. Cumchdach had jumped on him and forced his little brother to teach him how he'd done it. Seolta hadn't been able to stop laughing at first, but he was too proud of the trick to hold back on it.

And he probably knew his very angry big brother wasn't going to let him try it twice.

It was a piece of childhood foolery Cumchdach was suddenly grateful for. He touched the lock, hoping he could remember the details—and do it by touch only, with time against him.

He cursed as his fingers slipped. He could hear the men's shouting louder now. He forced himself to take it slower, to go carefully.

Finally, he had it set. He threw the lock against the ventilation cover and felt the vibration of the lock expanding. Then tugged, and began to breathe again as the belt lock held tight to the sides of the ventilation shaft. Before he could think twice, he pulled up on it and hauled himself skyward, fingers clinging to the edge of the shaft as he felt all around then opened the clips.

He had to swing himself up to get through the hole. Only desperation gave him the strength, ignoring the bashing of the shaft sides against his bruises and burns. Then he was through and placing the cover carefully back over the grating hole.

He began to pull himself along the shaft, slithering softly on the dusty surface and keeping as quiet as possible.

Soon he heard the men shouting below as they discovered his escape. He slithered faster. It wouldn't take them long to find out where he'd gone. Then a hatch cover popped open ahead of him and he slammed to a stop. Caught between, he had nowhere to go.

A head emerged from the hatch, one covered by a breathing mask, and water sloshed from below. That room down there was full of water. The newcomer grabbed both edges of the hatch and pulled himself up onto the lip.

This wasn't one of his captors. The man was too young, too slim. Then the man pulled off his breathing mask and Cumchdach surged forward, grabbing the newcomer and slamming him to the floor of the tube.

"Anton den Falasch. I should have known."

The boy made choking sounds. Barely a man, in Cumchdach's head he was still the sulky brat of a teenager who'd made Anna's life hell too often. But he was family, he belatedly remembered, and Cumchdach eased off his hand enough to let the boy talk.

"You've got it wrong," Anton said. "I'm here to rescue you. Anna knows about it."

"She made it out?"

The boy nodded and one of the tight knots inside Cumchdach relaxed. Then Anton fished in his wetsuit pocket. Cumchdach pounced on the sliver. "It's for you," the boy protested. "Loaded with all your public contacts. The marshals did it. It's clean."

"The marshals? They sent you?" It was hard to believe.

"Whatever you think, Anna is my sister and Rubhaicreach my city."

"Why would the marshals send you?"

"I'm trained in marine and cave rescue and I'm small enough to make it through any space. Others are coming too." He reached into his pocket again and pulled out another breathing mask. "We're wasting time. Can you swim?"

Cumchdach nodded, stunned.

"Put this on and come along. Now, before they figure out where you are. The marshals are waiting above and this whole section of tunnelling is unstable."

For a whole long moment, Cumchdach considered it. Then another implication struck him. "The marshals have a tracker on me?"

The boy nodded. "It's how we found you."

"Go back. And tell them Manascraoch isn't safe. There are still traitors there. They have to take Anna and Roo somewhere else. Somewhere safe."

"Tell them yourself." The boy shoved the mask at him again.

Cumchdach shook his head. "They're taking me to their bosses. If that means the heads of this whole conspiracy, it's too good a chance to throw away. The marshals can track me and arrest them." Breaking the conspiracy was the only way to make sure Anna and Roo were permanently safe.

The boy pushed the mask at him again, and Cumchdach pushed it back. "Get going. They mustn't know I've talked to you. And keep your sister and nephew safe."

The boy's mouth dropped open. "You trust them to me?"

"You're family, aren't you?"

Something changed in the boy's face. "Yes, yes, I am. And one day, I'm going to make your wife give me Falasch," he added with a grin. "When I'm ready for it."

Before he realised he was going to say it, Cumchdach said, "I think she'll welcome that—when you're ready." He clapped the boy on the shoulder. And the boy clasped his arm in reply then put on his mask and watched while Cumchdach slipped the sliver of his new com under his armpit into the small hollow there. It should be nearly invisible in most inspections.

The boy slipped into the water and Cumchdach silently replaced the hatch cover. Then he turned back toward his captors.

'Go safe, brother,' came to him via a mind link. His new com working, thankfully.

'And you,' he sent back. Then began to slither noisily back to the thugs awaiting him.

They caught him as he slid over the open hatch. A blaster shot through the tube behind him and one in front, forcing him to halt, belly exposed to the open hatch. Another blaster poked him in the waist.

"Get down here, now. The boys and I have had enough of your games and we'll soon forget orders."

Cumchdach slowly pulled his legs up and levered to slide down through the hatch. They weren't satisfied of course, grabbing his legs and jerking him down, to slam into the base of the tunnel.

"Got lost, did you."

He scowled at them. "Couldn't find a room that wasn't full of water. Hoped to find one back this way."

The leader eyed the bruises on his face and added a kick to his torso. "That'll teach you. Now get up. These walls aren't going to hold and we're not about to be caught down here because of some spoiled rich slug. Move, Ser den Coille." They hauled him up and had him running faster than ever in the wavering light.

Many times during that nightmare flight, he regretted not taking up Anton den Falasch's offer. The walls about them crumbled, small flakes of clay and rock spilling downward and making the floor slippery. Too often, he heard the thud of falling stones right after they passed through.

The men dragged him faster and faster. Finally they came to a doorway. It was an airlock.

"That's seawater out there. It's dangerous."

"You think we don't know that?" The man dragged him through the door, slammed it behind them. "Hold your breath."

Cumchdach grabbed at a lungful as the water poured in. They'd set the fill rate to maximum. Then the outer door was opening and they were pulling him toward a small flyer tethered in the opening.

Crash.

Panic hit the men's faces. More crashes and bangs ricocheted on the door. The inner tunnel had collapsed and a wave of water battered against the door lock. If it didn't hold, they'd all be caught in the wake.

The bosses might not get their moment of triumph.

The man grabbed him and he swam as hard as the rest for that open door into the flyer.

Then they were in and slamming the door shut. The pumps worked hard and soon they could breathe. The first man ran for the pilot's seat.

Then he heard a yell.

"The lock is gone." And a crashing wave hit their flyer.

CHAPTER TWENTY-SIX

Anna caught herself nibbling on her finger again and hastily pulled it out. What had she been thinking when she agreed to this mad plan? Anton was still a boy.

He's twenty-one standards. Older than you when you fell in love with Cumchdach.

He was still the baby brother who'd once toddled after her, demanding she pick him up then hugged her with all the strength of his tiny body—and she'd let him go into danger. She had put the survival of Cumchdach in the hands of her baby brother.

"I've done this kind of thing before. This storm isn't our first," he'd told her. She knew that and said so. She grew up with Rubhaicreach storms.

"Not like this one. They've grown worse since you left here."

Of course they had. The Survey had been trying for years to tell them what was happening to their world. And that left her feeling guilty and scared. She stomped down on it like she always did.

"He's one of our best," said the team leader, "and he's smaller than the rest of us. If anyone can get through those flooded tunnels, it's Anton."

Not even the marshals had sided with her. Dunan had eyed Anton, not fully trusting him she guessed, but had then surprised her with his nod. "He'll do." He passed a com sliver to her brother. "This has Ser den Coille's known public contacts. It's a secured marshal com. Undetectable to most scans."

Anna stared at it, fighting the need to touch it. A small sigh escaped her when Anton tucked the com into the secure pouch on his suit. The loss of com contact had been the worst part of this whole nightmare. That pulse of the marshals' tracker was poor reassurance. What if his captors had discovered it and tampered with it? The team could be heading into a trap and Cumchdach already gone or was— No, she refused to even think the word.

She was going to have to let Anton do this.

"You'll be wanting to get back to your baby," said Marshal Dunan in what he probably thought a caring, diplomatic voice.

"I'm not leaving until Cumchdach is safe." She crossed her hand over her aching breasts as if to deny the pull of motherhood. The medics here had helped her to express and assured her a short break wouldn't stop her feeding her baby. She wouldn't believe them until she had Roo back again, adding one more mark to the score she'd built against these conspirators. But Roo was safe in Manascraoch. She was staying. She thrust her chin out.

"What if something happens to you? Rubhaicreach is no longer as safe as it was. Not for a den Coille, or a rival den Falasch," said Marshal Dunan.

"You're trusting Anton," she said, sending her brother an apologetic look and ignoring the flush on his face.

"To a point," the marshal said. "The current leaders of Falasch are another matter."

Anton flushed, his mouth tight, and she suddenly realised he must have heard similar judgements many times before. From her, and from others.

"Our father may love us, but he is not a strong man, or a sensible one sometimes," she said to her brother and held out her hand to him.

His eyes widened in surprise. She kept her hand out and, after a moment, he took it, squeezing it once.

"Grandfather, on the other hand, was as tough as the rock this city is built on. He would have been proud of you," she added, and watched the shock of it hit her brother.

"Thank you, Na," he said very softly, for her ears only. It had been baby Anton's first name for her, and she flushed too, this time in pleasure.

"You will find my husband, and then we need to talk, you and I."

He nodded slowly. Then she watched him and his team set out. He was the smallest, the slimmest, and the youngest by a large gap. All were fit, strong, and from the way they checked their equipment, had done this many times before.

It didn't stop her worrying as her baby brother disappeared from sight. He was clearly competent. The reaction of the rest of the team made that clear. He was also young, with something to prove, and despite what she'd told him, she wasn't yet sure she trusted him.

Marshal Dunan lifted his head from a study of his com screen. "They're on their way back."

"And Cumchdach?"

Silence. An awful silence, the kind that meant nothing good. The marshal shook his head.

Before she could demand more, the lift chute signalled an incoming party. They were in the Rubhaicreach security headquarters. No one used that chute without permission.

She stood up and watched the exit, heart in mouth.

First out was the city's marshal liaison. She'd gone to First School with him, but he avoided her gaze. She waited, leaning forward with each new body broaching the chute exit. Anton was one of the last, then the team leader. She waited, peering into the chute. It cycled closed. No one else was coming.

She strode to her brother and shoved him in the chest. "You promised! Where is he?"

Anton was stronger than he looked. He rocked lightly on his feet but caught himself. Then she saw his face, saw the rigid clench of his jaw.

"He's dead?"

"No. No."

The leader stepped up to her. "The ser refused to come. They're taking him to their bosses. He thinks they include the leader of the conspiracy."

Her mouth dropped open and she gasped for breath. She locked her arms around her chest, trying to hold in the pain of it.

"And you *let* him?"

"He said it was the only way to keep you and your son safe," said Anton.

"He has a com, Sera, and we are tracking him," added the leader.

"Show me."

The team leader glanced at Marshal Dunan, who nodded. The techs made way and opened up their screens to her. One, small tracer line moved quickly. Down, away along the maze of back passages. The old, rarely repaired tunnels, known only to locals. She turned on Anton.

"Who gave them the secret of the tunnels? You?"

He shook his head, his too young face and body held as tightly as hers. "My mother and her supporters. They've been talking to Urbis groups for years."

"And our father?"

Anton shrugged. "He's the one who showed them to Mother. They were good business connections, she told him."

They probably were. From the start of this mess, it was clear that opposition to the Council's changes for the planet came from top companies. The ones most likely to be hurt financially.

"They betrayed our city, our world, and you did nothing?" She couldn't help herself, the words spouting from her. "Or do you too think the Council is spreading doomsday talk for their own ends? Are you one of them?"

Now colour bloomed on her brother's cheeks. He shook his head angrily. "Why do you think I joined this team? The kinds of storms we're getting now will destroy this city if something isn't done. But I don't control Falasch. I'm not even in the line of seniority."

"Don't give me that. Falasch has always been family run. You're tragging closely involved."

"Involved, yes. Running it, no. You left that to Da and my mam. Don't blame me for what happened. Not when you've been anywhere but here." Her brother flipped a hand at her. "Go back to your precious plants and your honoured new family. Den Coille has everything so perfect. It's easy for them."

"Under Council orders to cut back on their main profit source and with my own father's company stealing from them? Don't be an idiot."

"You're the idiot. You were safely away from here, and you threw it away."

"You can't throw away family and birth."

"Yeah?"

She stood as stiff-backed as Anton. Roots, you'd think they were a pair of kids again. Except she hadn't been a child for many years, and she'd had Cumchdach supporting her by the time her little brother was old enough to start flinging Gria's poison at her. Old enough to be past childish tantrums.

She forced her clenched hands open. "I am your sister, and Rubhaicreach will always be my first home." She took a breath as she said out loud what she'd too long denied. "But I now have other bonds as well. I am the wife of Cumchdach mar Bram den Coille, and the mother of Ruiseart mar Cumchdach an Anna den Coille. I am also an acknowledged expert on plant interactions, knowledge my planet needs. I can no more ignore those ties than I can my birth family and first home. That is what it means to be an adult—like us."

Her brother's cheeks reddened more, but not as angrily. She watched as he also forced his fingers open. "And I am Anton mar Eolas an Gria den Falasch." It was the first time since he was little she'd heard Anton use his full Mountainer name, and she couldn't stop the tear that quivered in the corner of her eye. "Rubhaicreach is my birth home and Falasch Shipping is my company. To them, I owe my duty and my heart."

She had to bow, the formal bow to acknowledge a vow. She had no reason to trust her brother, or not many, and would never forgive his mother for what she'd done here, but her brother spoke truth.

She was beginning to believe Falasch would be safe in his hands—in time and with help. The help only her support could bring. She'd have to talk to Grandam.

"You need to leave here, sister. It's not safe for you, and Rubhaicreach is in no state to stand up to the turmoil if you're harmed."

"You're asking me to leave to save my home city?"

He gulped. "Yes."

The local security head stepped in then. "Ser Anton gha Driach is correct, Sera Anna." The city was already connecting him with their grandfather, it seemed. "Too much has happened, and the details of the Falasch trial is about to hit the tunnels."

Anna jerked up. "You've heard the penalty?" The trial in the Arcadian courts over reparation for Falasch's defrauding of Den Coille was underway but what Den Coille were seeking hadn't yet been made public. Or so she thought.

"It's not announced yet," said Marshal Dunan.

"But," said Anna.

"Den Coille wants reparation. They are suing for control of Falasch and for a penalty payment sufficient to satisfy the Alliance Central required sanctions against Falasch Shipping.

"Payment? How much?'

He told her, and she gasped. "That will destroy Falasch."

The marshal made no apology. "It's likely they'll win, given the potential cost of the fraud to Den Coille, based on the value of the trade in Festin. It's Arcadia's most widely sold export commodity."

"You know this how?"

"The courts gave the marshals a warning."

"You know what will happen here when this is made public?" asked Anton, watching her. "Everyone in the city knows what you think of my mother. They'll be waiting to see what you do to us."

"They know me better than that."

Her brother said nothing. She'd been away too long. She hadn't lived full time in Rubhaicreach since she'd first left to study in Urbis. But she hadn't believed the city had renounced her.

"They know Grandfather. They know how much time he spent with me."

Her brother's mouth tightened at the reminder.

"They know, Sera Anna ingh Eolas bean Cumchdach," said the local team leader. It wasn't enough, he was telling her, and the marshal made no attempt to intervene.

She shook her head, torn as never before. It changed nothing about what she must do. "I can't talk about this now. We have to rescue Cumchdach. That comes first."

"Ser Cumchdach has made his decision, Sera, and the planet will be grateful if it works."

"Whether he survives or not," she said bitterly.

The marshal bowed in acceptance. "In exchange, we have to honour his wishes. You and your son must be kept safe. You are leaving here now, Sera. A marshal flyer is ready to take you home to Manascraoch."

"No," said Anton unexpectedly. "Ser Cumchdach warned there are traitors there too."

"But Roo is there."

Marshal Dunan suddenly flipped on his com and put up a cone of silence. Anna watched him talk in growing horror. Then the marshal snapped off the cone.

"We've got him in protective custody. He has a team of marshals with him."

"And the den Coille family?"

"Have been informed. Den Coille security protocols are now in place."

"What level?"

"Our people advise that Den Coille security is at level 1A."

Anna had to sit. Dunan shoved a chair in her direction and gently pushed her into it.

"Breathe, Sera. You are safe, and so is your baby. The marshals will ensure that."

"How can you when there are traitors everywhere?"

"Not in the marshals."

"But you're a Coaster too."

The man drew himself up, rigid as roots. "Lower boughsman these days, Sera."

And she remembered that visit to the lower boughs, the hopelessness and the simmering anger. "Why would you, of all people, put yourself at risk for a den Coille?"

He flushed. "It's my duty, Sera," he said stiffly. Then added, "You are the sister-in-law of Samhchair den Coille and have been vouched for by Councillor Seilach ingh Craobh bean Stobach den Bunachan. You didn't turn away from us that time you visited."

"I can't make any promises to the Coasters in exchange for my safety."

"No one's expecting you to." Now she'd offended him, by the tone of his voice.

"Marshal Dunan is a highly trained and valued serving marshal, Sera," said the marshal who had first found her. "His word is good."

Dunan said nothing to that, his face the blank mask they must teach in Marshal training school.

"But where am I to go?" she said.

More silence. Then Marshal Dunan stood up again. "The Coaster community is known to have no love for Den Coille, thanks to our displacement. Few go there now and those few distrust outsiders."

Anna shook her head. "Ripe for rebellion then."

But Marshal Dunan was obstinate. "They're not part of the conspiracy. There's no money in Coaster lands. Den Coille has the ownership tied up and, without festia trees, there are no credits to be gained there."

"I'll be safe?"

"Given your backing by the Sera Samhchair and the Councillor, yes."

Maybe, but her son's safety was at stake here. Anna opened her mouth, but the two marshals gave her no chance to argue. They hustled her away, and all she could do was wave frantically at Anton.

"It's to keep the city safe, sister," he called with a grim twist of his too young face. "You can fight me for it after."

Then she was in the flyer, watching the land of her childhood fall away and merge into the dense forested slopes of the mountains. Soon, below her lay patches of new plantings as waves crashed against the shore. This wasn't the usual approach to Manascraoch. The mid slopes had easier air currents and less fuel costs. She looked sharply over at the Coaster marshal, sitting ahead of her on the far side of the cabin. She could see the side of his face, then the back of his head as he turned to say something to one of the other marshals. He'd brought a full squad with him. She'd seen the change on their faces as they lifted off, telling of an incoming com message pack they were scanning—orders from Marshal an Fallon, she guessed sourly—then seen the sudden glance they shot at her and the straightening of their backs.

She was important, and she was a risk. It was the only message those looks could mean. The marshals remaining in Rubhaicreach had given a full salute to Dunan as they boarded, and the Coaster marshal returned it. Police transferring a dangerous prisoner—and she was the prisoner.

"Where is Roo now?" was her first question when they reached Manascraoch airspace.

"He and his nurse have been transferred to a marshal flyer. They're on hold above the city and will meet us in a safe landing spot before we head to the final location."

"Which is?"

But Marshal Dunan turned away from her and went back to whatever he was doing with his com. Their exact location was none of her business, it appeared. She was a danger to his people, and they weren't going to forget it.

"Why are you even taking me there if it could hurt your Coasters?" she demanded.

He kept his back turned and she slumped back in anger. "This had better be a safe haven, or I'm not staying there."

That had him swivelling around on her. "You'd be lost in no time in our marshes. They're not well mapped, even yet. The channels change daily." She saw a hard edge come into the narrowed eyes. "You're going there because it's the safest place for you while Ser Cumchdach completes his mission. He's in enough danger as it is; he doesn't need his family at risk and giving his captors another edge on him."

"I know that," she snapped back, "but keeping me in the dark doesn't help anyone. I can help you, Marshal, if you let me."

"That is a decision for the Commander."

She hated that rigid, security face. She'd seen it too often lately. "Cumchdach is my husband. I'm not likely to do anything that puts him in more danger. But you need to be honest with me so that I can make well informed decisions. His safety and that of our son are my first concerns."

Unlike the marshals, she felt like adding, but kept silent. The marshals obeyed the Council and the laws of Arcadia first; the wellbeing of its citizens coming a distant second. She'd learned that the hard way when Cumchdach and his family were imprisoned.

"Is he even still alive?"

The marshal gave a brusque head bow. "Yes, Sera, and is being taken to Urbis according to his tracker.

"And the com sliver?"

"He… is not responding," the man carefully admitted.

Her heart beat harder. "His life signs?"

"All still positive."

"But…"

"They are positive. He is alive and not in immediate medical danger."

She'd spent too much time with Cumchdach's mother and sister when they were worried about a patient. All that meant was he wasn't at risk of dying.

"For all you know, he could be unconscious or badly hurt."

"Not badly. His heart readings aren't sufficiently disturbed. That is all I can tell you, Sera."

"I want a promise out of you, Marshal. Or I call the den Coilles right now and have them block this flyer."

"That is not possible, Sera."

"I can't call them, or they can't block us?"

"Both," he finally admitted. "We are flying shielded. Only marshal transmissions can access us."

She really was a prisoner.

"It's for your own safety, Sera. We have no way of knowing who in Manascraoch is compromised."

It sounded so reasonable, that flat marshal tone of his with the voice of fact-backed authority.

She'd used that same voice herself when she wanted people to do something. She didn't trust it one syllable but for now had to give way. She looked out the window. They'd given her a seat on the side facing out to sea, where she could watch headlands and waves crashing on the rocks. A scene similar to her home. Maybe they thought it would help, but she badly needed to see the trees of Cumchdach's home, the rising slopes and mountain peaks towering above.

To see it unchanged, a constant reminder of how long she'd loved him.

Only there would be changes, the dense colour of festia trees giving way to the fresh greens of new seedlings, a new patchwork of shrub, grassland, and meadows to suit the natural shape of the mountain country.

A change that must be limited. Den Coille and Arcadia still had to make credits, and Festin from the festia trees earned too much in export returns.

Bram den Coille had asked her to help to find a new pathway for Den Coille. Help she'd yet to deliver, too caught up in the needs of a new baby and the political coils snagging her life. Truth was, she didn't even know if she could help them. The Survey and Den Coille scientists were first class. All she could hope to do was increase the efficiency of pollen production. Her project in Deuteron was giving exciting results under the watch of her best students and may give some answers. But that was yet one more call on her time. And then there was her home city, with the danger of the split threatening Rubhaicreach if the fraud trial's penalty lost them their independence.

No, when. Den Coille would win and must demand payment. For their own protection, they needed control of her family's business.

On top of it all and tearing at her heart, was the break from Cumchdach. She still saw no way back from that, no way out of the angry pain for a man who had failed to trust her.

He's putting his life on the line to keep you safe.

She shoved the thought aside and looked out the window again. The view was changing below. Fewer crashing waves, now it was lower headlands and rocky beaches, rising to dunes and the first of the coastal reeds. A stream rushed to the sea below her, gouging a sideways path along a gravel-covered bar, to erupt into the sea where the beach met the rock of a headland, as if refusing to be held back any longer. She peered down, trying to see what lay inland. The first sign of reeds, then a glimpse of a festia tree. Dark-leafed, but not as vibrant in colour as those up on the mountain slopes. Festia liked wet feet, but not the brackish water of lands so close to the sea.

This was not its natural home, but so valued was its pollen that Den Coille had pushed its planting right to the limit of its natural range, until a straggly caricature of the tree survived on the margins.

"Coming in to land," said the pilot's voice in her ear. She looked out eagerly, wanting to see her new home in this strange country. She had no real idea of the land at the moment, and felt disconnected as the flyer set down and she stepped out into the groomed surface of the landing site.

This was no Mountainer landing pad, with its ever moving platform set high in the trees. It was more like her own home, the hard, rocky ground of her peninsula. Only it smelled nothing like home. Here, she had the smell of the sea, as at home, but beneath her feet was the hard surface of plascrete, edged on all sides by foreign plants and the open fields of reed-covered marshlands, while the overwhelming smell was the dank mustiness of squelching mud.

The marshals dealt with everything. Once they left the crude shelter that was the pad's control room, office, and passenger reception all in one, they were met by a skimmer of a type she hadn't seen before. Two, fat tubes hugged the sides, and the middle was little more than the skeleton of a crate with metal sides, the overall appearance favouring utilitarian over aesthetic. The strange, dun-coloured coating, with splodges of mud and plants hanging from the edge of the tubing did nothing to enhance it. Marshal Dunan strode toward the contraption as if unsurprised by the lowly work vehicle, and the rest of his team followed.

She hurried to join them, helped by the hustling of a team determined to keep her firmly in their middle.

"What explanation did you give the reception office?" she asked as soon as they were under way.

"We're here on a routine inspection visit. The marshals do similar often enough."

True enough. The marshals were responsible for overall policing in all of Arcadia and tended to pop up anywhere. They didn't usually receive so little attention though. The local police force usually got wind of their coming and made sure everything looked spruce and under control before the marshals got there.

Not that the uniformed marshals were the only ones inspecting far flung posts, but they were the ones that caused a commotion. Yet here, they had passed through the entry hut with no more than a murmured request for clearance.

"Who did you tell them I am?"

"A technical specialist consulting for the service."

True enough, if lacking specificity or any indication that she wasn't here voluntarily. "And now what? Where are we going?"

"Down the coastline a bit. There's a small settlement still there that will take you in with no questions asked."

"Will they talk?"

"No. You're safe."

"And Roo?"

"Is already there. His flyer came in earlier."

They hadn't told her that. They'd deliberately made her think she was meeting him elsewhere. Marshals trusted outsiders rarely, and they didn't trust her one speck.

"Do you seriously think I'd do anything to hurt my own baby?"

Marshal Dunan looked at her face and a slight twist of his mouth said he'd seen the signs of her fury. Inconvenient for him, was it? This whole thing was a tragging sight more than inconvenient for her.

"It was thought to be the safest plan, Sera, in case anyone locked onto your flyer. This skimmer is of local make, the com systems linked to the local networks only. It's less hackable."

"You trust your own people, Marshal, but I have no reason to yet.'

"I trust marshal systems, Sera. These have been fully vetted."

She subsided, but couldn't relax. It had been so long since she'd felt safe, she sometimes wondered if she'd ever be able to again.

Then remembered that too short, special time with Cumchdach. Imprisoned by their enemies but, for the first time since this whole nightmare began, she hadn't felt alone.

She needed him so badly.

He had to be safe, had to get out of this alive.

She vowed then and there that when they did meet again, nothing would stop her. She was going to tell her husband exactly what she felt for him. That she'd loved him since she'd first met him as a young girl.

The worst he could do was reject her, said common sense. Only common sense didn't know how badly rejection would destroy her.

Their skimmer had changed routes now. They were headed into the marshes proper, and she glanced at Marshal Dunan. He was staring out the window, lost for a moment. Then jerked back and pulled up his com again, still using that tragging marshal privacy shield. But every now and again she saw him glance out the window.

"How long since you've been back here?" she heard herself ask.

"Not since we left. I was sixteen standards. My village was relocated to make way for a new plantation."

"All affected parties were compensated, I was told."

"Oh, yes. We were given new homes, a fund that paid our living costs. But jobs, a purpose, a history, and a culture? Those you can't compensate for, Sera. They can't be replaced easily."

"Jobs can."

"If someone gives you a chance."

"Like you were?"

He grimaced. "I was lucky. I had a good teacher. She recommended me for higher training and personally organised a scholarship. She also backed my application for the marshals."

"Why them?" Her stupid curiosity, always wanting to know *what next*.

"They're independent. The den Coilles don't own the marshals."

"They have influence on the Council."

"Not even the Council can order the marshals to act against the law, and laws aren't easy to pass. The den Coille's aren't the only ones with influence on the Council."

"You wanted to change things, or wanted to restore the old order? There's a difference."

He bowed his head in acknowledgement. "I wanted to give my people back their lands, and the Alliance orders gave us our first chance at that, but I want them back here with power of their own, control of their own fates. Corporates must be controlled."

This time, she was the one forced to bow her head. She came from the corporate side of the ledger, but her mother's family had always worked on the governance side of Rubhaicreach. Generations of her family had striven to balance the needs of Falasch against the needs of the city. It had worked until her father's day.

The engine's noise changed, slowing to approach a dock. They must be there, and she gratefully put aside her ponderings.

Where they were to stop wasn't obvious. No break in the wall of reeds appeared. But the skimmer came to a slow crawl and edged through the reeds. She watched as the stalks collapsed under the tubing then bounced up again after they'd passed. Hardy and resilient. She wondered if it was an adaptation to the strong winds that hit this coastline. Dunes could offer only so much protection. She kept watching their surrounds as they edged closer to what she hoped was their final destination, determinedly shoving aside her worries and finding refuge as so often before in the new plants around her. Her fingers itched to get out there and touch them, to discover their secrets.

Then the skimmer gave a final surge up onto a low bank, and the craft came to a halt in an empty clearing.

She stood and filed off with the rest of the team, looking around in confusion. "We're walking from here?"

Her boots already sank into the springy ground. The clearing was covered in a network of ground-hugging plants with tiny florets sparkling among the equally tiny leaves, and around them rose walls of forbidding, head-high reeds. She hadn't realised how tall they grew. Then she looked closely.

"They change colours."

It was subtle, more a shift of tone than colour bands, from palest sand to hints of tortoiseshell splodges among darker brown stems, to flashes of a deep, blue green. And she heard a constant hum and cocked her head.

"It's from the constant rubbing of the reeds. Even on a still day like this, the currents below the surface stir them. This land is floating, the soil only a few metres deep."

"Oh." She looked down and walked as lightly as possible, as if treading one of the smaller branches of the den Coille home tree.

The marshal grinned. "Don't worry, Sera. That dirt layer has a network of soil organisms, forming a tough mat. It won't sink far and easily holds our weight."

"Really? I need core samples." She reached for her com.

A shout from the far side of the clearing stopped her hand and she forgot all about samples or plants. Biarsuin emerged from the reeds, surrounded by others and, in her arms, her little boy waved his hands excitedly.

"Roo. Oh, Roo." She broke into a run. In an instant, he was back in her arms where he belonged, and her little man nestled his head into the hollow of her neck and tangled his hand in her hair.

"Mam's back, my mannikin. Mam's back, and she's not letting you go again."

Cumchdach groaned as his head hit something and pain shot through it. Then he opened his eyes and groggily wondered what by the tragging roots he'd been up to the night before. More importantly, where was he?

And where was Anna? The feel of her body against his was the only clear memory in his head. He sat up sharply, then slumped back as a wave of dizziness overtook him. That was when he discovered his wrists were bound by a restraining field. His attempt to use both hands to lever himself up failed appallingly, leaving him falling over and slumping again on whatever hard surface lay below him.

He banged his head again on something behind him. At least it was solid. He waited for the ringing to pass and his stomach to settle, then squirmed closer to it and used his feet, hips, and shoulder to work himself up against it. He didn't dare open his eyes until he was upright and sitting still.

He was on the floor of whatever place this was and the solid thing behind him was a wall. There wasn't even a blanket. Whoever had put him here wasn't hospitable. Then he looked down. The overall he wore wasn't his either. It looked like it belonged to a cleaner or maintenance worker.

Then it all came back to him. Anna!

She'd got away. Her brother had come for him and the marshals had sent him a com. She was safe, and on her way to Manascraoch.

No, not there, not with unknown infiltrators in the city. Had her brother delivered his warning? He must've. He *had to*. He slumped back against the wall. He was in the hands of the conspirators and on his way to meet the head bosses. Thanks to his moment of stupid nobility.

He had to keep Anna and Roo safe.

The marshals would hide them. They had sent the Rubhaicreach team and the com to his rescue. They would take Anna and Roo somewhere safe.

But they couldn't *keep* them safe. Not while this selfish conspiracy spread its dirt. A mad coalition of selfish brakkas who'd proven too many times they'd stop at nothing to keep their profits safe.

Once their bosses got what they wanted from Cumchdach, they had to kill him. He knew too much and was too determined to stop them.

Marshal an Fallon, you'd better come through this time.

The man hadn't let his family down so far. Not when it counted. It was what came before they rescued him that was the problem.

Cumchdach studied the room. Empty of anything. Not even water or food, or a service cupboard. He'd have to ask his captors for whatever he needed. They were taking no chances with him.

Good. That meant they knew he'd stop at nothing to save those he loved, and he grinned nastily. He clenched his arm to his side, feeling the slight touch of the hidden com but didn't activate it or send a message. No need to risk discovery, not before help was critical. But the feel of it there helped, and he shut his eyes again, listening hard to the sounds around him.

He was on some kind of flyer, he'd guess. Without using his com, he couldn't know the heading, but he would bet his yearly returns it was to Urbis. That's where the heart of this rot lay. Lurking in the twisted streets and crowded towers of the capital.

They must be taking the long route. That, or time in this box passed very slowly. Cumchdach tried hard to endure it, but a parched mouth and urgent needs finally made that impossible and had him limping over to the door and banging loudly for attention. They'd beaten him up worse than he'd hoped when he tried to distract them from Anna's escape.

They ignored him for a long time. Letting him suffer probably. Then he heard steps outside, a cranking of an old-fashioned lock, and the door opened. Four men faced him, all with blasters pointing straight at his gut.

"Water and a service closet," he told them. He'd be tragged if he was going to beg.

They stared back, no change in their faces. He switched to the more formal standard used by the Urbis upper groups, but they still stared back. Then one tilted his head as if listening to an incoming com message. After that, he pointed his blaster down the hall, to a small door at the end.

It was the most primitive service closet Cumchdach had seen, and none too clean. But at least it had water and sanitation. He washed his hands first, hoped the primitive san unit he used next killed basic pathogens, then used them to drink deeply of the water, not knowing when he'd get more.

The guard banged on the door before he'd finished, and he had to hurriedly cover up and clean his hands again before they yanked open the door and gestured for him to return to his cell.

The cell door slammed shut on him and he slammed his hands against it. He hadn't got even a word out of them and knew no more than before they'd let him out.

Did their refusal to speak mean they were off-worlders? The marshals had always believed Alliance parties were involved. The Alliance diplomat, Deputy Attaché Malgrave, was part of the plot that had entangled his brother Seolta, and the involvement of off-world companies in defrauding Den Coille backed it up.

Seolta was still investigating that side, with intermittent help from Alliance officials, it had to be said. The Alliance Central trial had finished the affair, as far as they were concerned, but all it had done was convict Falasch. Whether any Alliance companies were involved had been kept very carefully out of that proceeding—a condition necessary to bringing the fraud to trial.

Too many in habitat worlds hungered for a better life. Dangerously many, given few knew what it took to survive on Arcadia and the damage mass migration would do to this world. Seolta's wife had nearly lost her sanity the first time she'd stood under the open skies of Arcadia, and she'd known what to expect. Anyara ingh Gevard bean Seolta den Coille was one of the best biome specialists in the Alliance. On her visit to Arcadia, she and

Anna had spent hours talking in words that were a mystery to the rest of the family.

What he would give to be back listening to his Anna talk excitedly in words he didn't understand. He used to watch her face for hours when she was engrossed in her work, loving the light in her eyes and the passion in her voice.

If he got through this, he swore they'd be together again. Whatever Anna wanted, however she wanted it, but together. If he didn't make it, she would be safe and free to work, and their son would grow up in the warmth of her love.

A fitting monument to a man's life. He grimaced. He'd have liked to be part of it, but life had a habit of kicking you in the backside when you demanded too much. He'd learned that in prison under the boots of the Survey guards.

They'd been bullies for hire, like those who held him now. Paid mercenaries with nothing to gain by treating him well. All they had to do was deliver him alive to their client.

And still able to talk. Don't forget that bit.

Cold fear hit him then, in that lonely cell so far from everyone he loved. Always before, he'd had Anna, or his family. His three brothers, annoying sometimes, but loyal always. His sisters, Samhchair to talk sense to him and Fioruisghe to stir him up. His parents. His father may be the wiliest person he knew, but his mother was the wisest. He might be the expected heir to his father's position as head of the company, but the den Coilles were a team. None of them functioned well without the rest.

They're still there. Still working to help him. The marshals too.

And Anna. She would refuse to go into safety without a rescue plan in place for him.

But there was Roo. Who would she put first: her baby or her husband? And he remembered then the feel of his son when he'd first held Roo, the wonder, the joy, and the crushing weight of responsibility. A precious and tiny spark of humanity totally dependent on him and Anna.

She'd put Roo first. She had to, and he hoped and prayed with everything in him that she did. He'd do the same.

It didn't make the fear go away. He settled into the floor and shut his eyes, trying every trick he knew to get some sleep. Whatever was coming, he needed to be in better shape to deal with it.

It didn't work, of course, and he lay fuming, wishing for an end to it all. Just get on with whatever was going to happen when he met these invisible bosses, hopefully including the one at the top. The one he'd only ever seen in avatar. First thing he'd do, he decided, was call him out on his cowardice. Hiding behind his corporate stooges.

Concealing whatever about him made him less than compelling. The man used the full range of technology like a top-level sportsman used the full range of the court. Was there a reason for that?

What about the leader must be hidden? He'd learned from his father that there was a logic to most problems and misunderstandings in business; you only had to find it.

At least trying to work it out distracted him from his present reality, even if it gave him no answers. All he'd decided by the time the door slammed open again and the guards kicked him to stand, was that Ceart was right. His enemy was no corporate head. Nothing about this whole thing made business sense or felt familiar.

The leader came from another sphere entirely. One far more political.

Another kick too near his head had him scrabbling up and forgetting all thoughts of the leader. Surviving the next few moments took precedence. Two big men grabbed him, one on either side, as they released his restraints, dragged his hands behind his back, then applied them again. Another brought in a scanner and he tensed as they swept it over him.

"Clean," said the guard, and he stared ahead, throttling back his relief. He listened hard to their accent but got little from it. They sounded Arcadian, from the back streets of Urbis, he'd guess, but whether that was from a language program or their inborn accent, he couldn't say. It took a linguist expert to do that, although he had a suspicion his brother Seolta could pick it. His annoying younger brother had spent his youth picking up stray pieces of knowledge, collecting them like a gandy in its burrow.

Then the thrust of a blaster in his back and a shove by the men had him hurrying forward.

He tried to look for clues to his whereabouts when they marched him off the flyer, but all he could see was a landing cavern like any other and blank walls in the tunnel they hustled him down. It looked like the flyer entrance of any large office, without the usual welcoming signs or services.

It also looked disused, as if abandoned for many years, although the smears in the dust on the floor and the metallic smell suggested his flyer wasn't the first to dock here. A hideout used by the conspiracy?

Not long to go now.

The tunnel was a long one, mostly downward, and the metallic smell was joined by a dank mouldiness, as if passing under water. If they were in Urbis, he'd guess at one of the older industrial areas on the multitude of branching canals in the estuarine zone. When his feet splashed in a puddle and he saw the tell-tale smear of greasy slime on the wall from a leak, he knew it. Modern tunnels had sensors spaced along their length to check and seal any leaks, with automated ventilation. This air tasted of decay and age.

They began to walk uphill again, and not a gentle slope. The bruises and burns from his capture and the long sleepless night made their presence felt, and he had to fight to quell a huff of breathlessness. The guards made no concessions, dragging him along if he looked like slowing.

Even if he'd wanted to escape down one of the intermittent dark circles of a side tunnel, he doubted he'd manage it. Not with the pace they were setting and in his current state.

After far too long, they stopped in front of another door. One of the guards did something on a door pad and it slid open. Then his restraints were released and he was shoved in.

It was another cell. He squashed down the disappointment and drew himself up.

"Your bosses not ready to receive me yet?"

"You'll find out soon enough." The man slammed the door shut in his face and left him alone again. He was discovering he hated being alone, although he couldn't count how many times in his youth he'd prayed for just one moment of uninterrupted privacy. He looked around, exploring this latest prison. It looked much like the last, although this one had a service closet at least, as well as a crude sleeping bench. He wouldn't grace it with the name of a sleeper. Not when it was little more than a wooden bench with a blanket tossed over it. He slumped down on it, pulling the blanket up, then shoved it away with a 'faugh'. It stank of stale sweat. He wasn't the only one who'd been held in this barren room.

The deliberate cruelty was too familiar. Too like the last time he'd been imprisoned for no just cause, along with the all the den Coille and Winter families. It wasn't concrete proof, but enough for him to know, deep in his heart, that the conspirators were behind that too. His whole family still thanked the Survey field staff for their role in freeing them.

Fortunately he didn't have long to wait this time. He'd no sooner thrown off the blanket, settled his back into the coldness of the stone wall behind him, than the door opened and blaster-carrying guards again gestured for him to stand. He didn't bother trying to talk to them this time. He was too busy marshalling his thoughts and guts for the meeting to come.

They pushed him through a cleanser this time, clothes and all, and waited while the system made him appear respectable. No offer of a change of clothing, though. Maybe they liked that the crude overalls helped them to feel superior, or they hoped it made him forget who he was.

No chance of that.

He gritted his teeth and went with them.

If you're going to make a move, an Fallon, soon would be good.

The tunnels changed in kind. These ones were still old, but someone had tried to clean them up and the air smelled less dank. The flooring even changed to the softer tread found in offices.

Someone didn't like facing the reality of what they were doing.

Then they came to another door.

CHAPTER TWENTY-SEVEN

Anna kicked at the dirt, then swore as her heel sank down. The soft ground was too accommodating. Always retreating from her foot, instead of kicking back like the honest rock of her home city.

Nothing here made sense. She was in Mountainer country, but the only hills within walking distance were the dunes cutting the marshes off from the sea. The winds here slithered inside her tunic and wormed their way through whatever protective gear she donned. Soon, she'd be reduced to asking one of the locals for a loan of their all-enveloping shirts made of fibre from a local browser. It wasn't waterproof, but it kept you warm thanks to layers of air bubbles trapped within the special weave.

She kicked again at the ground and snarled in frustration. Then sighed. It wasn't the ground, the unfamiliar systems, the alien feel to everything that had her prowling down this avenue of reeds, followed hastily by her ever present security team.

No, it was the lack of news. The marshals were supposed to be monitoring Cumchdach at all times. They must have found him by now.

Where was he? And *how* was he?

Marshal Dunan was working security today, walking beside her with eyes constantly scanning all directions. She turned to him.

"You have any news?"

"Not yet, Sera. You will be told as soon as we do."

"You must know something."

"The Ser is on his way to Urbis, as predicted. That's all we can say for now. He is alive, and his vital signs are within acceptable parameters."

"Acceptable." She was going to choke soon. "What in tragging blazes does that mean? Near death, a touch roughed up, just fine and snazzy? If you can't speak in proper Mountainer, then try Standard. That should be official enough for you."

The Coaster marshal smothered the grin touching his mouth. "It doesn't change the message. That's all we have, Sera." His smooth voice was probably meant to sound sympathetic.

She swung around and walked back the way she'd come. "Talk to me again when you have real news."

Her skin crawled and every nerve in her body burned. He had to be safe. They needed to rescue him before their enemies hurt him.

If only she could do something. But his word and his son bound her here. Cumchdach had gone into this dangerous captivity only on the promise she and Roo would be taken to a safe refuge. Roo already had one parent in danger; she must not put his mother at risk too.

Work, that was what she needed. Work to keep her mind and hands busy.

She'd met the local couple who were the only others living in this abandoned village. The marshals said they'd refused to leave when everyone else was ordered out, and the Den Coille security agents sent to enforce that order had refused to manhandle the elderly couple onto the transporters.

"One home won't make a difference to the plantings," their leader had later told the Den Coille forestry head, "and they seem to know what they're doing. They claim they don't need help."

Anna had asked Marshal Dunan about that, and was relieved to learn that Den Coille had kept an eye on the pair, ensuring that supplies were made available if needed and medical help on hand. Though she suspected the couple had refused to thank anyone for it. Not when they'd been fine before the outsiders interfered, as the redoubtable old woman had told her last night.

They both looked healthy and well fed, more so than the exiled Coasters she'd met in the crowded conditions of the Manascraoch lower boughs. Which meant they knew how to live in this country, they knew how it worked.

Maybe in talking to them she'd find a way into this new plant biome—and a way out of her constant worry.

The couple were home when she knocked on their door. No modern door sensors here. They liked good old-fashioned knocks to herald the arrival of visitors, she'd learned. The old man welcomed them in, if a grunt and a curt wave of his hand to follow him could be classed as a welcome. He led her into a room that appeared to have little use. The formal 'company' room, she guessed. The Coaster version of the den Coille's great hall, where official visitors were hosted and outsiders were kept well away from the private family quarters.

This room was spotless, but lacked the feel of a place anyone lived in. A room for perching politely on the edge of a chair and exchanging necessary courtesies, not one for finding information and garnering trust. She sat, told the couple of her background, allowed Roo to be properly cooed over, and dutifully ate the cake put before her. One that had been pulled from their stores, she'd guess. A fancy type of cake for unwanted company. Preservation had done it no favours. A hint of what it had been lingered, but too little moisture remained to make it palatable.

When they had all finished their tiffen and the proper time had come for her to stand, say something meaningless and depart, she pulled the sleeping Roo in his backpack onto her shoulders, then grabbed the tea tray with the dishes and leftovers before the old woman could touch it.

"Here, let me carry that for you. It's wrong for one so much younger to stand and watch while you carry such a weight." She lifted the tray and walked through the door, leaving the old woman to follow. Anna lifted her eyebrows in query, and the woman pointed down the hall with a stunned look on her face. She didn't recover her poise until Anna set the tray on the table in the warm and cosy room at the back of the house, where a cheerful heater sat among an assorted mix of table, chairs, and kitchen benches. This room glowed with care and living. Not as grand, not as carefully curated, but much more welcoming.

"Oh, how lovely," said Anna, straightening and looking around, propping the still sleeping Roo by the table before beginning to sort the dishes into the wash unit.

"Here, you let me do that. That's not for the likes of such as you," said the woman.

"My grandam said everyone must know how to feed and care for themselves. I've done this plenty of times before," she said with her warmest smile. She liked this room and had a feeling she'd like the old woman equally if she could only get her to relax. "Not that I was always as careful as she wanted," she added with a chuckle, and almost caught the woman out in an answering chuckle. "You have grandchildren too?"

"Yes, three," the woman said, then clapped her hands over her mouth.

"In Manascraoch? I may have met them there."

"We heard you'd been down to the lower boughs."

Then the woman sat in the chair Anna guessed was her usual and gave her the same long look Grandam did when she guessed Anna was trying to cozen her. "What do you want with us, young woman?"

Anna finished putting the dishes into the washer then wiped the tray over and put it back with the others she saw in the nearby rack as she assembled her thoughts. She'd come here looking for a distraction, but this woman, the displaced people of this region, deserved more than that.

"I want to know how this area works, how the plants work with their environment. How it all works," she finished with a lift of her hands, feeling inadequate.

"Why? Your husband's in trouble. Isn't that top of your mind?" The sharp look in the woman's eyes said 'Do not lie'. "Our way of life has been trampled under to serve den Coille needs for too long," the woman added, making her warning clear.

Anna blushed. "You're right, and I apologise. I came here to hide, and I am not a person who can sit idly and wait. It will drive me bogswaddled. But this area does need studying. The festia will be removed, and something must replace them."

"Huh." The old woman had clearly heard that one before.

"This time it's true. Den Coille has no choice. The festia don't belong here. They're the stringiest specimens I've ever seen."

"We told your people that right from the start. Wet feet is one thing. Salty, wet feet is quite another."

Anna bowed her head in acknowledgement. Festia preferred living in the damp hollows of the slopes, but that water was sparkling and fresh, filtered through soil and ground plants, and constantly on the move downward, totally unlike the sluggish water of the marshes, mingling with the sea only a sandy line of dunes away. With each tide and seepage through the sand, the sea brought its cargo of salt and other minerals into the marsh water.

"So you'd start this puzzle. Then forget all about it when they free your husband and you flit back to the big city." The woman hmphed back into her chair, glaring at her.

"I don't abandon projects. This area may have been studied, but not well enough. Not for what's facing our world." Then rethought her words, thinking of the Deuteron farm project she'd had to leave so precipitately. "I can't always see them through personally, not the fieldwork stage, but I do make sure they continue under the control of scientists chosen by me. And I *always* follow their progress. Maybe not in a timely manner," she had to add, remembering the groaning desk load of work waiting her attention, "but I do follow them up."

The woman looked unconvinced.

"Ask Marshal Dunan," Anna said. This woman knew these lands. She needed this woman's long knowledge of how this place worked. More, Anna needed this project. Needed to give something back to these Coasters to thank them for taking in her and Roo.

"Hmmph, that boy. He's my grand-nephew you know. My sister's grandson."

"Has he ever lied to you?"

"He wouldn't dare."

"You are so like my grandam," Anna said. Then she clapped a hand over her mouth "I'm so sorry."

"No, you're not." The woman bent an eye on her. "A woman of sense, is she? This grandam of yours?"

"Oh, yes," said Anna, thinking of the stern matriarch who ran her family and city, "and I have *never* lied to her."

"I should think not, young lady. It's the one thing the years teach us. How to spot a lie. This project of yours. What do you need?"

There followed a more enjoyable time than Anna had expected to find since leaving Cumchdach all those months ago. After a while, the old woman bent to her com.

"Ianno, come in here. And you can bring that scamp of my sister's too, as long as his hands and feet are clean and he keeps quiet until spoken to." The old woman bent to Anna. "Call me Sera Mari. It's what everyone used to call me when the village was here."

Her husband and the marshal filed in soon after. The marshal, she noted, stood quietly at the rear until the old woman nodded curtly at him and pointed to a hard chair. He pulled it up beside her, into the spot she pointed at, then sat with a meek look on his face she didn't trust one bit. If Anna even once showed any sign of being a danger to the couple, the marshal would be in action before she had a chance. She'd had enough interactions with his boss, Marco an Fallon, to pick when a marshal was at full duty status and ready for immediate action.

"She wants to know about the plantings," said the old woman as soon as her husband settled into his own chair. "You're the best to show her."

"Do you mean a home garden?" said Anna. How anyone grew food crops in these conditions, she couldn't imagine. There were plants habituated to saline soils, but this close to the sea and surrounded by brackish marshes, she didn't know of any that would thrive.

"Guess you call it that," said the man with a grunt. "You can come with me tomorrow morning."

"After I feed my baby," she said firmly and saw the nod of approval from the woman. The man gave another grumpy sound. "You'll have to leave the wee one at home. Track's dirty, no place for a baby."

Next morning, she gave Roo his early morning cuddle and feed as soon as she heard his first whimper. Usually, she'd let him settle back to sleep and hope for an extra half hour before he woke fully and demanded her attention. Afterward, she swaddled him warmly, gave him another cuddle and a wet, sloppy play kiss before handing him off to Biarsuin, standing by with his favourite toy to distract him while his mother made her escape.

Outside, the old man waited, a sour look on his face. She refused to apologise for holding him up. That look would have been there regardless, she suspected. He did cast an eye over her clothing. The rugged boots and tough overall must have met his approval. Marshal Dunan had handed her one of the local capes last night, telling her she'd need it if she was going out with the uncle.

"Best get on," the man said, slightly less grumpy sounding. But that was all the consideration he gave her. Anna had thought herself fit, but the coastal elder gave her a lesson in endurance that morning. Slogging through rough marshes used muscles she didn't even know she had, and she slumped down on a hillock to catch her breath when he finally stopped.

"How much farther?"

"Here," he said, with a tilt of his head. She looked around in confusion.

"There's no garden here."

He stomped forward into the shallow lagoon in front of them. "Not Mountainer gardens," he said in disgust. "Not book ones."

She followed him, watching as he slowed and walked gently along the margin, peering into the water, then periodically stopped and clipped at something just below the surface. She looked down at her feet.

"Keep to the edge," he said. "This crop's near ready to harvest. Don't need all that work destroyed."

She stepped to the side hastily, then looked down again. The lagoon was very shallow, no more than ankle deep. Below the water's surface, a dark green mass spread out, with branching leaf-like protrusions sprouting from the base and waving in the current that drifted gently across it.

"It's edible?" she said cautiously.

He looked at her, then picked a piece and passed it over. This she was really unsure about.

"I'm a nursing mother."

"The mainna is safe. Best thing for you, better than manufactured muck."

She looked at the water and thought of all the organisms growing in it. The man gave her another look of disgust and chomped down on it, then began to turn away.

She looked at the weed in her hand. Then set her com to auto-alert and lifted it to her mouth. There was a security team on hover above her in a cloaked flyer. They'd be here in an instant if anything went wrong.

She touched the weed to her mouth, then nipped at the tiniest fragment. A taste sensation erupted in her mouth.

"Oh. That's so good."

A grin actually split the old man's face. "It's kept Coasters alive for generations."

"Why does no one know about this?"

"Don't want no outsiders coming here and taking over. We like it quiet."

"Outsiders came anyway. My husband's family came, and wrecked this area." It was a risk, that reminder, but the old man deserved the same honesty his wife had demanded. "If more knew of the riches of this area, the festia plantings could have been stopped and your people would've stayed here."

"To turn the marshes into some kind of factory place. Might as well be gone as let that happen."

She stopped, blindsided. Wasn't that exactly how Den Coille had got into trouble? How this whole part of the continent had got into trouble? Den Coille had turned their side of the mountains into a huge festin manufacturing site and Winter Solaris had done the same to the plains with their massive solar fields. Now both companies and both regions were having to find new ways to live and make credits to bring their region back to an equilibrium where people could live well. The path they'd been on had one end only, and it wasn't a great one for the either the planet or the locals living there.

"It changes nothing. Someone outside needs to know how your systems work, and I'm one of the best at that. You and your wife won't live forever. How much will be lost when you go?"

This time, she might as well have stabbed the man in the back. "You think we don't know that, young missy?" A relative term, given her years and her status, but she let it pass. "We're doing what we can. A few come back., but most can't—or won't. They're so downbeat in that tree world of yours, they've given up. We'd teach them if they'd only listen."

"An old professor of mine taught me something valuable once. If there's no record of something, it didn't happen. That's the fate of your knowledge, of all your people have learned here over the generations, if you refuse to let it be recorded. Teach me, and I'll make sure your young are brought into my classes to learn it."

"There's still some of us old ones left. Enough to pass it on."

"Here?" said Anna in surprise. She'd thought the marshes emptied out.

"A handful," the old man admitted grudgingly. "Most went to the trees with the young ones. Few are left who know as much as me and the Sera." The old man stared into the distance, seeing what, Anna dared not think. Cumchdach's people had not done well here, and that surprised her.

"Why did the others go with the evacuation if they could live better here?"

"They were fed a story. A good life waited, an *easier* life, said the company man."

Of course he had, but something was still missing. "And…"

That brought the old man's fierce stare back to her. But she'd had months now of outwaiting a baby determined not to sleep. The old man was nothing to Roo.

"And…?" she repeated.

"Gah!" His hand slapped the water, the one holding his weeding tool. "The marshes give us most things. It's a good life here."

"But not everything."

"Not the things the young ones wanted. A life spent doing more than bending over in the waters. Gizmos and such nonsense. The kind of schools we don't have here." He slapped the tool against his thigh, as if the slap of it could banish reality. "That takes credits, more credits than you can make selling fibre and food."

"Fibre and food are essentials. Den Coille has built its fortune on the pollen of the festia tree." The look the old man gave her then nearly had her stepping back, but she refused to give way to him. "Let me study the area. See if I can find something."

"More empty promises."

She shook her head. "No promises. That's not how science works. We ask questions, and try to find answers. Real scientists do not make empty promises."

The man's face went blank. Then finally he grumbled a barely heard, "All right."

Anna blew out a cautious breath. "Start with this crop here. How do you grow and harvest it?"

She spent the rest of the morning with the old man, weeding the lagoon crop, until her back ached and her head throbbed. At lunchtime, the old man glanced at the surface of the water and pronounced it time to move. "Tide's on the turn," he said, though how he knew that from the look and feel of this still lagoon and why it made a difference, she had no idea. So she asked him, and looked at the lagoon with new eyes afterward. She'd thought this a natural lagoon, untouched by humans, but discovered it was strictly managed.

"Water's not a constant thing," he told her. "Always changing. Temperature, minerals, current speed, salt levels. Some good for mainna, some lethal. Got to let it change. Too many other critters also need this lagoon. It's a balance."

That was the old man's answer to most of her questions, she would discover in the days ahead. Everything in balance. This was a wild ecosystem, with the old couple tweaking it here and there to take their share from it. Farming it, in truth, but not like any farming she'd come across. Not even the complex interactions on the Deuteron farm.

At night, she pored over the records of previous studies of the region, then battered the old man with more questions the next day. "You missed a bit," he'd growl, pointing at whatever task he'd set her. He made her pay for each speck of precious information, and her hands were growing as hard as his and the sera's. But never did he force her to neglect Roo or her other responsibilities, and soon she took to carrying her son in a sling on her back he devised for her from the tough marsh reed fibre.

"Mari used to carry all the littlies like that. Does the heart good to see it again."

Roo enjoyed the days as much as she did. The old man showed her how to let him play in the warm waters and muddy reed beds. She slathered protective creams on him, but the old man shook his head, plopped a hat on Roo and gave her a different cream. "Works better than that city stuff. The boy needs to feel the land to know it."

That was another of the man's maxims. At the start, she'd haul both herself and Roo into the cleansing unit on her security's flyer and set it to heavy duty to scour away all the day's grime, but after a while she gave up. Both their skins were stained with the mud and tanned from the sun, but the smile on Roo's face each morning made up for it all. She got to see the moats and the deceptive weirs the Coasters had installed to assist water flows, recognisable only by their unusually stable structure in the floating and squishy world; gathered the small invertebrates dwelling in the reed roots and floating among the mainna beds that were the Coasters' main protein source; helped Sera Mari break down the reeds to extract the tough fibres at their core and helped her shear the local raitens—herbivores distantly related to the plains nietens—that lived in the marshes and browsed on the tidal plants. Their undercoats were a soft downy fibre, uniquely comfortable and warmth-trapping, while the outer fibres repelled water and were used to make the capes native to the area.

It would have been a perfect interval if she didn't go to sleep each night worrying about Cumchdach, to wake sweating from nightmares about what he was enduring. Each day, the marshals told her the same non-news.

"He's still alive, Sera. He's in Urbis and being questioned."

"Has he contacted you?"

"Not yet, Sera." And a cold stab of terror plunged into her each day. Yes, it was a risk for him to use his hidden com, but why hadn't he said anything?

Cumchdach woke to another day of pain. Another day he'd managed to defeat his captors. He'd tried to keep track of the days he'd been here but had given up after they took away the shard of stone he'd been using to scratch a mark each night. He stared at those marks now.

They were proof. He would survive today.

He lay on the hard bench, keeping his breathing slow and soft, a trick he'd learned that first time in prison. Each moment before the guards discovered he was awake were precious. As soon as they realised, they'd be in here, prodding at him to stand up and forcing more of the muck they called food down his throat.

More of the drugged muck.

Had he told them anything important? He clenched his shoulder into his side, feeling the tiny prick of the hidden com in his armpit. Still there. Still operating, he hoped, after all the scans and brutal cleansings they'd done on him each morning before dragging him back to the cold, white room.

He called up the same image he'd brought into his head every morning of this hellish incarceration. Drew each line, each delicate tinge of colour, the shape of her brow, the calm look of exasperation she'd send him when he'd done something stupid.

Like letting himself be taken into captivity in the arrogant belief he was important enough to be hauled in front of the conspiracy boss.

The images were still there. Anna. His wife. And Roo, his son. He'd thought he was losing them once, their faces a blur in his head. That was after the first beating. The guards hadn't repeated it, not when it left him unconscious on the floor and they'd had to bring in a medic to reboot his breathing.

He'd heard about it afterward. Angry words echoing outside his door, but who was talking? That, he hadn't found out yet. These days, they clamped him into a chair and had a bot program hammer him with questions in a direct mind link. His brain would be lucky to survive it.

His body wouldn't. Not after he'd done what they wanted.

Then the door opened and another day began.

It started the same as all the others. The scans, the scouring, and the force feeding bringing the now familiar gluggy fog slowing his brain before the guards dragged him into the white room and locked him into the hard metal chair in the centre. Once secured, they slapped a com sliver onto his forehead and the bot voice invaded his head.

Some days, there had been other people in the room. Unidentified figures in the uniform of business. Crisply cut tunics and hard-edged trousers, the shade of the fabric the only difference, changing from dark grey to a silver sheen. The gender of the human changed, but not the personality. Avaricious, detached, but with a hint of nerves on the first visit. Some came more than once. On those visits, the nerves were gone and a smug smirk touched their mouths, like a naughty child who'd got away with it once and now thought theirself invulnerable.

No visitors today, not yet. The bot hammered its demands. Capitulate, accept the group wisdom, demand he understand what the Alliance rules for Arcadia were doing to the economy, see the whole thing as a plot by competing planets to weaken Arcadia and take its wealth.

Unfortunately, there were enough strands of truth in that last bit to make it harder to resist. They hadn't yet tried to get him to betray his family and company, but that was coming as soon as he showed the least hint of capitulation.

That was what kept him fighting back. They'd figure it out soon enough, though, and he woke each morning from a nightmare vision of watching his little sister, his mother, his baby brother, limping harder than ever, being dragged off for torture thanks to what he'd said.

Mam is tough, Fioruisghe is tougher and has proven it before, Aigherach is the toughest of them all. He'd endured the torture of their first imprisonment and hadn't broken, and his limp now was visible only to those who knew of it. The nightmares were a lie, brought on by the relentless pummelling of the bot's suggestions and the drugs they fed him.

It didn't make them less terrible.

His teeth had begun to clench too tight, his jaw rigid. One day he'd break his jaw. Then a sound broke the silence and a noise came from the door. It opened and the bot's voice ceased. He slumped in relief, too far gone in the drugs and pressure to care he was showing the newcomer a sign of defeat. He refused to look up, though, until one of the guards came and tugged his hair to lift his head. That hurt, but it was just one among too many hurts now to bother him.

"Ser den Coille. I can't say it's a pleasure to see you. This is all so unnecessary."

It was a woman. He recognised the accent but not the face. He'd met relatives of hers before, though, all with that same freckled face overlaying a mid-brown skin. A strange enough combination to make them unique. Like spotted folklar, someone had once quipped. The dappled predator of the Mountainer forests was vicious and devious. A good description of the agricultural conglomerate dominating the Estuarine region south of Urbis.

"Sera Piakja." The use of her family name was enough to cause a pause in her step, but she hastily covered it up.

"We haven't met," she said.

"No," he agreed, but kept it to that. She could make the first move.

Then she gathered up her composure and gave him the practised message she'd come to deliver. "We don't enjoy all this nonsense," her hand lifted to encompass the cold room and the hard-faced guards. "Please, let us help you to more amenable accommodations while we discuss the next phase of our relationship. It is in all our best interests."

If she included herself in that *all*, she had to be delirious. He stayed silent but stared at her, fighting against the fog of the drugs to appear in command of himself. It worked a bit, by the woman's glance at the head guard.

"He's had the usual breakfast," the man grunted and she nodded and relaxed. Then turned back to him.

"There is a suite upstairs for you. It has a proper sleeper, a cleanser, all the amenities of the finest city hotel. You and your wife would be far more comfortable there.

Just like that, the day changed.

"My wife is far from here," he said in the iciest voice he could manage.

"At present," she agreed, "but not for long. Our friends have helped us. She will be joining you in the next few days."

Anna was alive, was his first thought. A relief so vivid filling him, he couldn't breathe. Then the next bit. They knew where she was and were ready to seize her.

"My wife is well protected."

"Oh, yes, she is that. But not always."

Marco an Fallon didn't allow mistakes in his people. That was a lie. Wasn't it?

"I want to talk to your boss," he said.

"And who says you're not?"

He shook his head. "You're an underling. I know the feel of a leader." Any child of Bram and Scathach den Coille knew that from birth. His mother ran her hospital and his father the family company with a highly effective mix of intelligence, empathy and sheer will power. Leaders took responsibility for everyone under them. Not this woman. She lacked the courage.

Or a good leader did. What of the leader of a corrupt conspiracy? All he really had was that warning from his brother. The head was not from the business world, Ceart had said, and Aigherach had found no trace in his Higher School contacts.

Whoever it was, was good at hiding and well camouflaged.

"Make the appointment," he said.

She stared at him a long moment, and he began to think he'd failed. Then, "Take him back to his room. He needs time to think," she said with a nasty smile, "and to prepare for his wife."

He growled, lurching forward and cursing at the restraints. The woman walked to the door.

"You can't touch her," he yelled at the woman's back. She kept walking, the door clanged shut, and the guards grabbed him up again, dragging him down the hall and slinging him back into his room. By the time they brought him the thin soup they called dinner that evening, the morning drugs had worn off and, for the first time, he wished they'd put some in this mix as well. He'd spent the afternoon marching from one end of the claustrophobic room to the other, trying whatever he could to stop him crushing down on the com sliver in his armpit and calling in the marshals.

They hadn't mentioned Roo. Anna wouldn't leave their baby, not unless she was forced to. If they really knew where she was, they'd know where Roo was too.

If he was still alive.

They hadn't said his name. They'd have told him if they'd killed his baby. He didn't know what he'd do if they harmed his son.

Nor did they, and maybe that's why they hadn't told him.

Had they caught Anna when they caught him?

Anton would have told him.

If he was really on her side. He was Gria's son, and that made him suspect.

Arguments, counterarguments, a stew of emotions, of yeses and noes. What was truth, what did they have?

What did they really want?

Too many questions for sanity.

The guards pointed blasters at him when they next came into the room to check on him. It didn't stop him, and they had to use a paralysing blast to hold him back. Even then, he kept trying to get to the open door, cursing them with every street word he remembered as he clawed at the walls and floor.

They must be well paid mercenaries. They kept themselves to the odd kick before leaving, but one was to his gut, another to his kidney, and he had to coil over in agony when they left.

In the past, it would have been enough to stop him, but his Anna was in danger. All he could hope was that the com sliver was open for transmission, despite not being found by all their scans.

That was possible only if it was dormant, said the rational part of his brain, what still remained of it.

Hope said the marshals were watching him; reason said he was alone until he activated the com, and that would alert his captors. He had to hold off until he knew he was in front of their leader.

They knew where Anna was. They had threatened his heart.

Was it real?

CHAPTER TWENTY-EIGHT

Marshal Dunan was unusually silent one morning. Normally, he greeted her with a quiet "Morning, Sera," and a gentle tickle of Roo's belly as he lay in her arms. But this morning he sat down at Sera Mari's table and began eating without a word. Anna felt a kick to her heart.

"Any news?" she asked.

He shook his head. Not long after, he asked a stock question about her plans for the day. Which site she and the uncle planned to visit. No word about whatever it was bringing that crease to his forehead.

What had he heard?

She'd long learned not to waste energy on the impossible. High on that list was getting a marshal to talk if they didn't want to. She still asked once more, hands on hips and staring down at him as she was about to leave. "You've heard something."

The marshal stared back, saying nothing, until she had no choice but to nod curtly and leave. Her usual guard followed her, but today another pair joined them and she caught a glimpse of Marshal Dunan talking on his com as she left the room, his face that of a man giving orders. Then he stood and, soon after, she heard the faint whoosh of a shielded flyer taking off. Her airborne cover for today.

A chill wind nipped over the dunes and cut through clothing, with a hint of rain in the air. Given the kind of storms that could suddenly blow up on the coast, the weather was too chancy to risk her baby, and she was leaving him home today, despite her need to have him in sight and under her direct care at all times. The uncle would make sure they were under cover if anything threatened, but his idea of cover from the elements was far short of what any protective mother thought adequate for her baby. Sera Mari had taken one look at the skies and suggested Anna stay at home as well.

It was probably wiser, but she couldn't, not after that closed look on the marshal's face this morning. Couldn't sit idly inside while whatever was happening threatened Cumchdach.

They were heading out to repair a weir in the reed marshes. The storms had undermined it and allowed too much salty water to seep into the beds.

"Bugs don't like too much salt in their dinner," the uncle said when she asked him why they had to fix it.

She made yet one more note in her com. Find out about these *bugs*. The uncle was a fount of wisdom, but he dished it out sparingly. No more than one short sentence at a time. If she persisted, all he did was hand her another tool and tell her to get on with it. "Sun don't stay up forever," was one of his favourite sayings, pronounced in a terse grunt of a voice.

The weir looked fine to her when they got there but the uncle gave the scowl she'd learned to interpret as a curse on nature and its fickle interferences. The uncle might work with the natural world; didn't mean he had to submit to it. She buried a smile. The uncle also had no tolerance for what he called *city learnings* or those who thought it made them better than him.

Not that he didn't have good cause, after what the *experts* and money crunchers had done to his people. She bent down to help dig out the offending section and weave back in the reed roots that anchored the weirs in place and gave them a solid foundation. Then she lifted her head. A faint whine in the sky. Strange. The shielding of the marshals' flyer usually smothered all sound of its presence. She'd have to ask Dunan about it when she got back. She bent back to the weir.

A sudden crackle of sound broke over her com. Both she and the uncle jerked up and opened their coms.

"We've got company. Get under cover." It was the marshal's voice. Abrupt. To the point. Scarily so.

"Who?" she gasped back.

"Don't know, they're not talking."

"Roo," she cried and started running back toward base. It would take her a good hour of slogging. "Send a skimmer," she said into her com between pants.

"Too late."

That was all. Silence. She turned back to the uncle, still talking on his com.

"The Sera, does she say anything?"

"A flyer came in and strangers surrounded the house. The marshals are covering them and Mari's taking your people to cover."

"Where?" she demanded. Where was her baby?

"We've got a place. Follow me." He waved his hand at her, urging her to hurry. She stood, caught by a rare lack of decision. Get back to Roo? Save herself?

"Mari knows where to go. No good for the little one if his mam's in danger."

He was right, but it went against everything inside her. She hurried after the uncle. He took her deep into the marshes, slogging up to her knees in water and lost in a vast sea of reeds. They hadn't been this way before and she'd thought it untouched wilderness, but the uncle seemed to know where he was going. She tapped his shoulder yet again, pointing at her com sliver as she had so many times, and he shook his head. He hadn't heard, or Roo and his protectors were safe? Every time she opened her mouth to ask, he shook his head violently.

Whatever scanners their enemies possessed, they couldn't track them through this wilderness with its huge biomass. But human speech was unique, nothing like the other sounds of the marshes. She followed the uncle, slowing to match his cautious gait, wading softly through the water in a dreamlike movement that made a minimal wash, and carefully parting the reeds. The kind of movement that wasn't visible from above, just a breeze stirring the reeds. Even the nearby animals kept up their usual chirrups, a constant staccato of sounds she'd come to associate with the marshes.

Then the uncle stopped, held up his hand, and listened. He parted the reeds and she discovered they'd reached the edge of the beds, close up under a rocky cliff where the foothills began. He waited for a time as she crouched beside him in a welter of nerves. Then he hunkered down and moved out, motioning her to follow and stay low.

Open sky had never bothered her before, but crawling under it this slowly, leaving them exposed to whatever hovered up there?

Where were the marshals? Why hadn't they come to her rescue like they were supposed to? That was their *job*.

The uncle moved a bit faster and she scuttled after him, hugging the contours of rock and shrubs exactly as he did. They rounded a small clump of bushes, and he pushed into a cluster of clinging weeds. She was too afraid to question it. She pushed in after him, hating the slick strands that stuck to her face and clung to her clothing. Then they were through, and she fell into a black hole. The ground had dropped sharply into a damp cave carved into the hillside.

Her mouth opened in a scream, stopped only by the grubby hand of the uncle clamping down hard on her face. "Not a sound, Sera," he said in a voice a mere whisker above inaudible. She nodded slowly to let him know she'd understood and he lifted his hand.

Leaving her alone in blackness. There was a trace of light coming in through the gap they'd made in the vegetation, but little else, and the inky darkness blanketed her. Then she felt the uncle's hand in hers. He tugged at her, and it was one of her bravest moments to take that step after him and follow him into the unknown.

The ground was uneven beneath her feet, and more than once she stumbled, to be caught by the old man. He was fitter than his years, holding her each time until she could stand on her own. Then he tugged her on.

She had an impression of solid walls around her. The only sounds were a faint drip of water, the uncle's hand scraping over stone, and the faint patter of their feet on the solid rock under them. After a while, she reached out to feel the stony tunnel. It was smooth to the touch, as if sculpted from the surrounding rocks. Artificial, not natural. Then finally she saw a faint light ahead, and she began to breathe normally. The uncle led her out, and soon she found herself in a narrow grotto with a low bench at the front, lit by a narrow opening also covered by weeds. The uncle pointed to the bench.

"Sit. We'll hear from Mari soon."

There was no one else here. He'd given her no reason to think it, but she'd foolishly assumed he was taking her back to Roo and the others. She stared out through another curtain of weeds at a view over the marshlands and south to the couple's house. No sign of anything out of place. Where were the marshals' flyer and the strangers?

The uncle sat down on the bench and tugged at her tunic for her to join him. As if on autopilot, she plopped onto the seat without taking her eyes off the outside. "Where are they all?"

"Mari's gone to ground with your little one and the girl. The lad will be with them. The rest of the marshals and the strangers." He shrugged as if to say, 'what did it matter'. "She'll call when it's safe to come out."

Did the man expect her to accept that? To wait here while who knew what happened to her baby? Suddenly, a flash lit the sky near the house and then she saw a strange flyer, hovering over the house. A flare of flame lit up the clearing and she jumped up.

The uncle tugged her down again. "They've gone, no one's hiding in there. Mari knows better."

"They're in a hide, like this one?"

"Similar," said the old man.

"Where? There's nothing like these cliffs closer to the house."

The old man shook his head. "Like this, not same as." A grunt, then, "It's safe. Only locals know the way."

Her nerves came near to strangling her as she waited. She kept glancing at the uncle's wrist to see if his com activated, despite knowing it must be shielded. The marshals would have made sure of it. When she wasn't doing that, she stared at the house and their base. Where was Roo? Where was his security?

Where was the marshals' flyer? Why hadn't it swooped down as soon as the other flyer came close?

Then she saw movement outside the old couple's house. The uncle reached into the pack he always carried and pulled out a pair of distance viewers. He glanced through them, grunted in a way that made her feel worse, then passed them over.

Walking from the house were Sera Mari, Marshal Dunan, and Biarsuin carrying Roo. Her heart about stopped. Strange troops surrounded them and right beside her baby, holding a blaster to his head, stood a guard.

"They're holding a blaster to my baby's head. What kind of person does that?" The uncle said nothing, but she saw him watching his wife with a look on his face that almost matched her horror.

"How?"

"They've had help," said the uncle, in a voice that said he'd strangle whoever had done it. "Help from one of our own."

More people walked from the house, all in the same unknown uniform, some wearing helmets that she guessed had low light capacity built in. The uncle pointed his thumb at one of them, his mouth grim. It was a man, slightly stooped, but around the same age as Cumchdach's baby brother. His body had the same lightness to it, of muscles and bones not yet matured.

"You know him?"

"His folks lived a way up the coast. Heard he was hurt in an accident not long after they moved to the city."

"He'd have been treated. Should have been. That back, that's not right."

The old man shrugged, but his mouth twisted in a way that said it all. Free treatment was for citizens of the city, not barely tolerated refugees. The boy was bitter, then. No friend to the den Coilles. And today he'd taken his revenge by putting her baby in danger.

"Doesn't make it right," she said, and the old man gave a curt nod of agreement.

Then, above them all, another flyer materialised. The marshals had been there all along. So why had they done nothing yet?

"No need to until now. Young Dunan, he'd have told them what we do when trouble comes." The old man was looking at Marshal Dunan and, even from the distance, Anna could see the rigid way the man stood. Nor did she think it was the two blasters aimed directly at him. Not the way he was staring at Roo and the Sera.

The marshals' flyer came to a halt above the intruders, and a voice bellowed down.

"We are locked onto you. Release your captives."

One of the troopers looked up but not the rest. Their leader, she guessed as he lifted his wrist and gestured to the flyer to signal he had a message for them. She hadn't expected the man to put his com on general broadcast or the jarring broken voice to call out across the marshes.

"Our blasters are on auto. You shoot us, and the prisoners will be dead before we fall. No beam can break that built-in interval."

Anna stumbled back, her legs giving way. The uncle caught her.

"Hold up, Sera. The marshals aren't beat that easy."

"They're going to kill my baby." Then she saw the leader lift his wrist again.

"Anna den Coille. Surrender to us and we'll let your son and the others go free."

"Don't trust them," growled the uncle.

"I have to." They were holding a blaster to Roo's head. Her baby made no sign, didn't struggle in Biarsuin's arms. That was so unlike him. "How do I get closer?"

The old man studied her face. Then nodded. "Follow me."

"No, tell me. You stay here."

But all the uncle did was push his way through the weeds low down then slither along the ground until he was near the start of the reed beds again. She followed him, ignoring the mess she made of her clothes. So what if she turned up looking like a mud scrabbler if it saved Roo.

The intruder's voice rang out again, calling her to come out.

"Get back under cover," said a new voice through her com. "We have this under control."

She checked the call sign, then had her com double verify it. It came from the marshals' flyer. They must have a tracker on her.

"Not from where I'm looking, marshal," she sent back sub vocally. Her com picked it up.

"We will save your son, Sera. Get back under cover."

She kept moving, crouching low as they broke through the reeds. The old man moved fast this time, and she had to study him to see how he did it without disturbing the reeds. Then she copied his movements exactly. Her knees and elbows would be a mess after this.

It was worth it.

He stopped. "Tip of the island's up ahead."

He must mean the land where the old couple's house stood. She nodded back, then held up a hand to order him to stop. "The Sera will need you," she mouthed.

He looked at her for one long moment, and bowed his head in the formal acknowledgement of a Mountainer. Then he slithered backward and disappeared among the reeds.

She was alone.

She gave him a minute before reaching out to feel the bank. The intruder's voice echoed over the swamps again. She peered up through the reeds and saw the intruders and their prisoners.

"Last chance, Sera den Coille. Then we use the blasters." The man was the worst kind of coward, blaming his victims for what he threatened to do. "Stand in sight or we begin shooting."

"No," came another voice, and she saw a blur of movement.

She stood up quickly, as a shout and the unmistakeable sound of blaster fire split the air.

In front of the house, Marshal Dunan crumpled to the ground at Roo's feet. Then she saw the man beside her son press his blaster back against Roo's temple and heard her baby's whimper. The Marshal had just saved her son.

"Stop. I'm here," she called out, terror lending her voice volume. "Don't shoot again. Let my son go and I'll walk in."

She held her breath. It was a gamble, but she had to get those blasters pointed away from her son and the others. The marshals' flyer could do the rest.

A zap of heat spat mud from the ground in front of her.

"No tricks, Sera. We're not playing."

No, they weren't. Not with that ominous figure of the marshal at Roo's feet.

"No tricks," she said and began to walk toward them.

Out of the corner of her eye, she saw a small group of marshals slide down to the ground on jet pads. But they didn't touch the intruders, just surrounded them with their own scary weapons aimed directly at the strangers.

They couldn't touch them any more than she could. Not with those blasters on auto-fire so close to their prisoners' heads.

She kept walking, her pace slow in terror of setting off one of the intruders. Hands out to her side, posture as relaxed as possible when she was scared silly. *I'm no threat, it said.* The marshals began to move too, until the leader of the troop spoke again. "One step closer, and we'll kill them all."

No doubts about it now. Not when so many lives hung in the balance. Marshals usually had their weapons on stun, but not always. Sometimes they killed. Right now, she had no desire to push either group. Both looked trained and dangerous.

The marshals had the edge, or so she hoped. But bet Roo's life on it?

These mercenaries had infiltrated the Coaster hideout without alerting the marshals. That meant serious tech and highly trained troops.

Think, think.

It was near impossible, with Roo calling to her mother's instinct. She had a brain; *use it.*

Why were they here? She studied them as she walked closer. Biarsuin carried Roo, but nowhere could she see his carry bag, the one that held all the supplies a baby needed. Not held by Biarsuin nor by any of the mercenaries. Did they have supplies on board their flyer for a baby?

Or they had never planned to capture him, so hadn't bothered with supplies for him? No, the more she thought about it, turning over every option furiously in her head, the more she decided they'd come for her. *She* was their target. Why?

To use against Cumchdach. Endanger his child by taking him prisoner, and she had no idea what her husband would do. Anything it took to save his baby. Whoever held Cumchdach wanted him to do something, and for that they needed a lever against him, not a red-hot incendiary spark.

They wanted her. Their baby was a tool to capture her. Roo meant nothing to these people.

If pushed, they'd get rid of him.

She faltered, her gut clenching. She had to save her baby, everything else came second. She glared at the marshals. *Stand still.*

She'd nearly reached Roo. Biarsuin held him, arms clamped tightly around his body to stop him wriggling and her face blanched white. That's when Anna saw the blood on the nanny's arm. Another who had risked her life for Anna's son.

Another she had to make sure came safely out of this.

"Stop there, Sera."

She halted immediately. So close. Roo saw her and began to whimper. He might love Biarsuin, but his mam came first. He reached out his arms.

"Shh, little one. Mam's coming."

One of the mercenaries stepped up now, the one who'd been guarding Dunan's slumped body.

"Hold," said a marshal. "The sera is under our protection."

"And her son is under our control," growled the mercenary.

"Lift your weapons away from the baby."

"And let you kill us all? He's our best cover."

"Use me instead," said Anna. "An adult den Coille, a den Falasch, and a recognised scientist. I'm better cover than the baby."

She could almost feel the blast of anger from the marshals. "Sera, leave this to us."

"Can you free my son?"

"Not yet, but a standoff can last only so long. They must get tired."

"And the minute those troops falter, that blaster on my son's head goes off."

The marshal who'd spoken glowered at her, his eyes black as coals. But he didn't deny it. He couldn't.

Did none of them have children, or know what the sun and cold did to one? She watched Roo's face intently, saw the instant he began to droop. He'd fallen quiet as soon as he heard her voice, but her baby was scared and confused. Why wouldn't his mam take him, feed and cuddle him, all the things she *always* did when her baby needed her? She could feel her milk beginning to leak and cursed. It had only come back in fully the last few days here, and now she'd have to abandon him again. He may no longer need her milk to survive, but his feeds were important to both of them. She cherished those moments when she cuddled him close and taught him the world was full of love.

Now these troops had brought violence into her baby's life. She would never forgive them.

She began to walk forward again. It seemed to stun everyone, marshals and intruders alike. Enough to let her get right up to Roo and take his hand.

The man holding the weapon on him recovered too quickly. He grabbed hold of her, pulling her away and switching the blaster from Roo to her head in one fast move. A woman holding her blaster against Biarsuin still stood too close to Roo, but Anna didn't care. Her baby was free.

"You have me. Let my baby and the others go. Otherwise, this ends in death for too many of you."

The leader's face stayed as cold as ever but something flickered in his eyes. He wasn't stupid; he knew the odds here as well as she did.

"We can take you and the baby."

"Try that, and you won't leave Arcadian airspace alive," said the marshal.

Did that mean that more marshals were on their way, with equally advanced systems? Or were they bluffing?

Risking Roo's life on it? Not an option.

"If the marshals give their word you will be free to leave, will you release the baby and the others?" she said.

The marshal growled. "You can't trust them."

"It's mutual," replied the mercenary.

"Then we all stand here and let my baby get cold and sick? Not happening."

"He's wrapped up," said the mercenary.

She snapped him a glare, then turned back to the marshal. "Ask any of your squad with children. That wrap around him is inadequate for the chill factor here today." She saw one of the other's eyes take on that faraway look of using a mind link. The woman was a mother too, she hoped. It might be late summer, but the sea winds on this coast were never kind, and the first hint of Arcadia's long winter touched the air. Roo's hand when she touched it was already too cold, and she had a bad feeling his body would feel the same, despite Biarsuin's holding him snugly into her warmth.

She turned to the mercenary leader. "You came to this planet to do a job. You don't get paid unless you complete it. Take me, leave my baby with the marshals. They won't shoot you while you have me."

"Taking them all gives us more protection," the mercenary leader said.

"Not when they know you're likely to kill them as soon as you're out of Arcadian space. But we all know you came for me. You've been contracted to deliver me to your customer, and I'm guessing that's alive or I'm no use to them." She shut down all outside distractions, holding the mercenary leader's eyes. "Marshals are used to making hard decisions. They won't let you leave if there's a chance they can save some of your prisoners. But if there's only one, and one they know you have to keep alive until you reach your destination? Then you're safe until you deliver me."

"They'll follow us."

"Of course," snapped the marshal. "Sera, please leave this to us."

Anna concentrated on the feel of her son's hand, felt his tiny fingers and the stillness in him as he waited for her to take him, to make this all go away and keep him safe again. "You are not a second-rate outfit. You've been tailed before," she said.

The leader nodded. "It's still a problem."

"And if they give their word to leave you alone until you exit Arcadian space?

They'll still follow you after that, but this way, you will have an intact ship to escape in. You have a chance."

A slight lift of the man's mouth and he gave her a short tip of his chin. "A good argument." Then he turned toward the marshal. "We can do this slow and easy or fast and risky."

Anna looked at the marshal, who looked like he'd been forced to eat mud. "Marshal, is it agreed."

For a moment, she wondered if he'd actually refuse. He studied each mercenary, his eyes lingering over the still body of Marshal Dunan. She'd looked too, seen the slight rise and fall of the marshal's chest. The very slight rise. The man needed medical help, and soon. Then the leader of the marshals turned back to the mercenary chief.

"Dead slow, and hands in the open at all times. The baby and his carer come over first."

The chief spoke into his com and the mercenary on Biarsuin stepped back from her.

"Sera," whispered the nanny.

"Go, Biarsuin. Now." She deliberately released Roo's hand, but her eyes never left him as Biarsuin walked away, carried him away from her, to be engulfed by the marshals as they hurried him into their flyer. All she saw was a glimpse of his dark curls, surrounded by the shimmer that told of a personal shield the marshals wrapped around him and Biarsuin as soon as they had them.

"Now the sera."

It took so long, or so it seemed to her. The old lady turned and spat at her captor, then walked with head high and mouth grim to the marshals. Then the marshals walked over to their man and lifted Dunan between two of them, carrying his limp body. The squad leader looked even grimmer at the sight. The last she saw of him was a medic's stretcher rushing up the ramp of the marshals' flyer.

Now she was the only one left. Two mercenaries held her now, a large man and a tall woman. Both had a vicious grip on her arms. They'd leave bruises.

"We're leaving," said the chief, unnecessarily. They marched her to their flyer, blaster held to her head, and flanked her as they walked her into the interior. Inside, they clamped her onto a seat, blaster still held to her head, and locked her down. Then the hatch was closing, and the flyer was lifting. A bit afterward, they levelled out and their speed increased as the pilot threw their craft into a gut roiling series of sudden switches.

They put her into a seat in the middle of the flyer, still wet and filthy from her crawl through the marshes and getting colder by the moment. After a while, she took great delight in the stink of the swamp that pervaded the cabin, making the soldiers sitting beside her lean away.

But not far enough. Not enough to let her have a chance at freedom.

The marshals will follow her.

She was too far from a viewport to see their direction, and the lurching of her stomach was the only clue to the flyer's increasingly erratic path. They lifted up high, so they must be clearing the mountains and heading out of Mountainer country. Then sideways, down, up again and what felt like a complete change of direction, twisting one way, then another.

The cabin was silent. No idle chatter to be picked up by scanners. These were professionals.

Suddenly they shot up again, really high, then lurched forward at high speed. She thanked the roots her stomach was empty.

"We've lost them," finally announced the chief. He could have said it over a com link, but the cold blank of his eyes said he wanted her to know.

She was on her way to Cumchdach, with no outside help.

The pilot still bent over his com fields. Then lifted his head to the chief and nodded. "No signs on extended scans."

The marshals' reach covers the whole planet. Doesn't it?

It got harder to remember that when the troopers began to talk. Muted, low and in an unfamiliar language. Not standard, and no Arcadian tongue she'd heard.

They were off-worlders—and professionals. The marshals couldn't save her this time. But she might be able to save Cumchdach.

After what felt like hours, when she'd become seriously chilled, the flyer dropped down sharply then landed. The hatch opened.

Stale smells, dank odours. Gone was the fresh air of mountain and sea. The guards adjusted her restraints enough to let her walk but not to escape their control.

It was an old building with a taint like the marshes but overlaid with a sharp chemical bite. She was in Urbis, the rank decay and residue of a large population unmistakable. Her guards marched her down a derelict corridor, litter covering the floor, and stopped at double doors. They swung open and a new group of guards stood on the other side.

"The package, as promised," said the mercenary chief in Standard.

"You weren't followed?" said the one heading the new group.

"We know how to do our job." The leader sneered, making no effort at hiding his contempt. "Our credits?"

"Transferring now," said a small man on one side of the new group. All organisations needed their clerics, she decided cynically.

The leader checked his com.

"Through now," he confirmed. Then gestured to his troop. They shoved Anna toward the new guards.

For an instant, her restraints vanished and she had a violent urge to escape.

But that would doom Cumchdach.

The new guards locked her down again and two of them took firm hold of her arms. She was collecting a treasury of bruises.

"Come, Sera. Your husband is impatient for your arrival."

The door opened into a new room. They'd left him alone for too many hours, now they came in and dragged him out but, for the first time, they took a new turning. Along more decrepit corridors, then to ones that someone had tried to clear up and sanitise. It hadn't been very successful, the nose-biting smell of chemicals adding to the habitual mix of decay and vermin. Then they came to a new door, one that looked too much like the bland doors of so many company headquarters he'd visited in Urbis.

He was getting a bad feeling.

Cumchdach's guards shoved him forward. He thrust an elbow back and heard a grunt that gave him a buzz of satisfaction. He'd walk into that room on his own, whatever it held. Two guards walked immediately behind him and one in front. Did that mean they didn't trust him, or whoever was in this room was too important to let him enter untouched?

He had to get near the head of the conspiracy.

Inside the room, he stopped. It was a boardroom, and he nearly broke out laughing. They'd done the same to Ethan Winter. Did they think that coating their actions in corporate protocols made them legitimate?

He was shoved into a chair at one end, feet locked to the floor and hands locked behind his back with restraint fields. He wasn't going anywhere, not without outside help. At the other end of the room, an oval table took up most of the width of the room. Four people sat on the far side, their seats set higher than his like a judicial panel waiting to judge him.

Or a pack of carrion feeders waiting to strip him of anything of value.

He didn't recognise any of them, but their type was familiar. Second-tier assistants, the backroom types who too often pulled the strings in a less profitable company. The kind that never lost out if a company failed, flitting on to their next victim instead.

The chair in the middle sat empty.

He nodded toward it. "Your boss still hiding?"

"They will be joining us soon. Once we have the answer to some questions."

Cumchdach jerked his chin back. "Not happening."

He didn't like the smile on the woman at the far end. Too smoothly dressed, with the firm-fleshed face of someone who worked out more than regularly. The woman was an enforcer, he'd bet. Used to putting pressure on smaller outfits to get them to buckle.

"We are also waiting on another party," she said. "They are on their way now."

Then a guard carried in a second chair. Smaller than his, but with the same tell-tale signs of inbuilt restraints. He placed it to one side of the room, between Cumchdach and the woman. A spot where it was visible to everyone in the room but did nothing to block the line of sight of the panel or Cumchdach.

"Who might that be?" he asked, fighting to keep his voice cool.

"Your wife, of course. She is eager to join you. The den Falasches have always been keen supporters of our endeavours."

He surged forward, fighting vainly against his restraints. "That's a lie."

His chair stayed firmly in position and all he succeeded in doing was adding to the bruises on his body. The woman smirked. "It was her idea to come."

"You bring her, and you bring the marshals down on you."

The woman's smirk got wider, and less inviting. "Not with the special skills of our backers."

"You're using outsiders," he said in disgust.

"We do what is necessary," said one of the others on the panel. "And none of this is. If only the Ser would assist us."

"Never," said Cumchdach. These traggers knew what side he was on, thanks to the marshals' and their heavy-handed rescue of him at that last meeting. No point denying it. But now they planned to use Anna against him.

She'd never act against Roo or his family. And maybe, just maybe, she still felt something for him. That last kiss. It had felt so real.

He was getting her out of here, whatever it took. He squirmed in his chair as if the rigid stance was getting to him. It was, but he'd endured worse in prison. There, the tiny prick of the marshals' sliver, still in place. One activation, and they'd swoop down on this building.

But first, he needed Anna to be safe. And he needed the leader.

"I'm not talking to underlings. Get your boss in here."

He sat unspeaking after that, as they threw question after question at him. What did Den Coille plan? How badly were they hurting? Who else followed them? What did they plan to do to Falasch?

Goaded into speech and needing to buy time, he finally answered. None of their business, and the details of the Falasch restitution were still pending. Then they brought out the lies. The Council had been misled by scientists and Survey field staff intent on holding onto their lucrative jobs; the planned controls on companies would destroy Arcadia and bankrupt its business; the Alliance demands were driven by greed for Arcadia's space and wealth.

He said nothing. The Survey field staff had saved his family's lives, and he knew exactly what that had cost his sister and Caleb Winter. They knew their jobs and were honest to their backbones. If Survey field staff said Arcadia was in trouble, it was true.

The other two claims had too much truth in them. If Den Coille was finding it hard to meet the council's demands, others were finding it harder. Without help or drastic changes, too many companies were destined for destruction. As for the Alliance, that was a whole other cesspit. Luckily, it wasn't his to deal with. Seolta and the Ministry of Galactic Affairs had the thankless task of finding out exactly what was going on there and making sure none of it hurt Arcadia.

Right now, he had to keep his Anna safe. They hadn't mentioned Roo, so he must still be free and safe from them. But not Anna.

Then the tension in the room ratcheted up a notch and the door behind him opened.

CHAPTER TWENTY-NINE

It was Anna. That unique scent filling the air was branded in his heart. Today, it mingled with the rank smells of his captivity, but his senses always knew when Anna was near. He sat rigid, hands clenched behind him and knees locked to keep him still as he stared straight at his captors, watching as their gazes switched to the back of the room then focussed on his face.

He heard her footsteps, and the heavy feet of the lowlife troops guarding her. She moved from the door to the seat, coming into his view at last. He had to use every speck of the control he'd built growing up in his volatile family to stop his anger overwhelming him.

His Anna, his beautiful wife, was filthy and wet all over. She was dressed in the kind of work clothes she loved; tough, durable, and comfortable, was how she'd always defended them. They did nothing to hide her curves or her enduring appeal, despite the caked dirt marring her face or the traces of vegetation dripping from her sleeves.

"My dear," he said in his most polite, most unrevealing voice, "I see our hosts have been attending to your needs as expected."

For an instant, he saw a flicker in her eyes of someone lost. Then she caught his eyes, held them and sent back his challenge as she'd done so often in the past. "In a manner of speaking," she said in the voice she used to address graceless lab assistants and lifted one arm to examine the gunk gracing her lower sleeve.

"They must be unaware of your… zealousness in your pursuit of your research."

"A momentary misunderstanding, I'm sure."

Did she mean the marshals followed her? But no, she was here. They'd never have allowed her to be taken like this. They'd *promised* him.

Or had they?

Not in so many words. Not directly. A new fury lit his veins and he turned back to the panel.

"So you have my wife. As you heard, she is a busy woman and has other pressing needs to attend to. If we can hurry this along… Once everyone is here."

Their faces stayed unchanged and the door behind them stayed shut.

"Just a few more details to sort out, Ser den Coille."

"No," he said, as firmly as possible. "Not without your boss, and my wife stays untouched."

"For now," said a man at the other end.

"If you want my cooperation, you will make very sure not one more hair on her head is harmed. Nor is my wife in the habit of talking business while in her field clothes."

He stared back, fists still clenched and hating that shiver he caught before Anna gripped her jaw tight and clenched down on it. They could have put her through the cleanser they'd forced on him. She'd be warm and dry, if no happier.

He'd mastered the art of staring down others as a youth, against far harder opposition than these. His younger brothers and sister were as headstrong as it came when they had mischief planned, Seolta and Fioruisghe an unholy partnership leading the rest.

"Immediately," he said softly.

The enforcer woman looked to the other man who'd spoken, the one at far end of the panel. He must be the interrogator, the two of them a practised team, like his sister and brother.

The woman nodded. "See that the Sera is accorded the appropriate treatment."

"No," said Anna.

"They will bring you back," Cumchdach said, holding her eyes. "They have nothing to gain by doing anything else."

"Do not be so sure, Ser den Coille," said the man.

"Don't take me for a fool," Cumchdach said. "The instant you hurt her, you lose all leverage over me. Not if cooperating doesn't keep her safe."

"So you will cooperate?" said the woman.

He shrugged. "It depends on what your leader promises."

And was pleased to see the tightening of the woman's face. Not the answer she'd planned on.

Then tell your coward of a boss to stop hiding and come face me. Preferably before he was forced to call in the marshals to save Anna.

If that com still worked, after the scans and cleansings his captors had put him through.

It's marshal built. They have research labs second to none. It had to work. As for how fast they responded, he had no doubt Marco an Fallon had a troop nearby. The marshals acted quickly when they had to.

If it suited them.

He began making plans for how to get Anna out of here without help.

They tightened his restraints while Anna was out of the room. Not quite tight enough to act as a tourniquet but close. He could feel the blood buzzing at the constriction. A reminder of their power. It made the chair even more uncomfortable and ensured that if he did escape them, he'd be unable to walk.

Then Anna walked back in and they restored the first setting on his restraints. The rush of pain in his limbs had him clenching his gut to stop crying out. It cost him a first look at her. When he managed to look up, they had locked her down and her face was locked down harder.

Not from him though. She'd seen the pain in his face. He might keep it from their captors but Anna had known him too long. Her fists clutched the chair arms.

Were they doing the same to her? How tight were her restraints? He tried to sit straighter and pain ricocheted through his body, even as he saw her lean toward him. He subsided and shook his head. *I'm fine, a chiad,* he mouthed in Mountainer.

Her grim mouth said she didn't believe it any more than he did.

"Satisfied?" asked the woman enforcer, with a jerk of her head toward Anna.

"Not by a long shot," he snarled back.

"We're wasting time," said one of the pair in the middle who'd so far kept silent. Another man from the corporate world, his tapping on the desk too familiar. Still second tier, said that tapping. A man who'd had to sit frustrated through too many meetings.

Cumchdach never let his feelings be so obvious in a meeting with opponents. Not without a purpose, and not when a sign of weakness was a balm to an opponent.

He stared at the tapping fingers, until the man abruptly stopped. Then he plastered a smile on his face and looked directly into the eyes of the tapper. The man thrust his hand under the table and glared back.

At the other end of the table, the one he'd dubbed the interrogator leaned forward. "Your wife is here and properly attired."

In a manner of speaking, he supposed you could say that. She was clean, and had lost the pinched look and shiver, but the outfit they'd given her was a garish orange and cut badly. Nothing like her usual cool elegance when not in the field.

She ignored it, head back and studying each panel member as if they were interesting research subjects. He was so proud of her.

But she should not be here. And if he failed, her life was forfeit.

Of that he had no doubt at all.

"It's past time we got to the purpose of this encounter," said the interrogator in what the man probably thought a chilling voice. Cumchdach had faced the real wolves of the corporate world too often.

"Which is?" he said back in a proper chilling voice and saw the man blink.

"Your role in this planet's response to the Alliance demands."

Cumchdach lifted his shoulders. "Nothing to explain there. Den Coille has accepted the reality of the Alliance findings. Arcadia is in trouble and without change, our continued settlement here is finished."

"The Alliance have put that on hold," said the other woman in the middle. "The original findings were exaggerated. They will never demand changes that destroy the economy of this world."

"They weren't exaggerated, and they will," he said. "There are plenty out there only too ready to come here. We comply, or they'll ship us out and replace us. That is this planet's only option."

"According to whom? Your brother? He's proven so reliable," sneered the interrogator.

Had the man been one of those who used Seolta's post-imprisonment rage to lure him into their conspiracy?

"My brother—and my sister and her husband." That stopped the man a moment. Cumchdach saw the faint flush with huge pleasure. Fioruisghe and her husband Caleb Winter were the first to expose and defeat this miserable conspiracy. "I'm sure you will agree that their credentials as senior Survey field agents are impeccable."

The man grunted, as if conceding anything of the sort gave him heartburn.

"Lay it out," said Cumchdach, suddenly impatient. "What precisely is it you want of me?"

"We will come to that in good time," said the interrogator.

"No, we come to it now."

"You're in no position to make demands," the man reminded him in the kind of oily voice Cumchdach hated. He had no bargaining power here, the panel knew that as well as he, but he did have something they wanted and bluffing was a legitimate business tool that had occasionally served him well—in the past, when he'd had real power behind him.

Now, he bargained for Anna's life. All he had against them was a hope they never guessed that his own life didn't matter. Not as long as Anna survived.

Cumhdach gave a lift of his shoulders and leaned back in his chair, as relaxed as possible when your hands are bound behind you and your legs clamped hard to the chair legs. Then he stared insolently at the panel and settled in to wait.

Except a man moved in closer to Anna. A man holding a blaster, the kind with multiple settings.

He set it to Anna's hand and activated it. She jerked hard, a low sound breaking her iron control.

"That's enough. Leave her alone."

The blaster snapped off as the interrogator leaned forward. "Perhaps you will reconsider your attitude, Ser den Coille."

"Or you torture my wife? I don't let that happen to anyone under my care."

"Then talk," the man snapped.

"Bring in your boss," he snapped back.

Silence reigned in the room. The kind before a storm, when all the preparations are made and you don't know if they are enough. He kept forgetting to breathe. The man with the blaster stood far too close to Anna and that crease in her forehead said the zap had been from the setting that left pain to linger for hours afterward. He could see her trying to flex her hands.

Then the guard raised that blaster to Anna's head.

"No." He lunged uselessly. "None of you have clearance to order that. Bring in your boss."

The enforcer woman's lips twisted. He was right then. The guard was looking toward the door. Someone out there was giving orders. Someone who did have the authority.

"I'll talk to your boss. Leave her alone."

The enforcer's lips twitched upward, the nearest the woman was able to come to a smile, he thought sourly. He'd told them the one thing they needed. He'd do anything to keep Anna safe. But there was a limit to his acting ability. Watching Anna die broke it.

Then Anna spoke for the first time. "Cumchdach, no. Do not give them what they want, not if you want Roo to grow up in Arcadia."

"Sorry, sweetheart. Better he grow up with his mother, no matter where, than grow up motherless on Arcadia."

Her mouth dropped open. "He loves Biarsuin and he's young enough to forget me."

"No one—no one—can ever replace you," he said, holding her eyes. Then he turned back to the panel. "Bring in your tragging chief. He wants a deal; he'll get it. But my wife goes free."

The silence beat on his head. That blaster still rested against Anna's temple. Then, the door behind the panel began to open. He'd won. The boss was coming.

One of the panel stood to pull out the middle chair and a man stepped into the room. Cumchdach flexed his upper arm, squeezing down hard on the sliver buried in his armpit. Then he recognised the newcomer. A man he'd met once before as part of a business team.

A second-tier marketing manager.

The man took the empty chair at the table and looked down on Cumchdach. Then he nodded to the man by Anna and the man lowered his blaster.

"You have something to say to us, Ser den Coille?"

That was when more of Ceart's words came back to him. They all trust whoever it is. Single-minded and highly intelligent.

He studied the guards' and the others' reactions.

The guard on Anna still had the unfocussed eyes of someone listening to another person over their com. He might look at the newcomer but the man in the room wasn't the real head of the conspiracy.

Cumchdach had failed, and it was too late to warn the marshals. All he could do now was buy time to save Anna.

"What's your proposal," he said as if defeated.

"No," said Anna, sounding as defeated, as disillusioned.

Then one of the men flanking the so-called leader jerked up. "He's wearing a live com."

Chaos erupted.

"It's a ruse. You're not the leader," yelled Cumchdach to distract him.

The blaster stayed planted against Anna's head and her captor's finger moved against the control pad.

He surged forward, straining against the restraints. Ceart had broken them once.

Then an explosion rocked the side of the building, he surged forward with everything in him, and the blaster zipped past Anna's face as a woman aimed from the breach in the wall and shot the thing away from her. A storm of blaster fire filled the room. His restraints gave way and he ran for Anna, pulling her down and away from the firing, just as the guard's blaster shot out again. He pushed her behind him. She shoved back.

Both of them went down on the floor. A searing pain shot through his leg and he heard Anna scream.

She'd been hit.

Then he knew no more.

CHAPTER THIRTY

He woke to desolation. "Anna," he croaked as soon as he could work his mouth. But knew it for a waste of effort. She was gone. He'd failed at the most important job in his life; protecting the woman he loved. He lay back and shut his eyes. He hurt all over, his ankle leg the most, but nothing hurt as much as his heart.

"The sera is sleeping. She has been treated and will be up to a com call by this evening," said a woman's voice. He opened his eyes and looked up.

It was a woman in a uniform he recognised from the first time he'd been imprisoned and freed. A nurse in the Urbis Central hospital.

"Sleeping?" He'd seen Anna shot.

"She took a blast to the gut. A nasty one. Fortunately, the marshals got her to us fast enough to minimise the effects of it. She is not to move yet, though. You will be able to visit her tomorrow. Once your leg is fully stabilised."

"Visit? She's here?" Nothing made sense. He anchored his elbows against the sleeper to haul himself up. A hand shot out and the nurse held him down. "The medics have spent hours stabilising that ankle and fixing the rest of the damage done to you. Lie down, Ser den Coille. You are not allowed to waste all their hard work."

He studied the woman. He'd met her kind of nurse before. Care of her patient came before everything else. "My wife, she's really safe. She's alive?"

The woman frowned impatiently. "Didn't I say that? Stop worrying, Ser. You are in the best medical facility on Arcadia. We do not let patients die on us without proper cause. Your wife is sleeping, not dying. I would have told you if it were more serious."

She gave a huff, as if mortally insulted, and Cumchdach grinned. Thank the roots he'd got this woman for a nurse.

"Anna's alive," he said, just to hear the words.

"That's what I told you. Now lie back, shut your eyes, and get some sleep. The medics can't perform miracles, and patients who do not do as they are told make life far too difficult for us."

He did as ordered and felt the smile lifting his lips. His wife was here, safe, and alive. And that evening, he talked to her by com.

"You're safe," were her first words after she woke and saw his holo shimmering beside her. He wanted badly to touch her, but all he could do was lay the hologram of his hand over hers. "They told me you smashed your ankle when you broke free of the restraints."

"Is that what happened?" He'd been too worried about Anna to ask about his own injuries. His ankle hurt, but the nurse had said it was being treated, and that was enough for him.

Then he noticed the strained look on her face.

"You didn't mean to do that?" she said.

"I meant to get to you, a chiad. How, was irrelevant." He watched her face, saw the creases forming in her forehead. "I will always do whatever is needed to keep you safe."

"But they were shooting at you too."

He shrugged.

"They were trying to kill you."

"And you think I'd want to live at the expense of your life? To live without you? The woman I've loved since I was a boy? Never, a chiad."

Then the com cut out and his now least favourite nurse returned. "That's enough, Ser. Your vitals are outside acceptable limits, as are the sera's. You can visit her in the morning."

The woman had the gall to remove his com patch and tell him to go back to sleep.

Anna had been about to tell him something, he was sure of it. Something important. How did this nurse think he'd sleep while he waited to hear what his wife, his love, the heart of his life, was trying to tell him?

Next morning, he demanded to be taken to Anna as soon as the first human appeared.

"I'll put through your request, ser. The Sera Anna is in strict isolation. No visitors. Her state is still fragile."

"I'm her husband."

The young medic glanced at his com readout. To Cumchdach's jaundiced eye, he looked like he should still be in Med School.

"Our information is that you are currently estranged. We'll need to check with the Sera whether she agrees to a visit."

Then the boy put him through one of the more uncomfortable medical checks he'd ever endured. "Have you done this before?" he growled as the medic's fingers probed through the protective field. "That hurt."

"Yes, he has, *mo leanadh*, and it doesn't hurt that much."

"Mam!" He'd never been so glad to see his mother.

Scathach smiled serenely at the young medic, but Cumchdach knew her too well. Her face might show nothing, but those hands hiding away in the folds of her tunic said it all. Mam was upset, worse than upset. She'd lived through too many of her children putting their lives on the line.

"May I?" said his mother in what they all called her head doctor voice. "Just to reassure myself."

The young doctor reddened and stepped back. His mother nodded her head in thanks and copied his movements. She hurt him too, but he did his best not to show it. Not that he could fool her.

"Sorry, but you have made a bit of a mess of your leg. This is going to take some time, even after the healing fields have done their best. What made you take on a restraining field? It's shattered that bone to slivers."

"I had to get to Anna. They were firing at her."

"Aah." His mother had a lot of annoying faces. The one that said she suddenly understood a tragging sight more than her children wanted was one of them. At least she stopped mauling him.

"And you can wipe that grumpy frown off your face, young man."

Treating her children as if they were first schoolers was another of her annoying habits. She put on her calm smile and turned to the young medic. "A fine job you are doing here. My family is very grateful, and so will the Ser be once he recovers."

"They won't let me see Anna," Cumchdach blurted out.

"Aah," said his mother again. He went to rise. He'd get to Anna himself if no one was going to help, but his mother put out a hand and turned to the young medic. "I do think you will have to let him visit her if at all possible. My son has a distressing tendency to focus on one thing to the exclusion of all else. He won't rest until he can see for himself his wife is safe."

"As to that…" the young man stuttered.

"Is she awake and able to talk?"

"She's awake, yes."

"Then believe me, if you want either of them to recover, they need to see each other."

"But they're… We were told they aren't together…"

"By whom?" said his mother in her most dangerous voice.

The young man blushed even harder. "The gossip vids. It was in all of them," he said in a barely audible voice.

"I see."

Cumchdach almost felt sorry for the young man when his mother opened up her com. "Administrator, Scathach den Coille here. Please arrange for my son to be taken to visit his wife. The family will be most concerned if this is not facilitated immediately."

Soon after, the door opened and a hospital porter entered the room. His mother looked pointedly at the medic and the young man hastily fixed all the paraphernalia cluttering up Cumchdach's sleeper and body to enable his transfer.

"I'll be back later to see how you're getting on."

"And Roo?" asked Cumchdach before she could disappear. His mother's smile widened to the joyous one all her children loved most.

"Back in Manascraoch under triple security and loving all the attention. As soon as possible, we will have you both transferred back home and you can be with him there."

"Thank you." He did not want Roo anywhere else, not until the conspirators were caught. "And the traitors in our ranks?"

"We've caught three and are tracking down any others. Your father is not happy."

He had to chuckle at that, then clenched his bruised gut muscles. He could imagine his father's language. On the rare occasions he was driven to cursing, all his sons were known to stare admiringly. His vocabulary was truly awesome.

"It is not funny, young man."

Cumchdach lifted a hand in apology. "Our people will track them down in no time. Da will make sure of it."

"Yes, he will. If only to stop Marshal an Fallon finding them for him." At Cumchdach's gasp, she added, "Yes, they're involved. There were mutterings about *connections* and *tragging interfering outsiders* last time I asked about it. Now, go see your wife, then get some rest." With which final order, his mother exited the room and the orderly set his sleeper in motion. The man also told him to lie flat, but Cumchdach refused to meet Anna looking like a battered victim. He'd had enough of that the last few days. He'd beaten their captors; a few breaks weren't going to defeat him.

Then they reached her room. A nurse stood guard outside the door.

"Your wife is a long way from being well yet, Ser. Please, keep your visit short and do not upset her."

Why did everyone think he'd do anything to hurt Anna?

Then the door opened and his sleeper moved in. He pulled himself fully upright as soon as it stopped.

She'd been facing the far wall. Her skin was too like the grey of the coastal sands on a wet day, and bruises mottled her torso around the plate covering her wounds. A slight hum in the background told of the continuing work of the medics' machines, healing her abused body, and too many tubes ran into her veins. They did that when a person was too badly injured to take a non-intrusive infusion and needed high volume inputs.

She had nearly died. Anyone who told him different was lying.

He'd thought she *had* died.

He must have made a noise. She turned her head slowly on the sleeper pillow, and a smile lit up her face then was hastily smothered, and she watched in silence as they pushed him beside her.

"They won't let me off the sleeper," he said, heart thudding. "It's not as bad as it looks." He reached out his hand and took hers, folding his bigger hand around her wrist where the pulse beat. She might not want him, but he needed very badly to touch her. To feel her warm and full of life.

He swallowed. "You're in no fit state yet, but when you're better we need to talk. We can't continue like this."

Her eyes flared wide in shock and she dragged back her hand, hugging it to her.

"What did I say? Please, *a chiad*." She'd always told him anything, or he thought she had. But now, her face closed tight against him.

The nurse bustled forward. Cumchdach shoved up a hand. "Out, now. If you want your patient to recover, you need to give us privacy."

He might be terribly wrong, but Anna had been his best friend since childhood. He *knew* when she was hurting. And this wall between them was hurting her badly. More than her injuries. She'd helped him recover after his prison ordeal. The medics had cleared them all, but inside, he'd been a wreck. He was supposed to be the one who kept his younger brothers safe and he'd failed completely, forced to watch while Aigherach, the baby of them all, was brutally manhandled.

The nurse opened his mouth.

"No. Out," said Cumchdach. The door opened and another medic walked in. A senior doctor this time by the label on his tunic.

A medic he recognised. He'd been one of those treating them after prison. A marshal medic. They must be in the security wing of Urbis Central.

"It's all right," the newcomer said to the nurses. "You can monitor vitals outside the room, but otherwise a privacy protocol is now in place." The medic bowed his head to Cumchdach. "One hint that the Sera is in trouble and we will be back in force."

The medic stood back and waited until the nurses complied. Then he left as well.

The door shut and Anna struggled to sit up. Cumchdach shoved out his hand to stop her, but halted before he touched her.

"No, *a chiad.* You heard him. Let me say what I have to, then I won't bother you again. We can work out the arrangements for Roo after."

She lay back but looked so unhappy at being forced to look up at him that he lowered his sleeper so his head sat at the same height as hers.

He opened his mouth but Anna got in first.

"Did you mean what you said last night?"

"What?" All he'd remembered clearly was they were cut off before Anna could tell him something.

"About loving me since you were a child. It's still true? You're not being nice, or courteous, or because of Roo."

Suddenly, his whole life balanced on a fragile twig.

"Am I just Roo's mother to you?" she went on. "A left-over habit from youth you don't know how to break free of?"

How could she think that? "Roo is one of the two most important people in my life, the two who make my life complete." He swallowed, so scared he'd muck this up. "You are the other one. My best friend, my wife, a woman so beautiful you take my breath away. I love you so much, *a chiad.*"

"So much you couldn't tell me about the Restin case? You didn't even try to work it through with me. That's my home city, my family's legacy Den Coille is attacking."

"I know," he said miserably, "but you were so sick."

"Don't give me that. Don't make me so *small.*" A single tear drop hovered at the edge of her eye. "I trusted you."

"And I failed you. I was just so scared. You're *never* sick."

"Yes, the pregnancy hit me hard. That doesn't mean I was suddenly feeble minded. I *know* you, Cumchdach duine Anna." Then she stopped, and the tear was joined by another. "Or I thought I did. Until that day."

She looked so hurt, a shadow haunting her eyes, and he had put it there.

She could never forgive him. All he was doing was making it worse. "I'm sorry. I was wrong to come. You're in no state for this. I can't even promise you anything about the Restin case. What your father did; it hurts too many others." She tried again to sit up and he thrust out a hand. "Stay still, *a chiad.* Please." She lay back, eyes locked on him, and he pulled back his hand. "Whatever happens, I'm still your friend. Tell me what you want, and I'll do it. Keep going like this, separate formally, or divorce." He hated the word, but he forced it out. Divorce was rare on Arcadia, especially in corporate marriage like theirs, but if that was what Anna wanted…

That beautiful mouth had gone straight as the line of clouds on the Mountainer ridge line "Did I ask you to drop the Restin case? No." She shook her head violently and a machine squawked. She turned and glared at it, raising her voice. "If a single one of you dares come in here, I'll make sure you're broken down to garbage duty."

"Shush. You're too sick for this. Forget I said anything."

Anna turned that glare on him. "Will you stop talking, Cumchdach duine Anna. I don't work for you and you're not in *charge* of me." Her eyes snapped. "And close your mouth. It's not flattering."

He hastily shut his mouth as ordered.

"You think you know everything."

"Not everything. Why did you agree to marry me?" he suddenly said, the words out of his mouth before he could stop them.

Anna stared at him, so angry she forgot all the pain and the stupid weakness. How could he be so blind? He knew her better than anyone else. "Why do you think?"

"I don't know. I never have."

"You think you're the only one who can fall in love? Who found the one person who can make them whole." She threw up her arms, then scowled at the stabs of pain. Cumchdach opened his mouth but she glared at him. "The words might be hard for me to say, but it doesn't mean there's nothing there. I fell in love with you the first time I saw you. Yes, I was not much more than a child. But I knew then, and it's never changed. I love you, Cumchdach bean Anna, and I wanted your child. That's why I married you."

"A baby." His eyes were blank with shock. "Roo. That's all you wanted from me?"

"You're the only man I have ever wanted to be the father of my child."

"But we could have had a baby at any time."

She stared at him. Could he really be so obtuse. "Did you bang your head too?"

"What?" He shook his head. "This isn't funny. You refused to marry for so long."

"With who we both are? Of course I did. A union of Manascraoch and Rubhaicreach is no private affair. As for a baby…"

He'd drawn back from her. Looked about to leave, as if unable to bear what she said, and she braced her heart to take the blow of it. But then his brows drew together, and he made as if to get off his bed, only stopping when the squawk of his monitors threatened to bring the medics back in on them.

"Don't move," he snapped at the doorway as it threatened to open. It shut again, and he turned back to her. "That's the only reason you refused to marry me. We're more than our names."

She gulped. He was going to strip her bare. Did she dare let him?"

"I was scared," she admitted, the words dragged from her gut. "What if I was wrong, that one day you'd stop loving me?"

"What could make you think that? Don't you know that's impossible?"

She squirmed at that. "Is it? You're you. The heir to Den Coille."

"As you're the heir to Falasch."

"But you're also the eldest brother in a family that's everything mine isn't. Your family, they really love each other. Mine…"

He said nothing to that. He couldn't and they both knew it.

Cumchdach had never so badly wanted to dismember her sad excuse of a father. Didn't she know how much she deserved to be loved?

"*A chiad.*" He reached out and gently turned her head toward him. Then he leaned over, one hand on the side of his sleeper to stop himself tumbling onto her, and took her lips.

Soft, gentle, it started as the kind he'd plant on a cheek, but this was Anna and he had loved and wanted her so long. When her mouth opened to his, he sank into her warm depths.

The whining of another machine brought them back and he lifted his head, staring down at her.

"As soon as you're fit, we're going home. Together."

"And the Restin case? We will talk, and we will deal with it. Together?"

Her words might sound like an order, but Cumchdach saw the tightening of her face and the hidden fear. He lifted his hand and cradled her cheek, his thumb brushing the line of her lips. "Together," he promised again.

The door opened and a scowling nurse walked in, accompanied by the senior doctor.

"That is enough for today, Ser den Coille," said the doctor. "The Sera needs to rest now—and so do you."

"As you say, Ser," said Cumchdach meekly. The touch of a chuckle from Anna was the only reward he'd ever need. "Until tomorrow, *a chiad.*" Fortunately, no one argued.

The medical staff bustled around Anna, setting her to rights again, as was proper in a medical ward. The orderly moved to set Cumchdach's sleeper into motion to take him away. Anna reached out her hand. A mere touch of wrist and fingers. The pulse was frighteningly erratic in her wrist and he squeezed hard.

"I'm not going anywhere, *a chiad.* I'm just down the hall." Her too dark eyes, sunken in the hollows of her face, fixed on his.

"Until tomorrow, and all our tomorrows," she said, and he heard the whisper of hope in it. It wasn't enough, not yet. But it was the promise of enough.

"Sleep, *a chiad.* Until tomorrow."

He visited her as promised, but she was sleeping. The hollows under her eyes were dark with fatigue, and she looked so fragile, lying among all the paraphernalia of the medics. He took her wrist again, scared silly. "You promised me, *a chiad.* All our tomorrows."

The senior doctor came into the room then, a marshal doctor he would never forget. The man had seen him at his worst, when prison had left him battered and soul sick. He didn't have to pretend in front of this man.

The medic put a hand on his shoulder. "She's not dying, Ser den Coille, so wipe that look off your face." The man looked at Anna, then back to him with the smallest twitch at the corner of his lips. "Whatever you said to her yesterday, it helped. Sleep is what she needs now, more than all our sophisticated help."

"She will recover?"

"Yesterday, I wasn't too sure. Today, yes, Ser, she will recover. It will take time and rest. But she will recover."

"When?"

"Miracles come only once a month, young man. She will recover when she recovers."

"No, when can I take her home?"

The medic chuckled. "That's easier. As soon as it can be arranged. Your mother's hospital is as good as they come and can provide all the home services needed. She is far better off with her own people and her baby. We'll get her nursing again, too and that will help. Crossing a nursing mother is never a good idea, even when it's her own body doing it." The medic chuckled at that and looked again at Anna.

Cumchdach stayed by her side after that, sharing her room. The medic said it improved her vitals, and it certainly made Cumchdach feel better. It was there that Marco an Fallon found them the next morning.

"Marshal, how are you," said Anna.

Cumchdach wasn't feeling so kindly. It was the marshals who'd got him into this mess; and nearly got Anna killed. "About time. Have you cleaned up that nest of wernets yet?"

"I couldn't get in before. Your medics have been blocking us." From the scowl on the man's face, an Fallon wasn't used to being refused. "The documentation and other evidence found in the building suggests it held the heart of the conspiracy. We're tracking down their contacts now."

"Sol Winter?" Ethan, the middle Winter son had been a strong support to Cumchdach in prison and was now one of his closest friends. Any action against his father would hurt all the Winters.

An Fallon shook his head. "The records confirm he was involved earlier but has had nothing to do with the group since his son's intervention. We're more interested in the core, not any past associates, and the man has more than paid his dues." The Winter parents were imprisoned with Cumchdach's parents by the false Survey managers. Like him, they owed their lives to Caleb Winter and his wife Fioruisghe, Cumchdach's younger sister. "It's early yet, but so far it looks like we've broken them."

Marco an Fallon wasn't a man for false hopes but, for the first time Cumchdach remembered, the man looked optimistic.

"And the other person?" said Cumchdach.

An Fallon looked startled. "You caught the leader. He's the chief strategist with GenCorp." A name that didn't surprise Cumchdach. A major financier, it stood to lose millions of credits if too many of its clients went broke.

Cumchdach shook his head. "The mercenaries who brought in Anna. They were linked to someone outside that room."

"There was no one else," said an Fallon sharply.

Cumchdach tried to sit up straighter and cursed the weakness of his body. "Ceart told me he'd heard whispers. He said the leader wasn't from the corporate world—and those mercenaries weren't taking their orders from the man in the room." He glared at the sleeper and his stupid leg. "I don't care what that man claiming to be the head said, or even what he thinks. There was someone else behind him."

"The guards who brought me there," broke in Anna. "They were professionals, and I'd swear they were off-worlders. They spoke in a language I've never heard before."

An Fallon cursed, then apologised to Anna, before slapping open his com. "Block all outgoing ships leaving the planet. And give me a trace on all that left in the past week, along with everyone—and I mean *everyone*—on board. Also, track anyone leaving the office block around the time we broke in."

He went into private mode after that, issuing multiple orders. Deep lines scoured both sides of his mouth. At the end, he said a curt thank you.

Cumchdach shook his head. "I failed you." All that Anna and he had endured, and for nothing?

"No, Ser den Coille," said an Fallon. "From what we've learned in that building and from the conspirators we have in custody, it appears we've beaten those involved on Arcadia. The conspiracy as it stands is finished."

"But?" said Anna, grasping Cumchdach's hand.

"If someone escaped from us, there is always the possibility of another conspiracy starting up. We need to track them down and destroy them once and for all. Only then can Arcadia be safe." Then he looked over both of them. Cumchdach felt as if he'd been stripped to the bone, all his weaknesses and injuries exposed. "You two have done more than enough," said Marshal an Fallon. "The rest is up to others. To the marshals and our off-planet connections. For now, Ser and Sera, you have a baby to raise, one company to save and another to rescue from incompetence. The planet thanks you for your services and wishes you all the best."

Cumchdach gave a loud, *Hah.* "I'll believe that last bit if you get the Council to repeat it."

An Fallon gave the nearest he had to a smile. "It is not for a simple policeman to speak for the Council. But the marshals will not forget what we owe the families of den Coille and Winter. Thank you, Ser and Sera."

He bowed to both of them then left, leaving them sharing bemused grins.

"Did that man actually praise us?" said Cumchdach. Anna could only chuckle, before smothering a yawn, and Cumchdach forgot all about the marshal and his concerns. "Go to sleep, *a chiad,* if you want to see our son soon."

"Yes, dear," she said.

He scowled at her and pointed to her sleeper. "It would be nice if for once you meant that."

Anna chuckled, then yawned again, and soon her eyes shut. Cumchdach lay, watching her. She was safe, and healing. Then sleep took him too.

CHAPTER THIRTY-ONE

Two days later, they were both medevacked home to Manascraoch. Even better, Roo was there to meet them. Thanks to the medics' treatments, Anna was able to take him and cuddle him then, soon after, order everyone except Cumchdach out of the room and give her baby the best reassurance possible. Cumchdach watched her settling a desperate Roo to the breast, then marvelled at the peace that came over mother and son as the baby began to feed.

"Isn't he getting too old to need nursing?" he dared say after a while, worried that it would drain her too much. She was still far from well.

Roo turned a glare on him as if understanding every word before setting to again.

"He's not even a year old," said Anna as if that finished the discussion.

Cumchdach kept his silence but had a word later that day to his mother. Who was even more emphatic than Anna. "Leave her alone. She's had more to deal with the last year than any new mother should have to. The intervals with Roo soothes them both."

Having seen Anna's face as she watched her baby feed, Cumchdach couldn't deny the truth of that. But he also couldn't forget his first sight of Anna in hospital.

"Her medics are keeping a close eye on her," said his mother before he could say anything else. "Anna is fully aware of her needs and is cooperating fully with them. Go solve the problems of Den Coille. Your wife is perfectly capable of keeping herself and your son safe."

And where do I fit in? The unbidden thought brought a load of guilt. Anna had enough to deal with. He couldn't banish it, though, and went to his father. Bram just laughed. "Welcome to fatherhood, son. Support her and help her to do what her instincts tell her is needed. That's your job."

"Most mothers don't face what Anna has since giving birth."

His da put up a hand. "Most *fathers* get being second best out of their system in the first weeks after a baby's born. You and Anna weren't granted that. Anna's making up for it now. Leave her be."

Maybe, but that kernel of reserve in her was still there. It had always mattered, but he'd learned to accept it in the years they'd been together, to trust in what lay between them. But that was before he'd failed her.

Too few days later, he returned home from the office to find Anna surrounded by her lab staff, one hand stroking Roo as he slept beside her while her other scrolled through something on her com and a familiar crease settled into her forehead.

"What are you doing?" He glared around the room. "And what are all these people doing here."

She looked up and gave him the smile that meant her head was deep in her work. "Working with me." She returned to her com screens.

"You're supposed to be taking it easy." He'd deliberately left so much unresolved until she was stronger, all the Restin mess with her family, and now look at her.

She waved a hand at him. "There's too much to do. You have no idea what I learned from the Coasters. They have a whole economy and way of living with their environment we knew nothing about. No wonder they're all miserable in the lower boughs."

Cumchdach scowled. Samhchair had been nagging him about it too. "We're replacing the festia plantations on the coastal regions as fast as we can, but they can't go back to nothing. Our staff are working on it."

"Hmmm. Have them talk to me." With which his adored wife waved a distracted hand at him. "Now, get back to your work and leave me to mine. Next up, we're doing a full scan of all the mountain plantations. After what we found in Deuteron and Coaster country, I can't wait to find out what's in the rest of Mountainer country."

"You are not wearing yourself out. You nearly *died* not long ago."

She looked up. "But I didn't. I've never let you rule my life, and I don't intend to start now simply because we are married."

"What about because you love me and I love you?" Cumchdach felt like pulling his hair out. Anna simply pursed her lips.

"Yes, I do, and you nearly died too. Now stop being silly. I have work to do and so do you." She looked back to her screen, then must have noticed he hadn't moved.

"It's the end of the day. Time you shut down," he said.

She gave that a moment's thought. Then shook her head. "Soon. Roo's asleep. There's… something… in the chiller. Sure of it." Then she looked properly at him. "I need to talk to your father.

Those lower boughs folk aren't staying there a moment longer. He has to move them back to the coastal lands. I have work for them to do."

Cumchdach knew a momentary urge to kick Roo's cradle. Maybe she'd listen to her baby's cry. She certainly wasn't listening to him.

"Out," he said to the lab staff. "You've got families expecting you home." They didn't need telling twice. Anna watched them with open mouth.

"We haven't finished."

"Yes, you have."

He cursed inside at her too pale face and the slight grimace when she went to stand. "I don't know who said you were fit to work again, but I'm sure they didn't mean pulling extra long days and not looking after yourself properly."

He hadn't been as badly injured as she had, and a day at his desk had left him with an aching body and a clanging percussion in his head. The last of her techs shut the door with a bang and Cumchdach winced.

"What's wrong?" said Anna, finally ignoring her com.

"Nothing," he said, as if trying to hide something from her. She narrowed her eyes.

"Sit down. Put your feet up. And let me get dinner ready. You're no better off than I am."

Cumchdach let her fuss over him. If that was what it took to get her to take it easy, he'd play the injured man to the full. Their prepper was fully stocked and Mam had made sure it was automated. Within moments, he had her stretched out in her favourite chair, eating a healthy meal, and watching imperiously as he ate his dinner. Since he lurched up with a moan any time she tried to stand up or look at her com, she had to stay where she was.

Soon after, she stretched out her legs and let the chair cradle her. Minutes later, he grabbed at her plate as her eyes closed and she fell asleep.

"*A chiad,*" he murmured. "You are the most stubborn, infuriating, beautiful woman and I do love you so." He flung a glance at their also sleeping baby. "And if you dare wake in the next hour, *mo leanadh,* you are having water and food from your da. Not a drop of Mam's milk.

Roo must have heard him. He didn't wake that night ,and Anna looked much better in the morning. Of course, that just spurred her on to tackle more work. Not only the Coaster and Deuteron projects. To his secret terror, she'd also contacted Rubhaicreach. The Restin compensation trial wasn't over yet, but it wasn't far off.

He didn't mention it to her, but he wasn't about to let her wear herself out on the other projects. After two days of arguing, he had to give up. Or maybe it was the sharp words from his mother, forcing him to acknowledge that Anna did look better. It wasn't as if she was traipsing about in the field, said his Mam.

Not yet. He had no doubt that would come soon, though. He had a word with Da and Den Coille security about it.

A week later, life was nearly back to normal, if you ignored the undercurrent of fear he couldn't yet banish. They'd unearthed the Manascraoch traitors. The core of them came from the lower boughs as he'd guessed. Displaced, homeless, and angry, the youngsters were ripe for recruitment by the conspiracy. Cumchdach took all Samhchair's concerns to their da and, between them, they came up with a fast-track plan to get the refugees back to Coaster lands.

Anna glowed when he set the plan before her. "The Uncle and his fellow elders will soon set them back to rights," she said. Then her eyes took on that gleam he mistrusted. "He can organise them into field squads for me."

He might mistrust that gleam, but he also welcomed it. Proof she was growing stronger. Her unique smile broke out more often with each passing day, More importantly, she asked him to move back into their room, and each night he got to hold her as she slept, curling his body around hers and vowing before sleep took him that no one would ever hurt her again. But that had been all, so far. He couldn't yet banish the memory of how fragile she'd looked, or the bruises that had mottled her whole abdomen. They were starting to fade, but Cumchdach thought he'd see them in his mind forever.

Nor had the shadow quite gone from her eyes, and wouldn't until the tragging Restin case was resolved. He dreaded each incoming message from Urbis, and knew Anna retained a feed from her Grandam.

Not from her father. In that, nothing had changed, but she did surprise him one day when she mentioned she'd heard from her brother, Anton.

"You're talking to him now?"

She nodded. "Grandam and our docks staff tell me there's good stuff there."

"Do you trust him?"

She grimaced. "Part of me wants to. The other part can't forget he's Gria's son. I'm keeping an open line to him, and we'll see what happens."

Then, one evening as they sat with the family, Cumchdach's com beeped with a message, and his father's face jerked. Cumchdach slapped his com open in full privacy mode.

"It's the Restin case, isn't it?" said Anna. Tension gripped her jaw. She expected him to lie to her again.

After everything they'd been through?

"Yes," he said. Thankfully, Da kept silent. "The ruling has just come through. Den Coille has won everything they asked for."

Of course they had. When the Alliance was involved, no Arcadian court was going to be lenient. The courts might be independent; they weren't stupid.

"How much?" said Anna. He showed her, switching his system to include her com, and she gasped. "That will bankrupt Falasch. It will destroy the city."

"Not necessarily," he said desperately, knowing it for a lie. But what had her father expected when he set out to swindle Den Coille in the middle of a diplomatic situation as bad as they came?

It wasn't only Den Coille fighting for survival. It was their very planet, with too many dirty fingers in the mess both here and across the wider Alliance.

He tried. "Da?"

His father nodded. They hadn't had a chance yet to talk about it but Da always had multi-layered plans. He didn't disappoint this time either.

He coughed and Anna lifted her head away from the com screen. There were tears in her eyes.

"The amount awarded," said his father, "is equivalent to, as far as our finance department can ascertain, your father's share in Falasch Shipping as the principal shareholder."

"My father forfeits it to Den Coille, and the courts will be satisfied?"

Cumchdach wanted to take her hand so badly, but that look on her face said *No*. Said he was a den Coille tonight, before he was her husband, and all his foolish dreams turned to ash.

His father gave her a curt "Yes," in reply. Then, the head of Den Coille spoke to the heir of Falasch. "Unless someone can offer an alternative. Den Coille will not agree to any proposal that leaves Falasch free of supervision, not for some years," he added with a finality that both Cumchdach and Anna couldn't mistake. She'd grown up in this house as much as he'd grown up in hers, both her father's and later her Grandam's.

"Let me think on it," said Anna, as coolly formal as his father. She rose, and Cumchdach wasn't stupid enough to think he had any invitation to follow.

But then she turned around and looked him square in the face. "I'll see you in bed after you've talked to your father."

Cumchdach wanted to jump up and follow her straight away. *She hadn't cut him. Not yet.*

But he did need to talk to Da before he talked to Anna. She was leaving him to learn all the details, and trusting him to tell her afterward.

She was trusting him again. And expected him to do the same.

He throttled down his haste and turned to his father, who was watching him with an unreliable spark in those too knowing eyes.

"You two are working things out, then?"

"We're getting there," he said, and thankfully his father asked no more, just gave that curt nod of his that said the matter was under control. "As for the Restin case…"

Da leaned back in his chair. "I've sent you the full file, with our advisors' notes. You do know we have to take the penalty?"

Cumchdach grimaced. "Even Anna knows that, I think. But it doesn't mean we have to destroy them. Falasch has too long a track record and too many well established intergalactic contacts."

"We need them functioning as capably as they used to? Is that what you're trying to tell your slow witted Da?"

Cumchdach gave a sigh and slumped back. "You've already got a plan." Then he squared his shoulders. "I've a suspicion of what it is, but—it's best if you tell her. In the morning, when she's had time to get used to what's happened."

"She's known it's coming for long enough, and your wife is no dullard."

"Reality is always a shock when it arrives. Give her tonight. I think I know what she'd prefer, and it may be closer to what you propose than you imagine."

"We'll see," said his father. "In the morning."

Cumchdach knew he'd get no more. They'd already put in place increased security for when the trial results came through. The news would spread fast through the mountains, and he planned to keep Anna well away from Rubhaicreach until everything was settled.

He still asked about the security changes and listened as his father confirmed everything Cumchdach had already checked on. He was buying time and knew it, too scared to find out if she really meant that last invitation. *Look at you, for roots sake.* Hanging around like a nervous boy, waiting until she fell asleep in case she hadn't meant what he thought. Finally, his father stood up and said he was for his bed. Then outright ordered Cumchdach to do the same, so he had no choice. Fear still batted at him as he walked the familiar passage to his home quarters and let himself in as quietly as possible.

He first thought she was sleeping, lying so still in bed. In the gloom of what light filtered through their window, he couldn't see the bruising or the grey smudges staining the skin beneath her eyes. Could almost imagine she had never been hurt, if the images of her in that hospital bed weren't carved inside his head.

Then she lifted her head and waved her hand to bring up the lights and her beautiful dark eyes searched his. "You've fixed everything with your father?"

He shook his head. "He'll speak to you first."

That had her sitting up. "You made him wait?"

"No." Bare honesty was the only way forward. "I asked him to, and he didn't refuse."

Anna gave a strained snort and the tight knot inside him unwound a fraction. "Someday, it would be nice if your father wasn't already two steps ahead of everyone else."

"He doesn't trust Anton," Cumchdach had to warn her.

"I'm not sure I do either. But I have to try. I owe it to Grandfather."

And what else do you owe him?

She put out a hand, surprising him again. "He trusted me with the future of Falasch Shipping; doesn't mean he expected me to actually run it. Not full time."

Anna had been doing a lot of thinking the last few days as she watched Cumchdach's terrified steps on the path back to her.

It was the sheer depth of his fear that reassured her the most. He was being so careful. Soon, she'd relent, but not quite yet.

Because you are just as terrified.

She ignored the irritating thought. She had reason; she was risking everything.

As for her grandfather… She paused, old memories crowding her head. He'd talked to her about the family and their history, taught her the inside secrets of the company. But he'd done nothing to change the deeds of succession that left control in her father's hands. She'd studied them in detail and then asked an outside lawyer from Urbis for an opinion.

Grandfather couldn't stop her father inheriting the majority share but he could have moderated the conditions of it to give the board greater control.

Her grandfather had trusted his son, and had trusted her to find a way through to her own time with the company. He'd left the future of Falasch in her father's hands, and those of his children. Of all her father's children. Anton had gone to the same prestigious Higher School of Business in Urbis as Cumchdach, and her grandfather had made sure of that. He'd wanted her to go there, too, but hadn't fought her when she refused and enrolled instead in the UBS to study the plants she loved.

Well, he'd tried to fight her, she corrected with an inner smile. But he'd let her win that battle, and made no effort to block Grandam when she gave her the funds for it. Not that he'd have succeeded. Gria had been delighted, she remembered, thinking it left the way clear for her own offspring. Grandfather had let her, allowing her to think him too old and febrile to challenge it.

Grandfather was a power until the moment he breathed his last breath, and he'd known it.

"I have to give Anton a chance," she said now to Cumchdach, "but I expect you to help him."

The den Coilles would do a lot more than mere helping, she knew. Bram den Coille wasn't about to agree to anything less than complete supervision of whomever ran Falasch Shipping.

"Grandfather Falasch talked to you about business as much as he did me," she said. "It's possible he always expected you to take over Falasch. Or at least have a role in the management of it."

"Maybe," said Cumchdach. He had reason for his caution. Anna's grandfather had been almost a match for his own father in triple thinking. "Sleep on it," he told her. Not feeling up to useless arguments. She agreed. Whether to put off whatever must come, or just to enjoy another night when his hard body held hers, she refused to think. Her bruises were almost gone now and she rarely had to flinch from pain when he touched her, but he was still too careful with her.

She would have liked a night as they'd known in the past. Just one night.

Then it was the next morning, and they were off to the meeting with her father-in-law. With Bram mar Gliocas duine Scathach den Coille, the head of the Den Coille company and father to the den Coille family.

A family and a company her father had put at risk with his stupid schemes.

In return, Den Coille threatened the survival of her birth company and family, leaving her caught in this bog ridden no-man's land between them. She grabbed at Cumchdach's hand as they signalled at the door, wishing for the feel of her baby in her arms.

But Roo didn't belong here, not her innocent wee man. He belonged to den Falasch and den Coille, and would make his own choices when he was grown. For now, he must be free to smile his baby smiles at Grandam and his den Coille GranDa and GranMa.

Stop stalling.

She wasn't the only one. Cumchdach stood beside her, and made no attempt to walk in his father's door until Bram uttered a gruff, "Come on in, you two."

It sounded like her father-in-law was no more eager than her for this meeting. That could only mean she wasn't going to like what he had to say. She swallowed and followed Cumchdach in.

They all took their seats. Bram had selected to sit in his lounge chair in the window bay where the weak forest sunlight filtered through and made patterns on the floor. Of the other chairs, she took the one nearest the door and Cumchdach sat between them.

It was too much of a reflection of reality. She clutched at the worn fabric on the chair's arm.

"You've seen the court's ruling in full?" asked Bram first. She nodded. It had been shockingly clear, outlined in precise legal terms that left no room for doubt. Her father was ruined. She couldn't save him, even if she wanted to. But maybe there was hope for Falasch and all the people it supported.

"I take it Den Coille will not forgive the penalty?" she asked anyway.

"Not possible," said Bram. "Your grandfather would have told you the same."

"You will want payment sooner rather than later, then." Was that her voice, that strangled squeak? She'd hoped for a compromise, but her father-in-law's face gave no promises. "I must ask for time to find a buyer for Falasch." She couldn't meet Cumchdach's eyes, didn't want to look at anything in this room she had once thought a safe refuge in time of trouble. He went to move toward her, but she held herself in a tight ball and made it clear that wasn't possible. One touch from him and she'd shatter; she couldn't afford that. Not if her family and home city were to survive this day.

Bram folded his hands, one upon the other. "We might consider an interim compromise, given that your son will one day be the major shareholder in Falasch."

She shot up, shaking her head violently. "No. Keep Roo out of this."

"You misunderstand me," he said, in his even tone. "Please." He gestured to her to take her seat again and opened his com. "Our advisors have proposed an alternative."

She swallowed and sat back warily. She lifted her wrist, opening her com, and Bram sent her the file.

"You don't need to make a decision now. But we would appreciate an indication of your thoughts."

Her father-in-law had never spoken so formally to her before. Had never addressed her as the representative of her family's company rather than as one of his family. She swallowed again, holding on tight to everything thing inside her, and began to read.

Halfway through, she looked up with a shocked gasp, and for the first time she glanced at Cumchdach. He sat staring at her, hands clenched onto his chair.

"Did you know about this?"

He nodded, pale faced. "Some. Just… consider it, please."

She began reading again.

At the end, she closed her eyes and stared into the words bouncing inside her head. The plan was simple enough. Den Coille took her father's share, and with it, control of the company. But they were prepared to bring in Anton in a management role, under Den Coille supervision, and work toward him taking the lead role in running the company after an unspecified period of years, depending on his and the company's performance.

She opened her eyes again and studied Bram mar Scathach's face. It still gave her nothing. "The alternative to this?"

"The Council seizes control of Falasch. Nothing else will satisfy the Alliance sanctions."

She'd guessed it, but to hear it was a whole different matter. She swallowed and fought for courage. "My brother. What will it take for you to let him take charge?"

"Perform, and put Falasch first," was Brams brutally short answer. "Any sign of your father's greedy incompetence, and he will be out, permanently. The Alliance won't accept less."

"And my father and the rest of his family?" she forced herself to ask. Not even for the company could she speak Gria's name.

A scowl tracked Bram's face. "We cannot leave him destitute."

"Unfortunately," she heard Cumchdach mutter.

"He is still a den Coille family connection, is still Ruiseart's grandfather. He will be paid a living stipend from Falasch. But he and his family must leave Rubhaicreach and move to Urbis. The company will not survive any continued meddling from its previous manager."

"No further penalty? And Gria?" A hard look crossed Bram's eyes.

"That is for the marshals," he said.

She leaned back in her chair, a sour taste in her mouth. He was right. Her stepmother must have been involved with the conspirators. Too big a part of her wanted to punish the woman, wanted to see her pay, and pay again, for what she'd done. But Bram was right. Justice was different from revenge; she just had to hope the courts gave her a small piece of it.

"Thank you," she said stiffly. "Den Coille is being more than fair, and I hope my brother lives up to your trust. I cannot give you a final answer yet—I need to talk to the board and the rest of my father's family. But if we accept, you have my word that I will do my best to ensure that Falasch honours the plan."

"Anna. You are family," said Bram den Coille in the soft voice she was more used to. "There is nothing owed by you to Den Coille. Make all the calls you need and give us an answer tomorrow."

She rose stiffly, feeling all the aches of her injuries. Then a hard dose of reality hit her. "When everything's decided, I have to go to Rubhaicreach. They need to hear it from me in person, not second hand from a Den Coille agent."

"No." Cumchdach erupted from his chair. "You're going nowhere near that place."

"It's my home."

"And look what happened the last time you were there."

Suddenly, Bram den Coille shoved up a hand. "Wait," he said using the tone they'd both been brought up to obey. She turned to him as he touched his com.

"The Marshal Commander just landed on our private pad,' said the voice of the head of Den Coille security. "Please advise what action to take."

"Let the man in, of course," said Bram bean Scathach to his com. "As if we're about to pick a fight with the head of the Federal police force."

"How long have you known he's on his way," demanded Cumchdach.

"Since he landed," said Bram, fury in his voice. "One day, I really want to know how the marshals avoid our security. And sit down, the pair of you. We'll have to finish this after an Fallon is gone, but he'll be wanting to see you both as well."

All too soon, the marshal walked into the office, escorted, she was surprised to see, by Cumchdach's mother. The look her mother-in-law sent Bram and his nod back said she'd been asked to come. And that they still didn't trust the Marshals' commander in chief.

Cumchdach watched the marshal enter, cursing the man. He didn't have time for this now. He had to stop Anna going back to Rubhaicreach. Didn't she remember she'd nearly died there?

It's her home.

No, it isn't, he argued stubbornly with that annoying voice in his head. *This* is her home now.

But so was Rubhaicreach.

He still didn't want her going back there. Not when everything was in turmoil and too many of its people had reason to resent her and anyone from Den Coille. He watched his mother wave the marshal to a chair as she took the one that was hers always. The one right beside his father.

"You have news, Marshal?" said Da.

The man sat down carefully, showing nothing as usual, trag him, and holding his body carefully. The way that said he was ready to react to a threat. "There have been developments in the investigation into the conspirators. Specifically into identifying those involved."

"And?" asked Da. "Why does that bring you here?"

"After what your son did for us, the den Coille family deserved to be told before the news breaks. What little will be allowed out."

His father lifted an eyebrow but didn't look surprised. "Sensitive?"

"As hot stones," said an Fallon. "There are players who will never pay what they should. But they will be watched."

"Most of the names I gave you were second and middle tier management," said Cumchdach. "Their heads. Were they involved too?"

"Variable," said an Fallon. "The clever ones can't be connected."

"But you think they all were?"

"Most. Some we can take action against. But others…"

"Politically out of the question?"

"They will be monitored."

"And the Council?" asked his father.

"Ah," said an Fallon and his father leaned forward.

"A problem?"

An Fallon squared his shoulders. "Three councillors and an Upper House representative have agreed to resign."

"Which Representative?" asked Da in his most dangerous voice.

"Ser Coinneas den Cleireach."

The Upper House Representative for the Mountainer region. Beside Da, his mother jerked forward in her chair.

"That wermet. All the times he refused my requests."

"He was always very helpful to Den Coille," said Da, but Cumchdach saw the hard glint in his eye even as he teased his wife.

His mother's smile answered that hint of steel. "You never trusted him either."

"You think me a fool, *mo stochri?*"

"Far from it, *mo stochri,*" she said softly. and Mam's smile held all the love that made his family, his refuge.

But when they both turned to an Fallon, it was the head of Den Coille and the matriarch of their family that faced the Federal marshal.

"It's not enough, is it, Ser Marshal. You can arrest all the conspirators you want. It won't change what people think. Not inside their hearts." Mam was the one speaking, but his father held her hand as he sat upright beside her. His parents had long been the strong unit at the heart of their family. Now they stood together for the planet, and Cumchdach reached blindly for Anna's hand.

"Your family are safe, *mo stochri,*" she murmured to him. "No one is being arrested today."

He only hoped she was right.

"Coinneas den Cleireach was the only Representative stupid enough to be caught," said his father, "but how many think like him? They're elected officials, a reflection of the hearts of Arcadians, and too many think the Alliance is bluffing."

"It's not," said an Fallon.

"Not all families have seen the proof of that as starkly as ours."

"Or paid as dearly for that knowledge. The marshals are aware of that, Ser and Sera." An Fallon crossed his arms. "The Survey do their best to spread the message about the environmental crisis, but after their protest march and all the public scandals that followed, too many wonder who was right; the field staff or the department heads."

"Did the council get rid of the false managers to stop them talking, you mean?" said Da in his driest voice. "Anyone's free to read the trial records. They're all on the public links."

"Few do. That's the problem. Most don't have the time, getting the short version from whichever vidcast they follow instead."

His father grunted. Having been on the receiving end of too many popular vidcasters, no den Coille had much faith in them. "We need results. People—and the Council—need to see a successful company working within the Alliance demands. Show them that the environmental problems are real, but the changes needed are not the end of a good life here. Just a different one."

Anna's hand tightened on his. "Shush, *a chiad*," Cumchdach said. "No one's expecting you to save Den Coille. That's *our* job."

"Are you sure," she said, looking over at his father.

"Cumchdach has the right of it," he was relieved to hear Da say. "Though any ideas of yours would be gratefully accepted."

"That's just it." She twisted her hands together, and Cumchdach pulled her closer.

"Enough, Da. Anna's only just recovered."

"I can talk for myself, thank you," said his wife with the same glare she'd given him when he tried to help her control her first flyer. "I've looked at this from every angle possible. But," she said to his father, "I don't think I *can* find a miracle fix for you. Yes, I can improve the performance of the Estuarine farms. Given their current hidebound systems, that's not a problem. But Den Coille's research staff and the local Survey are already the recognised experts in festia production. I can fine tune it, but not enough to compensate for the loss in plantings, and the Coaster ecosystem will take years before it produces an economic surplus. You need to find something else."

Cumchdach was so proud of her courage. He tugged her close to his side, just as Samhchair knocked on the door, carrying Roo. His son saw Anna and gave a tired whimper as Samhchair handed him over.

"I think he needs his Mam," she said, much to Cumchdach's relief. Anna immediately abandoned the discussion and took her son in her arms. Roo snuggled into her, giving the room a swift glance of triumph before burrowing back into his mother's hold with another piteous whimper. There was more than a touch of his Grandfather Bram and Uncle Seolta in his son, and Cumchdach had to smother a smile. Right now, he was more than grateful for it.

"Time for a nap, little man," said Anna, lifting him up and taking him out with her. The door closed and Cumchdach turned back to his father.

"I mean it, Da. Anna doesn't need you pressuring her to save our company. She's got enough dealing with the fallout from Falasch Shipping."

His father looked as frustrated as he'd ever seen him. "We need to do something, son. Starting with talking to the Council," he added with a glare at the marshal.

"That would be very helpful," said an Fallon in his blandest of voices.

"But it's not enough?"

The marshal didn't bother replying. Cumchdach leaned back in his chair, thinking furiously. Something Anna had said niggled at him. He stared at the far wall, covered with the unique whorls of Mountainer carvings, but seeing nothing.

"She's right, you know."

"Who, and about what?" said Da grumpily.

"Anna, about our research labs. They are experts, and not just in festia production. And expertise is a valuable product in its own right."

"We control all festia production. That knowledge is no use to anyone else."

"No, but how we're changing the mountainsides to adapt, the new systems we've discovered, *is* useful knowledge. Our production levels haven't gone down at the same rate as tree loss."

"No." Then his father leaned forward, his face alight. "No, because most of the festia we're losing are trees planted in less than perfect zones. We've kept the best, and increased their harvest output. Fewer trees but with more pollen. I'm beginning to see what you mean, son." One of his father's hands plucked at the arm of the chair as it did when he was deep in thought. Then he gave a shake of his head. "We need to get the best of our advisory staff onto this. I want all the ideas I can get."

"There's also what Anna learned in the Coaster zones. They won't want us turning their marshes into maximum output farms, but maybe we can work with the Coasters to develop uses for their surplus. Work with them and the environment to find new products. It'll be like the chaullnia flowers all over again."

"More isn't always better," chanted his mother with a chuckle.

"And remember those shrubs Anyara found on Deuteron? The ones she claimed were related to festia. If that can be proved and their pollen output maximised, we can use our knowledge of festia production to set up a joint project with the Deuteronians."

Da looked even happier, and even Marshal an Fallon momentarily relaxed his stern face. "It sounds a good plan, Ser Cumchdach duine Anna. One to set in place as quickly as possible. Then you can address the Council."

Cumchdach shook his head hard at that idea. The Council chamber was not his forte. "That's Da's job."

"Thank you, son," said his father dryly. But it was too true to be denied. Da had wrangled with the Council many times before; he knew the players and which levers to push. An Fallon nodded in agreement.

"There's a full Council meeting in ten days. I'll ensure you are added to the agenda, Ser Bram bean Scathach." The marshal had a few more details to tell them, then he rose and returned to his flyer, with a polite word of refusal to his mother's offers of hospitality. "I have too much work waiting in Urbis," he said, and that would be only too true.

Ten days gave them precious little time to settle the Falasch matter. No sooner had the door shut on the marshal than his father began pulling up lists of staff to send to Rubhaicreach to take over Falasch. "I suspect the company's in a mess, despite the long-term staff's best efforts."

"Those few Eolas retained," Cumchdach reminded him, and that brought another scowl to his father's face.

"How a sensible woman like Anna bean Cumchdach came from that piece of excrement, I'll never know."

CHAPTER THIRTY-TWO

Anna might have left Cumchdach to his discussion, but she hadn't forgotten it. Or her decision to go to Rubhaicreach. She owed her people that, after what her father had done. Someone in the family had to step up. That's what she told Cumchdach the next morning, with the inevitable response.

Under all the shouts, the bluster, his fear shone out. He was so terrified for her. She'd seen it before, but not as clearly.

It was so real.

Because of it, she allowed all his protections. A level of security that had even his father raising an eyebrow. But one thing everyone else made clear, much to her husband's disgust. Cumchdach was not allowed to set foot off the marshal flyer taking them there. No one had the heart to stop him going with her, but a solid bank of opposition met his vow to stand beside her when she spoke.

"Too inflammatory," said his father in his dry voice. "You'll just put Anna at more risk."

That alone silenced Cumchdach.

Roo was staying safely in Manascraoch, though.

Ironically, the sun was shining when her shuttle descended onto the landing pad of her home city. A rare moment of brilliance, the sparks off the sea's wavelets giving life to the bravely flowering natives tucked among the tough shrubs of the plateau. Even the little rete flowers lifted their smiling faces toward her. Lots of them, carpeting the sides of the pathways as they should, thanks to her intervention.

They'd left Cumchdach in the large marshal flyer high overhead. A full, operations control centre flyer, packed with the kind of technology she hated being needed in her home city.

Cumchdach hadn't wanted to let her go, holding her tight for as long as possible and only letting go when she gave him a kiss and a promise she would be back.

"You'd better." She could see the effort as he dropped his arms and stepped back from her.

The shuttle landed, she took a breath, and nodded for the hatch to open. Her gut churned as she fastened on her widest and brightest work smile. Grandam would be proud of her—she hoped.

The silence that met her was the first warning. A full squad of marshals surrounded her, and she knew the crowd waiting at the landing site was packed full of marshal and Den Coille agents, but she still had to force herself to walk out there. She was to speak from the main gateway of the den Falasch family home, where all Falasch announcements had been made as far back as anyone could remember.

It meant she had to walk through all the winding, crowd filled pathways of the upper plateau, with that eerie silence following her. Once, she heard a child's voice, too suddenly hushed, but that was all. Even the seagoing aerial creatures kept silent, their usual squawks cut off as they flew above her head.

Everything waited on her, waited and reserved judgement. She should not have to feel grateful for the squad of marshals surrounding her, not in her home city.

At the gates of her family home, her father's troops awaited her arrival. The marshals said nothing to them that she could detect, just slapped their weapons into place and gestured the Falasch troops out of the way.

She held her breath. Then her father's squad moved away and the marshals took their place. It did nothing to help her nerves as she mounted the steps. A tingle over her skin said the podium was protected by a security shield.

She still felt vulnerable, staring out over the crowds. Shields didn't stop everything. At the top, she thrust out her chin as she slowly turned and stood to face her people. Those personally invited stood in the front ranks: Falasch employees and associates. All those whose income and lives depended on what happened here today. But beyond them, it felt like the whole city had turned out; men, women, children, crowding over the boulders, roofscapes and pathways of the upper plateau. Stupidly, she was relieved to see her beloved plants and gardens were so far untouched.

How long that remained once she started talking…

She heaved in a breath.

"You have all heard the outcome of the case brought by Den Coille against Falasch Shipping." Her father had already been notified by the courts and she'd asked the marshals to send a copy of the findings to Anton, not trusting her stepmother to pass on the ruling untouched. "The fraudulent sale of Festin as the counterfeit product, Restin, was proven in the case brought before the Alliance Central courts, and the Arcadian courts have now found Falasch liable, with a penalty to be agreed with Den Coille. Your coms are receiving the ruling now." A slight nod, and the marshal control centre on the flyer confirmed transmission. She saw a mass swinging of heads to wrists and the glazed look of those reading a com message crossed all the front ranks. Then the silence was broken. A low, gut deep sound, like the slow rumble of the only earthquake she'd ever felt. This one brought the same clench of fear.

But still no talk. Instead, one by one as they finished reading, the faces turned back to her. Waiting.

For her to tell them this was all a mistake? That Den Coille was going to forgive this attack on their company? She heaved in another breath and began talking again.

"The courts have now signed off on final details. The actual amount granted to Den Coille is retracted. I can tell you it was more than Falasch can pay, even by selling the company. However, Den Coille has agreed to accept a lesser amount on the condition that my father's shares are surrendered to Den Coille, and the Falasch board has accepted their offer." She rushed on before any could react.

"Den Coille will be the principal shareholder in Falasch. However, they have a long history of doing business with Falasch and value Falasch's expertise in the transport sector, including that of its employees. Den Coille has no wish to lose that or break up the company. The business stays, but with changes. You will all receive a com message in the next few days, setting out how those changes affects you."

"The marshals. How long are they staying?" yelled out one brave voice.

It was the head of the dockers, a man who'd known her since she was a baby.

"They're staying as long as they think fit," she said. "They have no reason yet to trust Falasch."

"And the other agents?" called out another. The union representative this time. "Den Coille have security crawling all over the peninsula."

"Staying also," she said coldly. "Den Coille values its people. Their security will stay as long as any risk remains to Den Coille staff seconded here."

"So Manascraoch finally got this city too," a voice spat out, and a low hum ran around the crowd. Beside her, the marshals dropped into a ready stance and a scared silence fell over the crowd.

Then, one old lady walked up onto the podium, shoving aside a marshal in her way, and with not a single security guard with her.

"Grandam, no," said Anna.

Her grandmother had never taken orders, not even from her grandfather. She stared at Anna, and Anna dutifully conceded the podium to her as the agitators fell silent.

"Don't you dare say that, Sarmadur mar Obar. I minded you as a baby. Manascraoch didn't take this city; we *gave* it to them. How many of you knew we were robbing Den Coille blind? You, you?" She thrust a finger at the crowd, unerringly picking out the troublemakers. "Blame Den Coille, blame that silly woman Eolas mar Driach married, or the man himself when he ran Falasch. But every one of you who knew about the fraud and let it happen? Each one of you is just as guilty."

Grandam's hands clenched the lectern. "Don't take it out on my Anna and the den Coille family. Eolas duine Gria knew exactly what he was doing when he set out to cheat the wiliest man on the mountains, and he's lucky to get off so lightly. But right now, our city needs you. Rubhaicreach and Falasch were once great, and can be again." She drew herself up, thrusting out a hand to stop the harried assistant rushing up to help her. "Den Coille have offered us a chance, and we are going to seize it." Then Grandam ran her gaze over the crowd. Anna had felt the force of that look often enough when growing up, and she and her cousins had been stupid again.

It was like she saw into your soul and knew every single black deed written there.

"Rubhaicreach needs you," said Grandam, "all of you. Make sure you stand up and answer its call."

Then her Grandam walked off the stage, and Anna had to step up to the podium again. Only this time the leader of the marshal troop stepped up beside her, and the rest of his troop stood to attention, eyes set on the crowd below.

The gates of Falasch house opened behind her. She didn't have to turn her head. This whole farce was tightly scripted—though no one had expected Grandam's contribution. Her father and his family walked out, surrounded by the city's police under the supervision of even more marshals. She daren't turn her head. So far, she'd held herself together, but seeing her own father treated so was more than she could take.

Nor was she allowed a facade of self-respect. The troopers marched them to the front of the podium, and the head of the Falasch board—a second cousin of hers, the son of her grandfather's sister—pulled up a com scroll and began to read. Much of it repeated what she'd said, detailing the board's response to the court's findings. Her father was stripped of any position in Falasch but was to be granted an income as was his right as a child of the family. Then came to the clincher, just as a series of packing containers began to trundle into the house.

"The family of Eolas mar Driach duine Gria den Falasch is required to vacate the Falasch homestead immediately and remove to Urbis. As next heir in line, occupancy of the house is granted to Anna ingh Eolas an Sumhneas o Falasch bean Cumchdach den Coille, and the board sincerely hopes that she and her family will take up residency at the soonest possible."

The man snapped shut his com, and turned away from her father, who was protesting loudly. But it was the shock on her stepmother's face that most stunned Anna. Didn't the woman realise the cost of her power plays?

"And where do you expect us to live? On the streets?" demanded her stepmother.

The board Chair refused to meet her gaze. "Your accounts have been scrutinised and the board is satisfied that the family has sufficient funds in reserve to tide them over until they can establish themselves in Urbis. The income allotted is more than adequate for the family." The board member turned back to her father and lifted a wrist. "The details of the settlement are being transmitted to you now, Ser Eolas mar Driach."

Her father glanced down at his com, pulled up the message and showed it to his wife, then snapped it shut. She went to open her mouth again.

Anna only just heard his words, spoken softly to his wife. "Not here, Gria. Not in front of them all. We will discuss it when we get home to Urbis."

They had an apartment there. Gria had never liked Rubhaicreach, despite revelling in the power her husband's position gave her, and had always kept a bolt hole in the city. But to hear it called *home* by her father…

She studied her family then, seeing the fury on her father's face, the shock on her stepmother's and the frozen disbelief on the twins. Alone of them all, Anton looked shattered. The only one who looked as if leaving the house was leaving his home. As her brother walked through the doorway, he lifted a hand to touch the old doorpost that had guarded generations of her family. A brief touch, then snatched back as his head came up and his face hardened.

They hadn't told him. She'd trusted the marshals, trusted Cumchdach. Even stupidly, trusted her father and his wife. But no one had told her brother he didn't have to leave, not if he was prepared to work with Den Coille.

Maybe even one day take over Falasch, if he proved true to that hint of promise she'd seen in him.

The Falasch troops lined up, forming a guard to protect the family as they moved over to their waiting flyer. Her father was the eldest son of the family; honour said he must depart with dignity.

Honour, and the held breaths of all those citizens standing watching, the tension of the day thrumming against her skin. She stared straight ahead, refusing to be seen taking part in her family's shame.

Their own fault.

No, not theirs alone. She'd tried. But she had failed. She knew her father; she was his daughter and enough of him ran in her veins that she understood what drove him. Her father was no leader, but birth had thrust him into a position he was not made to fill.

Yet her father loved his wife, his children. Maybe he even had some kind of love for her. She'd never been sure about that. But he'd trusted her to protect his family, and she'd failed him. Both of them knew it was she who had inherited her grandfather's strength.

She might have learned to accept that, but it didn't erase the guilt wracking her today.

The hatch on the Falasch family flyer swung open, as a second troop of marshals marched out of the large marshal flyer parked beside it. All heads, including hers, swung around. This new troop wore full dress uniform with their ranks displayed, unlike their usual plain blacks, and that was never a good sign. Then she recognised the man leading the troop.

Marshal Dunan strode in front, showing no sign of his recent injuries and wearing the insignia of a Senior Commander, one rank below the Commander himself. A select group of elite marshals answering only to an Fallon. They marched up to her stepmother, stopping in front of her, and Marshal Dunan pulled up a formal com scroll. The first troop of marshals surrounded the family, isolating them from the Falasch troops.

Then the new squad surrounded Gria, and Dunan began to read from the scroll.

"No," cried Anna in horror. "This wasn't in the agreement," she shouted, running from the podium, stopped only by the strong arms of a marshal blocking her way. Her father was yelling as well, trying to get to his wife, and more marshals held tight to him.

"What are you doing?" she called out to Marshal Dunan. "Den Coille never asked for this."

Dunan wore that look she'd come to dread on a marshal's face. The one too like a cyborg, giving nothing away and closed to all emotion. "This is a federal matter, Sera. The Sera den Falasch has been charged with matters relating to actions taken against the rule of the Council."

Just then, her father broke away from his guards, and a rock flew through the air. She felt the whoosh of it. Then another body flew in front of her, and she was flung to the ground. A clatter, and a large rock rolled to a halt beside her. One wearing a bright splash of blood red.

Cumchdach watched the meeting from above with hands clenched against the control panel. He should be down there. Then more marshals arrived, they arrested that stupid woman who'd married Eolas, and it turned into a tragging bog fest. A hand swung up, a rock flew through the air, and Anna's tragging brother flung himself at her.

All he could see after that was Anna lying on the ground as the crowd surged forward, her marshal guard sprawled on top of her, and her brother spread out beside her. She'd gone down under the weight of the two men and only the quick thinking of the marshal, ordering a security shield up, saved her from more attacks.

They should have had one up all along. Who cared if the tell-tale shimmer added to the tension? Anna would have been safe.

Not from her brother.

"Put us down. Now," he yelled at the pilot. The marshals might be in charge here, but this was a Den Coille flyer. The pilot glanced at the marshal standing beside him.

"Hold your position," said the marshal, "if you value the sera's life."

"Put down, if you value your own life," said Cumchdach. "That's my wife down there."

Thank the roots, the man listened. The marshal could do nothing to stop a pilot, and no marshal would be stupid enough to fire on a flyer holding the principal heir to Den Coille. Cumchdach palmed his weapon, just in case, though he doubted he'd succeed against a trained marshal.

"Land there." He pointed to the bare patch between the security shield and the rest of the officials.

The man gulped but followed his order as the guards below hastily scattered.

"Down. No casualties," said the pilot with a decided quiver in his voice.

Cumchdach was already rushing toward the hatch and slamming the opener. He ran down the ramp. The marshal had picked himself up, but Anna was still on the ground, with her brother lying beside her and another man bent over her. As soon as he reached her, he snatched her away from the man.

Two big hands grabbed him by the shoulders and the unmistakeable hold of a restraining field hauled him back as the first man caught Anna and lowered her back to the ground. He flashed a medic's logo at him, and behind him, he heard heavy boot steps.

"Anton den Falasch was trying to save your wife, not attacking her," Marshal Dunan shouted. "Don't be more an idiot than necessary."

"Anna?" said Cumchdach, eyes fixed on her pale face.

"Safe," said the medic. "Stunned by the fall, but nothing serious."

Cumchdach tried to move. "Let me go."

"You going to be sensible?"

"When I've made sure my wife's all right."

Thankfully for his sanity, Dunan nodded at his troops, and the restraining field disappeared. He crouched back down and cautiously touched Anna's cheek. She turned toward him, her eyes blank, then opening wide. Then, her face softened. "Cumchdach," she whispered, and sighed as he gathered her close into his body.

"You're safe, *a chiad.* You're safe," he murmured, and didn't know whether he spoke to her, or himself.

Anna came to again as the bands of a stretcher locked around her body, and it began to move. A hand held hers, anchoring her. A hand she would always know. She opened her eyes, to meet those of her husband. "You're still here," she said stupidly.

"Of course I am. Always."

"Is that a promise?" Where the words came from, she didn't know. "Forget I said that," she said hastily.

But his hand tightened, and his eyes held hers. "Yes, *a chiad*, it is a promise. You are my wife, my own one, and I will always be here. It is all I have ever wanted."

She didn't know what to say. "But I seem to give you only trouble."

His mouth dropped open. "You give me trouble? I've done nothing but make your life hard this last year."

"No, you haven't." In her life, she'd only ever had two people she trusted never to let her down. Grandam and Cumchdach. But with Cumchdach, something deep in her had always waited to be proved wrong. Had waited for Cumchdach to leave her—just like her mother had.

"Ser and Sera, we need to get out of here now."

The marshals brought reality back with a crash. "I can't, not yet." Grandam wasn't safe—and she needed to talk to her brother. She used her elbow to lever herself up. Cumchdach tried to stop her of course, but she shook his hand off. "I need to see what's going on."

He hated letting her. She could see the tightening of his jawline that was his giveaway. Barely perceptible—Cumchdach den Coille had early learned to hide what he felt from outsiders, and right now, he was surrounded by them—but he'd been best friends with her since childhood and her lover all her adult years.

A thought that gave her the courage she needed. Cumchdach had to help her, though, or she'd have failed, still too lightheaded to sit unaided.

Then she saw her brother, flat on the ground and being treated by medics "Anton!"

That tightening of Cumchdach's jaw increased. But it was the marshal who spoke. "Ser Anton ghar Driach blocked the rock aimed at you, Sera. It caught his head. The medics are preparing him for urgent transport to the Rubhaicreach hospital."

"Will he be all right?"

"So the medics advise."

"You have to let me stay until he's out of danger. And his family," she made herself add. Despite the headache pounding at her, the memory of Gria being arrested stood out too clearly. She looked around, but the Falasch flyer no longer waited on the landing pad and the hatch of the marshals' flyer was securely closed and readying for lifting off. Another dark shape hovered overhead, waiting to land to take its place.

"They have already left. The civil situation here is too risky for them to remain," the marshal said.

"We have to leave too, Anna," said Cumchdach.

He'd carry her himself if she refused, said his face. Marshal Dunan beat him to it. A gesture to her medics and the stretcher started moving.

"Wait. Anton, did he get my message?"

Dunan's mouth tightened this time. "All transmissions to the junior den Falasch were blocked."

"He doesn't know, then. He thinks you're taking him away too."

"Most likely."

"You have to get that message to him. He has to know he can stay. Promise me."

This time, it was Cumchdach who answered. "We will. He's protected us twice now. I owe him."

"He deserves a chance," said Anna.

A tic appeared at the corner of Cumchdach's jaw. The one that only showed when he was under the worst of stresses. "He gets a chance, and all the help our people can give him."

"He will get the contract, Sera," said the marshal.

"Thank you. And Cumchdach." Her poor husband had been pushed far enough. "I do love you. Take me home, please."

The tic disappeared and her stretcher suddenly began to move a whole lot faster. The medics beside her had to run. In no time, they'd left Dunan behind, and were inside the Den Coille flyer and lifting off.

"Home, pilot," said Cumchdach. "Back to Manascraoch."

Only when they breached the cloud layer and turned toward Manascraoch did Cumchdach breathe easily. Below him, a large Den Coille freighter was settling down onto the official Rubhaicreach landing site, with the company's security guards emerging first. Even as the crowds were disbanded by the marshals and local police, Den Coille staffers were moving into the Falasch offices and taking over the business. Anna had given them a list of the Falasch staff she trusted most; the competent and sensible ones the new managers needed to stay on. He could only hope they'd agree, helping steer the company through the transition.

But he now admitted what he'd refused to in the hectic days leading up to this, as he'd listened to Anna and searched through what they knew of Falasch Shipping. They needed a den Falasch on board, and Anton den Falasch was the best option. Yet only when the boy—no, man—saved Anna, did Cumchdach begin to have real hope.

She was safe, and she was coming with him.

What came next?

He looked down and caught the sparkle in Anna's eyes that said she was laughing at him.

"You could have been killed," he said, affronted.

She nodded. "But I wasn't, thanks to Anton and all your planning." She narrowed her eyes. "You are going to be nice to him?"

"Of course. The company needs him…and he's your brother."

"Yes, he is. My grandfather would have been proud of him."

Cumchdach thought of the old, sharp-eyed patriarch who'd run Falasch Shipping with a will of iron. "Yes, I begin to think he might have been."

Then Anna's eyes fell and her teeth worried at her lip.

"What is it, *a chiad?*" Was she in pain?

"I do love you, Cumchdach duine Anna, and I owe you an apology."

"What? No, you don't."

"I do. You have never let me down, but something in me still waited for you to leave me, like my mother did." She swallowed. "I was wrong, and I apologise."

He barely dared breathe. "And now?" Was this what she'd hidden from him all these years? Curse her family and their years of unthinking cruelty. Then he saw the smile bloom on her face.

"Now, it's like I've lost a weight I didn't know I was carrying. After everything we've been through…" She heaved in a breath, her face lifting to his. "You stay, and keep on staying, no matter how hard it gets. I trust you, Cumchdach duine Anna, and I will love you to the end of my days."